DINNER AT MINE

CHRIS SMYTH

SIMON & SCHUSTER

London · New York · Sydney · Toronto · New Delhi

A CBS COMPANY

COUNTY LOUTH
LIBRARY SERVICE

Acc. No. ...4346990...
Class No. ...AFP...
Invoice No. ...4/140237...
Catalogued ...8/06/12...
Vendor ...JLS...

First published in Great Britain by Simon & Schuster UK Ltd, 2012
A CBS Company

Copyright © Chris Smyth, 2012

This book is copyright under the Berne Convention.
No reproduction without permission.
® and © 1997 Simon & Schuster Inc. All rights reserved.

The right of Chris Smyth to be identified as author of this
work has been asserted in accordance with sections 77 and
78 of the Copyright, Designs and Patents Act, 1988.

1 3 5 7 9 10 8 6 4 2

Simon & Schuster UK Ltd
1st Floor
222 Gray's Inn Road
London WC1X 8HB

www.simonandschuster.co.uk

Simon & Schuster Australia, Sydney
Simon & Schuster India, New Delhi

A CIP catalogue record for this book is available from the British Library

ISBN PB: 978-0-85720-505-6
ISBN Ebook: 978-0-85720-506-3

This book is a work of fiction. Names,
characters, places and incidents are either a product of the author's
imagination or are used fictitiously. Any resemblance to actual
people living or dead, events or locales is entirely coincidental.

Typeset by Hewer Text UK Ltd, Edinburgh
Printed and bound by CPI Group (UK) Ltd, Croydon, CR0 4YY

Dinner at Rosie and Stephen's

COUNTY LIBRARY

LOUTH

SERVICE

One

'Did you remember to get yuzu juice?'

'What?'

Rosie looked up from the chopping board and called louder out of the kitchen door.

'Did you remember to get yuzu juice?'

In the hall, she heard Stephen slam the front door and drop his bag on the floor with a thump.

'What?' Stephen asked again, testier this time.

Rosie's voice never quite carried out to the hall. She chopped a few more beetroot wedges before replying again, listening to Stephen's footsteps coming towards the kitchen.

'What are you saying?' he demanded as he appeared in the doorway, flushed and slightly out of breath from the journey home.

'Hello, darling,' she said, putting the knife down to go over and give him a kiss on the cheek. 'How was work?'

'Hello,' he mumbled back at her, exhaling sharply.

Rosie couldn't detect any alcohol on his breath. 'What were you saying?'

'I was just wondering whether you got a chance to go to that Asian delicatessen near your office.' Rosie could feel him staring at her as she moved back behind the chopping board. 'Do you remember that I asked you this morning to try to find some yuzu juice?'

'What the hell is yuzu juice?'

'It's a sort of Japanese fruit. Something like lime, I think.'

'Oh God, are we having people round?'

Rosie sliced another beetroot before answering, watching Stephen as his eyes moved round the kitchen, taking in the large pots on top of the stove, the casserole in the glowing oven and the detritus of garlic husks, aubergine tops and unidentified trails of seeds scattered along the worktops.

'Yes,' she said. 'You haven't really forgotten, have you?'

'Oh bugger, we're not doing that stupid *Come Dine with Me* thing, are we? Is that tonight?'

Rosie chopped the next beetroot in half quite brutally.

'We just don't usually . . . on a Friday . . .' Stephen tailed off.

'You said you'd do pudding,' Rosie said.

'Did I?'

'I thought something with figs and honey might be nice. It would go with the rest of the meal.'

Rosie felt the evening's first twinge of anger as she watched him standing there, working out when to say what they both knew he was going to say.

'How about a crumble?'

Rosie replied in a flat voice: 'There are pears in the fruit bowl and blackcurrants in the fridge.'

'Pears?' Stephen looked alarmed. 'I don't know how to—'

'Jesus, Stephen, I thought we could do something at least slightly different. It's hardly a huge departure from apples, is it?'

'All right, all right. When are they coming?'

'About forty-five minutes. You'd better get on with it.'

'Where's Jonathan?'

'I put him to bed early.'

Rosie gathered up the pile of cold, boiled beetroot slices and scattered them into the bowl of lentils she had taken out of the fridge to warm up. She added chopped onion, lemon juice and maple syrup and tossed the salad more aggressively than the recipe suggested.

Stephen stopped and turned on the way out of the kitchen. 'By the way, I'm afraid I . . .'

'Yes, all right,' she snapped. 'I can use lime and mandarins instead.'

'Sarah! There you are!'

She was still closing the front door when he rushed out of the living room to confront her.

'Sorry, Marcus, I had a ton of marking to do.'

'Did you get my message?'

'I've been in such a rush . . .' Sarah shook herself out of her coat, feeling tiredness begin to advance as she hung it up. If she sat down now, she wouldn't want to get up until Sunday afternoon. 'I thought I'd just nip upstairs to get changed, then we can go straight out,' she said.

'So, what do you think?' Marcus said, a little impatiently.

'I thought I'd wear my green dress. Are you going to change into something nice as well? That would be—'

'No – I mean about our approach.'

'Approach to what?'

Marcus gave her that stare she hated, the one that combined frustration with private amusement.

'You didn't read my message, did you?'

'I've been so busy . . . It's been a difficult day.' She fought to keep the edge out of her voice.

'Well, it was you who said yes to this.' Marcus prodded expertly at the sore point.

'Don't be like that . . .' The edge was there now.

'I'm not. I just want to agree our approach.'

'Approach to what? We're just going round to Rosie and Stephen's for dinner.'

'No, we're doing *Come Dine with Me*. It's a competition. We need to work out how we're going to win.'

'Marcus,' she said as she pushed past him towards the bedroom, 'we're just going out to have a nice dinner with our friends.'

How could she be exasperated with him already? They hadn't even made it past the hall.

'I'm not worried about our turn yet, but we have to know what we're going to say tonight.'

Marcus followed her into the bedroom. He seemed so cheerful. Was she being unreasonable? No, because he was never cheerful these days except at someone else's expense.

God, that was a horrible thing to think about someone, wasn't it?

'Look, Marcus,' she said, trying to sound conciliatory. 'I just want to have a nice, enjoyable evening talking to our friends.'

'Well, that bit's up to them. Depends how enjoyable you find talking about kitchen appliances. Or how the baby's constant drooling is actually a sign that he's terribly advanced for his age.'

'Please don't be rude about our friends, Marcus. I really hope you're going to be polite.'

'Of course I'm going to be polite.'

'Good.' Sarah took off her suit jacket and began unbuttoning her blouse.

'That's the approach I was going to recommend, you see? Be very friendly, and say complimentary things about the food.'

'Marcus …'

'But afterwards be quite strict about scoring it. We won't mention the flaws, but we need to make sure we remember them.'

'Marcus …' She tried to look stern, but knew this would be difficult, standing there in her bra.

'Look, I'm not saying we should cheat, or be unfair, or anything like that. Just, you know, precise. Make them earn the marks.'

'Do you have to take it so seriously?'

'There's no point in doing it otherwise.'

'What about having fun?'

'That is the fun. Honestly, Sarah, I think it's you who's not getting into the spirit of things. Have you even looked at the menu?'

'Marcus, I've not had time.' She turned away from him to take off her trousers. Maybe he had a point. She was hardly in the mood to be the life and soul herself, was she? All she really wanted to do was have a large glass of wine and go to bed early. In fact, that was more or less all she ever wanted to do now. Perhaps it wasn't Marcus; perhaps it was the thought of going out into the cold again and talking for hours that was making her irritable.

'Chilled Spinach Soup with Avocado and Crunchy Bacon Croutons to start,' Marcus read. She hadn't noticed he was holding a notepad. 'Well, add bits of fried bacon to anything, it's going to taste nice, isn't it? So we really need to hold them to a higher standard there.'

'Marcus . . .'

'Then Breast of Duck with Pomegranate Molasses and Okra. Who knows whether they'll pull that off? It reeks of Trying Too Hard.'

Sarah exhaled sharply. No, it was definitely him that was making her irritable. She was standing there, wearing only her underwear, and what was he doing? Waiting in the doorway reading out a menu. He wasn't even looking.

'And serving it with Candied Beetroot and Lentil Salad? I don't think that's going to work. Not the same sort of flavours at all. It doesn't even go with the vegetarian stew.'

'Marcus . . .' Not that she felt up to doing anything, obviously, but he hadn't even noticed.

'Then Ricotta with Figs and Honey for pudding. Well, it's definitely not fig season. I can't stand green figs; there's no point to them at all if they're not black and oozing and that isn't going to happen at this time of year. Not a good sign.'

'Marcus, they've cooked for us before. You enjoyed it.' She rummaged through the wardrobe, looking for the green dress.

'Actually, I remember it being distinctly mediocre. The lamb was overcooked and the salad was watery. If there's no improvement on that I don't think we've got much to worry about.'

'Is this because you find Rosie and Stephen boring?'

'No, not at all. It's nothing to do with that. It's just part of the competition.'

Sarah struggled to zip up the back of her dress herself, not wanting to ask him for help. 'Look, just be nice for me. Please? It will be so embarrassing if you are rude about the meal.'

'Weren't you listening? I'm going to be nice about the meal. And then if it's bad, I'll give it a very harsh mark afterwards. OK?'

Sarah snagged the zip on her finger and swore silently. 'Let's just go. I don't want to be late.'

A damp, aubergincy waft escaped from the pot when Rosie lifted the lid. She prodded at the contents anxiously with a wooden spoon, and a chunk of vegetable bobbed gently in the stew. It was too watery, she decided, not nearly gooey enough. Maybe it would be all right in another hour. She turned up the heat and dumped in another few spoonfuls of tamarind paste and most of what was left in the jar of honey. She wouldn't be needing it for dessert now. The mixture bubbled thickly as she stirred it, burping up a sickly sweet gust much more powerful than she had anticipated.

Immediately, Rosie decided she had overdone it. The dish was ruined. The evening was over already and the competition lost. She might as well throw everything away and tell everyone to stay at home.

Calm down. The soup looked fine. The salad was almost ready. The duck breasts were washed and seasoned. Rosie turned the heat down again under the stew and put the lid back on. But why wasn't Stephen back? He hadn't even started the crumble. She had wanted him to be part of it, but really she should have just made the dessert she wanted herself.

Rosie took out a box of crackers and began arranging them on a plate, a dollop of black tapenade on each. It wasn't part of the menu plan, but she found the repetitive motion soothing. After two dozen crackers, she promised herself, she would start on the crumble.

'Right then,' Stephen said as he came back into the kitchen. 'What have I got to do?'

'Just make the crumble. I've left all the ingredients out.' Rosie waved the olive-covered knife at the end of the worktop, where pears, blackcurrants, butter, flour and sugar were laid out in the order specified by Nigel Slater.

'OK, then.' Stephen headed towards them.

Rosie noticed that he was holding a large glass of wine. She thought of saying something as he set it down next to the fruit, but he seemed to have cheered up and, with the guests about to arrive, there wasn't time for an argument. He should really have offered her a drink, but he would just say that she never wanted one when she was cooking. She didn't, but that wasn't the point, was it?

Instead, she asked: 'Is Jonathan asleep?'

'He was,' Stephen replied. 'I'm sure he'll doze off again.'

'Oh Stephen ...'

'Look, I didn't mean to wake him, but once he was up, well ... you know. I don't usually see him at all during the week.'

Rosie listened for a moment, but couldn't hear crying. 'Never mind. You seem a bit more cheerful anyway. Was work OK?'

Stephen grunted. Rosie watched his brow furrow down the middle as he chopped the pears in half. He hadn't bothered to peel them. Was it too late to say anything? Probably. He filleted the seedy cores and threw the fruits, roughly quartered, into a deep dish.

'Thank you for making the crumble,' Rosie said. 'You always do it so well. I'm sure everyone will love it.'

'Who's actually coming tonight?'

'Sarah and Marcus.'

'Oh God.'

'Sarah's one of my oldest friends ...'

'There's nothing wrong with Sarah.' Stephen chopped two more pears in quick succession.

'Marcus isn't that bad.'

'Yes he is. He's a cock.' Stephen chopped the next pear with particular force.

'Well ... Anyway, there's Barbara and Justin. She's a friend of Sarah's, a potter, very artistic. I don't know much about him.'

'Jesus, is there anyone I actually know and like coming to this thing?'

'Yes – Matt.'

'Oh – Matt.'

Rosie looked carefully at Stephen's profile, but couldn't gauge his reaction.

'I thought you'd want to have Matt here. He's your friend.'

'Yes, he is, isn't he?'

'Darling, I don't know why you're being weird about it.'

'I'm not being weird about it.'

Rosie had run out of things to do and her fingers were twitching uselessly.

'I thought you'd like to have one of your friends here.'

'But you didn't think of asking me?'

'You've been so busy recently ... and when we talked about doing this, you said that was fine as long as I arranged it all.'

'I didn't know that meant you'd be speaking to Matt, did I?'

'Darling, please don't make such a big deal out of it.'

'I'm not making a big deal out of it.'

Stephen turned away to find the mixing bowl, rolling up his shirtsleeves very deliberately. Rosie noticed the cuffs were beginning to fray. She frowned to think he was going to the office like that. Was that one of the ones she'd bought for him last Christmas? No point saying anything now. She made a mental note to buy him another couple of shirts next time she was in M&S.

'Look, perhaps I should have asked Mike and Tony instead,'

Rosie said. 'I was thinking of it. But then I thought there would be too many men. Is that homophobic? Oh God, it might be. But I don't think so; it's just about balance, isn't it?'

Stephen asked: 'Is Matt bringing a girlfriend, then?'

'No, that's the other thing. I've asked Charlotte from work.'

'Do I know her?'

'Yes, Charlotte – she's the accountant. I mean, you haven't met, but I know I've mentioned her to you. I think she and Matt might get on really well. Don't you think?'

'I've never met her.'

'No. But I think they're similar types.'

'So now you're trying to set Matt up as well.'

'No ... not exactly ... I just thought they'd get on.'

'Why do you care about Matt's love life?'

'I don't ... I mean ... I think you're reading too much into it.'

'Am I?'

'Stephen, for God's sake ...'

'Can you turn on the taps, please?'

He had finished kneading the flour, butter and sugar, and held his white-dusted hands in front of him piously, like holy relics. Rosie obeyed, mixing the water to the right temperature. Stephen washed his hands, dried them, and scattered the crumble mix over the pears.

'Thank you,' Rosie said. 'Would you mind laying the table now?'

Stephen picked up his wine and left the kitchen without replying.

*   *   *

'I'm sorry, madam, you'll need to complete Approved Application Request No. 3742b.'

'But you won't send me the damn form!' Barbara shouted into the telephone.

'I'm sorry, madam . . .'

'How do I get it?'

'You will need to send a Certificate of Provisional Approval of Extension of Leave to Remain.'

'And how do I get that?' Barbara's knuckles were white from clenching the phone. Justin wanted to reach out across the sofa and touch her, try to calm her down.

'You need to apply for that from the Home Office, sending them Supplementary Information.'

'Such as what?'

'Such as a job offer or marriage visa.'

'I don't have those!'

'I'm sorry, madam.'

Justin did reach out now. Barbara flicked his hand away.

'There must be something else,' she said.

'You can complete Approved Application Request No. 3742b.'

'Jesus!' Barbara shouted even louder.

The woman's voice on the end of the line was muffled, but Justin could still make out her words and tone of dogged neutrality. He felt sorry for her, really. It wasn't her fault, after all. She didn't make the rules. She just had to sit there all day and listen to people like Barbara shout at her. Probably didn't get much more than the minimum wage for it either. Perhaps Barbara should tone it down a bit.

'But don't you realize how stupid that is?'

'I'm sorry, madam. I'm just explaining the rules.'

'You're making me really fucking mad here, you know that?'

'I'm sorry, madam, but if you continue to swear at me I will have to terminate the call.'

Justin reached out his hand again, but looked at Barbara's face and thought better of touching her.

'I'm not swearing at you, I'm ... I'm ... All right, I'm sorry.' Barbara closed her eyes and took several deep breaths. Justin felt proud of her. 'OK, to get the extension of leave to remain, never mind the approval form, what else do I need?'

'First, you will need to complete a Financial Independence Declaration, including three recent bank statements proving you have funds beyond the required minimum.'

'How much is that?'

'Eight hundred pounds, madam.'

'All right. Anything else?'

'There is an application fee.'

'And how much is that?'

'Eight hundred pounds, madam.'

Barbara threw the phone across the room. Justin got up from the sofa and went to pick it up. He made sure it wasn't broken before giving Barbara a comforting pat on the arm. She tensed but didn't pull away.

'Don't get upset, honey,' he said. 'It wasn't her fault.'

'Don't get upset? I am upset! Your stupid fucking country and its stupid fucking bureaucracy!'

'It's the system. It's all based on fear. There are some

campaign groups fighting for a fairer way of doing things. We could join them.'

'I don't care about campaign groups! They're going to kick me out.'

'I'm sure they won't. Just be grateful you're not an asylum seeker.'

'That's really comforting, Justin. Jesus!'

Justin couldn't see what he'd said wrong. He tried patting her arm again. She brushed him off and stood up.

'Barbara, I'm sorry, just tell me what to do and I'll—'

'I think I'm going to go and lie down,' she said, suddenly subdued.

'All right. We can get a taxi tonight if you want.'

'A taxi? Where?'

'To your friend Rosie's for dinner. Didn't you see the menu?'

'I can't go to a stupid dinner tonight! I'm not in the mood.'

'I think we really ought to. She's doing a vegetarian thing specially.'

'Can't you tell her I'm not coming?'

'She's your friend – I've never met her.'

'Jesus!'

Justin craned round on the sofa to watch Barbara stamp across the hall of their tiny flat. Maybe it was best to let her go for the time being.

'I've got to send some e-mails about the Malawi project,' he called after her. 'I'll come and get you after that.'

*   *   *

Rosie sniffed anxiously at the steam that billowed up when she took the lid off the rice. Was it fragrant? She thought not. The sweetness of the currants was just about there, and a hint of allspice, perhaps, but overall it was more of a wet cloud than a delicate Middle-Eastern aroma.

With a wooden spoon, she fished out a couple of grains and bit them gingerly. They disintegrated at the first touch of her teeth, leaving a grainy paste smeared on her tongue. Rosie felt the edge of coming panic. Massively overdone. Massively.

It's OK, she told herself quickly. It's only rice. She drained the pot thoroughly and flicked in a few more sultanas and wisps of dill before putting the lid back on. Maybe it would solidify if she let it stand.

Too many dishes, that was the problem. She hadn't kept her eye on the pilaf and now it was overcooked. The stew had been more difficult than she thought, and who knew cooking beetroot was so complicated? Eight people was too many really, especially with the vegetarians ... She should finish the salad now, before they came.

Wait, though – how was the stew doing? It sounded all right. Rumbling with slow, deep bubbles. When she stirred it, the stew moved reluctantly, the glistening chunks of aubergine moving across the pot like dark icebergs through an oily sea. Much better.

But when she tasted it, the tang wasn't as intense as she'd hoped. Not bad or anything, just ... Where was the evidence of the hours of chopping, and frying, and stirring? What was the point if the effort wasn't, well, not on display exactly, but definitely implied? Rosie scraped out what was left of the pine honey and stirred it in. That should help.

It was almost twenty-five past seven now, and the table still wasn't laid. What was Stephen doing? She wanted to call out to him, but she'd have to shout to be heard upstairs and then he'd ask why she was screaming at him, and they'd probably have to argue about that until the guests arrived, and the table still wouldn't be laid. Thank God Magdalena had come that afternoon and the house was tidy.

As she went back to the bowl of lentils Rosie thought fondly of her new coffee table. Smooth, dust free, and with nothing on it yet but a vase of red tulips. She would go out and look at it in a minute.

But first she had to stir the non-yuzu juice into the lentil and beetroot salad. She had bought two limes just in case. Not that she expected Stephen to forget, but . . . just in case. It was a rare ingredient. She'd never tasted it, but the recipe said it was some-where between lime and mandarin, so she squeezed a clementine over the lentils as well before stirring the salad again.

It didn't taste too bad, actually, but all the same it was definitely lime and orange. She'd been hoping for an uniden-tifiable zing, and imagined herself saying casually, 'That? Oh, it's just a splash of yuzu juice . . . Don't you know it?'

With the gleaming purple chunks of beetroot poking out of the dark-green lentils, it certainly looked good. Lemon juice and maple syrup next. There was a lot of sugar in this meal, wasn't there? Oh well, she didn't have to list her ingre-dients; they'd never know. Rosie stirred them all together until the salad looked suitably artless.

Damn. She had forgotten the onion. There was definitely a red onion around somewhere. It wasn't in the fruit bowl, or in the veg tray. Perhaps in one of the cupboards? There were a few onion-skin flakes by one of the big pots, but they were old and desiccated. Why were they still there? She would have to have a word with Magdalena. Rosie slammed the door on them and quickly pulled open all the drawers along the side of the kitchen, closing each one more violently than the last as no onion was revealed.

Had she remembered to buy it? Yes, it was there on the list and she remembered picking up only one because she was sure there were already a few in the kitchen. But there weren't. And now she couldn't find the one she'd bought.

Rosie breathed deeply and ran her hands through her hair, forgetting they were still covered in lemon juice. She winced, then retraced her steps from the morning: unpacking the shopping; putting the ingredients away; trying to stuff the plastic bags in the ever-growing collection bursting out from under the sink; giving up; guiltily putting them in the bin because she didn't want to go out to the recycling . . .

She stared into the rubbish. Beneath a layer of beetroot skins and aubergine stalks she could see the orange glint of a Sainsbury's bag. She looked at it for a moment. Then with her thumb and forefinger she reached in and pinched the edge, pulling at it experimentally. She felt weight at the bottom of the bag. Slowly, she pulled the bag from under the damp vegetable peelings and opened it, revealing a shiny red onion at the bottom.

Rosie looked at the onion for a few more seconds.

It seemed fine. It had been wrapped in the plastic bag, mostly, so it was protected. There was nothing harmful in the rubbish. And no one was watching.

She cut up the onion quickly, and once she had scattered the slices into the salad and scraped the peel into the bin, covering up the plastic bag, the tension in her shoulders subsided.

With a teaspoon she tasted the salad. Good, but . . . well, it was mainly lentil, wasn't it? Maybe a bit more maple syrup? She measured out two overflowing teaspoons and stirred them in.

Oh dear, now it was a bit sweet. Was there any lemon left? She squeezed what was left of it over the salad, picking out the pips by hand. Hmm, that was now a bit sharp. More syrup?

Rosie looked at the time. They were late, but so was she. Thank God she'd already got changed. As long as her hair had survived the lemon . . .

The Gruyère loaf that stood cooling on the side looked dense and misshapen. Rosie cut it into thick, irregular slices to serve with drinks. The chunks fell apart as she laid them out, even though she'd been so careful about the timing. Bloody thing. Why hadn't she just got some nuts instead?

After hanging up her apron, Rosie set out the loaf along-side the crackers on the coffee table. The quiet tidiness of the living room immediately soothed her. Every time she looked at her Noguchi coffee table and Accent Wall with its fresh wallpaper, she felt a sense of contented calm.

It had taken two months of disruptive painting and decorating work, twice as long as they'd said it would, but

Rosie felt that room was worth it. She had been looking forward to having guests in here ever since it had been finished. Not that she wanted to show off, exactly, but she was certain that they'd be impressed.

She crossed the hall to the dining room. The table still wasn't laid, but soon it would be beautifully arranged with plates designed by a younger member of the Conran family and cutlery made by a German modernist. Perhaps the evening would be a success.

Rosie started sharply at the firm ring of the doorbell. The tone was too insistent, she thought; it always made her jump. Perhaps she should try to find something softer. But never mind that now. She smoothed down the front of her dress and went to answer the door.

COUNTY LIBRARY
434697
LOUTH
SERVICE

Two

Marcus watched Sarah and Rosie embrace warmly before saying hello to Rosie himself and engaging in a much more awkward kiss.

'Sorry if we're a bit late,' Sarah said.

'No, not at all. You're the first ones here, actually.'

'Oh I'm sorry . . .'

'No, no, I was just starting to wonder where everyone was.'

Marcus tried to identify the jumble of smells coming from the kitchen as Rosie led them down the hall, but couldn't get much beyond a vague, sweet spiciness. He did not think the aroma was intimidating.

'Smells lovely,' Sarah said.

'Thank you. I hope you'll like it. I'm just putting the last few things together. Let me get you something to drink.'

'Oh, yes – we brought some wine,' Sarah said, scrabbling around in her handbag. Marcus couldn't understand how she carried it around with her like that, with all that useless stuff in it. She could never find anything, even a bottle of wine, for God's sake.

Rosie took it without looking at the label.

'Well, here it is,' she said as they paused in the doorway of the living room. 'Our sitting room is finally finished. What do you think?'

'Oh it's lovely,' Sarah said, before stepping in.

Marcus experienced a moment of uncertainty when he saw the sofa, a sleek understated design that he didn't recognize or dislike. He had not previously suspected Rosie of having good taste, and the adjustment was disconcerting.

But then he entered the room fully and saw the expanse of patterned paper on the opposite wall. She probably got the idea from a TV makeover show, he thought, and the idea relaxed him. The paper was beautifully made and obviously expensive, but the coloured floral pattern, he felt, was too loud and fussy. It felt like a pub that was trying too hard to be trendy. He smiled to himself as he sat down on the sofa.

'How gorgeous!' Sarah was saying. 'It really brightens the place up.'

'We're very pleased with it,' Rosie said. 'I say "we" – I'm not sure Stephen's even noticed.'

'Where is Stephen?'

'He's probably just saying goodnight to Jonathan.'

'How is Jonathan?'

'Wonderful. We're sure he'll be talking any day now.'

'What a shame we missed him!' Sarah sat down next to Marcus. 'What's this?'

Marcus had already inspected the bready nibbles lying on

the coffee table – Noguchi! Did people still buy those? – and was quietly confident that it would be bland and doughy.

'It's Rosemary and Gruyère Loaf. Dig in. I'll get you some drinks.'

Sarah picked at a piece of loaf while Rosie went to the kitchen.

'Try it, Marcus, it's very good!' she said through a mouthful of sticky crumbs.

Marcus studied a chunk. The consistency was better than he had expected. He had put it to his nose to sniff for rosemary when Rosie returned with two small glasses.

'I thought we'd start with some sherry. I know it's a bit old-fashioned, but I think it goes really well with the loaf.'

'What a good idea,' Marcus said, surprised to find he meant it. The bread wasn't as heavy as he had anticipated and the fresh tang of the cheese was topped off with the warmth of the rosemary. He sipped his drink and found the dryness of the sherry cut nicely through the cheesiness.

'Very good,' he conceded.

'I'm so glad you like it! How's the sherry? I've really got into it recently – I think it's due for a comeback, don't you?'

'It's good,' Marcus accepted.

Rosie had not sat down. 'Look, I know it's rude, but do you mind if I leave you alone for a couple of minutes? I've just got to finish the starter and get Stephen down here.'

'We've got everything we need,' Sarah replied, sherry in one hand and loaf in the other.

Once Rosie had left the room, Marcus opened his notebook.

Sarah looked at him in horror. 'What are you doing?'

'What?'

'Bullet points? Don't you think that's going a bit over-board? What are you writing?'

'I'm reminding myself to mark them highly for the loaf, actually; it's nicely done.'

'You've put more than that.'

'I'm going to have to deduct points for leaving us like this. Less than perfect hosting.'

Sarah let out a disappointed sigh.

Marcus resented her for it. What right did she have to pity him in that martyred way? He retaliated by marking Rosie down on the redecoration. Sarah had always said he should be less judgemental about other people's taste – but she hadn't always been so disapproving about it. When had that started? Her thin lips were pinched tight beneath a hard frown that accentuated the creases at the corners of her mouth. She seemed to be losing her sense of fun. Even if she had always complained he was too snide, at least she used to enjoy it. What had gone wrong with her?

'OK, I've finished. Happy now?' Marcus stuffed the pad into his back pocket.

'Just promise me you won't get it out at the table.'

'What, you want me to sneak off to the toilet to make notes in secret?'

'Why do you have to do it at all?'

'If it's that important to you—' Marcus began, ready for an argument. But he stopped when the metallic bark of the doorbell cut through the room.

They listened for a long time, but heard no one go to answer it.

'Do you think we should go?' Sarah asked.

'I think that might come across as rude.'

They waited in silence for a few moments more, before the doorbell sounded again. This time footsteps in the hall followed and Marcus heard two male voices greet each other undemonstratively. He stood up as the living-room door opened.

'Hello, Stephen, we haven't seen you yet tonight.'

'Hello, Marcus,' Stephen said without audible enthusiasm. 'Do you know Matt?'

Marcus looked at the tall, broad-shouldered man he had brought in. 'No, I don't think so.'

'Marcus and Sarah, this is Matt.'

'We've met,' Matt said to Sarah.

'God, it's been years, hasn't it?'

'Yes, a long time,' Matt said with a faint smile. Marcus smiled inwardly at his broad northern accent. Lancashire, was it?

After Stephen had got sherry for Matt and himself, he restarted the conversation abruptly. Marcus thought he sounded like he was doing a foreign language role play.

'So, Matt, how are you?' Stephen asked.

'All right, thanks.'

'How's work?'

'Pretty good. Quite busy.'

'Did you get that big case you were trying for?'

'I did, actually. Starts next month. Should pay the mortgage for a while. Especially if I win.'

Stephen laughed dutifully. 'But you do usually win, don't you?' he asked.

'I've got a decent record,' Matt said. 'What about you, Stephen? Did you get that promotion you were applying for?'

'No.'

'Oh.' Matt inclined his head. 'Sorry to hear it.'

Matt took a square of loaf. They lapsed into silence.

Marcus took a long sip of his second glass of sherry. His left hand groped towards another slice of the Gruyère loaf. He had eaten half of it now. Probably rude to have any more. But he was going to get pretty drunk if they didn't start eating soon.

'I didn't see you at Rosie's thirtieth, did I?' Sarah asked.

'No, I wasn't there,' Matt said.

'It was a good party, wasn't it, Stephen?'

'Mmm.' Stephen nodded.

'Of course it must be a couple of years ago now.'

'I think I was abroad,' Matt said.

'On holiday?'

'No. For work.'

'Well, you missed a fun night.'

'So I hear.'

Marcus could not have been more relieved to hear the doorbell ring. Stephen leaped to his feet with equal gratitude.

'I'll get it.'

Marcus heard a female voice he didn't recognize, and Stephen returned with a tall blonde woman, with a florid complexion, whom Marcus judged just the wrong side of statuesque. Stephen introduced her as Charlotte.

Marcus girded himself for more small talk when Rosie

appeared at the door, looking flushed and carrying a small bowl of olives.

'Hello, everybody. Sorry I've abandoned you. Don't worry – everything's going fine with the food. Nearly there now. Have you all met? Oh good. Stephen, are you getting Charlotte a drink ... well done. Now, could you be in charge of these?' She handed him the bowl.

Stephen handed Charlotte a glass of sherry, offered round the olives and returned to sit quietly in his corner seat.

'Cheers,' said Charlotte, the glass reaching her lips before she had finished the word. 'What's this?' she asked after a generous draught.

'Sherry.'

Charlotte shrugged and drank some more. 'So, Rosie, how does this whole thing work?' she asked.

'You've seen *Come Dine with Me* on TV?'

'Sure.'

'It's just like that. We all take turns at cooking, give each other marks out of ten, and someone wins.'

'What, is there a cash prize?'

'No, apart from that. It's just for the fun of it. And the glory, of course.' She laughed briefly.

'Right, but I have to cook for everyone?'

'Yes – didn't you read the e-mails?'

'Because on TV there're just the four of them. What are there, six of us here?'

'And Barbara and Justin.'

'We're not doing eight evenings, are we? We'll be sick of the sight of each other by then.'

Rosie grinned nervously. 'No, the plan was that we do it in couples. So just four dinners, like on TV.'

'Doesn't seem very fair if I'm on my own and there are two of everyone else.'

Rosie's anxious smile got wider. 'Well, the thing was, you see, that I thought you might cook with Matt. I thought I said in the e-mail ...'

'Who's Matt?'

Marcus took a quick gulp of sherry to hide his grin. A slow red blush was creeping up towards Rosie's ears.

'Stephen, I thought you said you'd introduced everyone?'

'Well, I did, but ...'

'I'm Matt,' said Matt.

He and Charlotte stared at each other appraisingly.

'It's a bit of a surprise for me as well,' he told her. 'But pleased to meet you anyway.'

Three

Christ. What the hell was going on? Charlotte turned to stare at Rosie, who snatched up the bowl of olives again.

'Shall we go and sit at the table?' Rosie said. 'I'm sure the others will be here in a minute.'

She was leading them out of the door before Charlotte could say, 'Fucking hell, no, what the fuck do you think you're doing?'

Charlotte fumed silently. Wasn't there something a bit more humiliating Rosie could have tried? What about sticking her in a shop window with a neon sign saying: 'Sad and Lonely – Reduced to Clear'? Or having some business cards printed up with 'Charlotte Wells – Getting More Desperate Every Day'? And why the fuck did Rosie think she'd want to be set up anyway? Particularly with one of her husband's arse-crushingly dull friends. Jesus, what are they going to do at the end of the evening? Lock her and Matt in a room with some Barry White playing and a box of Milk Tray? Or is this going to be a car keys in a bowl situation?

Fuck.

There's no way I'm going to get through four nights of this, Charlotte thought. Absolutely no way. How awkward can you get? Maybe I just won't talk to him all evening, just to let him know how things stand. But then I'll have to talk to the others. Christ, I bet Stephen's already talking about house prices. No, it's home improvement now, isn't it? And that little git in the black-rimmed glasses – Marcus, was it? – I just know he's going to start asking everyone's opinion on the new Rimsky-Korsakov exhibition or some such bollocks, and then, when you say you don't know, act all smug and bore everyone to death about it. Look at him, you can just tell.

Christ, why did I agree to do this? Was I drunk? Well, I soon will be.

Charlotte reached for the nearest bottle sitting on the side table of the dining room, relieved to find it already open. She abandoned her sherry glass for something bigger.

'That's quite a decent New Zealand Pinot noir,' Stephen said as she filled her glass towards the brim.

Oh Jesus. Just let me drink my booze in peace, will you? Why do all these boring couples assume I'm desperate to join their self-satisfied, delightfully decorated, 'oh I know the best little wine club' world? I'm not. I don't care about your Ascot-style patio garden extension. I don't care that little Johnny's learned to crap. And I certainly don't care about your pitiful attempts to offload your embarrassing male friends on to me.

'Thank you,' she said to Stephen as she tasted the wine. 'Very nice.'

They were hovering round the dining-room table, as Rosie explained the seating plan. Charlotte ignored the instruction to sit opposite Matt and plonked herself down in one of the empty seats, silently thanking whoever it was that hadn't turned up yet. Rosie looked flustered for a moment, but Charlotte stared her down.

'Did you like the living room?' Rosie turned to Marcus to restart the conversation. 'We spent ages agonizing over the colour, didn't we, Stephen?'

'It's certainly very striking,' Marcus said. 'Didn't I see something like it on one of those TV programmes?'

'No, it's a new pattern that was only launched this season.'

Oh Jesus. Charlotte hid her face with her glass. Kill me now. It's even worse than I thought. There's no way I'm doing this again. No way. Even if I have to fake leukaemia, I'm not doing three more evenings of this. I'm not sure I'm even going to make it through tonight.

'Of course, the builders were a nightmare. They took twice as long as they said they would, and made a terrible mess,' Rosie said.

'You don't have to tell me about builders,' Marcus interrupted. 'I deal with them all the time. The trick is to always double everything they say. That way you won't be disappointed.'

'Are you in the trade yourself, Marcus?' Matt asked.

Charlotte snorted a little through her nose as she stifled a laugh.

'I'm an architect,' Marcus said stiffly.

'Oh, right.' Matt's face was unreadable.

Charlotte studied him again. He wasn't that bad to look at, she thought. Tall, beefy, but not fat. Nice, soft, wavy brown hair. Something clever-looking about his face, but, for some reason, really dirty eyes. If she hadn't already decided not to, Charlotte thought she might have quite fancied him. Not a sexy accent, though. Still, maybe if he didn't say too much . . .

'I've tried Barbara's phone, but there's no reply,' Rosie said. 'I don't want to start without them, but you must all be getting hungry?'

'I'm starving,' Charlotte said.

'Stephen, can you bring in the rest of the loaf and crackers, please? And should I bring out some crisps or something as well?'

'Anything.'

'It would be a shame to ruin our appetite for the meal, though,' Marcus said, grinning.

'Sarah, do you have Justin's number?'

'No, I don't think so.'

'I vote we start,' Charlotte said.

'Maybe give it five more minutes . . . I'll get you the crisps.'

'Who are these people anyway?'

'I know Barbara through Sarah. She's very nice.'

'I met her at my Pilates class,' Sarah explained.

'Oh yes, that reminds me,' Rosie said. 'You'll need to know for your meals – Barbara and Justin are vegetarians.'

Vegetarians! Immediately, Charlotte decided not to like the late-coming couple.

'I'm sure I told them seven thirty,' Sarah said.

'They've probably got lost,' Charlotte declared.

'Why do you say that?'

'Because they're vegetarians.'

Matt laughed. 'How does that follow?'

'It's the sort of thing they'd do. Vague and inconsiderate.'

'I didn't think you'd met them.'

'No, I mean vegetarians. Can't be trusted.' Charlotte took a long gulp of wine.

The doorbell rang. Everyone jerked upright.

'There they are!' Rosie leaped up and rushed to the front door. There were urgent, apologetic voices in the hall.

'Sorry, everyone,' Justin said, sticking his head round the door. 'We got a bit lost.'

Four

'Maybe I should have given you clearer directions,' Rosie said.

'No, it was my fault,' insisted Justin, savouring the acceptance of blame. 'We got off the bus in the wrong place.'

'I'm sure it's easy to do.'

'I hope we haven't held everyone up.'

'No . . . not too much.'

'We have, haven't we? I'm so sorry.' Justin felt a warm glow of self-sacrifice seep through him. 'I knew I should have looked more carefully at the instructions.'

'You could have phoned me once you were lost and Stephen would have told you the way.'

'Yes, I should have done,' Justin agreed. 'But I didn't want to disturb you. My mistake.'

'Never mind. Let's go straight through. Barbara, can I take your coat?'

'Thank you,' Barbara said, handing over her bead-embroidered jacket.

There was no question of telling people what had really happened. It would have been too upsetting for Barbara, and Justin didn't want to worry the others with talk about deportation. So he had decided to take the blame for lateness on himself.

Of course there was an element of guilt at mentioning the buses at all; public transport was always being picked on and belittled, and Justin hated to add to the blame. On the way over, he had considered claiming to have been held up at work, but that wouldn't have been fair on his colleagues.

'Sorry again, everyone,' Justin said as they entered the dining room, with its two conspicuously untouched place settings. 'It was my fault.'

He thought he heard the blonde woman at the end exclaim something.

'Never mind, let's just sit down, shall we?' Rosie said. 'Sorry to rush, but do you mind if I bring the starter straight through?'

'No, that would be great.'

'Stephen, can you give me a hand, please?' Rosie said, already retreating towards the kitchen.

'Sorry to keep everyone waiting,' Justin said again, as he sat down.

There was silence. Charlotte topped up her wine glass and offered the bottle to Barbara and Justin.

'Just a bit for me, please,' Justin said. 'Early start tomorrow.'

'On Saturday?'

'It's my volunteering morning.'

There was another short pause.

'OK, here we are,' Rosie said, decelerating sharply as she arrived back at the table with a tray of soup bowls. 'Our first course: Chilled Spinach Soup with Avocado and Bacon Croutons.'

She began handing out the bowls and, as Justin's mouth opened, added: 'And, of course, the vegetarian version with celery chunks instead of bacon for Justin and Barbara.'

Justin closed his mouth.

'It looks wonderful,' Sarah said.

'Right, then,' Rosie concluded as she sat down. 'Cheers, everybody.'

Everyone raised their glasses and the table fell quiet. Spoons scraping against china bowls occasionally disturbed the hush.

'Well, what does everybody think?' Rosie asked, an edge of anxiety in her voice.

'It's delicious,' Sarah said.

'It's lovely, Rosie,' Justin said. 'Really fresh-tasting.'

'Oh good.' Rosie exhaled.

'The bacon's a nice touch,' Matt volunteered. 'It's good to have a bit of crunchiness.'

After a moment's thought, Marcus said: 'It makes a change to have a cold soup, doesn't it? Particularly when it's not really summer yet.'

Sarah looked at him sharply.

Rosie said: 'Do you think so?'

'Yes. And I suppose it's so much more convenient if you can make it all a couple of days in advance and stick it in the fridge.'

'Yesterday, actually.'

'It's definitely not too cold, though, so you judged it well, taking it out of the fridge in time.'

'Marcus . . .' Sarah began.

'I'm just giving you my impressions,' Marcus replied with a defensive shrug. 'Anyway, Justin, you were telling us about your charity work.'

'No, I wasn't.'

Justin realized this might have been a bit abrupt. The question seemed aggressive to him, but perhaps that was unfair. He didn't really know Marcus, and he probably meant well. 'I mean, I don't want to bore everyone.'

'It wouldn't be boring,' Sarah said. 'I'd like to hear about it. You work for AfricAid, don't you?'

'Yes, but in the office it's all about lobbying work – talking to governments, organizing donors, putting together support packages for victims of violence or persecuted activists in Africa. At the weekend it's nice to actually meet some of the people this is happening to, to see who you're trying to help.'

'Where do you do that?'

'There's a refugee support centre in Stamford Hill. It's so hard for them, adjusting to a new way of life in an alien country.'

'What do you do there?'

'Oh not much, really. Offer advice, help with bureaucracy, that sort of thing. Often, I'm not really needed. They'd much rather watch TV. Which is fine. But I just like being there, you know? It reminds me why I'm doing it.'

The clink of spoons on china once again filled the dining room.

'Tell me,' Marcus asked, wiping soup off his upper lip with a napkin. 'How effective do you think your campaigns are?'

'It's hard work, of course, but we do think we make a difference.'

'You don't think you're just treating the symptoms? Interfering from outside, making cosmetic changes that aren't really lasting?'

'Marcus . . .' Sarah said again.

'No, it's all right,' Justin said. 'It's important to be able to correct those arguments openly. There are a lot of misconceptions around international advocacy work. Most importantly, everything we do is alongside local partners. We're not forcing change on these societies; we're trying to help forces for change that are already there. That's the first thing. Secondly, we do make lasting changes. Our project in Malawi, for example—'

'Does anyone want any more?' Rosie asked. 'Sorry to interrupt, Justin, but there's loads left, so does anyone want a top-up before we move on to the main course?'

'No, thank you, Rosie,' Justin said. 'It was delicious, though. Now, what we did in Malawi—'

'Marcus?'

'No, thanks, Rosie. I've still got plenty left.'

'Oh sorry, I'll let you finish, then.'

'Actually, I'd like some more if we're going to have to wait for the main course,' Charlotte said.

'Great.' Rosie reached out to take the empty dish from Charlotte, and handed it to Stephen. 'Would you mind getting

Charlotte some more?' Wordlessly, Stephen got up and took the bowl through to the kitchen.

'Anyway, in Malawi—'

'Oh look, sorry, Justin, but before we get too drawn into things, maybe we should just sort out some ground rules for the competition. Is that all right?'

'Yes, fine, Rosie, of course.'

In fact, Justin was a little disappointed at being interrupted. It wasn't that he liked talking about his work as such, but these were important issues. People needed to know. There was a lot of scepticism out there about what aid groups and NGOs like his were doing – maybe they hadn't been good enough at communicating it – and Justin liked to take every chance he could to tackle public mistrust. But it was OK, he told himself. There would be another opportunity.

'Is everyone all right with doing one dinner a week?' Rosie was saying. 'I thought four in a row might be a bit much . . .'

'It certainly would,' Charlotte said with feeling.

'Great, and for the scoring,' Rosie continued, 'shall we just get each couple to give a mark at the end of the night?'

'Why by couple?' Charlotte demanded. 'Why can't we give our own marks?'

'Well . . .' Rosie said, avoiding Charlotte's eye. 'Maybe . . .'

'If we're cooking in couples it does make sense to score that way too,' Marcus said.

'I don't see why,' Charlotte said.

'It doesn't really make any difference,' Matt said. 'It's easy enough to take an average of two scores and give that as one mark.'

They paused to work this out.

'Matt's right,' Sarah said.

'More importantly,' Marcus said, 'we can't do it at the end of each night, otherwise by the end everyone will know exactly what scores they need to give to win. We mustn't find out what marks everyone has given until the end.'

'How do we do that?' Charlotte took the refilled soup bowl from Stephen, then thrust her empty glass back at him.

'What do they do on TV?' Rosie asked.

'They have producers watching them on TV, don't they?' Stephen said, ignoring the glass.

'True,' agreed Rosie.

'Can't we all just tell Rosie?' Justin said.

'No!' Marcus and Charlotte said together.

'Why not?'

'That would give her an unfair advantage,' Marcus said.

'Yes, no, not me,' Rosie said. 'Maybe someone impartial.'

'Who could we ask? It would have to be someone independent.' Marcus said this with the impression of deep thought. 'Someone we all trust.'

'Don't you think that's going a bit over the top?' Stephen said, eyes still averted from the empty glass.

Charlotte reached out towards the fresh wine bottle herself. 'Maybe we should all put our scores in sealed envelopes,' she said. Stephen reluctantly filled her glass to halfway. 'Then we could open them all at the same time on the last night.'

Justin thought she might have been joking here. Surely no one was taking the competition that seriously?

But Marcus said: 'That's a good idea. Still vulnerable to

fraud, though – anyone could make a new envelope at any point.'

'Honestly, Marcus!' Rosie looked pained. 'I don't think any of us are going to resort to fraud.'

'But that's what it would be, Rosie. Sorry to be harsh.'

'Really gorgeous soup,' Sarah said.

'Of course, we could give the envelopes to someone to hold,' Marcus mused. 'But that just leaves us with the same problem as before.'

'I tell you what, Marcus,' Matt said. 'Let's create a dedicated e-mail address where we all e-mail our scores. That way, no one will have them early, and no one can change them.'

'Good idea, Matt,' Rosie said, standing up. 'Now has everybody finished?'

There was silence for a moment as Rosie collected the bowls and stacked them into a precarious pile.

'So who has the password to this account, then?' Charlotte said.

'Exactly,' Marcus agreed.

'Couldn't we all have it?' Sarah asked.

'Of course not,' Marcus snapped. 'Then we might as well just tell each other the scores.'

'Looks like we'll need a referee, then,' Matt said.

Charlotte took another sip of wine. 'Why don't we have a password that each of us only knows part of?' she said. 'It would be like those films where the three guys each have a key to the treasure vault and no one can open it unless they're all there.'

'Yes!' Marcus exclaimed. 'Great idea. What do they call that?'

'A tontine, I think,' Matt said.

'No, that's where they have to wait for everyone to die and the last one alive wins all the money,' Marcus corrected.

'No, it's the key thing,' Matt said.

'I'm sure it's not.' Marcus got to his feet. 'Rosie,' he said as she came back with a steaming dish of rice. 'Can I use your laptop?'

'Marcus, you can Google it later,' Sarah hissed.

'I'm not going to Google it. I'm going to set up the account.'

'Well, I'm going to serve the main course,' Rosie said with a grimace of distress. She added: 'What account?'

'I'll show you.' Marcus left the room.

Rosie stood forlorn in the space between the door and the table. Justin felt a little sorry for her. She'd put in so much effort and, really, maybe Marcus could have waited. But then, if it was a competition, even a friendly one, maybe it made sense to sort out the rules at the beginning.

'It's all right, Rosie,' he said. 'We won't blame you if it starts to get cold.'

'Is that the main course?' Charlotte pointed doubtfully at the big dish of rice. 'I'm still starving.'

'It's just the pilaf. I'll bring out the main dish when . . . What is Marcus doing?'

'Setting up an e-mail account to keep the scores secure,' Matt said.

'Oh.'

Marcus returned holding the laptop open in front of him. 'Right, here we are. I hope you don't mind – I found this in the spare room. I've created dinneratminescores@gmail.com. Everyone can remember that. Rosie, do you want to go next?'

'What?'

'Just put in two digits, anything you like, then pass it to Charlotte.'

'Do we all need to do this now, Marcus?' Rosie asked.

'Just one half of every couple if you like.'

The laptop was passed round the table in solemn silence, Rosie to Charlotte then to Justin. He used the first two digits of his birthday. Was that too obvious? But what did it matter – who would be trying to guess? He pushed the computer on to Matt.

'Finished?' Rosie asked when the laptop was returned to Marcus.

'Hold on,' Marcus said. 'It says I need to use some letters. Let me pick one.'

'Can you put the laptop away now?' Rosie asked with brittle politeness.

'I'm on Google now anyway, so I'll just look this up . . .'

'Marcus . . .' Sarah said.

'Oh,' Marcus said to Matt, sounding disappointed. 'We were both right about the tontine.'

Five

'Barbara,' Rosie slammed the wooden salad bowl down in the middle of the table, 'why don't you tell us about your exhibition?'

Sarah watched Barbara, who had been staring into the middle distance, slowly focus on Rosie. 'Really, it's not much of an exhibition,' Barbara said. 'Just a couple of pieces on display in the local café.'

'Never mind. I'm sure everyone would love to hear about the work,' Rosie insisted, still standing up. 'Barbara's a potter,' she explained to the rest of the table. 'She makes such gorgeous things. That vase is one of hers.' Everyone obediently studied the irregular, brightly coloured object on the sideboard.

Sarah had never been sure she understood Barbara's work. It was pretty, of course, most of it anyway, but the deeper themes that Barbara agonized over somehow weren't apparent to her. She had asked Barbara about it once, but Barbara had said you weren't supposed to describe it, you were supposed to feel it.

'How did you become a potter?' Rosie asked. 'I've always meant to ask.'

'At college,' Barbara replied.

'Right.' Rosie waited. 'And when did you come to England?'

'Three years ago.'

'Why?'

'To study at Goldsmiths.'

After a few monosyllables the conversation drifted on to other things. Sarah wondered if something might be the matter. Barbara was so lively when she was in a good mood. Maybe it was the new people. Beneath it all, Sarah suspected, Barbara was quite shy. You wouldn't think it for someone so creative and beautiful, but she was a very serious person. It took a long time for her to get comfortable with people; it had been almost a year of seeing each other at Pilates before she was really relaxed around Sarah.

Although, it seemed to be quicker with Rosie. Sarah had introduced them only a couple of months ago, and now they were seeing each other just the two of them. Rosie had already been to see Barbara's exhibition. Sarah hadn't. She had been planning to ask Rosie to go with her.

It was great that they got on so well. Of course it was. Barbara didn't know that many people over here, and it could get lonely in a foreign country. It was wonderful that she was becoming friends with Rosie. But why didn't they ask her along when they met?

Sarah immediately felt guilty for thinking this. What was she worrying about? That Rosie was trying to steal her friend?

Ridiculous. It was probably just that Rosie had a free after-noon, and Barbara was self-employed. They would have known Sarah was at work and not wanted to bother her. Of course.

'Here we are, everybody. Sorry about the wait.' Rosie came back carrying two plates, trailed by Stephen carrying two more. 'Duck Breast with Pomegranate Molasses.'

'Oh that looks lovely,' Sarah said as Rosie set down a plate in front of her. Thin slices of duck breast covered in a thick sauce sat nestled next to a mush of long, green vegetables – what did they call that? Was it okra?

There was a silence round the table. What had they been talking about? Sarah hadn't been listening. Oh dear, that was bad, wasn't it?

'...And for the vegetarians, Aubergine and Tamarind Stew.' Rosie was back with the last two plates. 'Please help yourself to the pilaf, everyone, and the Candied Beetroot and Lentil Salad.' Rosie pulled in her chair and reached for the wine bottle. 'Bon appetit.'

Sarah realized she was absolutely starving. She gulped down a slice of duck breast very quickly. But that wasn't right, was it? Rosie had gone to such effort that she ought to savour it properly. Sarah filled up a bit on rice before trying again.

'Rosie, this is lovely,' she said. 'The sauce is so unusual.'

It was very good, she thought; a bit cold, maybe, but definitely tasty, and it was great to be adventurous and try something new. Sarah wasn't sure if she really liked pome-granates, but how was Rosie to know that? And they were probably very good pomegranates.

It seemed so petty to grade the food like a piece of sub-standard homework. Maybe they could forget about the competition and just say something nice in their e-mail? Sarah sighed quietly as she thought about suggesting this to Marcus.

'Very nice, Rosie,' Matt said. 'The duck's great. Properly pink in the middle.'

'You don't think I've overcooked it?' Rosie asked. 'I was a bit worried.'

'Not at all,' Matt said.

'Maybe a bit,' Marcus said. 'But duck's very hard to get right. Well done for giving it a go. What's in the sauce?'

'It's pomegranate molasses with a bit of cinnamon and some herbs. Very simple.'

'Yes, I thought I could taste cinnamon. But I wasn't sure if you'd have deliberately made it that sweet.'

Rosie turned away from him. 'Justin, Barbara. How's yours?'

'Great, thanks,' Barbara said.

'It is very nice,' Justin said. He chewed another mouthful before adding: 'Though I sometimes think it's a shame that we're not all eating the same thing.'

'Then you shouldn't be a vegetarian, should you?' Charlotte said sharply.

'I don't condemn people for eating meat. But I just think sometimes they should stop and discover how good vegetarian food can be. This tamarind, for example, is a great flavour.'

'Goes very well with lamb, I reckon,' Charlotte said.

'Let's not argue about that,' Rosie said. 'Has everyone had some salad?'

Justin inspected the salad bowl full of beetroot and lentils before taking some, then passing it along.

'It's very good, Rosie,' he said. 'Has it got lime in it?'

'Yes,' Rosie replied. She looked strangely tense as she said it, Sarah thought.

Sarah had nearly finished. She ought to slow down. It wasn't healthy to bolt your food, was it? Rude, too. But she was still hungry. It had been such a tiring day. How did Rosie possibly manage to cook all these courses on a work night? But she worked part-time, didn't she? That would be nice. Of course she had Jonathan to look after, and that was obviously a full-time job in itself. But still . . .

Sarah wondered if she hated her own job. No, that was a stupid thing to think. She loved teaching. Of course she did. She was making a difference. That sounded trite, but it was true. Giving something back.

Marcus sometimes said that giving something back was really taking it out of her. He was always so pleased with himself when he said it, but she supposed that might be true. She was tired all the time now. It wasn't the kids' fault, of course. They were just being themselves. But sometimes . . .

This morning, for example, Dr Cowley had said she should have been tougher. But was it really right to start calling the children liars?

Khalida had been texting in class, while Sarah was trying to teach them about the suffragettes. Sarah had asked her, politely, to stop it and pay attention to the lesson.

'Khalida, please stop that.'

Khalida had not replied.

'Khalida, please stop that!'

Very slowly, Khalida responded: 'I'm texting my little sister, miss.'

'Do that after class.'

'No, miss, I need to do it now.'

'Khalida!'

'She's pregnant, miss.'

'Really?' This had thrown Sarah. Little Aisha? She couldn't be more than thirteen, could she?

'Yeah, miss, she's got a doctor's appointment and she's scared, see? I said I'd text her.'

'Oh I see. Well, I suppose . . .'

'Miss, miss, Khalida's lying!' Sureen burst out. 'Her sister's not pregnant. She's texting her boyfriend.'

'Shut up!'

'Calm down, everyone,' Sarah said. 'Now, Khalida, you wouldn't lie about something like that, would you?'

'No, miss.' Khalida smirked aggressively at Sureen, flaunting her phone.

'Well, what about your mother? Where's she? We've got Mrs Pankhurst to get through. Couldn't you do it after class?'

'No.'

'I see. Well, be quick, then. Now, everybody, if you turn to page sixty-three, you'll see that Mrs Pankhurst was arrested again the following year for hitting a police officer. What do you all think of this kind of— Lauren, put your phone away.'

'But, miss,' Lauren looked up wide-eyed from her screen. 'My sister's pregnant.'

'Really? . . . No she isn't. Just put it away.'

'But, miss!'

'Dylan, you too.'

'Honest, miss, I have to. It's Tyler's mum . . . she's pregnant!'

'Fuck off!' Tyler lunged across the desk at Dylan.

'Boys, stop that! Stop it!'

Some teachers would have started shouting at this point. Sarah didn't believe in that. It just brutalized the children, didn't it? If she didn't give them a good example of calm and rational behaviour, who would? They were good kids, if you gave them a chance.

By this stage, all the girls had their phones out and Rihanna was in tears.

'What's the matter?'

'Kelly's called me a slag on Twitter. Said I slept with Jack. But it was only hands.'

'Kelly, is that true?'

But Kelly wasn't listening. She had formed a tight gaggle with three other girls, exchanging gossip with whoops of delighted outrage.

By then the boys' fight had spread to the back of the class and Dylan was using *Changemakers: Political Struggle in Twentieth-Century Britain* to club Tyler round the head.

After that, Dr Cowley had to get involved. Sarah winced at the way she screamed at them, but it did stop the fighting. Sarah felt like a failure.

'Don't you think so, Sarah?'

'What?'

Rosie was looking at her expectantly, but once again Sarah had no idea what they were talking about.

'Oh yes, probably,' she mumbled. 'This really is delicious.'

Marcus rolled his eyes at her as he got up. Had she said something embarrassing? Was it obvious that she'd been daydreaming?

'I'm just going to the toilet,' he announced.

Why had he said that so loudly? Because he wasn't going to the toilet, was he? He was reaching into his pocket for his notebook, even before he got to the door. Oh dear, it was so rude. At least he wasn't doing it at the table. He'd been so mean already this evening. Poor Rosie. Why was he being so competitive? But then he always was. He was going to be awful when it was his turn to cook. Sarah didn't want to think about it. He'd be unbearable for days before and afterwards.

Things hadn't been going so well recently. He was intense about his opinions, and Sarah had always liked that; it was admirable, uncompromising. But lately . . . well, it wasn't that he'd got more stubborn, exactly. More that he had stopped taking her opinion seriously.

No, that was unfair. Wasn't it? But Sarah certainly found it very hard to talk to him now. She hadn't even thought of telling him about the fight in the classroom. He would have made it clear that he considered it her fault. He probably wouldn't have said it directly, but it would have been obvious. He would have been impatient. Unsympathetic.

Sarah wished she had told him. If he'd put his arms round

her, soothed her, made her feel better, she wouldn't be thinking these things. But she couldn't see that happening.

It was a bad time for his practice, that was true. There wasn't
much work coming in, and his last project had never been
built . . . But when had that been any different?

She brooded on this until Marcus returned, tucking his
notebook into his back pocket, with a broad smile across his
face.

Matt watched him sit down. 'You've been gone a long
time,' he said. 'And you certainly seem to have enjoyed
yourself.'

Charlotte tried to suppress a snort of laughter, and drops of
red wine came out of her nose.

Six

Stephen had reached the stage of the evening when he kept his right hand resting on the base of his wine glass between sips. He had finished his main course and was sitting back in his chair, arm stretched out to grip the glass. The wine had padded the corners of his earlier irritability and he felt sated and much better disposed to the conversation.

Matt was telling a story about the stupidity of one of his clients, a man who was trying to sue a supermarket that had sold him a bag of pistachio nuts, because the packet did not warn him to take the shells off before eating them. Stephen emitted a warm, alcoholic chuckle.

The worst of the evening was over now. The tense preparation and the stilted, effortful small talk had all been washed away by the passage of wine. Stephen was enjoying himself. Certainly, he would have preferred to have his feet up on the coffee table watching *Lewis*, but he was having a tolerable time. With most of the food out of the way, conversation was flowing a bit easier too, keeping itself going spontaneously rather than through determined questions from Rosie.

'So I asked him, "What actually happened when you ate the nuts?" and he said, "I cut my lip." So I said, "Just remind me how much you want to claim for that." He looked at me and said: "Two hundred grand. What? It was quite a bad cut."'

A ripple of laughter spread round the table. Stephen sat up sharply as he heard Rosie laugh louder than the rest. What did that mean? Why was she simpering like that at Matt? But she was standing up now, and Stephen decided that the overeager laugh was a sign of tension, a way of trying to leave the table without appearing rude. He settled himself back in his chair, and had another sip of wine.

He knew she was going to check the crumble. He knew that, really, he was supposed to be doing that. Sod it, though. He was comfortable now. She would be fretting about it anyway, so there was no point both of them running about. Besides, the busier she was, the less anxious she got. Stephen poured himself some more wine.

'Here we are, everybody,' Rosie said, setting down the bubbling crumble dish. 'Stephen, could you start serving while I get the cream?'

Reluctantly, Stephen let go of his glass and cracked the top of the crumble with the big spoon. Thick seams of sugary fruit juice bubbled up between the golden peaks of crumble, which separated into textured continents of browned, rocky crumbs. Stephen congratulated himself. He had judged the mixture just right.

Rosie returned with the cream. Stephen had served out all

eight portions before Marcus said: 'I thought we were having figs?'

'We were, but I just couldn't find any that were good enough today,' Rosie said smoothly. 'The local organic shop had an excellent batch in recently, but they'd run out this morning and I thought there was no point trying to do it with sub-standard figs. So Stephen stepped in and made a crumble.'

'Stephen, this is delicious,' Charlotte said, her voice muffled by a huge mouthful of creamy fruit.

'It really is,' Matt said. 'I've nearly finished mine.'

'Yes, it is nice,' Marcus said. 'Good to have some hearty British fare after all that Mediterranean stuff, eh?'

Stephen ignored him. Rosie had gone to fetch the dessert wine.

A glass of Vin Santo washed the crumble down nicely, Stephen thought. One blanket of sticky, sugary warmth wrapped round another, but with the crunchiness of the crumble top there to give a bit of bite. Stephen helped himself to seconds. Almost everyone asked for some more, and he eked out the last charred scrapings from the rim of the dish with quiet satisfaction. He did make a good crumble. He offered the dessert wine round again before draining the last of the bottle into his glass and sinking back into his chair.

A stuffed lull settled over the table. All efforts were now focused on digesting the thick mix of doughy crumble, leaving little energy to spare for conversation. Laboured breathing spread out around the room.

Despite his discomfort, he appreciated the silent companionship of surfeit. Everyone, he felt sure, was happy and relaxed, content to let the evening coast pleasantly towards a quiet end.

'I know!' Rosie said. 'How about a game?'

Stephen groaned inwardly.

'What about charades?' Rosie went on. 'It's been ages since I played that.'

'I don't think I can move,' Sarah said.

'Really?' Rosie coaxed.

'Definitely not,' Charlotte decreed.

Rosie looked crestfallen. Stephen decided to risk some teasing. 'Rosie's no good at charades anyway,' he told the guests. 'She always picks *Ferris Bueller's Day Off*.'

Rosie gave the company a brittle grin. 'Yes, but Stephen always picks the film we saw last.'

This was true, Stephen had to admit. Although often he couldn't remember what the film was called.

'Well, Marcus always picks film titles in German,' Sarah said. 'It's very annoying.'

'I didn't realize you spoke German,' Rosie said.

'I don't,' Marcus replied. 'It just makes them harder to guess.'

'That's cheating!' Charlotte protested.

'There's no rule against it,' Marcus said. 'I've checked.'

'Look, do we have to play a game?' Charlotte asked. 'Are we really so boring that we can't think of anything to say to each other?'

There was a pause.

Stephen knew he ought to say something, but couldn't

think what. All he wanted to do was let the conversation wash over him, stirring only if he spotted something interesting floating by.

'I just thought it would be fun,' Rosie said.

'How about Shag, Marry, Kill, then?' Charlotte said. 'Or, I Have Never.'

'Or, Mr and Mrs,' Rosie suggested.

'No!' Stephen cried, at exactly the same time as Charlotte.

'What about that one where you all have to write the name of someone famous on a piece of paper?' Sarah suggested. 'Then you take it in turns to put a name on your forehead without looking at it, and you have to guess who you are by asking yes or no questions.'

'That sounds great,' Rosie said. 'I'll get some paper.'

Stephen put a lot of thought into his choice. He wanted someone who was unquestionably a household name, but who wouldn't be immediately obvious. That way he could keep people guessing for ages, and they'd be kicking themselves when they didn't get it.

In the end he went for Kofi Annan. Instantly recognizable, but not at the front of anyone's mind any more.

Justin was the first to draw. He unfolded the torn scrap of paper at arm's length and slapped it quickly on to his forehead.

'Move your fingers,' Charlotte said.

Stephen craned forward to read the name. It didn't resolve itself. He peered closer.

'Who the hell is that?' Charlotte demanded.

'I've no idea,' Matt said.

'Marcus!' Sarah exclaimed.

'What?' Marcus asked. 'Why are you assuming it was me?'

'Has anyone else ever heard of Farkas Molnar?' Sarah demanded.

'You've given it away now!' Marcus protested.

There were blank looks around the table.

'He was the foremost Hungarian disciple of the Bauhaus!' Marcus protested. 'No? No one?'

'Can I put this down now?' Justin asked, fingers still clamped to his head.

Sarah nodded and Justin tore up the paper and picked another. Paris Hilton, it read.

'Happy now?' Marcus muttered.

Rosie drew next. Stephen felt a twinge of excitement at seeing the name.

'Good one,' Sarah said, nodding.

'OK. Is it a politician?' Rosie asked.

'Yes,' Sarah said.

'British?'

'No.'

'Is it Kofi Annan?'

Stephen went off the game after that.

He stopped playing but they seemed to carry on fine without him. Stephen breathed out huffily, but found himself wheezing. Perhaps that second helping of crumble had been a mistake. He'd eaten it too quickly and was starting to feel very bloated. Maybe some wine would help. Soothe his stomach.

No, in fact it just increased the pressure. Bugger it. He was going to feel this tomorrow. He listened tetchily as Sarah quickly identified Martin Scorsese. Matt was the last to guess, pretending not to mind at all as Charlotte goaded him.

Stephen watched Matt with dyspeptic malevolence. After all these years, how had he only just found out? Rosie said he was making too much of it, that it was all so long ago and what did it matter now? But if that was the case, why had she never told him about it? Why had he only found out by accident from the big mouth of some woman he hardly even remembered from college?

Of course, Stephen had always known that Rosie and Matt had gone out together. Briefly, they said. It was during the first year of university, and only for a couple of months. Rosie said it was nothing really, just a fling that clearly wasn't going anywhere. And that was fine. Sort of. Rosie had told Stephen about it when they first got together and he'd got over it then, even felt an unaccustomed superiority over his friend: he, Stephen, had made it work with Rosie after she had dumped Matt.

Only, it turned out, she hadn't dumped Matt. No, he had dumped her. And Stephen had only just discovered that. Rosie had apologized for not telling him. But it sounded more like she was apologizing for him finding out. She said she hadn't wanted it to be awkward at the time, and later, well, there was just never the right moment. Stephen could understand that, he supposed, not telling the truth when you were twenty-one. But what about the decade since? Yes, it had started as a small lie, but it had been getting bigger every year since.

Not that he was worried, exactly. If they were going to run

off together, then, as Rosie said, they would have done that by now. He didn't doubt that she loved him. He was angry, yes, but it was more that . . .

It was that Matt had gone along with it. That was the really insulting thing. Matt obviously saw it as Stephen taking up with one of his cast-offs, in that egotistical way he had. But instead of saying so, he decided that Stephen's confidence was so fragile he had to pretend that he had never wanted Rosie to go. He'd not actually said as much, but he'd definitely let Stephen think that. It was so bloody condescending.

And all the possibilities it raised about the break-up. What if . . .

Oh God, why was there no more wine? Brandy, though. There was plenty of that in the drinks cabinet.

'Darling, could you help me with the plates?' Rosie asked as Stephen hauled himself to his feet.

'In a minute,' he mumbled as he moved, more unsteadily than he expected, to the cupboard in the corner. He offered the brandy round and it came back with almost half the bottle gone. Jesus, how much wine had they got through? It had been good, though, hadn't it? Must make a note to order more of that next month. What was it called? Don't put the empties in the recycling without checking. Better tell Rosie to do that later; he'd be bound to forget.

He reached out to accept the conveyor belt of dirty bowls being handed down from the end of the table. They clashed against each other loudly as he tried to stack them. 'Oops,' he muttered.

'Darling, do you want me to carry those?'

'No, I'm fine.'

Rosie laughed nervously.

Stephen reached out to take the two bowls being offered to him by Barbara. As she bent forward, arm outstretched, he noticed how the thin material of her strappy top clung to the curve of her breast, while rumpling out in the middle to show an inviting scoop of cleavage. Great figure she had, really. Very pretty all round. Hadn't said very much this evening, but that was kind of sexy, wasn't it? Not knowing what she was thinking.

'Stephen? Will you offer people coffee?' Rosie picked up the dishes in front of him. She added under her breath: 'The dishwasher's full. If you're not going to play, can you do some washing up?'

Stephen blinked at her. He got up slowly. Maybe a walk would do him good.

When he returned from the kitchen, everyone but Charlotte and Rosie had gone silent.

'She is!'

'She is not!'

Scraps of crumpled paper littered the table, but the game seemed to have halted.

'Yes, she is,' Rosie insisted. 'Nadia Comaneci is a world-famous gymnast who's won five Olympic medals.'

'That doesn't make her famous,' Charlotte replied. 'It's not even a real sport.'

'Yes, it is. Rhythmic gymnastics is a very physically and mentally demanding sport.'

'Come on! It's just exercise. Keep fit.'

'No, they're very different things.'

'They're the same thing,' Charlotte said loudly.

'Look, Charlotte, I used to do rhythmic gymnastics at school . . .'

'There's a surprise.'

'Charlotte . . .'

'Go on, then. Explain.'

'Rhythmic gymnastics is a complex, synchronized sport about displaying grace in time to music.'

'While waving ribbons?'

'Sometimes.'

'That's callisthenics. It's keep fit.'

'It's not the same thing at all. Rhythmic gymnastics is an Olympic sport.'

'So? Table tennis is an Olympic sport. Doesn't mean it's not ping-pong.'

What the hell was going on? What were they talking about? Stephen couldn't understand it. Was he even drunker than he thought?

'What do you know about it?' Rosie asked.

'Not much.' Charlotte shrugged.

'There you are, then.'

'But I do know it's the same thing as rhythmic gymnastics.'

'Why don't you go and Google it?' Marcus suggested. 'That ought to settle things.'

Charlotte and Rosie both glared at him. How on earth had this argument started, Stephen wondered. What were they even arguing about?

'I don't know why you always think you know better, Rosie.'

'I don't always think I know better. It's just that on this, I do.'

'Why can't you ever accept that you don't know something?'

Rosie let out an exasperated sigh. Sarah lobbed a question into the lull. 'Er, Rosie, did you say something about coffee?'

'Stephen's making it.'

'Oh, are you, Stephen?'

'Um. I suppose I could. Who wants some?'

While he waited for the kettle to boil, he wondered where that had come from. He didn't even know Rosie had ever done rhythmic gymnastics. Why was she suddenly so passionate about it? Maybe she was just drunk. Unusual, that. Would it mean she'd feel like sex later. Was he up to that? Stephen wasn't sure. How many people had wanted coffee? Sod it — there were enough cups for everyone.

In the dining room, no one was speaking.

Rosie scrambled up to pour the coffee. 'Is everyone having some?'

'Not for us, thanks,' Justin said. 'Coffee after six o'clock always makes it impossible for me to sleep.'

'You should have said. Stephen would have made you some decaf.'

'No, thanks, we're fine . . . In fact, we should probably be getting off soon.'

'Already?' Rosie sounded slightly disapproving. 'We've got some herbal tea if you prefer.'

'No, thank you. It's a shame, I know, but I have to get up in the morning. And Barbara's very busy tomorrow too, with the new exhibition.'

'Of course ...'

Justin stood up. 'Well, I don't want to have to disturb everyone all over again in a few minutes, so we'll say our goodbyes now. It was nice to meet everyone and I suppose I'll see you all again ... when is it?'

'Next week. Probably. If Matt can ...'

'I'll check on Monday, Rosie.'

'Thanks, Matt. Well, it was lovely to meet you properly, Justin,' Rosie said as she got up to kiss him goodbye. 'Stephen, will you serve everyone else their coffee?'

In silence, Stephen passed round the white cups while Rosie showed Justin and Barbara out. As soon as the front door shut, Charlotte said, 'Jesus, that man is annoying!'

No one disagreed. Rosie came back in.

'Aren't they lovely?' she said.

No one disagreed.

Sarah said: 'I hate to do this to you, Rosie, but I think we'll have to go too.'

'Oh no, really?' Rosie said.

'If everyone's going, I'll be off too,' said Matt.

Stephen waited quietly with Charlotte while Rosie took the others out to the hall.

After a while he asked: 'More brandy?'

'Thanks.'

Stephen poured himself another glass as well and immediately wanted to go to sleep. How long was she going to stay? Could he go to bed anyway?

'That was very sudden,' Rosie said in a breezy tone as she came back in. 'Just us now ... Oh good, I see Stephen's offered you another drink. Look, Charlotte, I'm sorry about all that, earlier. I don't know what came over me. Perhaps it was too much wine. But whatever it was, I'm sorry.'

'You're still wrong,' Charlotte said.

'I . . . maybe you're right. I'll look it up later. So how have you been, Charlotte? It's good to have a chance to talk.'

'All right.'

'Because I know at work it's hard to speak properly . . .'

'I think I'll go as well,' Charlotte said, flicking the last of the brandy down her throat. 'Now that I've given Matt a chance to get clear.'

'Oh look, I'm sorry about that. Is it going to be too embarrassing? We can do separate nights if you want.'

'He can do it on his own. I don't think this is my sort of thing.'

'Oh no, Charlotte! Come on, it will be fun. Matt's not that bad.'

'I'm sure he's fine. That's not the point. I'm going to get a cab.'

Stephen waved silently as she left. He didn't seem to be expected to stand up.

'That was a total disaster,' Rosie said when Charlotte was gone.

'It was fine,' Stephen replied, leaning back in his chair.

'I can't believe I got sucked into that stupid argument. It's not like me. Charlotte was just being so annoying, being stubborn for the sake of it, and I . . . But she was probably just getting her own back about Matt, so it was my fault, really. Oh dear, it was all going so well until then. Have I ruined everything?'

'I'm sure it was fine.'

'But why did everybody leave so suddenly?'

'They were probably tired.' Stephen yawned expansively.

'Shall we clear up? Maybe I should have done it on a Saturday. But I just thought it would be nice for people on a Friday ...'

'It was fine.' Stephen was thinking about how little he wanted to clear the table. Rosie had begun gathering glasses.

'And what about Matt? You got on all right, didn't you?'

'It was fine.'

Rosie gave him a concerned look. 'Are you sure?'

Stephen grunted.

'And was the food OK? I thought I might have put too much salt in the soup.'

'It was fine.'

'But the duck was definitely overcooked, wasn't it? I knew I should have waited until after the soup to start it. Was it ruined?'

'It was fine.'

'The pudding was good, though – thank you for that – and people did seem to be enjoying themselves for a while, even Marcus. How do you think it went, overall?'

'It was fine.'

Rosie took a handful of glasses through to the kitchen. Stephen reluctantly stood up and followed her, taking an empty coffee cup to show willing. Rosie piled up banks of dirty glasses and crockery above the rumbling dishwasher.

'Do you think we should do these now?'

'No.'

'I think I will.'

'Just put them in the dishwasher tomorrow.'

'I think I'll make a start. I want to get the worst of it out of the way.'

'I'm going to bed.' Stephen put his empty brandy glass by the others and left the kitchen.

From: Matthew Phillips <matthewphillips@newgreenchambers.
     co.uk>
To: Dinner At Mine <dinneratminescores@gmail.com>
Sent: 23.51
Subject: Dinner with Rosie and Stephen: Assessment

Comments:

Food:

Soup: Tasty, good combination of flavours, although slightly
     too cold.

Main Course: Excellent duck with highly imaginative sauce.

Side Dish: Adequate.

Salad: Not to my taste. Too many lentils.

Dessert: Extremely enjoyable; fruit soft, crumble very crisp.

Wine: Pinot noir, with nice balance of fruits.

Hosting:

– Effort: Excellent.

– Conversation: Satisfactory. Mostly enjoyable, although no
  particularly stimulating topics.

– Ambience: Mostly good. Pleasant home. Awkward lulls
  well covered.

Scores:

Soup: 7

Main: 9

Side: 6

Salad: 5

Dessert: 9

Wine: 7

Hosting: 7

Overall average: 7

Matthew Phillips

Barrister

New Green Chambers

Sent from my BlackBerry®

From: Charlotte Wells <charliewells2@gmail.com>

To: Dinner At Mine <dinneratminescores@gmail.com>

Sent: 00.12

<No Subject>

Thanks for dinner, Rosie and Stephen. To be honst, you lose points for trying to set me up. And for keeping me wiating for my dinner for so long. That explns why I'm so drunk now. Fuck, the buttns on this screne are annying. Wine tho was very good. And there was lots of it.

To be fair, the food was p;retty tasty. I did like the soup. The duck was pretty good as welll. Dessert was ok, but a bit too heaby by that point.

I have to say iThe geusts were pretty boring. Is that your fault? You did invite them. And you actively encouraged them to talk. So that's bad. Wait, Im home now.

Score: 6

Sent from my iPhone

From: Marcus Thompson <marcusthompson@
        taylorwilsonpartners.com>
To: Dinner At Mine <dinneratminescores@gmail.com>
Sent: 00.51
Subject: Dinner

The evening began promisingly, with excellent aperitif snacks which went well with the sherry. However, the good impression was rather marred when we were left on our own for long periods waiting for a dinner that was very late in starting.

When the meal finally began, I was disappointed that a good overall concept was slightly betrayed by the execution. The soup's taste was mostly bacon saltiness and it was too cold.

Although the pomegranate was a good flavour, and well integrated into the dish, it was let down by overcooked duck. Okra was also not a suitable side dish as it has a similar bitterness; the pomegranate demanded a fresh taste to cut through it. The rice was over-boiled.

The lentil salad was enjoyable in small quantities, but too much beetroot is difficult to stomach. There was also far too much lemon juice in the dressing.

The crumble was not what was advertised, for which points must be deducted. It also did not fit the tone of the rest of the dinner. While it was sweet and not too cloying, overall this course was a disappointment.

The hosting was, on balance, good, although the faults identified earlier pull the final score down from seven to six.
Score: 6
Marcus

Any information in this message is strictly confidential and intended solely for the person or organization to whom it is addressed. If you have received this message in error, please notify us as soon as possible and delete it and any attached files from your system.

From: Justin Davidson <justindavidson@AfricAid.org.uk>
To: Dinner At Mine <dinneratminescores@gmail.com>
Sent: 14.32
Subject: Dinner last night

Sorry this is a bit late, we were so tired last night. And then this morning I had volunteering. I don't really have much time to write, but I'm so busy with this Malawi project this afternoon that I'd better send something now. (Not that I'm complaining – it's an excellent programme. I'll tell everyone about it properly next time.) I think I remember that no one is reading this yet anyway, so I hope it won't matter being a bit late.

Thanks very much for a lovely meal. I think we liked the soup best. It was fresh, tasty, and chilled just the right amount. The main course was very tasty too, and we do appreciate that you made a proper vegetarian dish rather than just leaving the meat out of what you were having. Tamarind is one of my favourite spices too.

If I had to make any criticism at all, I'd say the stew was maybe a bit dry. But that's probably our fault, isn't it? We were so late that it must have been cooking for half an hour longer than you wanted. I'm so sorry. It must have been really annoying, so we won't mark you down for that at all.

What else? I'm sure the wine was very nice, but I'm not much of an expert. You were excellent hosts, of course, very generous. So overall, 7. Is that a bit harsh? 7½ then. No, make it 8.

See you next time.

Justin

Dinner at Matt's (with Charlotte)

Seven

'Oh honey, hi!'

'Yeah. Hi. Honey.' Barbara gripped the phone tightly to her ear.

'Aren't you at your exhibition?' Justin asked, sounding puzzled even over the crackle of the line.

'Yes.' Barbara waited.

'Look, I'm sorry I'm not there yet. I am coming . . . It's just this Malawi thing.'

'Yeah.'

'I need to get this chapter done tonight before it goes out to review. I think I'm nearly there.'

A gust of wind funnelled down the street, setting the buds on the spindly trees shaking. Barbara stepped back to take shelter in the café doorway.

'I am coming,' Justin repeated.

'Sure.'

'How's it going?'

'You know. Fine.'

'That's great!'

Barbara looked through the bright windows of the café. Three people drifted listlessly around the floor, peering at her pots. From outside, she could see a thin coating of dust over the pot nearest to the window. Would it have killed Mary to dust them? And some flowers, some flowers would have been good. But Mary might not have watered them. Dead flowers would have been even worse.

'Yeah,' Barbara said, breathing out very heavily. 'It's going great.'

'I'm really glad, Barbara!' Justin said. 'Are there lots of people there?'

'Some. It was a slow start.'

There had been three tables occupied when Barbara arrived: an old guy reading a newspaper, two young mothers interested in nothing but their chocolate muffins, and two grad-student types. Barbara had thought the two students were staring at one of the vases, but when she moved over to the counter it became clear that they were staring at her.

'Well, I'm sure it's warming up,' Justin said.

'That's probably the free wine.'

'Ha!' Justin laughed desperately. 'Are those people there?'

'Which ones?' Barbara knew who he meant. She was annoyed he couldn't remember their names.

'The ones from the gallery . . .'

'No.'

'I'm sure they're coming, though.'

'Yeah,' Barbara said, staring through the brilliant windows, knowing she couldn't be seen. 'Just like you are.'

'Exactly!' Justin replied quickly. 'It's still quite early, isn't it, and they're very busy people. I'm sure they'll come.'

'Maybe,' Barbara said, not quite smiling to herself. 'After all, right, they said they'd come, didn't they? So why wouldn't they come?'

'Well, exactly,' Justin said. He sounded relieved that she agreed.

Barbara couldn't think how to reply. Through the window she could see the two textile artists who rented space in the same studio as her, drinking wine and ignoring the pots. They were laughing about something. Barbara thought it must be her, then told herself not to be so paranoid.

Linda, the German one, had brought a sample of her own work. Barbara could see the bag wedged protectively between her feet. She didn't know whether to be insulted or flattered that Linda actually thought the gallerists were coming.

Barbara hadn't invited many people – it was pretty stupid to have a 'launch' when the pots had been in here for a month. She had only agreed to it because Marcello, who liked to call himself Barbara's agent, had said it was a good excuse to get Dieter Tunhelm there. She'd brought people to see the exhibition before, of course. Rosie had been in the first week, and said it was marvellous. Barbara guessed that was pretty nice of her. But because of that, Barbara had felt obligated to say yes when Rosie had suggested this dinner thing. Barbara had been a bit surprised when she'd asked. She didn't even know Rosie very well – found her a little intense, actually. But she liked Sarah OK, and Justin had liked the idea of showing off his cooking.

'Honey?' Justin said down the indistinct line.

'Yeah?'

'I'd better get on with finishing this . . .'

'Sure.' Barbara resisted asking how long it would take.

'I'll try to come as soon as I can . . . You know I'd come now, but with this dinner tonight I won't get it done later, and there's the conference on Monday, so I've got to get it finished.'

'Sure.'

'I knew you'd understand. It will go on for a while yet, won't it?'

Barbara looked back across the expanse of scuffed wooden floor inside the café. 'Yeah, maybe.'

Barbara waited.

'But look . . . um, if I don't get it finished, shall I just see you at Matt's?'

Barbara didn't feel like protesting. 'Sure,' she said.

'Thank you for understanding!' Justin was suddenly enthusiastic. 'I knew you would.'

Barbara didn't feel angry. There was no point arguing anyway; you couldn't win against starving children. And, actually, it would probably be easier if Justin didn't show up. Justin did have a lot of great points. He was nice, sweet, kind. She had been so attracted by all that when she had first arrived in London, the unthreatening stability of him. It would be embarrassing, though, having his enthusiasm in that almost empty room. Barbara wasn't sure if she would be more embarrassed by the café or by him.

'We've got the whole weekend, haven't we?' Justin went on. 'Sunday morning, you could give me a private tour.'

'Sure.'

'OK, great. Well, you know where Matt's is, don't you? I gave you the address. Just in case . . .'

'See you, Justin.'

'Bye, honey. I love you . . .'

Barbara ended the call and stared out at the street for a while. She had met Justin when she had gone with a friend from Goldsmiths to an Amnesty event that Justin had organized. She'd been impressed by his zeal, his energetic earnestness, and she'd gone back the following week. Eventually she'd asked him out. He wasn't like a lot of guys she knew in the States; it wasn't all just a way of getting her into bed, even if that meant pretending to be interested in her work. Yeah, say what you like about Justin, at least he didn't fake an interest in that.

A sharp rapping at the glass jerked Barbara out of her thoughts.

Linda, the German textile artist, was looking at her with a pained expression and gesturing for her to come inside. Barbara smiled weakly, looking past her, back into the café. She noticed that someone had put a stack of flyers for a student play into one of her pots. Outrage flared and quickly subsided. It seemed somehow appropriate.

Barbara took a step back and appraised her pots from the street. They suddenly looked far more like lumps of clay than works of art. Inert, lifeless, ill-formed. They were an embarrassment. Amateurish garbage. Was this really what she had spent five years doing?

Linda gave up on Barbara and went over to the bar for

another plastic cup of Chilean red. Barbara decided this was a moment of clarity. She had lost her way as an artist. Something had to change. She spun round and walked away from the café. Her jacket was still inside, but she didn't look back.

Eight

Rosie's mind once again went over the matter of the yuzu juice. She was thinking about getting hold of some and making the salad again, just to see what the difference was. She was convinced now that the extra zing would have made all the difference, lifted the meal to another level. It definitely would have been worth extra points. Would it mean the difference between winning and losing, though?

The problem was that there was no way of knowing how well the others had scored her. The question had been hovering there all week. She was worried now that when she saw them later on, she wouldn't be able to think of anything else. It was going to be torture.

'Yes, yes!' she said, to Stephen's muffled shout.

Marcus would have been stingy with his score. She could tell that immediately. It perhaps wasn't even so much to do with the food as a way of asserting his superiority, or making it more likely that he would win. She knew he fancied himself as a foodie, but God, he had been annoying, hadn't he? Did he think she hadn't noticed the notebook? Well, that would be repaid.

Was she being uncharitable? No. That was the point of the game, wasn't it? To win. Was that why she had suggested it in the first place? The thought struck her. Was she just looking for a socially acceptable way to prove she was a better cook than her friends? No, surely it was just a way to have some nice evenings, and make a bit of a change from a normal dinner party?

And even if it wasn't, what was so wrong with that? Everyone had agreed to the rules.

Rosie ran her hand through her hair.

And Matt? Well, he probably wanted to win without trying, didn't he? Gliding along like a swan while everyone else was paddling furiously underwater. That wasn't quite right, was it? But it would be just like Matt.

Take the menu for the night. Peruvian Ceviche. Well, that sounded great, didn't it? Exotic, fresh, a hint of culinary danger with the raw fish. But, actually, you just needed to get some very nice fish and squeeze some lemon on it. Easy, really. It would be tasty, though, that was the thing. Same with the main course. Navajo Roast Lamb. Navajo! How unexpected and intriguing. The thing was, it was probably just roast lamb. With a few strange spices. All you had to do was buy the right things and set the timer on the oven. Was that cheating or was it just clever? That was the thing with Matt – it was so hard to tell.

Still, Rosie was confident. The vegetarians would swing it for her. Marcus would be mean with everyone and Rosie herself was unlikely to give Matt a better score than he had given her. So it would come down to Justin and Barbara. They had really enjoyed the last meal. And then there was Charlotte. Had she ever actually cooked anything? Rosie had never seen any evidence that her culinary skills went any further than adjusting the settings on the microwave. If she was making something tonight, it would be the NY Espresso Chocolate Cake. Very hard to get chocolate cake wrong, but maybe Charlotte could manage it.

'Mmmmm!' she said.

That was mean. There was no reason to think Charlotte was a bad cook, was there? True, Rosie had never eaten a meal prepared by her, but then most of their socializing had been done after work. She could actually be quite good.

Why hadn't she mentioned Matt to Charlotte before last week? In her head, it had seemed much less of a set-up. Just because two people were single, it didn't mean they couldn't have dinner together, did it? With six other people there!

Yes, all right, it was the cooking together. That did look like a date. But there was nothing to be done about it. The rules were the rules. Both of them were adult enough to see that, surely?

Still, she should have asked them properly. Charlotte,

particularly. She always got very defensive about the suggestion of set-ups, as if they were an insult to her pride, a sign that people thought she should be the object of pity. Rosie couldn't see it. It was just a practical way of looking for a partner, wasn't it?

Maybe she should have invited Mike and Tony. Things would have been much more relaxed. There wouldn't have been the tension with Charlotte, and now Stephen was upset at suddenly discovering what had happened with her and Matt all those years ago.

Of course she felt guilty about not telling him, but it hadn't seemed a big thing at the time. Stephen had said she should have told him then, but she knew he'd have been much angrier ten years ago. Yes, he was upset , but he'd get used to it, wouldn't he? And then there would be nothing more to hide.

Rosie arched her back slightly as she stretched out her arms.

Best not think about that now, though. She wondered again where the tensions with Charlotte had come from. Things hadn't been quite right between them at work for a while, and then there had been that weird argument last week. When had it all started? Of course, Rosie had gone out less when she came back from maternity leave. What did Charlotte expect? She had a child to look after. Then there had been all the jokes about going part-time. Charlotte made digs about how Rosie wasn't trying any more. It did get to her, and maybe that was why she had fought back the other night.

But that didn't mean Charlotte was wrong. Rosie came home worrying about work much less these days. Which was a good thing in many ways, but it wasn't because she had suddenly mastered her job. More that problems didn't seem so important, or she knew that if she wasn't there the next day, they'd usually find a way to sort it out.

It wasn't that she was worrying about Jonathan instead. He was a delight at the moment, sailing through teething and on the cusp of his first words. Perhaps it was tranquillity, then.

Was that it? Was she slowly going to drift away from work and become a full-time mum, watching professional life recede slowly into the distance, never to be seen from close-up again? Instinctively, she found the idea was horrible. How boring would it be? How boring would she become, with nothing to talk about but her children? But then, the battles of office life didn't seem worth winning any more. Rosie had lost the stomach for them.

Maybe that's what infuriated Charlotte. They used to spend quite a lot of time bitching about the various bosses and, after a few glasses of wine, some of their colleagues as well. They still did it, sometimes, the first one anyway, but Rosie's heart wasn't in it. Did that make her a nicer person? Or just a more boring one?

Rosie ran her hands absent-mindedly up Stephen's back.

What would Stephen say if she gave up work entirely? Probably something about money. But would he like the idea that she was going to devote herself to the family? Or would he panic that she was going to become a dull housewife? Rosie realized she had no idea. Should she ask him?

Stephen pulled his weight off her and rolled on to his side, panting slightly.

'Are you all right?' he asked, pulling away the duvet to cool himself down.

'Yes, of course.' Rosie reached forward to stroke his hair. She noticed that it was thinning slightly at the back of his head.

'You didn't seem very into it.'

'Of course I was!'

'Really?'

'I'm sorry, darling.' Rosie smoothed down a stray lick of hair against his forehead. It stuck to the film of sweat on his skin. 'I suppose I might have been a bit distracted.'

Nine

Who the hell were these people? Charlotte barged between two laden trolleys being rolled pensively down the cheese aisle. Why were there so many of them? Who does their shopping on a Friday night? Don't they have anything better to do? Jesus, get out of the way!

Charlotte pushed round a fat man in a blue tracksuit who was staring thoughtfully up at the wall of butter. Can't you see some people are in a hurry, she thought. How can anyone take that long to decide? It's just butter! Is this your idea of a night out? Charlotte snatched up a block without looking at the label and threw it into her trolley.

Fuck, was that the time? How could it be ten past seven already? Christ, this was going to be tight. Charlotte looked at the printout she had made minutes before leaving the office. Flour next. Where the hell was that? Why couldn't they put all the cake ingredients next to each other?

Charlotte moved quickly down the end aisle of the supermarket, barging roughly past a woman comforting a screaming toddler, and swerving to avoid knocking over an old lady.

It wasn't supposed to be this rushed. Charlotte had worked out that if she arrived at Matt's by six thirty there would be plenty of time to prepare the cake, and she could put it in the oven as soon as the main course came out. Shopping wouldn't take more than twenty minutes so, really, there was nothing wrong with sneaking in a quick drink after work.

The second had been the problem – it quickly led to a third. So here she was, standing in Tesco fifteen minutes before she was meant to be serving dinner, staring at fifteen different types of flour. She looked at her list. She had written 'flour'. Plain, self-raising, sourdough, brown or spelt flour? What the hell was the difference? Why was there always so much fucking choice about tiny little things like this? Why didn't they just write on the packet which one you used for what?

Charlotte grabbed the cheapest packet and threw it into the trolley. Sod it. What was next? She looked at the list. Sugar. That was probably around here somewhere. Charlotte wheeled her trolley to the end of the aisle, looking up at the boards hanging from the ceiling. There was no mention of sugar. An attendant in a blue tunic directed her to Aisle 6, and Charlotte trudged back half the length of the supermarket swearing, mostly under her breath, at the shoppers in her way.

What next? Eggs. Fuck, they were back by the flour. There had to be a better way of doing this. Charlotte spun her trolley round, clipping the frame of a cart carrying another small toddler in the fold-out seat. The child started crying. Its mother looked round to see what the problem was, but Charlotte was already gone.

As she accelerated again towards the far end of the super-market, Charlotte looked longingly down the dessert aisle. Rows of cakes, chocolate éclairs, tarts and pies stretched away towards the tills, their cardboard packaging glistening with chiller-cabinet condensation. What was the point of doing it yourself at all? It just wasn't efficient. Teams of dedicated people had put years of effort into doing it for you. This whole competition was ridiculous.

Right, eggs. Six was enough. Organic? Free-range? Cheap? Fuck it, they were only bloody chickens. OK, what was the time now? Twenty past. Fuck.

Never mind the coffee. Matt would have some of that. So just chocolate to go. Don't say that's back at the other end ...

But another man in a blue tunic told her that it was. She followed him past the bakery, past rows of wines, breakfast cereals and toilet paper to the aisle next to the glistening desserts.

'There you are, madam,' the man said with proprietorial pride, indicating a shelf of thin, foil-wrapped bars. 'Which kind were you after? Milk, plain, white, organic, Mexican chilli ... ?'

'For a cake.'

The man stared at her blankly.

'Thanks anyway.' Charlotte reached past him and grabbed a couple of bars of something with the word 'Belgian' on the front. Right, that was everything. How long did she have to get back to Matt's and bake the thing? Seven minutes. Hmm.

She made for the tills. The ones nearest the doors were a crush of quarrelling families with trolleys groaning under the weight of junk food. Charlotte squeezed round them, but the checkouts beyond had long queues of giggling students with six-packs of own-brand lager and double-size bottles of Bulgarian wine. They'd probably all pay with cards, wouldn't they?

She pushed on towards the far wall again, scanning the tills as she went. But the queues started to get longer towards the household goods sections and then stopped. The last five tills were closed.

Charlotte stopped, swore, and looked back along the line of checkouts. She should have joined one of the queues of students. At least they weren't buying much. She jerked the trolley round, weaving through the growing lines.

Then she made an abrupt right-hand turn. A man with a trolleyful of lager swore at her. Charlotte ignored him, wheeling her trolley past the arrays of doughnuts and cream cakes and pausing in front of a large chiller cabinet packed deep with chocolate puddings.

The pictures on the packets looked much nicer than anything she was going to make. One in particular caught her eye: a thick, round pastry tart, with specks of hazelnut flecking the expanse of dark chocolate within the crisp golden crust.

Charlotte glanced up and down the aisle to see who might be watching. She looked at her watch, then at her trolley, and back to the tart.

Ten

Matt snapped on the kitchen spotlights, banishing grey dusk behind the suddenly reflective windows, and flooding the worktops with glossy yellow rays. The surfaces were clean and bare, with a chopping board, knife and glass bowl stacked neatly on the edge of the sink.

Exactly two hours earlier, Matt had made a series of one centimetre slits all over his leg of lamb and rubbed the sumac marinade into the meat, taking care to get plenty of it in the holes he had made. Then he had wrapped the lamb tightly in cling film and put it in the fridge to let the flavours sink in.

In the meantime, he had finalized the opening arguments for his case on Monday, had a shower, and watched an episode of *Curb Your Enthusiasm* on Sky+. Now he took the lamb out of the fridge and set it in the corner to reach room temperature again. He put the oven on to heat, drained the farro grains he had put in to soak after marinating the lamb, and put them on to boil.

He chopped some courgette, garlic, spring onions

and chilli. Matt knew he would need more chillies and some spring onions for the salsa, but he had always felt it turned out quicker if you just followed one recipe at a time. He fried everything briefly, then took it off the heat and stirred in the boiled grains, some lemon juice and a bit of mint. That would do for the vegetarian starter. It looked a bit too much like a side salad, so he added some more torn mint. Maybe he would serve it on individual plates, so he didn't have to use a salad bowl. With a dollop of harissa on the side of the plate, it would look much more like a proper course. He put it aside to cool.

Matt liked to think he was a competent cook. Not an excellent one – he knew he didn't have the instinctive feel to be really good, to be able to throw ingredients together and produce complex and interesting flavours unguided – but he was very good at following a recipe.

He wasn't too worried about the meal. The main dish was a reliable staple for when he had to entertain. It was hard to go wrong with a great big leg of lamb. Cover it with plenty of unusual spices and you could lift it out of the ordinary without too much effort. The starter he had made before, for his last dinner party. That was over a year ago, but it had turned out pretty well.

Next, there was more chopping to be done. Matt lined up a row of peppers, onions, aubergines, fennel, tomatoes and potatoes next to his walnut chopping board, delaying slightly the tedious process of cutting them up. He had expected Charlotte to be here by now, and had planned for her to have done most of the vegetable chopping. This hadn't been formally agreed, but from what Charlotte had said about her cooking skills, it would have been a mutually beneficial compromise.

Matt began with the red peppers, cutting them into long, thin strips. Where was Charlotte? It was well after seven now, and surely it would take her at least forty-five minutes to make the dessert. Matt decided there was no point worrying about it. He couldn't call because he didn't have her number. They had arranged this evening in a couple of peremptory e-mails in which she still seemed to be smarting about the indignity of Rosie setting her up.

For dessert, he had a back-up plan of fruit salad. A punnet of peaches, a pineapple and an array of berries had been delivered by Ocado that morning and Matt reckoned if Charlotte didn't show up on time they would make a decent end to the meal. Possibly, on the same principle as the lamb marinade, he would douse them in some kind of unusual spirit. Maybe that stuff he had brought back from South Africa. Certainly, he would try to negotiate compensation for having to cook single-handed. He would open the discussions at an extra five points, and probably settle for two.

Not that Matt really minded doing things on his own. It was how he worked best, just him and a stack of ring binders in the muffled quiet of his office high above Lincoln's Inn Fields. He had spent the morning preparing for a straightforward negligence case on Monday, and made quick progress. In the unruffled hush of the empty office, Matt worked fast. From outside, there was a faint, soothing background rumble of lorries moving along Holborn.

The only problem Matt could foresee was the judge.

The case was likely to be heard by His Honour Judge Featherston, who was known to the legal profession as an utter bastard. He was capricious and liked to bully counsel who made arguments that he found weak. The best way to counter him, Matt thought, was to be excessively deferential, and refrain from any jokes.

He might also have to tone down his accent. It was rumoured that Featherston thought regional accents a sign of weak-mindedness. So it was probably safest to modulate it into something less northern and less noticeable, aiming to become indistinguishable from the Home Counties tones of the rest of the bar.

Some people would find this humiliating. Some, Matt knew, would refuse to do it. Matt didn't let such things bother him. It was just something that needed to be done to give himself the best possible chance of winning the case. He was quite happy going the other way as well; several times in the past he had played up his northern accent, hoping to exploit the awkwardness of judges who were uncomfortable with even the slightest hint of minority status.

After finishing his preparation, Matt had returned home confident that he was going to win. He gave himself half an hour to send three e-mails before starting on the lamb.

With the vegetables chopped, Matt began to heat some oil in the frying pan and chucked them all in. He stirred them until he could hear the gathering hiss of the oil warming up, and when it started to spit he turned the hob down to cook them more gently, covering the pan with a high lid. At this point, without Charlotte, there was no alternative to cooking two things at the same time. Matt went back to the board and chopped some more peppers, spring onions and tomatoes for the salsa. While stirring the paella vegetables on the right hob, he used a griddle pan to char the skin of the chillies on the left. He soon got bored with waiting for them to blacken all over and tore them up by hand, throwing them into a bowl with the rest.

He added rice to the paella, and while that was browning he added olive oil, mint, vinegar and sumac to the salsa, roughly blending them with a hand-held food processor. He tasted a bit off the end of the blade and added some more salt. Then he put it aside with the salad.

It was about time to put the lamb in now. Matt unwrapped it on a roasting tray and put it into the roaring oven. No need to look at it again for an hour. He went back to the paella. This was always a satisfactory time in preparation, Matt thought, once all the side dishes had been done and there was no need to juggle the early stages of one recipe with the later stages of another. What was left to do involved following two simple sets of instructions, one after the other.

Matt waited until the rice had browned, then added a bit of water and a good slug of white wine. The mixture still felt a little dry when he stirred it, so, with the permission of the recipe book, he added another large glass of wine.

Quarter past seven now. The guests were supposed to arrive in fifteen minutes. Where was Charlotte? Matt supposed he ought to be worrying. He wasn't, though; in fact, he was relieved that he hadn't had to make conversation for an hour while cooking. That could have been a bit of a strain. If she

turned up now, there would just be a bit of chat – she'd probably apologize, he'd say not to worry – and they wouldn't have
to talk any more until after they had both drunk a lot of wine.

Matt wondered why Charlotte had agreed to have a go at
a cooking competition. She really didn't seem very interested
in food. If she was doing it for a laugh, she hadn't seemed too
amused last week. Maybe Rosie had talked her into it. He
found it hard to imagine Charlotte being persuaded to do
much she didn't want to do.

Of course, there was another explanation. Matt hadn't
really minded the obvious set-up. He wasn't much given to
embarrassment, and if people wanted to offer women to him,
that was fine. Charlotte had seemed a bit annoyed. Perhaps
she was just thrown, perhaps it was a ploy. Certainly, Matt was
confident that it was nothing to do with him. Objectively
speaking, he was comfortably better-looking than she was.

Matt wondered if he would end up sleeping with her. She
wasn't too unattractive. Rosie was clearly better-looking,
though. How long had that been now? Ten years, at least. In
many ways she looked better now – elegantly dressed, more
stylish. She was ageing well.

It was a shame Stephen had found out what had happened
between them, really. It had made him so stiff and formal.
Perhaps he was angry because they hadn't told him. Well, that
would have been Matt's responsibility a decade ago, but ever
since then it was Rosie's problem. Stephen would probably
get over it. Once he'd satisfied himself that Matt wasn't going
to make a move. Not that Matt was thinking of it. That time
had gone now, hadn't it?

Obviously, neither Rosie nor Charlotte was beautiful like Barbara. She really was gorgeous. But yes, Charlotte had something. If it wasn't exactly good looks, it was definitely something. She looked like she would be good in bed. Matt thought about that for a moment. It wasn't unpleasant.

The pineapple stood firm and reassuring in the corner by the fruit bowl. Conjuring an extra course from nothing at very short notice – that had to be worth extra points. If she didn't turn up at all, there was a chance he could win this thing.

Maria had been earlier, and the flat was looking tidy. Matt emptied his cutlery drawer to lay the table, giving himself the cracked and faded Donald Duck knife and fork his brother had brought back from Disneyworld while Matt was still a student. He counted out the eight wine glasses he possessed. The two at the front of the cupboard were clean and well-used, but by the time he reached the pair at the back there was a noticeable layer of dust. When had he last taken them out? At least a year. He had had some friends from bar school round – but that had been the Christmas before last. There had been five of them then. Maybe he had never used the other three glasses.

He rinsed them clean and put them on the table. It looked a bit cramped and Matt regretted not thinking to get out the extension panel earlier. But it was half past seven now and they would be arriving any minute. It was too late. Matt went back to the kitchen to check the paella, and a cloud of steam billowed from the pan when he took the lid off. It moved nicely when he stirred it. Nearly there.

He reckoned it was probably time to start the ceviche. The snapper was thick, firm and inviting when he took it out of the fridge. This was the only ingredient of the meal he had bought in person, at a reassuringly expensive fishmonger in Borough Market. Matt got out a new chopping board and began cutting the snapper into strips.

From the hallway, he heard the faint ringing of his mobile phone. He washed his hands and went to answer it. The phone was still in the pocket of his suit jacket, its old-fashioned ring-tone muffled by layers of expensive tufted wool. He didn't recognize the number.

'Hello?'

'Matt, it's Charlotte. How do I get into this place?'

Matt wondered how she had his number. She must have asked Rosie. What did that mean? 'Where are you?' he asked.

'Downstairs. Outside. I think this is your flat anyway.'

'Are you by the blue gate?'

'What blue gate?'

Matt laughed silently to himself. 'OK. Can you see the Brazilian corner shop?'

'No.'

'Try turning round.'

'Yes, all right. Got it.'

'So opposite that is a bike rack . . . yes?'

'Er . . . wait . . .'

'And about fifty metres north of that is the blue gate.'

'Which way's north?'

'Towards Costcutter.'

'Hold on . . . Ah!'

'OK, press the button for 17B when you get there, then press "Call".'

Matt waited too long for her to have not reached the door, and thought maybe she was somewhere else entirely, then he heard the buzz of the entryphone.

'Hello? It's the seventeenth floor. I'll leave the door open.'

Charlotte's reply was inaudible, but she didn't buzz again, so Matt assumed she was in. As he went to put the phone away, he noticed two text messages from Charlotte's number. The first had been sent an hour ago, the second half an hour after that. Both said she was running ten minutes late.

'Sorry! I know I'm a little bit late,' Charlotte said as she came in through the open front door. She was slightly out of breath, even though she must have taken the lift. Her cheeks were flushed, but her expression was businesslike, a combination that Matt found unsettling. She wore a dark denim jacket cut to accentuate her wide hips.

Matt gave her a quick kiss on the cheek and offered to take the jacket. She handed it to him and swung her oversized handbag to the floor.

'Is anybody here yet?'

'No.'

'Good. That would have been embarrassing. Where's the kitchen?'

Matt showed her through.

'Mmm. That smells good. What is it?'

'That's the paella. It's for the vegetarians.'

'Oh,' Charlotte said, with a disappointed look at the pot. 'What are we having?'

'Roast lamb. It's in the oven.'

'Great. And what's that?' She pointed at the chopping board.

'Snapper. For the ceviche.'

'Right, good. You seem to have everything under control. I'll get on with the pud, then.' Charlotte swung her Tesco carrier bag on to the worktop. It lay there, shallow, flat and square.

Charlotte didn't look at Matt as she took the box out of the bag. On the waxy cardboard packaging, Matt read: American-style Chocolate and Hazelnut Tart.

'What?' Charlotte said, without looking round. There was an aggressive edge in her voice.

'I didn't say anything.'

'I was in a hurry, all right? I was going to make it myself, but I just ran out of time.'

'Right. I've got stuff for a fruit salad if . . .'

'No. We're having chocolate tart.'

'O-kay,' Matt said slowly. 'You don't think anyone will notice?'

'I've thought of that.'

'Have you?'

'Why don't you just get on with your fish, OK?'

Matt shrugged. 'All right.' He turned back to his chopping board a split second before he started grinning. How would they react to such an obviously shop-bought dessert? It could be quite funny. After he'd seen their faces, Matt could always bring out the fruit salad. And what if they fell for it? That would be . . . But they wouldn't fall for it. Nothing home-made was that smooth. He chopped the rest of the snapper in silence before throwing it into a shallow dish and squeezing lemon over it.

'Do you have a salad spoon?'

'Er . . . yes. Second drawer down. Why do you need a salad spoon?'

Charlotte did not reply.

Matt turned round to see she had lined up the tart on the edge of the worktop, its crust just protruding over empty space. Charlotte smacked the crust at an oblique angle. Small chunks of pastry fluttered on to the floor. She turned the pie round a few degrees and repeated the procedure. The perfectly corrugated factory crust gradually became lumpen and irregular, with bits missing and ridges at uneven intervals.

'You've done this before, haven't you?'

'No.'

Charlotte now flicked the back of the spoon lightly over the soft chocolate filling, whipping up gentle drifts on its glassy-smooth surface.

Now she turned to Matt. 'Right,' she said, putting the plastic packaging in the bin. 'I'm ready.'

Matt peered over to look at the tart. With its careful flaws, it did look significantly more home-made.

'You might even get away with that.'

'Get away with what? I made it this morning.' Charlotte defiantly met Matt's eye. He was on the point of thinking she had really made herself believe it when she started to laugh.

Matt joined in. 'That was pretty good,' he said. 'But you'll have to go one better when Rosie asks you what's in it.'

'Oh fuck, yes, what was it? Some kind of nuts?' Charlotte reached round and began scrabbling in the bin for the cardboard packet. 'Yes, here we are: hazelnuts.' She squinted at the tiny list of ingredients on the side. 'What else? Emulsifiers, stabilizers, inverted corn syrup, diglycerides of fatty acid . . . can't really mention those. . . So, sugar, chocolate, and pastry (flour, butter, vegetable oil, stabilizers). Will that do?'

'How about some dulce de leche?'

'Sounds good. What is it?'

'It's like a South American sweet paste.'

'I like it.'

'It will sound better than just saying you put sugar in.'

'Dulce de . . . what was it?

'Dulce de leche.'

'Dulce de leche it is.' She dropped the packet back into the bin. 'Shall I open the wine?'

'Hold on.' Matt nodded at the bin. 'That's going to be too obvious.' He finished trimming the fish and threw the offcuts on top of the packet with a shower of spring onion leaves, working it down into the mulch of pepper seeds and onion skin. 'That ought to do it.'

'Great,' Charlotte said. 'What a culinary team we make.'

Matt laughed. After all his efforts, he had the right to be offended, but what was the point? Anyway, this would definitely make the evening more fun.

When Matt had finished the ceviche, he found Charlotte in the living room, unabashedly going through his bookshelf with a large glass of wine in her hand.

'Found anything interesting?' he asked.

'No,' Charlotte said. 'You've got a lot of law, haven't you?'

'Well, I am a lawyer.'

'But why have them at home? It's a bit sad, isn't it?'

'I suppose it is. But in my defence, the shelves at my office are filled with my first-edition collection of the *Twilight* series.'

Charlotte snorted without looking round. 'Oh look, these aren't about law. *The Men Who Stare At Goats*, *Fear and Loathing in Las Vegas*, Niall Ferguson, Richard Dawkins, Malcolm Gladwell . . . Don't you have any novels?'

'I don't really read much fiction.'

'Wait, there's some here. Tolstoy, Dostoevsky, Dickens . . . These are part of a set aren't they?' Charlotte picked one of them out and looked at the back cover. 'Yes, "The Twenty Essential Novels of the Educated Mind – a Classic Press Presentation Edition".'

'My mum gave them to me.'

'That's sweet. Have you actually read any of these?'

'Some of them.'

'How many?'

'Some.'

'Which ones? I don't think this one's even been opened. Understandable, I suppose, when you spend most of your time with these fascinating legal textbooks.'

'Have you read any of them?' Matt asked.

'No.'

'Well, then . . .'

'Oh wait. I think this Thomas Hardy was on the A-level syllabus at school.'

'Did you enjoy it?'

'No.'

They both laughed.

'Can you give me hand with the table?' Matt said. 'People are supposed to be here by now.'

They went into the kitchen. 'How are eight people supposed to eat round that?' Charlotte looked scornfully at Matt's folding table.

'It will be a bit cosy.'

'If we all only use one arm each it might be all right.'

'It's not that bad . . .'

'Yes, it is. We can't eat round there. We'll be forking things into each other's mouths by accident.'

'There's a middle section which goes in to make it bigger . . .'

'Well, why haven't you used that?'

'I forgot about it earlier. I don't think there's time now . . .'

'Of course there is. They're not even here yet. I'll stall them if I have to.'

Matt hesitated, but realized she was probably right. He went out to the cupboard in the hall to search for the extra panel. As he pulled it out from the back he knocked over a tube of tennis balls. They bounced off the front door in quick succession, half rolling into the kitchen and the other half into the living room. Why were they in there? When had he ever played tennis? Charlotte kicked them back too hard and they ricocheted around the hall until Matt knelt down and grabbed them one by one. Straining now to avoid getting flustered, he stuffed them back into their tube, threw it hard into the corner of the cupboard, and took out the panel.

'When did you last use this, then?' Charlotte asked as Matt began wiping the dust off it.

'I can't remember.'

'And how do you fit it in?'

Matt stared at the table. There was some sort of flap underneath, wasn't there? Or maybe you had to move the legs first . . .

'You can't remember, can you?'

'No.'

'Oh dear,' Charlotte said with obvious glee. 'Dinner on the sofa it is, then.' She sat down on one of the dining chairs with her glass of wine and settled in to watch Matt's efforts.

Matt laboriously removed all the cutlery and glasses, turned the table on to its back and crouched down to inspect it. Dusty instructions in Swedish were dotted around the base.

'Oh dear. This could take a while.' Charlotte grinned broadly.

'No, I think you just pull this . . .' Matt tugged on a block of wood, which remained resolutely immobile. 'Hmm, OK. Perhaps these screws have to be loosened first . . .' Matt wrapped his hand round a chunky metal nut and twisted.

'I bet this wasn't how Rosie prepared for her guests to arrive,' Charlotte said.

Matt hesitated for a second, then laughed. It was either that or get annoyed, and he didn't want Charlotte to see him irritated. She would almost certainly find it amusing.

'Probably not,' he said.

'I bet she spent the time worrying that the two candles on the dining table weren't exactly the same length. Or fretting about whether all the napkins were the exact same shade of taupe.'

'To be honest, that has been preying on my mind.'

Charlotte clasped her free hand to her face in mock horror. 'Don't tell me yours don't match!'

'Well, I've got a couple of white serviettes. I think the rest are left over from a Hallowe'en party. They may have cartoon pumpkins on them.'

'Uh-oh. I don't think Rosie is going to stand for that. You might as well just give up now.'

'Quick, then, draw spiders on the other two. At least that way it will look like a theme.'

'Dah-ling!' Charlotte exclaimed, in what Matt supposed was meant to be an exaggeratedly posh voice, but to him just sounded like a high-pitched version of her own. 'Don't you know insects are in this yah? Cath Kidston's new range is simply covered in woodlice!'

'I think this needs a spanner.' Matt got up and went back to the cupboard in the hall, where he kept his small bag of tools. Charlotte started laughing as he came back in clutching an adjustable wrench.

'I'm guessing you don't entertain very much.'

Matt yanked at one of the nuts, hoping Charlotte couldn't see how much effort it took to loosen it. He felt pricks of perspiration form on his forehead as he manoeuvred the panel into place.

Charlotte laughed. 'What I would have done ...'

An electric buzzing interrupted her advice.

'Was that the bell?'

'Yes, it was,' Matt said, tightening the last nut.

'Oh.'

Matt thought she sounded disappointed. He got to his feet and wiped his hands on a tea towel. 'I'll go and get it, shall I? Can you put the stuff back on the table? Make sure you give me the Donald Duck cutlery.'

With derisive laughter in his ears, Matt went into the hall and buzzed open the door without bothering to ask who it was. While he waited for the lift to ascend he noticed a stray tennis ball in the corner, and kicked it back into the cupboard.

He opened the front door in time to see Justin get out of the lift and look left and right a couple of times before realizing Matt was watching him.

'Hello, Justin. Barbara not with you?'

'No, she's coming separately ... I've been at work. She's not here, then?'

'No.'

'Oh dear, are we late?'

'No, you're the first to get here.'

Justin looked at his watch. 'Well, everyone else is late, then.'

'Do you want to come through?'

Matt led him into the flat, pausing as he passed the door to the kitchen so that Charlotte couldn't avoid being seen.

'Hi, Charlotte! Great to see you again,' Justin said.

'Yeah, hi.' Charlotte gave him a reluctant kiss on the cheek.

'I'd better finish off in the kitchen,' Matt said. 'Charlotte, do you mind getting Justin a drink?'

'Oh, lovely. I'll have a glass of white wine, please.'

Matt reached over to the fridge for the bottle and handed it to Charlotte in one smooth movement. 'Great. You can take some crisps out as well if you're hungry.'

Charlotte gave Matt a look of shocked malevolence as she accompanied Justin into the living room.

Matt took his time tidying the worktop. Then he began to re-lay the table. It had been quite fun with Charlotte, actually. She was a good laugh. Well, let's see how it goes. It could be a long evening.

Matt lingered over the place settings. He had no desire to go and talk to Justin. The lamb was browning nicely in the oven. About twenty more minutes, probably. The paella could go on simmering indefinitely. He wouldn't plate up the ceviche until everyone was here. So it was time for a glass of wine. Matt poured one from the bottle of red he had opened earlier. Pretty good. Charlotte had probably topped herself up. He certainly wasn't going into the other room to check.

Charlotte charged back into the kitchen and slammed the door behind her. 'Bastard!'

'What?'

'Leaving me in there with him like that. Jesus, that man is boring.'

'You've only been in there five minutes.' Matt put his wine glass down on the worktop.

'It felt like a decade. I can't believe you just palmed him off on me like that!'

'You were about to do the same to me.'

Charlotte considered this. 'True.'

Matt leaned back against the sink. Now that the table had been expanded, it was a bit cramped with them both in here. 'How did you get away, then?' he asked.

'Oh, I said you had some cashew nuts. Do you have some cashew nuts?'

'No.'

'Never mind. I'm not going back.'

They looked at each other. 'Have you got some wine?' he asked.

'I've got some in there, but I can't go back for it now.' She stared at him.

Matt poured her another glass. He'd have to wash up one of them before the others arrived.

'Need any help with anything?' Charlotte asked without enthusiasm.

'Nope, it's all done.'

'You are efficient.' Charlotte sprawled into a dining chair, allowing Matt to move away from the sink. 'What were we talking about?' she asked.

'You're not going back?' he replied.

'No. You?'

Matt sat down next to her. 'I think it was books,' he said.

'Can we say it was TV shows? I was watching this brilliantly awful thing yesterday . . .'

Soon, the doorbell went again.

Charlotte sighed in irritation. 'I'll go and get it, shall I?'

Eleven

There were several small Somali children playing football in the courtyard below the tower. Justin watched them approvingly. He had been feeling concerned since he first looked up Matt's address on Google Street View. The flat was on the top floor of a former local authority block halfway up St John's Street in Islington, not far from Clerkenwell, and Justin had always thought it was wrong for such places to be sold off, exiling the poor from anywhere nice, diminishing the stock of good-quality council homes and making central London a rich-only zone. He had been worried about whether it was right for him to eat dinner there.

But seeing the children use a tree tub and a dustbin for goalposts made Justin scold himself for being so judgemental. Maybe, in fact, Matt's decision to move here showed a worthy commitment to socially mixed living, a desire not to use money to run away from the less fortunate, but to join them in pushing the authorities to make conditions better for all. If it was right to send your children to a state school, perhaps it was right to buy in to a council estate as well. Justin took the working lift as confirmation of this. He resolved to apologize at a suitable point in the evening.

Surprisingly, there was no one else there when he arrived. Charlotte seemed in a bit of a huff as she poured him a drink. Perhaps she had quarrelled with Matt. Was she actually his partner? Presumably she was, although she didn't seem to know where the wine glasses were. Perhaps she hadn't moved in yet.

When they were sitting down, facing each other over glasses of wine, Justin asked, 'So how long have you two been together?'

'We're not.'

'Oh. I . . . Well, I thought . . .'

'It's Rosie's fault.'

'Is it? I'm not sure I understand how . . .'

'Never mind. Where's your wife? I've forgotten her name.'

'Barbara. She's not my wife. We have decided not to get married until gay couples everywhere in the US have the right.'

'Oh.' She looked at him with obvious mystification.

'Barbara feels very strongly about it and I'm fully in support of her,' he explained.

'Right,' Charlotte said in a tone he couldn't read. 'Is she coming?'

'Yes. But she's launching her new ceramics exhibition first.'

'Oh.'

There was a pause after that. Justin thought Charlotte might ask a bit about the exhibition, but she didn't. So instead he asked, 'What kind of work do you do?'

'I'm an accountant.'

'Oh.'

Justin didn't want another silence, so he thought he should carry on. 'Is that for one of the City firms?'

'No. It's the same place Rosie works. We design and manufacture kitchen appliances.'

'I see. Do you enjoy it?'

'No. Not particularly. But that's work, isn't it?'

Justin was a little shocked by this, and couldn't think of anything to fill the next silence. The humming of the Sky+ box seemed to be unusually loud. Charlotte took several sips of wine while Justin fiddled with his glass.

After a while, Charlotte asked, 'Are you a fan of *Come Dine with Me*?'

'Oh we don't have a TV.'

'Right.' That tone again.

'We both feel it tends to be a distraction from the more important things in life, you see,' he explained.

'Can I get you another drink?' she asked.

'Oh, er, no, thanks. I've hardly even started this one.'

'Are you sure?'

'Yes, honestly, I'm fine.'

'How about some nuts, then?' Charlotte stood up.

'No, I—'

'I'm sure I can find some peanuts or something. You must be getting pretty hungry.'

'Actually, I'm intolerant to peanuts. If I eat one, I start to swell up and—'

'Cashews, then?'

'No, really, I'm fine.'

'Let me see what I can find. Maybe Matt has some kind of organic snack.'

Justin thought it would be rude to object this time. Charlotte left the living room very quickly.

For a while, Justin remained perched on the edge of the sofa, his body bent forward at the forty-five-degree angle he used to signal interest in a conversation he was finding diffi-cult. After Charlotte had been gone for several minutes, he stood up and immediately noticed the view that appeared once he was looking down out of the window. In the bruise-coloured dusk, the landmarks of the City dazzled against the forest of lights stretching off in every direction. The Gherkin and the other skyscrapers seemed incredibly close, as if they shared with the tower block a high-rise space that ignored distances occupied by lesser buildings.

Coming closer to the window, Justin could see what must have been Smithfield market almost directly below. To the left he saw a strange warren of thick stone walls with ancient beamed roofs that seemed oddly out of place among the concrete and brick. Away to the right he could make out the top of the glowing dome of St Paul's, cradled in a ring of taller office blocks. Although it was a small flat, Justin now understood what Matt saw in it. How wonderful to have the whole city spread out below you like that.

Justin turned away from the window. Odd that there was no one else here. Perhaps he should have gone to Barbara's exhibition after all. He looked at his watch. Ten to eight. Where was Charlotte? Well, never mind. Justin put down his wine and opened the battered Eastpak rucksack he always carried with him. If he could start reading over the section he'd written that morning, then that would set him up well for the weekend. Relaxing into the sofa, he began to read.

He had barely got halfway through the statistics on mosquito-net penetration in rural Malawi when the doorbell went. Soon, he heard Barbara's voice in the hall. Reluctantly, he put the report back in his bag and stood up as Barbara and Charlotte came into the living room.

'Hi, my love,' he said.

'Hi, Justin,' she replied.

They smiled at each other but Barbara didn't come over to kiss him.

'Would you like a glass of wine?' Charlotte asked.

'Yeah. A large one, please.'

'Red or white?'

'Whatever. Red.'

When Charlotte left, Barbara flopped down in the recliner and exhaled noisily. 'What a shitty day.'

'What's the matter?'

'The launch was a disaster.'

'I'm sorry I didn't come.' He sat down facing her.

'It wasn't that. That's not important.'

'I'm sorry anyway. Did that gallery owner . . . I'm afraid I've forgotten his name – did he not come?'

'Dieter Tunhelm? Of course he didn't. But I don't care about any of that. I was standing there, drinking wine out of a plastic cup, looking at my work, and I thought: this is all a bunch of crap.'

'Oh no! Some of it's very nice!' Justin leaned forward to show her how strongly he felt.

'It's just twelve ugly lumps of painted clay. What's the point of it?' Barbara waved her arm dismissively towards the television. 'They say, if at first you don't succeed, try again. They say, if you work hard enough, you'll be successful. But what if you're a talentless nobody? They don't say anything about that.'

'You're not a talentless nobody!' Justin insisted.

'I think I'm done with it.'

'No!'

Barbara wasn't looking at him. 'And so I just left. I couldn't take it any more.'

'That's a little bit mean for Mary, don't you think? She put a lot of effort into—'

'And then I walked around for a long time thinking I just wanted to go home. But I didn't. I came here.'

Justin patted her on the arm. 'That was the right thing to do.'

'And now I'm thinking I don't want to spend an evening talking to these people.' Barbara's face hardened. 'And you know what I thought? If it wasn't for you, I wouldn't be here.'

Justin smiled affectionately at her. 'That's a sweet thing for you to say.'

Barbara stared at him again. 'I didn't mean . . .'

She stopped as footsteps came towards the door. Justin was surprised to see it was Matt bringing in the wine.

'Here you are.' He put a glass down next to Barbara. 'Hey, are you OK? You look like you've had a bad day.'

'Yeah, you know . . .' she mumbled.

'What happened?'

'It doesn't matter.'

'No – tell me.' Matt sat down on the recliner's footstool and pulled in closer.

Barbara shrugged. 'All right . . . I had my exhibition launch today.'

'It didn't go well?' Matt asked in a soft, understanding tone.

'No.'

'What was it? Was someone rude about it?'

'It wasn't anyone else's fault. It was just me. I looked at my work and I realized it was just garbage.'

'That must have been tough.' Matt patted her knee.

'I'm sorry. I don't know why I'm telling you this.' Barbara straightened in the chair.

'No, it's good. Look, I hope you don't mind if I say this – but things probably aren't as bad as you think.'

'They're pretty bad.'

'The thing is, this is a common response among artists. They work on a piece for so long, really throw everything into it, and then when they are done they can hardly bear to look at it. That doesn't mean the work's no good. Not at all.'

Barbara seemed to consider this. 'You think so?'

'Absolutely. In fact, I think I was reading somewhere that the same thing happened to Picasso. He made ceramics, didn't he? Well, I read that he was so disgusted with what he'd made one summer, he told his assistant to smash everything in the studio. Fortunately, the assistant didn't do it, just stowed them all away somewhere, and when he brought them out again after Picasso's death they were recognized as some of his finest works.'

Barbara brightened. 'Really?'

'Yup. Now, I'm not sure I can promise you'll make as much cash as that assistant did . . .'

Barbara laughed. She had a warm and open laugh, Justin thought. It made him happy to hear it.

'But all I'm saying is, things will turn out a lot better than you think now,' Matt said.

The doorbell went.

'I'd better go and get that.' Matt stood up, patting Barbara's knee again on the way.

When Matt had gone, Barbara looked at Justin questioningly. Justin was touched.

'What a nice thing for Matt to say,' he said.

Twelve

Rosie could see Charlotte puzzling over the table settings while Matt poured out wine in the kitchen to her left; in the living room to the right Barbara and Justin faced each other in silence across the coffee table. That was poor hosting, she noted with a hint of triumph. Definitely a potential mark against.

Was it wrong docking points in the hall before she had even got her jacket off? No, that was part of the game, surely.

In fact, if Matt didn't come and hang it up for her soon . . .

'You can come and sit at the table straight away,' he said, taking Rosie's jacket from her. 'It's about ready.'

'Can't we have a look round? I haven't been here before.'

'Sure. If you like. There's the living room. Go on in.'

'Hello!' Rosie waved at Justin and Barbara. She registered the bookshelf for further snooping, but went straight to the window.

'What an amazing view!' she exclaimed. It was fully

dark now, and towards the horizon the lights of the city merged into the stars, twinkling gently through the haze of distance.

'It's great, isn't it?' Matt said, joining her. 'It's a small flat, but I've always felt this makes up for it.'

'It must feel like you own the whole city!'

'Well . . .'

'No, it's fantastic. I bet you wake up every morning thinking London is there for the taking.'

Matt didn't reply to that. They stood side by side for several moments, watching the lights in silence.

It wasn't until the doorbell rang that Rosie noticed Stephen standing behind them. She moved away quickly. Not that, you know, but it might look . . .

'I'd better go and get that,' Matt said.

'Yes, of course,' Rosie agreed. She moved towards the bookshelf while Matt let in Marcus and Sarah. By the time he called them all through to the table, she had not found anything she could picture Matt enjoying reading.

Rosie had to turn sideways to squeeze into the folding chair jammed up against the wall by the extended table. Sarah and Marcus were already ensconced at the far end, and if either of them needed to get out, everyone would have to get up. Justin and Barbara had a bit more space on the other side of the table.

'Do you mind if we push the table out a bit?' she asked. 'We're a bit squeezed on this side.'

'We haven't got that much room.'

'Just a bit.' Rosie began pushing before Justin could object further. It was a bit rude of her, yes, but she wasn't the host any more. 'Thank you so much,' she said.

The other end of the table jutted past the fridge, deep into the kitchen where Matt was arranging something on to plates. Rosie noticed, with a sense of satisfaction, that two of them did not match.

The fish glistened under the bright halogen kitchen lights. Rosie was unreasonably irritated to see that the non-matching plates had been given to the vegetarians, as if they were meant to look different.

'This looks lovely, Matt,' Sarah said.

'Thank you.'

'Is it organic?' she asked.

'It's fish,' Marcus snapped back at her before Matt could respond.

'So?'

'It swims wild in the middle of the bloody ocean. How could it be organic?'

'I don't know. It's about not having any nasty hormones and stuff in it, isn't it?'

'No.' Marcus rolled his eyes. 'It's about how something is farmed.'

'Well, fish can be farmed.'

'Yes, but . . .'

'Is it farmed, Matt?' Sarah asked.

'It's from the fishmonger Jamie Oliver uses,' he said. This seemed to end the conversation.

Rosie took a forkful of fish. The flesh was firm and meaty, but as she bit into it she was pleased to discover that the citrus overpowered everything else; she could barely taste the delicate flavours of the uncooked fish over the acrid tang of lemon and lime. She took another bite. No, this one was hardly better, the marinade still overwhelming everything else.

Rosie grew in confidence. The starter wasn't a threat, and she couldn't believe Charlotte's pudding would be, so it would all come down to the main dish. And surely roast lamb couldn't compensate for two indifferent courses? It was reliable, yes, always likely to score well, but it was never going to be spectacular, was it? Rosie watched Justin and Barbara eat their salad. Some kind of puffy grains dominated; they looked dry and bland. That surely wasn't going to rescue Matt.

Rosie took a third forkful. The ceviche was almost half gone now. Just as well. That one tasted of nothing but lemon. Poor fish. To have died simply to become a way to mop up lemon juice. Rosie pushed the last bit round her plate and smiled.

'Mmm!' Sarah said. 'It's so light and powerful at the same time.'

'Thanks.'

'It's really subtle and refreshing.'

'Yes, it's very nice,' Stephen added in a low mumble. 'Very fishy.'

Well, Rosie thought, that was politeness, wasn't it? It didn't really mean they liked it.

'I must say, Matt, this is actually pretty good,' Marcus said. 'Simple, but very nicely balanced.'

Rosie was thrown. That sounded sincere. Grudging, yes,

but that only underlined the point. Not 'It's very lemony, isn't it?' or 'Mmm, the lime really comes through, doesn't it?', but straightforward praise. And if Marcus liked it, maybe Rosie was wrong. Maybe the others did too; maybe the course was going to put Matt out ahead. What hadn't she noticed? Was her palate missing some kind of subtlety?

'Rosie, what do you think?' Matt asked.

'Oh it's lovely,' she said emphatically. 'Really very good.'

'It's so easy to make,' Charlotte said.

As they discussed the dish, Rosie began to feel better. She had praised it, but she didn't like it; perhaps the others were doing the same. Marcus still had to cook, so there was no point making himself unpopular by slagging it off. Had they all been lying when Rosie cooked? Surely not. They really had seemed impressed. Even Marcus had liked some of the pomegranate molasses . . .

But that's what they'd want her to think. How good was she at telling when her friends were lying? Pretty good, she thought. But then, they hardly ever lied, so . . . But of course, maybe she was actually very bad at telling, and they lied all the time.

It suddenly seemed desperately important to have a way of knowing who wasn't being honest. Rosie looked suspiciously round the table.

'. . . but I've never been too bothered by the idea of getting older,' Sarah was saying. 'It just seems so trivial in the end, doesn't it?'

Hmm, Rosie thought.

'It's the helplessness I can't stand,' Stephen said, unexpectedly animated. 'Just drifting away from youth, quite slowly, actually, but watching it, examining it, knowing there's absolutely nothing you can do about it.'

'I like not having to pretend to be young any more,' Justin said.

'But you do, you do,' Stephen said. 'New generations spring up behind you, all optimistic and hopeful, and you're expected to keep up with them.'

'Jesus, Stephen, you're not even the oldest here,' Marcus said.

'Who is?' Justin asked. Everyone looked round the table. Justin continued: 'Charlotte, how old are you?'

'Fuck off.'

'Matt, what about you?'

'Matt's younger than I am,' Rosie said.

'No! Really?'

'No need to sound so astonished, Justin. Some people are.'

'No, I just meant . . . you know. I assumed he was older . . . Sorry, Matt, I only meant, sort of, late thirties.'

'That's all right. I don't mind people assuming that. I can always put them right if I need to. Can't do that if it's the other way round.'

'I suppose Barbara must be the youngest here,' Sarah said. 'You're what, twenty-seven?'

'Twenty-eight,' Barbara replied without emotion.

'A good age,' Stephen said wistfully. 'Old enough to feel mature and settled, but young enough to still feel unrushed.'

Barbara looked unimpressed. Stephen said nothing more. Rosie wondered what was wrong. Sometimes he got like that, but not usually after so little wine. She hoped he would enjoy himself tonight, get into the swing of things. It always cheered him up if he could end the evening thinking he'd been witty and talkative.

Sarah looked tired. Was work getting her down? Or was it something else? Rosie felt like a bad friend for not knowing. She resolved to find out. Probably not this evening, and this weekend would be difficult . . .

'What about you, Marcus?' Stephen asked with a touch of relish. 'Does anything about the inexorable slide towards decrepitude and death bother you at all?'

'Oh you know, not really,' Marcus said with studied casualness. 'Nothing beyond the usual waking up in the middle of the night sobbing over regrets and lost chances. That sort of thing.'

'Marcus gets depressed every birthday thinking about what he hasn't achieved,' Sarah said brightly. 'Comparing himself to other people and the things they have done by that age.'

'What do you mean? Like, by my age Alexander the Great had conquered half the world?' Stephen asked.

'Not even Alexander the Great,' Marcus replied. 'I mean, you know, Norman Foster. Now that is depressing.'

'Do you know what I always think when I worry about getting older?' Justin said.

Something about his tone made Rosie very reluctant to hear the answer.

'I think that, by my age, about a fifth of men in sub-Saharan Africa have already died.'

'Well, I can see how that would cheer you up,' Marcus said.

'It's a serious point. For one, it puts things into perspective, makes me feel lucky to have everything that I have. But it also makes me angry at the unfairness of it all. Drives it home to me that it's our job to go out and do something about it.'

No one seemed to know where to take the conversation after that. Rosie noticed that Charlotte was grimly emptying her glass. Of course, she probably was the oldest, Rosie realized. How old was she? Rosie wasn't sure. Thirty-five, perhaps? Did she look it? Well, probably not. Not until you thought about it anyway. There weren't too many lines on her face, but the plumpness helped with that.

Was that a bitchy thought? No, it was true, wasn't it? She was flushed red now, which was giving her skin an uneven, blotchy quality, but it was probably just the wine.

Certainly, she didn't look middle-aged, though. Not like Marcus. He was going bald at the front of his head and grey at the sides, and he had that odd, angular type of face which it was hard to imagine ever being young. Those glasses didn't help either. He looked about forty, but then he had done ever since Rosie met him. Maybe he would look exactly the same in thirty years and people would start remarking on how well he looked for his age.

Sarah seemed so worn as well. It wasn't really anything physical, although her skin was definitely sallow, but it was the expression her face had relaxed into as much as anything. Careworn and nervous. Like fun wasn't her natural state any more. Rosie wasn't sure whether to feel sad that someone her own age could look so youthless, or secretly pleased that she looked much better.

The conversation hadn't restarted. After a while Matt stood up. 'Has everyone finished? Shall I take the plates?'

Rosie watched him stand up. His face was naturally craggy, and his skin had a rough, worn sheen to it, but it was still taut. There was just such a focused, contained quality to him that young people didn't seem to have. Matt had always had it, though. There was none of the doubt that so many people had when they were young, and none of the buoyancy you saw in others.

Matt piled up all eight plates and began washing them up. Rosie realized these must be all the plates he had.

Charlotte wasn't getting up to help him. What did that mean? Had they had some kind of falling out already? No, Rosie didn't think so. When Charlotte didn't like someone, it wasn't hard to tell. There was none of that tension. She was just distracted.

In fact, the body language was quite good. They had been sitting next to each other for a start. Close together too. Angled slightly towards each other. Wasn't that a good sign? That's what it said in *Marie Claire* anyway. They weren't quite touching, but there had been a couple of glances that suggested a private joke. They were definitely getting on well.

It would be so much more convenient if they became a couple. Then Rosie could start inviting them to ordinary dinner things. It wouldn't be a special effort to see either of them any more; there'd be no more single-friend awkwardness. They could start going to the cinema together, or even the theatre. Rosie allowed herself a moment's pride. Perhaps it had been some sort of instinct.

Charlotte snapped out of whatever trance she had been in. 'Who wants some more wine?' she asked.

Thirteen

Justin looked round the table, silently asking if anyone wanted to take up his offer of a discussion on global inequality. No one did.

Marcus enjoyed the hush. Matt and Charlotte were over at the kitchen worktop and the others seemed content to let the conversation drift. He was in good spirits. It had been a satisfying day at work; they hadn't won the competition for the flats in Nottingham, but Piotr had agreed that they probably would have done if they'd gone with Marcus's idea in the first place.

A cloud of hot spice-laden air filled the room as Matt opened the oven. It was a thick, fatty scent that seemed almost edible itself, and Marcus realized how hungry he was. The starter had been quite pleasant. He had been assuming that Matt would trip up somewhere along the line, but it was competently done. Nothing special, of course. There was no complexity to the flavours, just a pleasing unity of fishy, lemony freshness.

But Marcus hadn't been expecting much, and he had enjoyed it. Now he was looking forward to the lamb. The fish had been insubstantial, and a hearty lump of roast meat seemed a good way to follow. Not much in the way of fine cooking, no, but that was ideal really; Marcus could enjoy a tasty dinner without worrying whether he could match it.

'That smells gorgeous, Matt,' Rosie said as Matt took the leg out of the oven and perched it on the front of the hob, swaddling it quickly in silver foil. 'And it looks amazing. I'm surprised you could fit it into the oven.'

Matt laughed briefly. 'It was a bit of a struggle.' He took the two odd plates off the drying rack and carefully loaded them up with paella from the casserole dish wedged behind the lamb at the back of the hob. He handed them silently to Charlotte, who plonked them down in front of Justin and Barbara with all the enthusiasm of a geriatric nurse distributing bedpans.

'Smells great,' Barbara said. 'What's in it?'

'Vegetables,' Charlotte replied.

'Peppers, onions, aubergine, fennel, artichokes, a bit of saffron, turmeric, parsley. That sort of thing,' Matt clarified, still facing away from them as he took another tray out of the oven – was that avocado Marcus could see roasting in there? – and tipped the contents into the salad bowl that occupied the only free bit of worktop. He handed that to Charlotte and she put it on the table.

'What's this?' Justin asked.

'Salad,' she replied.

'Avocado, alfalfa, lettuce, some Monterey Jack ...' Matt

tailed off as the lamb teetered on the edge of the hob as he removed the foil.

'Do you need a hand with that?' Marcus asked.

'I think I'll have to do it on the table.' Matt picked up the leg of lamb on its carving board, manoeuvred it over an empty spot on the table, then put it down heavily in front of a startled Justin and Barbara. Justin couldn't keep his eyes off the steaming lump of meat.

'It's very . . . leg-like, isn't it?' he said.

'It is a leg,' Charlotte replied.

'Sorry to dump it in front of you,' Matt said. 'But there wasn't really space to carve over there. I hope you don't mind.'

He picked up the carving knife and plunged it into the haunch, releasing a bubbling spurt of bloody juice. Justin flinched.

'You all right?'

'Well, actually, you know, I'd rather . . . but no, it's fine.'

Marcus was a little disappointed to see politeness win out.

'You sure?' Matt asked.

'Yes, fine.'

But Charlotte persisted: 'No, what? What is it?'

'Nothing.'

'Come on, what?'

'Well,' Justin shifted in his seat. 'I suppose it's just that I'd prefer it if you didn't do that in front of us.'

'Nearly done,' Matt said, doling out hunks of meat on to plates.

'What, roast lamb offends you, does it?' Charlotte asked, leaning back and folding her arms.

'We're vegetarians, you see.'

'I'd noticed.'

'So, you know, yes, we prefer not to have dead animals in front of us.' Justin's tone became a little less apologetic.

'It's not a dead animal. It's roast lamb,' Charlotte said.

'I certainly hope it's dead,' Matt said.

'Looks pretty dead to me,' Marcus agreed.

'Yes, but it's cooked,' Charlotte insisted.

'That doesn't make it any less dead,' Justin replied.

'But that's not the point, is it? That's like saying that your paella is just a bowl of dead peppers and dried-out rice grains.'

'That rice is not dried out,' Matt interjected. 'I'd say it was succulent.'

'Yes, it looks very nice, Matt,' Justin said.

Matt continued quickly: 'Charlotte, could you serve out the beans?'

This seemed to be the moment to break the tension. Matt began apportioning the lamb and Charlotte seemed fully occupied adding fava beans and flatbread to the plates and sending them round the table.

Marcus watched his own portion approach as he weighed up his options. The argument had threatened to ruin the atmosphere of the whole evening – he didn't want to see such promise go to waste. Clearly, if Justin and Barbara became embroiled in a bitter argument about meat-eating, they were unlikely to give the meal top marks. And for everyone else, a tense confrontation wasn't going to help the evening run smoothly. Rosie already looked uncomfortable, and Sarah too seemed on edge. If this carried on, she was unlikely to resist Marcus's attempts to mark Matt down. He would be right to do so. That was before they had even tasted the meat, which was never going to seem at its best during an argument about whether or not it was murder.

'Please start,' Matt said as he moved the hacked-up lamb to one side. Half the bone was now picked clean, gleaming whitely between hunks of gristle.

No one said anything as they took their first bite of lamb. It was, in fact, pretty good, Marcus thought: tender, juicy, well-infused with interesting spices. Of course it lacked a bit of subtlety, just sitting there on the plate with beans, salad and flatbread, but for what it was, it was good. The silence continued. It wasn't obvious how to compliment the lamb without restarting the argument.

Marcus said: 'Matt, Charlotte, this is really good. Tender and flavoursome.' He nodded. 'You vegetarians are missing out.'

'We can smell it, actually,' Justin said.

'Good, isn't it?'

'It's rather invasive.'

'Oh, is it?' Charlotte asked quietly, filling her wine glass to the top.

'Yes.'

'Annoying you, is it?'

'It is a bit. Barbara, what is it that Samina calls it?'

'Passive meat-eating,' Barbara replied.

'What!' Wine slopped over the rim of Charlotte's glass.

'Yes, it's when you're given no choice about ingesting

particles of meat because they're ambient, like smoke, in the air.'

'I've never heard anything so stupid in my life,' Charlotte declared.

'I'm sorry you don't like it, but it's true,' Justin said firmly. 'You're making me breathe in meat.'

'It's tasty, though, isn't it?' Marcus said. 'Are you sure you won't have a slice, now that you're eating it anyway?'

'Marcus . . .' Sarah warned.

'Come on, it was just a joke. Tell me, is it a moral or a health issue for you?'

'Both,' Justin said.

Charlotte snorted.

'Barbara, what do you think?' Sarah asked.

It took her some time to respond. 'I guess everybody has to make their own choices about killing animals. But I just don't think that I could ever eat meat. It's so heavy, and greasy, and full of stuff that's bad for your body.'

'Bollocks!' Charlotte said. 'We've evolved to eat meat.'

'You know, I think we've evolved to make choices. And I want to choose not to eat meat.'

'Well said, Barbara,' Justin commented, in a way that Marcus thought was faintly patronizing.

'What about my choices?' Charlotte jabbed her fork towards Barbara.

'I'm not criticizing your choices . . .'

'Yes, you bloody well are! You called it passive meat-eating! As if we were all sitting here with twenty Bensons each on the go, wafting them under your nose.'

'We're not saying it's necessarily equivalent to smoking in the health sense,' Justin said. 'It's more in moral terms, about what we want to eat or not eat.'

'What, so it's only in moral terms that I'm a baby-killer?'

'I didn't call you a baby-killer . . .'

'It's what you think, though.'

'Well, a living creature has died for your meal . . .'

'I knew it! I knew it!' Charlotte shouted in triumph. 'You come into my house and call me a murderer . . . !'

'This isn't your house—'

'But I'm still a murderer?'

'Look, I'm not saying . . .' Justin's tone lost a little of its edge.

'How can you condemn it without even trying it?' Charlotte demanded.

'I'm not saying it doesn't taste nice . . .'

'Because it does.'

'I'm saying we shouldn't kill other animals for our own pleasure. I don't need to try it to know that. Just like you don't need to try killing people to know that's wrong.'

'You see?' Charlotte pointed her fork at him accusingly. 'He is calling me a murderer!'

'Ach!' Justin exhaled in frustration. 'Like Barbara said, it's about choices. We choose not to make animals suffer and die for our dinner. You choose to do so.'

Matt interrupted. 'Maybe I choose to change the subject.'

Justin laughed politely. 'Perhaps that's—'

'No,' Charlotte insisted. 'I haven't finished. I've just thought of something. Why is it only you who gets to choose?'

'We all get to choose.'

'No, I mean tonight. You come over here and make me – Matt, anyway – cook you a whole other meal. It's not even the same thing without meat in it; it's a whole other meal.'

'And very nice it is too, Matt,' Justin said. 'Very tasty.'

'Thanks.'

'So why doesn't it work the other way round?' Charlotte continued. 'Why can't I come round to your house and demand that you cook me a steak? Or a nice joint of rare roast beef?'

'It's not really the same thing.' Justin's voice was tetchy again.

'Yes, it is. It's exactly the same thing. You don't want to eat meat. I do. Why do you get to have a special meal cooked for you and I don't?'

'You're being ridiculous.' Justin's head quivered.

'Why?'

'You can eat vegetarian dishes. And if you just tried them, you would probably really like them, because actually there are some great recipes . . .'

'But you know what would make them better? Meat.' Charlotte filled up her wine glass again.

'That's the difference, you see?' Justin said with clear exasperation. 'You can eat something without meat. We can't eat something with meat. So we have to have something else or we would go hungry.'

'You said it was about choices.'

'It is.'

'Well, I've made my choice. I choose sausages. When I

come round to your house, I want a plate of big, juicy, pork sausages.'

'All right, Charlotte,' Matt murmured.

Justin laughed very deliberately. 'No, it's OK . . .'

'I'm serious. Big, glistening sausages. Or a chop. There's a choice for you. I'd settle for a grilled lamb chop with a good bit of bloody pinkness in the middle. That's what I want.'

'Charlotte, come on,' Rosie said in a soothing tone. 'You know it doesn't work like that.'

'But why not? That's my point. I think it should. Sausages or chops. Got that, Justin?'

'Yes, I heard you.'

'Good. So we're agreed. You're going to do it?'

'No, Charlotte, I'm not going to do it.'

'Why not?'

'Because I think meat-eating is wrong and I find meat disgusting.'

'You're not going to get a very good mark off me if that's your attitude.'

'If it's a choice between a bad mark and my deepest values, I think I'll just have to take the risk.'

Sarcasm didn't seem to come naturally to Justin. The intonation was all wrong. Marcus thought he must be really angry to try it. In fact, it was probably Justin's equivalent of overturning his chair and storming out.

Marcus, naturally, was delighted. The atmosphere was truly ruined now, and clearly Justin would make sure this evening didn't win the competition. But the bonus was that Justin and Barbara's night was almost certainly out of contention as well, if Charlotte kept up her threats. There was always a chance of her apologizing, it was true, but somehow Marcus couldn't see that happening. At worst, she would glower scornfully and mark down whatever vegetable concoction she was made to eat. At best, the whole row would start again next time.

How was everyone else taking it? Even though it was ruining his hosting, Matt looked like he was finding it pretty amusing. Stephen looked a little bored and, interestingly, so did Barbara, even though she was supposed to be an active participant in the argument. She was just sitting there, chin propped up on her hand, staring into the salad bowl. Marcus wondered what she was thinking. It was so hard to tell. She seemed to have said almost nothing on both nights. Was she shy? Tired? A bit dim? Secretly contemptuous of everyone round the table?

Marcus bristled at the thought. At least he was willing to say something.

'Can I help you with the clearing up?' Rosie asked. She and Sarah were wearing the same pained expression, which Marcus found viscerally insufferable.

'No, leave it,' Charlotte commanded as Rosie reached for Stephen's plate.

'Honestly, it's no trouble . . .'

'No, we're going to have seconds,' she said.

'Oh, it was lovely, thank you, but . . .'

'Matt, will you give everyone some more?' Charlotte instructed.

'Not for me, thanks, Charlotte,' Sarah said. 'I'm absolutely full.'

'Matt, give her some more.'

Matt hesitated for a moment, then went over to the carving board. This time he didn't put it on the table. Lukewarm helpings of meat were passed round in grim silence.

Justin and Barbara declined seconds of paella and for a while no one ate anything. Sarah tried to stifle a cough that seemed unnaturally loud against the silence. Then Stephen cut a chunk of lamb and put it in his mouth. Was he trying to defuse the situation, or was he still hungry? Matt followed him, then, still looking pained, so did Rosie and Sarah.

The sticky sounds of meat-chewing spread round the hushed table, seeming to get louder the longer no one spoke.

Marcus tried to chew more quietly, but felt the squelching noise must be echoing round the hard surfaces of the kitchen. The meat, herby and flavourful the first time round, seemed to drain of all taste until it became just a fatty lump of animal flesh in his mouth. Marcus forced it down. He could hear everyone else doing the same, gullets pulsing and twitching like trapped rodents.

This was brilliant. The bitter, tasteless seconds were all anyone would remember of the main course. The evening was going down in flames.

Charlotte eventually broke the silence. 'I'll just open another bottle of wine,' she said.

As soon as she stood up, Rosie began clearing the plates. Charlotte looked round, disapproving, but then got distracted by the corkscrew.

Matt scraped a big pile of uneaten lamb into the bin and stacked up the dirty plates in the sink.

'Who's for dessert, then?' he asked.

Fourteen

Stephen was grateful for the lamb; it was solid and filling after a starter that had been too insubstantial to make much of a dent in his hunger. He had needed a large meal after a difficult day, as much for comfort as for sustenance. After his first plateful he had reached that pleasant state of repletion that he knew never lasted long before tipping over into exhaustion.

He had wanted to use this window to throw himself into the conversation, be engaging and amusing for at least a few minutes. But that silly row about vegetarianism shut him out. He had no interest in joining in on either side – he had always liked eating meat, but didn't want to make a moral point out of it.

Stephen had finished well before everyone else and thought it was probably too early to ask for more. What had he had for lunch? Oh yes, a sandwich from the canteen. Crayfish and rocket. It tasted exactly the same as the prawn cocktail salad sandwich they used to have, but was one pound more expensive.

But then, all the sandwiches in the canteen tasted similar – two slices of soggy bread moulded round a rubbery filling coated in fatty mush. Stephen ate them in rotation: Farmhouse cheese and pickle; Wiltshire smoked ham; Coronation chicken; New York-style pastrami; Crayfish and rocket. Eating them in order saved wasting time thinking about what to have on any given day, wondering about which he hadn't eaten for a while, or looking fruitlessly for an alternative.

The lamb really was very good. He had felt a twinge of jealousy when Rosie had praised it so extravagantly to Matt. But tasting it had placated him, because he had to admit that it deserved the compliments. Even cooling a bit, the soft hunks of meat were tender and full of flavour, with that unusual mix of spices and just the right amount of fattiness. Stephen paused with a few chunks left on the plate. He wondered why no one else seemed to be enjoying it.

Charlotte brought over some more wine and Stephen picked up his glass to accept a refill. While his attention was elsewhere, Rosie quickly cleared away his lamb without asking. Perhaps she was hungry for dessert. What were they having? Matt brought over a pot of cream. That was a good sign.

'Do you need a hand with anything?' Rosie asked.

'No, thanks. It's all under control.' Charlotte took a large chocolate tart from the fridge and placed it at the centre of the table. 'There we go.'

'That looks amazing, Charlotte!' Sarah said.

'I wish I'd saved a bit more room,' Stephen agreed.

Rosie frowned. 'I thought we were having Espresso Chocolate Cake?'

'I was experimenting for a while,' Charlotte said easily, 'and decided this went better with the meal.'

'But the menu ...'

'You can't be tied down by a piece of paper, Rosie. It's all about the taste, isn't it?'

Rosie bent over and inspected her slice of tart carefully. 'Did you make this yourself, Charlotte?'

'Of course. Does everyone want a piece? There's not even any meat in it.' Charlotte thrust a plate towards Barbara.

'Are you sure about that?' Justin asked. 'Did you make the pastry as well?'

'Of course.'

'And you didn't use any animal fat in it?'

'Er ... no. No, I didn't.' Charlotte said it firmly.

'Really?' Rosie asked. 'What did you use, then?'

Charlotte stared at Rosie, and blinked slowly. 'Flour, mostly,' she said.

'Just flour?' Rosie arched her eyebrows.

Charlotte shrugged. 'You know, water and stuff as well.'

'What about butter?'

'That too.'

Rosie compressed her lips in the way Stephen saw her do when talking to the builders. 'How did you make it stick?' she asked.

Charlotte stared defiantly back. 'You have to knead it for longer,' she said simply.

'That's so much healthier, isn't it?' Sarah said.

'Yes, exactly.' Charlotte turned to Sarah with a wide grin. 'It's very important to be healthy.'

'But you definitely made the pastry yourself?' Rosie asked.

'Of course. Really, Rosie, you're being—'

'What did you do with the dish?' she asked.

'The dish?'

'Normally you would serve a tart like that in its baking dish,' she said. 'In fact, I don't know how you'd go about getting it out.'

'Really?'

'Yes. What's your secret?' Rosie settled back in her chair and interlocked her fingers.

Charlotte looked away and coughed delicately. 'Well,' she said, after pausing for a moment. 'I just turned it upside down. And used a knife. That's why the crust's a bit damaged, you see? Look.' Charlotte pointed out the scratches, chips and irregular lumps that scarred the pastry case. Rosie leaned forward and inspected them.

'OK.' She leaned back. 'But why did you need to take it out of the dish at all?'

'I borrowed it,' Charlotte said, grinning again. 'I had to give it back.'

Rosie narrowed her eyes to squint suspiciously at Charlotte. Charlotte held her gaze. They stared at each other for some time.

'I'll finish serving, shall I?' Matt reached his arm deliberately between them, breaking eye contact. Stephen caught Charlotte cracking a slight smirk as she looked away.

Stephen smothered his slice of tart in cream. He glanced sideways at Rosie as he did so, but she didn't even notice. She was glaring at what was left of the dessert and her whole body was rigid. Stephen could sense her frustrated determination. He found it incredibly sexy.

He loved it when she was like this: resolute, single-minded and moving with restrained power beneath her dress, like a panther tensing to pounce. It made him think of the time just before they got married when she'd had an argument with her boss about a pay rise. She'd filled herself with righteous fury, marched into the MD's office and walked out with double what she'd originally asked for. Then she'd come home half ablaze with delight, half still simmering at the original injustice, and they'd had sex on the living-room floor. Thinking about it, Stephen began to sweat slightly.

At that moment, he wasn't really sure what she was getting angry about – did she think Charlotte was lying about the cake? – but her black and red dress pulled tight over her breasts with every deep, irregular breath. Under the table, he reached out and stroked her thigh. She batted his hand away without looking at him.

The rejection smarted. Stephen poured himself another glass of wine and attacked the dessert. It was good – a deep, textured, chocolate goo, broken up with crunchy chunks of hazelnut. The cream sunk through each mouthful of chocolate, giving a cool freshness to each sticky bite. But the richness was so intense that Stephen quickly hit his limit, and with every mouthful began to feel his stomach straining against his trousers. He took a few more forkfuls, regretting now the seconds of lamb. As his breathing grew laboured, he reluctantly accepted he would have to stop. He put down the fork and reached for his glass, taking very small sips to ease the pressure on his digestion.

'This is very tasty, Charlotte,' Sarah said. 'The hazelnuts in it are great. They really break up the sweetness.'

'Good, that's what I hoped,' Charlotte replied. 'Much better than espresso, I reckoned.' She grinned at Rosie.

'Yes, without them the sweetness could become too over-powering, couldn't it?' Marcus said. He seemed to be enjoying himself, Stephen thought.

'Tell me, Charlotte,' Rosie asked. 'Did you put molasses in?'

'Nope.'

'Because it isn't just sugar, is it? How did you get such a rich sweetness?'

'That would be the secret ingredient.'

'Secret ingredient? What's that?'

'It's a secret.'

'Ha, ha. Very good. Go on, tell me.'

Charlotte caught Matt's eye. She nodded at him.

'I know it's got some dulce de leche in it,' he said.

'Yes, that was it,' Charlotte admitted. 'Dulce de leche.'

'Really?'

'Honestly, Rosie. Anyone would think you were accusing me of not making this myself.'

'Oh no, of course not.' Rosie shook her head very quickly at the thought.

'Good. Because I spent a long time baking this, you know.' Charlotte sipped her wine.

'Oh yes, it shows. I wouldn't for a minute suggest you were passing off a shop-bought tart as your own. Not for a minute.'

Rosie shook her head again, slowly this time, then stopped. 'Only, you're always saying you're no good at cooking.'

'Well, you know ...' Charlotte waved a hand modestly.

'And the funny thing is, I bought a tart just like this from Tesco only the other week.'

'Really? What a coincidence.' Charlotte did not flinch.

'Oh no!' Sarah protested. 'This is much nicer than anything from a supermarket!'

'I'm glad you think so,' Charlotte said.

'Yes, with prepared food you get this horrid sort of packaged preservative taste.' Sarah screwed up her face. 'It's unmistakable. That's why I never eat them. And of course they're terribly bad for you.' She tutted. 'Honestly, Rosie, stop being so suspicious. It's very rude.'

'Yes, Rosie, really!' Marcus admonished, while grinning. 'You can tell it's not professionally made – it's far too lumpy and irregular for that.'

'Yeah, cheers, Marcus,' Charlotte said.

Rosie opened her mouth to say something, but decided against it. She stood up. 'Excuse me for a moment.'

On her way to the toilet, she stopped by the door and peered very closely into the bin.

'All right, Rosie?' Charlotte asked.

'Fine.' Rosie straightened up quickly.

The conversation took a while to get going again after Rosie had left the kitchen. Justin still looked grumpy. Stephen thought this should be the moment when he stepped in and got properly involved in the evening. But his window of gregariousness was closing. His full stomach had made him irritable, and then a wave of tiredness hit him, quenching the party spirit and leaving only the fizzling nausea of an impending hangover.

Sarah finished her last bite of tart and put down her spoon with an excited clatter. 'Ooh, I know,' she said through a sticky mouthful of chocolate. 'Shall we play another game now?'

'Fuck no,' Charlotte replied.

Slightly stunned by Charlotte's vehemence, Sarah fell silent until Rosie came back, when Sarah said she needed to go to the loo as well. Marcus and Stephen had to stand up while Rosie hung back by the door. The act of dragging himself upright gave Stephen another throb of discomfort in his stomach. He accepted it was time to go home.

As Sarah squeezed past them, Marcus asked, 'Do you entertain often in here, Matt?'

'Not this many people.'

'No, I'm sure it's normally more intimate.' Marcus looked at Charlotte as he spoke. Matt laughed politely. Charlotte wasn't listening.

'How long have you had this place?' Marcus asked.

'About three years.'

'Tell me, do you know who designed this estate?'

'No, it's a sixties tower block, isn't it?'

'Oh no, I would say early eighties,' Marcus said.

'If you say so.' Matt shrugged.

The conversation petered out after that. Neither of them seemed willing to put in the effort to keep it going.

Stephen had been here only once before and he was

startled to hear Matt say he had been in the flat three years. It was a nice enough place, but Matt could clearly afford better. Stephen, who felt a twinge of anxiety every time he thought about his mortgage, resented the thought that Matt was piling up far more cash than he knew what to do with. Even worse was the thought that he was investing it all somewhere, and would suddenly turn out to be a multimillionaire.

Stephen was fairly sure he wasn't jealous of Matt. Well, maybe he envied his money. Professionally, Matt probably was doing much better than Stephen, and he had the cash to go with it. But that was just income. That wasn't Matt. What did he have to show for it? Living alone in a sparse flat at the top of a council block.

Then there were the women. Matt always seemed to have someone new. But what was the point of going through all that effort, risking so much embarrassment, just to throw it all away and start again every time? Even now Matt was probably trying to sleep with Charlotte. Stephen could tell from the appraising way Matt looked at her. God, it must be so tiring.

'Does anyone want any coffee?' Matt asked.

'No, thanks,' Justin said. He had clearly been waiting impatiently for this cue, because he added very quickly, 'In fact, we'd better be going.'

'Are you sure?'

'Yes, I'm afraid so.'

Matt didn't push the point.

Fifteen

Thank God they'd gone. What a couple of clench-arsed prudes. Charlotte smiled into her glass of wine. God, that had been fun. The looks on their lemon-sucking faces! Why didn't people have arguments like that more often? It was so much better than chit-chat about house prices and whatever boring rubbish they had talked about at Rosie's. And it was exactly what they deserved too. Even the mention of the words 'vegetarian option' brought up Charlotte's hackles, made her picture moralizing killjoys. And she wasn't wrong, was she? Worst of all, they were always so dull. To Charlotte's mind, being a bastard was forgivable; being boring never was.

Charlotte couldn't remember exactly what she'd said, but she knew she'd won the argument. That was why Mr and Mrs Lentil Tofu were scuttling off home to their organic veg box. He was more of a dick, obviously, but she was fucking annoying, with her floaty, I'm-too-spiritual-for-you hippy bollocks, as if she hadn't noticed that she'd tied her halter-neck so

tightly that it practically screamed 'Please look at my tits!'.
Fuck it. They were gone now. Maybe everyone else could
start enjoying themselves as well.

'More wine, anyone?' she asked, louder than she expected.
'Or is it time for some shots? Did I see a bottle of sambuca in
your drinks cupboard, Matt?'

'I hope not.'

'Whatever it was, bring it out.'

'Not for us, thanks,' Rosie said, standing up. 'We'd better
be going.'

Stephen grimaced and began struggling to his feet.

'You sure?' Charlotte gave her a crooked smile. 'Maybe
some tequila?'

'No, we've got to get back. The babysitter, you see.'

'Oh, right, the babysitter.' Charlotte laughed. 'Well, give
my regards to Julian . . . No, what's his name?'

'Jonathan,' Rosie said tightly.

'Yes, Jonathan, that's it.'

'Thank you so much for dinner, Matt,' Rosie said. 'It was
lovely.'

'And me! Don't forget my delicious tart.'

'Yes,' Rosie said.

Charlotte managed to wait until they were out of the front
door before bursting out laughing.

Matt sat back down at the table with a bottle of clear spirit
in one hand and four shot glasses in the other. He was holding
them all easily in his left palm, Charlotte noticed. They were
big hands, weren't they? Powerful arms too, she could tell,
under that horrible shirt. He was a big guy.

'Who wants some of this? God knows what it is. I bought it in South Africa.' Matt poured out four glasses.

Marcus raised his palm. 'I think we're all right ...'

'Go on.' Matt pushed two glasses across the table. Sarah sniffed at hers and recoiled.

'OK?' Matt held his shot ready. 'One, two, three ...'

Christ, that was revolting. What the fuck was in it? No, better not to know. Charlotte coughed, opened her screwed-up eyes and saw Matt watching her.

'Like it?'

'Fuck, no.'

'What about you guys?'

Charlotte was enraged to see that Marcus and Sarah hadn't downed their glasses. Sarah had hardly touched hers. What sort of wet-blanket fuckwits sipped random shots? Jesus.

'A bit strong for me,' Marcus said. 'But you carry on.'

'Marcus,' Sarah whispered, 'do you think we ...'

'Yes,' Marcus responded slowly. 'I suppose we'd better be making a move. It's been a long day.'

Matt stood up to show them out.

'"Thank you very much for the dinner. It was very tasty,' Sarah said. 'I'm sure you'll score highly. The conversation was definitely, um ... interesting.'

'Did you have coats?'

'I'm not saying it wasn't entertaining,' Marcus added, 'but I don't think you can count on their vote.'

Christ. A wanker and boring, Charlotte thought. He could even be worse than the veggies.

'Oh but the tart was delicious,' Sarah said. 'You'll have to give me the recipe.'

Once they had gone, Matt came and sat down in the seat next to her, close enough for Charlotte to feel the rush of air as he let himself land heavily in the chair. He was holding a bottle of brandy.

'Shall we switch to this?'

'That stuff was revolting.'

'It was. Sorry about that.'

'What was it?'

'I don't know. I got it at duty-free.'

'Jesus. Well, it sure flushed out Mr Smartarse McWanker over there.'

'That's good, is it?' Matt stretched his arm across her to pour a glass of brandy.

'He's a wanker.'

'I suppose he is pretty annoying.'

'She's all right. Bit of a drip, though.'

Charlotte noticed her glass was almost full, while his contained only a small measure. She reached across for the bottle and filled his right up to the brim. He did that smile he was always doing. He probably thought it was enigmatic, but she found it annoying. It was growing on her, though.

'Cheers,' he said, splashing brandy on the table as he raised his glass.

'Cheers.'

'Well, I don't think we've won,' Matt said, leaning back in his chair. 'But it was good fun.'

'What do you mean? Of course we won. Didn't you see the

faces on those vegemites when they left? They looked like
someone had just told them tofu was made of African orphans.'

'I meant I don't think we'll be getting top marks from them.'

'Fuck the points. There's more than one way to win a
competition, you know.'

Matt did the bloody smile again.

'And the tart,' Charlotte said. 'They bought the tart.'

'They did.' Matt laughed. 'Just like you.'

'Ha, ha.' Charlotte made a face.

'It was pretty funny, actually. I think we both did well not
to laugh.'

'Did you hear it when Sarah asked for the recipe? That was
fucking hilarious. She really meant it.'

'Well, it was a nice tart.'

'Bit sticky for my taste, actually. But there we are.'

'Try Sainsbury's next time, then, eh?'

'Waitrose, please.'

Matt inched his chair in a bit closer as he laughed. 'I'm not
sure Rosie was convinced.'

'No, but she couldn't prove it, could she?' Charlotte took a
long sip of brandy. 'You have to be able to prove it.'

'Do you?'

'You're the lawyer. That's how the law works, isn't it?'

'Well, it depends which field of . . . Basically, yes.'

'There you are, then. Why should dinner parties be any
different?'

'All's fair in food and law?'

Charlotte had to pause for a minute to work this out.

'That was rubbish,' she said.

'I thought it was quite good,' Matt protested.

'No. It was rubbish.'

'I'll shut up, then.'

Charlotte nodded. She could see Matt had been leaning slowly towards her, close enough now to see the late-night line of bristles on his jaw. There was a musky scent of sweat and garlic. She could hear him breathing, deep and regular. She could still go home.

But fuck it, it wasn't like she was ruining anything special here. And it had been bloody ages as well. Screw it, no point in over-thinking things.

Charlotte watched Matt's dark eyes move closer. What was he thinking now? Besides the bleeding obvious. Better not to know. The eyes got closer. Charlotte felt a definite buzzing charge coming from them. It wasn't just the booze. He'd better hope he lived up to them.

'Do you want to come through to the other room?' Matt said softly. 'The view's amazing at night.'

Oh no. Don't speak. The accent could ruin the whole fucking thing.

'I'm fine in here. No need to bother with that.'

Charlotte reached out and took him by the back of his head. Thank God there was no hair gel, only thick tufts above the hard swell of the skull. She pulled him in.

He looked a bit surprised to begin with, but he soon got over it.

From: Rosie and Stephen <rosieandstephen@home.co.uk>
To: Dinner At Mine <dinneratminescores@gmail.com>
Sent: 23.34
Subject: Dinner

Hi Matt and Charlotte,

Thank you so much for dinner. We had a lovely time. It was so nice to see your flat – the views are amazing! Glad to see that cooking together worked out so well!

We both found the lamb delicious. You will have to tell me what you marinated it in. However (and please don't take this the wrong way – I say it only because that's the nature of the competition), I'm afraid to say that I found the fish very disappointing. It was positively drowned in lemon juice. The pudding was not to my taste. I'll leave it there. Although Stephen liked it.

I also feel bound to dock marks for your hosting. I know that you don't entertain very often, and that you've never done so together, but you really shouldn't leave guests on their own. Also, while I was willing to overlook the two odd plates, I think that using three different types of unmatching bowls was going too far. Of course, far worse than that is deliberately picking quarrels with the guests. Quite apart from what they thought, it made things very awkward for the rest of us. So we have decided to give you a six.

Yours,

Rosie and Stephen

From: Marcus Thompson <marcusthompson@
        taylorwilsonpartners.com>

To: Dinner At Mine <dinneratminescores@gmail.com>

Sent: 00.10

Subject: Dinner Score

The conception of the dishes was too simplistic. However the execution was effective, producing a pleasant, fresh starter with a good balance of plain flavours. The main course was satisfying, with good-quality meat, competently seasoned and cooked. It had, though, lost much of its appeal the second time round.

In addition, the side dishes were uninspired and too basic. A ladleful of beans and a piece of bread is unpromising to begin with, particularly so when the beans are all texture and no taste. The side salad's use of roasted avocado did show a certain imagination, though, and the overall score would have been better if there had been more of this.

The tart was over-heavy and could have been presented more attractively. It looked rather stark sitting on its own in a dish. It relied too heavily on sweetness and not enough on counter-flavours. The pastry was dry. As such, it might as well have been from a supermarket.

As a recognition of my part in the incident, I will not penalize you too harshly for the bad feeling generated by the argument. We were also late, which no doubt delayed the start of the meal. As a result our score will be generous, I think.

Score: 6

Marcus

Any information in this message is strictly confidential and intended solely for the person or organization to whom it is addressed. If you have received this message in error,

please notify us as soon as possible and delete it and any
attached files from your system.

From: Justin Davidson <justindavidson@AfricAid.org.uk>
To: Dinner At Mine <dinneratminescores@gmail.com>
Sent: 08.46
Subject: Dinner on Friday

Dear Matt and Charlotte,

I was too busy working on Saturday to have any chance of writing this, and I think that has turned out for the best. I'm ashamed to say that I was extremely angry when I left the dinner on Friday. I was thinking all sorts of nasty things which I am not proud of, and will not share with you. A little distance has given me a chance to calm down and recognize that perhaps I was partly at fault for the argument. Perhaps I should have understood that, while Barbara and I are both deeply committed to vegetarianism, as guests in a meat-eater's house it may not have been the best moment to make our case. So I offer sincere apologies for our contribution to disrupting the harmony of the evening.

Apart from that, we both enjoyed ourselves. The paella was very tasty and I certainly appreciated the variety of vegetables and spices it contained – five a day on its own! Barbara particularly enjoyed the unusual salad that came with it. The salad to start was nice too, and the harissa was a great touch, but I did feel that maybe it was one salad too many. But, of course, you are not used to vegetarian cooking, so you did very well in the circumstances. I didn't eat much of the dessert, so I can't really judge that. The wine was very plentiful. So, on balance, 6½.

Did we agree that it was our turn next?

Justin

P.S. I promised Barbara I would take off half a point from the score I wanted to give, as she is a bit less forgiving than me about what happened, which is, of course, her right.

Dinner at Justin and Barbara's

Sixteen

'The problem with Ed Ruscha is that he limits too many people's idea of America to highways and empty spaces.' Marcus tapped his exhibition guide against the wall panel as he said this, satisfied with the pithiness of his own judgement. He turned to Sarah. 'Don't you think?'

'Probably,' said Sarah, not really looking at the painting.

'Of course, he did a lot to create that aesthetic,' Marcus continued, moving back to study the painting from a different angle. 'So I don't say that as a disparagement of his work. It's just that the whole open road, badlands stretching off to the horizon, fifties motel in the distance sort of look – it's become a cliché. When people look at it, they don't really see it; they tap into those ideas. Probably trying to think of the name of the film it reminds them of.'

'Mmm. Maybe.' Sarah glanced at the canvas quickly, before her eyes drifted back towards the exit.

'Am I boring you?'

'No, of course not,' Sarah said. 'You know I appreciate your views on art.'

Marcus studied her for traces of sarcasm. 'Well, what, then? Aren't you enjoying the exhibition?'

'No, it's interesting . . .'

'You don't look interested.'

'I'm fine, honestly.'

'Right, then, I'm going to carry on.' He gestured towards the next room.

'It's just that I've got something I need to tell you,' she said.

'Is it about Jasper Johns? You were in front of that one for a very long time.'

'No. It's nothing to do with the exhibition.'

'Can't it wait, then? We've got a whole room of Abstract Expressionists to go.'

'How long do you think you'll be?' she said with a trace of irritation.

'I don't know. A while.' He was within his rights here. They were here to look at the art, after all.

'Don't be too long.'

I'll be as long as I like, Marcus thought. 'Why don't you go and look at the Warhols again?' he said. 'You like those.'

Sarah didn't protest, so Marcus moved on round the corner to the next section, admiring as he always did the beauty of the poured-concrete walls. Sometimes he thought the gallery building was more appealing than what was on display there – the way the sober elegance of the grey concrete had retained the delicate grains of the wooden panels that had been used to set it. The contrast between the mass of the material and the surprising lightness of the finish was always deeply pleasing to him.

Sarah didn't follow. She was still standing by the Ruscha, looking lost and nervously tearing strips off her gallery guide. Marcus felt a pang of annoyance. How often had she been here since he bought her the membership for her birthday? Once with him, but never on her own, he was sure. He'd had to start using the pass himself to make the membership worthwhile.

He slowed to a halt in front of a Combine, where half a bicycle glued to the canvas seemed to burst out into the gallery, dragging with it the painting's clutter of old poster and daubed red squares. Of course there was something dated about Rauschenberg these days, Marcus always thought, but you couldn't help admiring the force of it. He leaned in to read the notes on the wall, which contained a quote comparing the artist to Picasso. Marcus immediately tried to think of a way to dismiss the comparison, but with Sarah not there and no one to tell, it seemed a bit pointless.

He moved back to critique the work from a wider angle. This done, he continued round the gallery.

Marcus was appraising a De Kooning when he sensed Sarah standing behind him.

'Don't you think the problem with this, is that—'

'Marcus, I've got something to tell you,' she said.

He broke away from the painting and turned to look at her. She was staring at the ground and the exhibition guide was torn to shreds in her hand.

'What do you mean?'

'I think we need to talk.' She still wasn't looking at him.

'Can't it wait? This is the last room and—'

'I'd feel better if I got it off my chest now.'

'You sound like you're about to confess something.' Marcus laughed nervously. Was she going to admit to an affair? Marcus quickly dismissed the idea. It was ludicrous.

'I sort of am, in a way.'

'What? Tell me.'

'I've applied for a job at Hampstead College. I've got an interview next week. It's a private school.'

Marcus laughed loudly. A man in rimless spectacles turned round to look at them disapprovingly.

'I'm glad you think it's funny,' Sarah said.

'No, it's not that, it's just . . .'

'Just . . . ?' She was irritated now.

'Nothing. I wasn't expecting you to say that.'

'I know.' Sarah's head sank to her chest.

'Well, good for you. Can I carry on looking at the exhibition now?' Marcus took half a step towards an interesting-looking picture on the far wall.

'Is that it?'

'We can discuss it afterwards if you like.'

'Marcus . . .'

'All right. What's the pay like?'

'It's about fifty per cent more than I get now.'

'Excellent! Good work, well done. Now come and look at the brushwork on this with me.'

Sarah reached out and grabbed his arm as he moved off. 'Wait, what do you mean, "excellent"?'

'What? It's a lot of money, isn't it? I mean, I know you're not a fan of private schools generally, but you can't deny the pay's good.'

'What do you mean, "not a fan"? I think they're socially divisive. Don't you?'

'In principle, yes, sure. But I know you've not been enjoying your job recently, and things are bound to be easier in a nice middle-class school, aren't they? And the cash will be useful. We could go to China this summer. I've always fancied that. Some of the new buildings in Shanghai . . .'

'Jesus, the money! Is that all you care about!'

'You're the one taking the job!'

They had both raised their voices. Several people were now tutting at them, quite loudly.

'Look, we're disturbing everyone else,' Marcus said. 'If we have to talk about this now, I suppose we'd better leave.'

'Yes, please.'

'See? I knew you were bored.'

'Let's just go.' Sarah was already striding towards the exit. Marcus followed slowly, looking longingly up the free-floating staircase towards the secondary exhibition on Russian Constructivism.

Outside, Sarah decided it was too cold to sit by the river, so they went to the members' bar at the top of the Festival Hall, standing silently next to each other in the lift up.

The bar was very quiet, with two other couples talking in hushed tones at the far end. They sat down at a table overlooking the water and Sarah ordered a cappuccino.

Marcus thought about doing the same, but as it was mid-afternoon he ordered an espresso instead. Sarah sighed audibly.

'So, to recap,' Marcus said. 'You've been offered an interview for a more comfortable and better-paid job, and this has put you in a terrible mood.'

'Marcus, please don't be flippant about this. Do you think I'd be doing the right thing?'

'Sure, if you'll be less miserable, why not?'

'No, I mean is it morally right?'

'Jesus, you're not the Archbishop of Canterbury! It's just a job.'

'But I'm trying to do some good in Dalston. What would I be doing at a private school?'

'Perpetuating the edifice of class privilege, obviously.'

'Marcus!'

'You'll be educating some kids. What's wrong with that?'

'Yes, but it's not the same, is it?'

'Well, if you feel so sick about it, don't take the job.'

'But I don't, that's the thing! I applied for the job!'

Marcus watched her pale skin flushing with small islands of colour. But the tired, anxious expression on her face seemed to suck the life out of her features. Sometimes he really found it difficult to put in the effort needed to understand her.

'So what's the problem, then?' he asked.

'Marcus! You're not being very helpful.'

'Aren't I? What do you expect me to say?'

'You're always telling me how you didn't like the school you went to.'

Marcus couldn't understand why this was relevant. 'So you

don't want to take the job because my classmates were a bunch of cocks?'

'But that's the sort of students I'd be teaching.'

'Maybe, but all teenagers are pretty annoying, aren't they?'

Sarah didn't reply. They stared out over the river in silence for a while. A couple walking across Hungerford Bridge burst out in private laughter as they passed a busker playing the saxophone. Marcus wondered what the tune was.

Abruptly, Sarah asked: 'Do you find my moral principles ridiculous?'

Marcus couldn't stifle his laugh.

'So you do?'

'I find that question ridiculous.'

'You're not taking this seriously!'

'Of course I am. I know changing schools would be a big step for you.'

'No – you're not taking my moral dilemma seriously.'

Marcus laughed again. He couldn't help it. 'Sorry, well, no. Especially not when you put it like that.'

'Everything's a joke to you! Why don't you care about this?'

'You're overreacting . . .'

'No, I'm not. All you think about is your holiday in China. I want to know if I'm doing the wrong thing.' Sarah was breathing heavily. 'Thank you,' she added as the waitress set down the cappuccino in front of her. 'And then what about the kids? I'd be letting them down. I'd just feel so guilty about it.'

'At the moment you seem to be feeling guilty about not feeling guilty, so it won't be much of a change.'

'That's the fucking problem with you!' she flared up suddenly. 'You don't care about the wider world unless it affects you! As far as you care, it's all just the setting for an art house film.' She took a short, tight sip of coffee. 'Look at someone like Justin. He's dedicated his life to helping other people. That's what I thought I was doing. Now I find myself about to give that up. And all you talk about is what to do with the cash.'

Marcus drank some of his espresso, a little startled by her vehemence. He recomposed himself.

'I'm still struggling to see why this is my fault,' he said.

'You're not being helpful. It's like you don't even care enough to challenge me on it.'

'Wait, let me check if I've got this right. You're having a go at me because I'm not having a go at you?'

Sarah gave a yelp of frustration.

'No, no, if that's what you want . . .' Marcus pressed on. 'All right, I can't believe you're even thinking about taking this job. It's a betrayal of all your principles.'

'Marcus . . .'

'No, it would be wrong. Morally wrong. You'd be giving up on the poorest children to go to pamper a load of spoiled brats and entrench social inequality for another generation.' He picked up his coffee cup and drained the espresso. 'There – happy now?'

'For fuck's sake, Marcus!'

'I can't win, can I?'

'You're so . . .' Sarah tailed off into frustrated inarticulacy. She gave a short, angry growl, jumped up and stormed towards the lifts.

'Sarah . . .'

'I'll see you at home,' she called. 'Or wait . . . why don't you go straight to Justin and Barbara's? I don't want to speak to you any more.'

Marcus didn't get up to follow her. The couples at the other end of the bar were staring at him, but quickly looked away when he turned round.

Marcus took another sip of coffee, realizing too late that he had already finished it. He felt a prickle of annoyance as the grounds seeped between his lips.

But the feeling soon began to subside. Sarah would get over it. She was stressed at the moment, obviously. If the new job stopped the tantrums, it would be well worth it.

Best to give her a bit of time to calm down. Marcus looked at his watch. Still not yet four. The afternoon stretched ahead, precious hours alone before the dinner. He could go back and do the Russian Constructivists. And at his own pace too. Marcus felt a surge of pleasurable anticipation at the thought.

Seventeen

Jonathan stared at the plastic monkey as it revolved slowly on the turntable. A tinny American voice sang an educational song about zoo animals. When the song finished, Jonathan reached out and knocked over the monkey.

Stephen stood it upright for the fifth time. Although the tune was beginning to get on his nerves, he felt oddly proud of his son's suspicious attitude towards the toy. Still eyeing the monkey warily, Jonathan pressed the big red button on the front of the plastic dashboard, and the song began again.

Stephen gazed at his son with the same total concentration Jonathan gave to the monkey. He was on the verge of speaking now, properly speaking, and Stephen felt a thrill of excitement every time he thought about having a conversation with his son. He was obviously a clever child, and Stephen was convinced that sentences were piling up in there, waiting to rush forth as soon as the dam was breached.

What would he say? Stephen felt sure there would be a lot

of questions. Jonathan's wide brown eyes often seemed puzzled by what was going on around him, but never quite confused. There was always an edge of calculation in there, Stephen thought, a sign that the world was being processed and understood. He reached out and stroked the soft, wispy hair on top of Jonathan's head. Jonathan didn't look up. He waited until the end of the animal song, reached out, and knocked over the monkey.

The educational value of the song was clear, Stephen admitted. It ran through the names of various zoo creatures and illustrated them with sound effects. But he couldn't quite see why Jonathan found it so riveting. Perhaps it was the combination of movement and sound. Stephen tried pointing to the tiger and the penguin when they were mentioned, but Jonathan wouldn't take his eyes off the revolving monkey.

The song restarted its insistent jingle. It really was annoying. Stephen hadn't yet met a parent who didn't become sick of it after five minutes. What grated on him most, though, was the bit about the zebra. The word was pronounced in the American way, zee-bra, and although the woman singing it sounded very friendly, Stephen was irritated that the manufacturers hadn't bothered to record a British version. Presumably they re-dubbed the song for France or Sweden. So why not for Britain? They were training his child to speak with an American accent. Between the toys and the cartoons, it was no wonder kids got confused about what country they lived in and ended up calling 911 in emergencies.

But then Jonathan looked up and smiled proudly at him after knocking over the monkey, and Stephen's annoyance evaporated. He bent over, picked Jonathan up – getting heavier all the time – and gave him a hug.

Soon the boy squirmed free, sat back down on the floor, and pressed the red button. The tune was lodged deep in Stephen's brain, going round and round his head in an endless loop. He tried to tempt Jonathan with some stuffed toys and a book about caterpillars. Jonathan showed no interest. He waited until the end of the song, then knocked over the monkey.

Jonathan had been given the toy a couple of weeks ago, and Stephen now found the song often popped into his head during the day. When that happened at work he didn't find it so annoying, because it always made him think of Jonathan. The song reminded him why he was there in the office, that the petty frustrations were all worth it, really.

On Thursday, Stephen had been told that Sujay, his graduate trainee, was being appointed a Sixth Floor Liaison Officer, even though Stephen himself had never even been on the Higher Floors e-mail list. That was when Stephen didn't mind having the song about zoo animals going round and round his head. It took him outside his humiliation, reminded him why he put up with it and, as usual, showed him why it wasn't so important by comparison. Before the insistent jollity of the parrots and the lions, his mind would have been a bitter stew of resentment and anger, bafflement at how the company kept going when it was run so badly. How Matt almost certainly didn't have to put up with this at work. As it was, he came back to his desk with a list of tigers, elephants, penguins and meerkats running through his mind and so was able to wonder instead about how meerkats got in there.

Stephen hated thinking about work at the weekend, particularly on a Saturday morning, when two days with his family still stretched ahead. It was the best time of the week. His son always seemed to have learned so much in seven days.

Jonathan pressed the button again. There were footsteps in the hall, and Rosie appeared in the doorway.

'Is he still playing with that thing?' she said. 'The song drives me absolutely nuts.'

'It's not so bad,' Stephen replied.

Rosie was wearing that cape-like jacket thing he liked, the one that gave her a glamorous sixties look. Every year she got it out at about this time, when she put away her winter coat; a sign that spring was almost here.

'Don't you think it's a bit repetitive?' she said.

'Well, I do, but I'm not the target market. At his age they enjoy repetition.'

'I can't stand it,' she said. 'Maybe you could get him to play with those wooden alphabet blocks my mother bought for him?'

'Watch what happens when the song ends. He does this every time.'

They waited as the simple melody played itself out. Jonathan reached out and knocked over the monkey.

'There, you see? Every time.'

'Oh my God!' Rosie clutched her hands together. 'Do you think he's autistic?'

'Rosie! Don't be ridiculous. He's fine.'

'Maybe I should take him to the doctor, just in case.'

'"And what are the symptoms, madam?"' Stephen intoned

gravely. '"Well, he keeps knocking over a plastic monkey."
"Hmm, I see. That sounds serious."'

'It's not funny, Stephen.'

'Yes, it is.'

'Your son might have autism!'

'He doesn't, though.'

Rosie tutted. But a smile broke out anyway and there was
Stephen's favourite dimple, the one on her right cheek that
he always associated with happiness. It appeared from nowhere
whenever she was enjoying herself, as real but transient as a
soap bubble. No, he didn't envy Matt at all.

'Is there anything you want from the shops?' she asked.

'Are you going now?'

'Yes. Have you seen my Bag for Life?'

'No.'

'I'm sure I left it in the hall, but it's not there. I'll have to
take some plastic bags from under the sink.'

'They'll give you some in the shop, you know.'

'Not in the organic shop. I asked for a plastic bag in there
once and they looked at me like I was a war criminal.'

'Then go to Sainsbury's.'

'We have to support the local shops.' Rosie went out into
the hall to get her handbag. 'I have to go now, or the butcher's
will be shut.'

'What are we having for dinner?'

'Stephen! We're going to Justin and Barbara's tonight.'

'Oh yes.' Stephen's anticipation of the weekend dimmed
markedly. 'The vegetarians.'

'Don't be like that, Stephen. I'm sure it will be nice.'

'Can you get some steaks, then? You know the nice ones they have there?'

'Yes, OK,' Rosie said as she searched in her handbag for the keys. 'We can have them on Monday. Bye.' She came over and kissed Jonathan and Stephen in turn.

'See you in a bit.'

Stephen reached down to pick up Jonathan again. Steaks on Monday. That was something to look forward to. Stephen felt unreasonably happy at the thought.

Eighteen

Charlotte opened first one eye – all fine – and then the other. Woah. Not so good. The bedroom was suddenly blurred and unstable. Furniture reared up from the floor while the light from the window whirled around the ceiling. Queasiness welled up from her stomach. She shut both eyes quickly and rolled over on the pillow, waiting for the anxious roaring of blood in her ears to subside.

She could feel her flesh quivering as it sweated out alcohol. She knew if she tried to move it would be painful. For a moment, lying with both eyes closed, she tried to keep the sickness at bay, pretending that if she just stayed still it would somehow disappear. Even as she thought it she could feel her head throbbing and bile rising towards her throat. If she didn't move, the surge would pass. Even breathing made her whole body shiver. Suddenly her skin seemed hypersensitive, the press of the pillow on her cheek like broken glass. Sightless, she felt like she was twisting, falling into a vortex of nausea.

She tried again to open her eyes. First, the left one. The

room seemed clear, and Charlotte anchored her vision on the bedside alarm clock. Then the right eye followed. Immediately the clock dissolved and she felt her innards roiled by a fresh wave of sickness. She screwed her eyes tight shut.

What was going on? She fought to bring her breathing under control. In the hide beneath the duvet she could smell the stale alcohol on her heavy panting. More slowly this time, she tried again. Left eye: fine. Both: the room whirled. Was she still drunk? No, the headache was too bad for that. Was she going blind? Was this an early stage of some tropical disease? Would she be dead within the hour? Bugger. She didn't want her alarm clock to be the last thing she saw.

Charlotte tried again. Left eye: very good. Close it. Now right eye: very blurred. Left eye: good. Right eye: blurred.

Shit. She'd gone to bed with one contact lens in, again.

Charlotte closed her right eye for the time being and considered getting out of bed. Her nerve endings squealed in protest at the idea. Hmm. This hangover seemed like a bad one. She turned over very slowly and reached over to the bedside table, groping in the drawer for pills. She felt the reassuring crackle of silver foil. But the first packet turned out to be Strepsils, and the second was empty. She tossed them to the floor in disgust.

There was a wet glass lying by the side of the bed, a thin trickle of water spilling on to the carpet. Good. She'd obviously had some water before falling asleep. But the glass was now empty and the back of her throat was parched and ticklish. Was there anything else to drink?

Charlotte flopped forward on to her front, feeling a

metallic stabbing pain in her chest. Shit, what was that? A heart attack? Nope. She had fallen asleep in her bra and the underwiring was digging uncomfortably between two ribs. Charlotte groaned. She hadn't fallen asleep in her clothes again, had she? She looked down. Well, not exactly. Those were definitely pyjama bottoms.

What had happened last night? Charlotte tried to concentrate. After-work drinks as normal. Louise had been on good form, bitching about how unfair it was that Jodie was getting a bigger pay rise, even though everyone knew she was useless. Then some guys from Commercial had come down and they'd moved on to that pub near Warren Street. When they'd got kicked out of there, one of the guys – Dave, was it? Andy? – had taken them to an underground bar where they were playing loud Latin music. Dave/Andy had bought shots of tequila. So that had become the drink of choice for the rest of the night.

What had they eaten? Ah. That would be the problem. Charlotte felt a wave of hunger, which turned quickly into nausea, but then back to hunger again.

She had finally left when Dave/Andy had tried to get a samba routine going, lurching unsteadily round the dance floor, desperately chasing the beat with his hips. Louise had joined in, but Charlotte had gone home. She was drunk, but not drunk enough to samba.

That must have been well past three o'clock, at least. Even the illegal minicabs were beginning to drift home. What time was it now? Charlotte shifted her head until she could see the glowing red numerals of the alarm clock: 12.47. What did that mean? It was afternoon. Lunchtime anyway.

Jesus, she was hungry. No, nauseous. No, hungry.

Charlotte listened to her own uneven breathing for a while. This was an even worse start to the weekend than last Saturday morning. Whatever she'd felt then, at least she'd been able to open both her eyes without wanting to puke.

Her right eye was beginning to ache with the effort of holding itself shut, so she swapped, closing the left and looking at the blurred world through the right. The soft focus made her feel better. Her nausea could float freely now, without banging up painfully against the sharp corners of the room.

Come on. Time to get up. Food. Water. Pills. Charlotte pulled back the duvet and slid one leg experimentally out of bed. It reached the floor without incident. She sent the other out after it and used an elbow to lever herself upright.

For a few seconds she had to sit still on the edge of the bed, until the roaring in her ears subsided again. Her damp skin felt cold against the harsh air of the bedroom. Maybe this was a bad idea. Charlotte looked back down at the soft, tousled warmth of her sheets. She was about to let herself collapse back on to them when another pang of hunger propelled her upright. By the time it became nausea, she was halfway to the bathroom and it was too late to turn back.

At the sink, Charlotte slipped out the contact lens, stung her face with cold water and dug out some packets of pills from the back of the cupboard, rifling through them for para-cetamol. There was only one compartment in the plastic wrapper left unpopped. What about aspirin? She found a packet, but that too had only one pill left.

Sod it. She popped one of each into her palm and

swallowed them straight down with a cupped handful of water from the bathroom tap.

Her glasses were on the ledge under the window, and as she put them on Charlotte caught sight of herself in the mirror. Her skin was puffy, with red blotches down her cheek and a dark-yellow patch under her eye. She made herself look closer. The flesh below her chin sagged, but above it the skin was waxy, imprinted into lumpy mounds by the pillow. Her eyes were still not fully open, sunk into deep trenches ringed with wrinkly fortifications. She looked exhausted. No, worse than that – she looked old.

Christ. Jesus. Charlotte stared at herself. What a hag. She couldn't keep doing this. She wasn't young enough any more. She didn't recover like she used to. The nausea seemed to spread to her bones. How long was she going to carry on doing this? Would she still be out on the lash in twenty years? With all the twenty-one-year-olds laughing at her behind her back? Maybe they were doing that already.

At least she had woken up in her own bed this week, though. That was progress, wasn't it? Well, no, actually, it was the norm. And would be for decades ahead . . . decades of waking up alone with hangovers that got steadily worse until they turned into a terminal illness.

Charlotte slammed the bathroom door behind her. Jesus, what maudlin bollocks. Bacon. That was what she needed. Charlotte took off the bra, put on her warmer pyjamas and a dressing gown, and went down the hall to the kitchen. The fridge was largely bare, but at the back there were two stacked packets of smoked bacon, the remains of a three-for-two offer.

The top packet was open, but the three rashers left in it had acquired a rainbowy sheen. The meat below looked lifeless and grey. Charlotte checked the use-by date. It wasn't that long ago. She sniffed it. Nothing. It always looked better once it was cooked anyway.

She threw the bacon into a frying pan with a big chunk of butter. When the butter began to melt, she stirred the pan, coating the bacon all over. Within minutes the kitchen was filled with a fatty sizzle. Charlotte perked up immediately. She searched for mushrooms or tomatoes, but found only a tin of baked beans in the cupboard. They would do. Beans were better for a hangover anyway. Someone had told Charlotte recently that beans and ketchup each counted as one of your five a day, which cheered her up so much she decided not to check if it was true.

She tossed a couple of slices of white bread into the toaster, and when the bacon was browning at the edges she broke in the last egg without sniffing it first. The kitchen filled with thick, warming smells and Charlotte felt a stab of hunger which this time brooked no opposition from the nausea. She made a cup of tea and tipped the contents of the frying pan on to a plate. The egg landed upside down with the yolk bleeding into the beans. Delicious.

Charlotte flipped on the TV as she ate, pausing at a programme in which overemotional teenagers discussed their break-ups and crushes direct to camera. One boy, describing how his girlfriend of three weeks had dumped him, began to weep unashamedly. What wimps. No wonder teen bullying was on the rise if this was what fifteen-year-olds behaved like these days.

The pills and the fry-up had kicked in now, and Charlotte was feeling much better. Two days of recuperation lay ahead. Did she have anything on tonight? Oh shit. Another bloody dinner party. Charlotte mopped up the sticky red and yellow residue on her plate with another piece of bread.

She hadn't heard from Matt since last week. She could have been annoyed, but it would have been for form's sake. It was obvious that neither of them wanted anything more. Actually, she now felt that they'd handled it quite well.

The previous Saturday she'd woken up late too, with a moment of panic at the unfamiliar surroundings. When she had realized where she was, she had been relieved to find herself alone in the bed. It was a bad moment to be making small talk.

She had lain there in the half-light, wondering what to do. Occasionally, she heard Matt's footsteps walking past the door. Was he trying to let her know that he was still there if she wanted to come out? Or was it just a small flat?

Charlotte didn't move. The stale smell of Matt's sweat rose from the sheets, along with a strange aftershave she couldn't imagine him using. There was a glass of water by the bed. Had he brought it in that morning or was it left over from last night? Charlotte downed it. The room felt fetid. Charlotte wanted to open the curtains, maybe the window too, but she didn't want to attract Matt's attention. What the hell would they say to each other?

The footsteps paused conspicuously outside the bedroom door. Charlotte slumped back down and closed her eyes. Matt opened the door; light flooded in from the hall. Feeling his eyes on her, Charlotte didn't stir. She was pretending to be asleep and Matt, she was fairly sure, was pretending to believe her.

After a while he left without saying anything. Charlotte wondered how long she would give it before cracking. She didn't want to go out there drowsy and hungover, but what was the alternative? She lay staring at the bare walls. There were no posters on them, and the only clothes on the floor were her own. Everything else was tidied away. Charlotte suddenly wanted very badly to be in her own flat.

Outside, the front door slammed. Charlotte listened. The footsteps had stopped and the flat was silent. Had Matt gone out?

Charlotte waited five minutes. Nothing. The bastard! He'd just fucked off and left her there!

But no, this was what she wanted, wasn't it? She slipped out of bed and found a dressing gown in Matt's freakishly neat cupboard. Cautiously, she opened the bedroom door. The hall was quiet. She approached the kitchen, but it was obvious there was no one in it. Matt had already done most of the washing up, and a big stack of plates and glasses was drying on the worktop. The extended table was now very bare, apart from a note in the centre.

Morning, Charlotte.
I've just nipped out to get some stuff for breakfast. I shouldn't be more than half an hour if you can stick around
Matt

Charlotte admired its neutral simplicity. It committed him to absolutely nothing, and while it raised the possibility that she could leave, that couldn't be classed as rude because the decision was hers to make.

Charlotte had put her clothes on and got the hell out.

Now, the fry-up gone, Charlotte dumped her plate in the sink. She poured herself a bowl of Frosties for pudding and settled on to the sofa with more tea and the remote control.

If it wasn't for Matt, she would make an excuse and stay in tonight. No, that wasn't quite what she meant. It was just that if she didn't turn up, he would think it was because of him. Charlotte zapped through the TV channels. So she would have to go. It would be bloody awkward, obviously, but she wasn't going to be the one to blink first.

Nineteen

The minicab driver didn't offer to help Justin get the chairs out of the boot. Justin struggled under their weight and had to find a lamp post to lean them against while he went over to the driver's window to give him a ten-pound note. The man drove off without giving Justin his pound change. Justin thought of protesting, but the man didn't seem to speak much English. If he was a recent immigrant, he probably needed the money anyway, Justin decided.

The folding chairs were much heavier than they looked, and Justin found he needed to loop his arms beneath the backrests to be able to carry them over his shoulder. As he let himself in the front door he had to turn sideways and shuffle carefully into the hall to get them inside.

Justin had borrowed the chairs from Gautam, a friend who lived nearby. It was very kind of him, Justin thought. Especially since he hadn't been invited to the dinner party. Justin had explained that he would have asked him, only it was a competition, you see, and it had to be the same people every time . . .

Justin felt bad too that he hadn't felt able to ask his neighbours if they had any spare chairs. He experienced a familiar pang as he walked past the front door of Mrs McCluskey's ground-floor flat. He really wanted to get on with his neighbours, but she did make it so difficult. Justin trod as lightly as he could on the way past, hoping that today she would not dash out and complain that his footsteps were too loud. He had never had a conversation with her in which she hadn't complained about that, or about him walking around too late at night, or playing music, or running the washing machine at the weekend. Of course it wasn't her fault; she was obviously lonely, and had probably had a difficult life. Justin had tried to ask her about it more than once, but she'd told him to mind his own business. He suspected hers might be a council flat. That made him feel a bit better about it.

Justin made it past Mrs McCluskey's front door and started up the stairs with a great sense of relief. He had been dreading telling her he was having people over for dinner and with four folding chairs over his arms there was no way he could lie about it. As he turned on to the first-floor landing, Justin accidentally scraped the chairs on his left against the wall. He checked anxiously to see if he had damaged the paintwork, but there were so many marks and chips that he couldn't tell.

Inside the flat, Justin set up two chairs, one on either side of the large Buddha's head that stood where the TV used to be. What was it Gautam had said? Make sure the metal pins don't fall out when you unfold them. But they seemed pretty sturdy, Justin thought.

The cluttered living room seemed very small even with

just two of the chairs unfolded. Justin put as many books as he could fit back on the shelves and stuck the rest in a corner. He collected a pile of pillows, shawls and clay-etching implements and put them in the bedroom. When you could see it, the carpet really was quite frayed, he thought.

Justin stared at the room, trying to work out where all the guests would fit. He had never had this many people over before, apart from a couple of meetings of his letter-writing group, and they were usually happy to sit on the floor. They certainly didn't judge his taste in soft furnishings. Well, it didn't matter, did it? It was only a matter of not having much money. No one could condemn him for that, could they?

Justin and Barbara ate their meals at a side table wedged against the wall behind the sofa. Justin moved the table into the bedroom and pushed the sofa back against the wall. That would work, wouldn't it? Six chairs, and two people on the sofa. The coffee table wasn't really big enough for eight plates at once, but he and Barbara didn't mind eating off their laps.

There was a grey, dusty patch of carpet where the sofa had been. Justin bent down to pick the pen caps and five-pence pieces out of the matted dust before getting out the hoover.

With the machine on, he didn't notice Barbara coming in until she walked past him into the kitchen.

'Hello, honey!'

Barbara didn't reply. Justin heard her turn the tap on. He went over to the kitchen, a narrow slit jutting off the end of the hall.

'Are you all right? I didn't know where you were.'

'I was out.'

'Your phone was off. I was worried.'

Barbara didn't reply. She was hunting through the fridge, irritably pushing aside the ingredients Justin had bought for dinner.

'Have you seen my wheatgrass juice?'

'It's in there somewhere.'

'There's all this stuff in the way.'

'That's the stuff for dinner. I thought you were going to help me with the shopping.'

Barbara poured herself a glass of juice.

'I was going to start cooking soon. Do you want to do it with me?'

'Not right now.' Barbara walked back out of the kitchen without looking at Justin, even though he had to step back to let her pass.

'It's just that it would be great if you could do some of the chopping. Just at the beginning.'

'I don't really feel like it.' Barbara put her juice down on the coffee table, leaving a wet mark on the weathered wood. 'Where's my shawl? I left it right here.'

'I put it in the bedroom while I was tidying up.'

Barbara gave an irritated sigh and marched across the hall to get it, forcing Justin to move out of her way once again.

'Are you OK?' he asked when she came back.

'I'm fine.'

'You just seem a bit ...'

'I'm fine, OK!' Barbara glanced at him quickly for the first time since she had got in, then settled on the sofa, tucking her legs up and wrapping the big shawl round her shoulders several times until only her head, feet and hands protruded.

'I know you're still upset about the exhibition,' Justin began tentatively. 'But it was more than a week ago now. Maybe it would help to talk about it?' He let his voice rise into a questioning tone, hoping it would draw Barbara into filling the silence that followed. It didn't.

'It's just that you've been like this all week and I don't think it's very productive. You can't ignore everything, my love. There's that letter from the Home Office, which I know you haven't replied to . . .'

'I need to be on my own for a bit,' Barbara snapped at him without looking round. 'OK?'

'All right.' Justin retreated quickly into the kitchen. He didn't really understand what was wrong. To Justin's eye, Barbara's pots looked exactly the same this week as they had last week. She'd got upset about her work before, of course, declared it was all shit and stormed off crying, but usually everything was better by the next morning. He'd never seen it last this long before.

Justin got the bag of plump, glistening aubergines out of the fridge and lined them up ready for chopping. The sight cheered him up. They looked delicious. Not for the first time, Justin wished you could eat aubergines raw – just pick them up and bite a big chunk of the purple flesh. He turned on the oven to heat and chopped quickly, throwing the neat rounds into a roasting tin and pouring over plenty of olive oil.

He felt for Barbara, of course he did. But, as hard as he

tried, Justin found it difficult to be properly sympathetic. After all, they were only pots.

Oh God, that was a terrible thought, wasn't it? Justin had always considered himself as a great respecter of the arts. They were a vital part of a flourishing society, and they could be such an important part of how a civilization understood its place in the world. He'd seen their value among traditional peoples, and knew the West could learn a lot from that. He had always respected Barbara's decision to devote her life to cultural production.

Still, though. It wasn't as if she was worrying about starving children, was it? Might it not be a little bit self-indulgent to be moping about like this because you'd decided some ceramics didn't express you properly? It wasn't as if she was doing anything productive with the time, either. Where had she been this morning, for example? Justin had had to do all the shopping himself. Not that he resented that. But it had taken much longer than it would have done with two of them, so he hadn't been able to look over the chief exec's presentation to the donor conference on Tuesday. Now he wouldn't get time, and that actually was about starving children. What if the AIDS project in Karonga District lost funding because Justin hadn't spotted a mistake? He was already starting to feel guilty about it. Was Barbara?

Justin concluded, with some disappointment, that she probably wasn't. She was certainly a concerned and active citizen, and her moral clarity had been one of the things that had first attracted him to her. But for some reason, when it came to her work, the Barbara who went on anti-war marches and joined

Free Tibet groups on Facebook disappeared. Whenever Justin asked her about the significance of her pieces, it was always something personal, always very close to her own experience. Self-centred, even.

Maybe that was the problem! Justin was struck with the sudden thought. Maybe that was why she was so unhappy with her pots: she realized they weren't going to change anything.

Justin put the aubergines in to roast. They would sit happily in there for half an hour, giving him time to get started on the main course. He found some onions and chopped them roughly, while heating some more oil in a frying pan.

But he hesitated before putting the onions in to brown. He turned the hob off, rinsed his hands vigorously, and left the kitchen.

Back in the living room, Barbara was still curled up on the sofa in her shawl, reading a book. She didn't look up as Justin came in. He walked round until he could see the title: *Nourishing the Self Within: A Five-Step Journey to a Truer You.*

On the table beside her were a stack of other books: *Romancing the Ordinary*, *Your Soul's Plan*, *Everyday Greatness* and *Dare to be You.*

'What's that you're reading?' Justin asked carefully.

Barbara didn't reply.

'It looks very –' Justin paused – 'interesting.'

Barbara turned a page in silence.

'Are they new? I haven't seen them before.'

'I borrowed them from Marcello.' Barbara said this without looking up.

'Oh right. Why was that?'

'He thought I might find them useful.'

'OK.' Justin nodded. 'But they're ... They're self-help books, aren't they?'

'Marcello calls them psychological fulfilment manuals.'

'Does he?' Justin came across and sat next to Barbara on the sofa, putting himself in her eyeline so she had to look at him. 'Barbara, are you OK?'

'I'm fine.'

'Because you can tell me. Whatever's wrong.'

'I'm fine.'

'I mean, I'm sure those books are full of excellent advice, but maybe I could be of some help too ...'

'I'm fine.' She started reading again.

Justin nodded meaningfully. 'In fact, I was just thinking while I was in the kitchen. I know you've been down about your work recently. I know it's been making you miserable. And I wasn't sure what I could do.'

'Just give me some peace, OK?'

'But then it occurred to me. Just now. Maybe you're dissatisfied because you're not being radical enough.'

'Thanks, Justin.'

'No, no, I didn't mean it like that. What I mean is – your pots are all very pretty, and I know they're full of meaning to you, but none of your work is politically engaged. There's no message.'

Barbara looked up from her book. 'They're pots, Justin.'

He pushed on: 'So what I thought was that maybe you should make your art more strongly about animal cruelty.'

Barbara let her book drop to her lap and stared at Justin. 'Animal cruelty?'

'Yes. I mean, it could be something else. Global poverty. Inequality. Homophobia. But I was just thinking how strongly we both feel about animal welfare, and how tonight is going to be such a great opportunity to show people the benefits of a meat-free diet, and I realized that maybe you could do that with your art too.'

'Jesus Christ, Justin.' Barbara pulled off her shawl in three awkward tugs and jumped off the sofa. 'Sometimes I just ...'

'What?'

'"Make some pots about vegetarianism." Fucking hell!'

'What did I say wrong?'

'I just can't believe you. I really fucking can't.' Barbara snatched up *Nourishing the Self Within* and stalked out of the room.

'Barbara, wait!'

'Leave me alone!' She crossed the hall and slammed the bedroom door behind her.

Justin thought about going after her. But when she was in a mood like this it was usually best to let her cool off on her own. He returned to his onions.

'Hello!' Stephen opened the door to the babysitter. 'How—'

Lily was standing on the step with her phone clamped to her ear, and raised a shushing index finger to him.

'Hi,' she said, giving him a quick, distracted smile, before returning her attention to her phone. 'Mmm-hmm ... No! ... He didn't! ... No, she did ... What a bastard! ... Exactly ...

And all the time he was . . . Poor Ellie! . . . No, where is she? . . .
We should get her out . . . No! . . . Yes . . . I know!'

Stephen left the door open and Lily followed him into the
living room.

'You've got to tell him . . . Is he going to be there? . . . No,
I can't . . . I'm babysitting . . . Yeah, that's right . . . No, they're
not that bad . . . Look, I've got to go . . . Yeah, I'll text
you . . . Bye.'

She ended the call without needing to look at the phone.

'That sounded exciting,' Stephen said.

Lily shrugged. 'You know, the usual,' she said.

'Er, right. Do you want anything to drink? Tea?'

'Do you have squash?'

'I'll have a look.'

Stephen went to search the kitchen. He couldn't find any
squash, so came back with a glass of organic apple juice. Lily
was hunched over on the sofa, her thumbs moving in an
instinctive rhythm over the phone. Stephen put the glass
down next to her and sat waiting for her to finish. The silence
would have been awkward, but she showed no sign of noticing he was in the room.

Five minutes later she looked up, blinking. 'Oh, right, sorry
about that. I've just found out that Freddie is going to this
party with Olly, so I had to tell Beth that Nat would be there.'

'Oh,' said Stephen. 'Why?'

'Because Beth was hoping to get together with Freddie
tonight, so I had to warn her that he used to go out with
Nat.'

'Right. Well, I see the urgency, then,' Stephen said. He

didn't know if it would be considered polite or creepy to ask more. 'What an exciting social life,' he said instead. 'I feel like we're very boring by comparison.'

Lily shrugged, as if to say: Well, of course. You're old.

Stephen waited, hoping that Rosie would come down and save him from having to make any further conversation.

Lily turned on the TV. 'Got any food?' she asked.

'There's stuff for sandwiches in the fridge. Or you can phone for a pizza.'

'Great.' She flicked through the channels. 'How's Jonathan?' she asked. 'Is he all right?'

'Rosie's just putting him down now. He's stopped screaming, so I expect he'll be asleep soon.'

Lily carried on flicking, up through the weird shopping, foreign and music channels that Stephen had never seen. He didn't think he had been missing much.

Soon he heard the reassuring creak of Rosie's footsteps coming down the stairs.

'He's asleep!' she declared in triumph as she came into the living room. 'Stephen, are you going to wear that jumper out?'

'Yes, I think so. Why?'

'OK, then. It's up to you.'

Stephen went upstairs to change.

'Thank you so much for coming early,' Rosie said to Lily. 'I don't know what we would have done if you hadn't.'

'S'all right,' Lily mumbled, pausing at a hip-hop video in which girls in micro-shorts danced energetically in thick steel cages. Rosie pursed her lips at the TV.

'I just refused to drive this time, you see. Stephen never does when we go out, and it's not fair that I'm not allowed to have anything to drink. So we're going to get the bus there.' Rosie said this with some pride, but Lily didn't seem to be interested. She began texting again.

'Anyway, I hope we haven't ruined your evening,' Rosie went on. 'I'm sure you'd much rather be out having fun.'

'It's OK. I'll probably go to Gemma's party later.'

Rosie frowned. 'You know we won't be back until quite late? Maybe even midnight.'

'Yeah, no problem. Only losers turn up before midnight.'

'Goodness, how energetic! What time do these parties finish?'

'Dunno. Depends on how good they are. Sometimes we go on to an after-club in King's Cross.'

'Gosh, I wish I had your stamina! I'm delighted if I make it past eleven these days.'

Lily shrugged, as if to say: What do you expect? You're old.

'It must be fun, though. What sort of music do they play?'

'Commercial Dance, Electro, Dubstep,' Lily said, sounding bored. 'A bit of R 'n' B.'

'That sounds like fun,' Rosie said with a shudder of distaste. 'Oh Stephen, that looks much better, doesn't it? I bought that jumper for his birthday,' she explained. 'It's cashmere.'

'Yeah, great.' Lily didn't look up. Her eyes flicked from TV to phone.

'OK, well, have a quiet evening. This bit, at least! Call us if anything goes wrong.'

Lily waved the back of her hand in goodbye.

As they walked to the bus stop, Rosie said: 'Do you remember when we were that age and could go on partying until dawn?'

'Seems like a long time ago,' Stephen said.

'It's amazing, isn't it, the way she seems to be permanently on the way to a party, or dealing with the fallout from the last one?'

'It does make me feel old.'

Rosie grabbed his arm as she was struck by a thought. 'Oh God, Stephen, do you remember that club in Soho we used to go to when we first came to London?' The dimple appeared on her right cheek as she broke into a wide smile.

'The one where the jukebox was that fifties American car?'

'That's right, and that old man was always trying to sell everyone fake drugs.'

'He can't have been too much older than we are now.'

'Oh don't say that!'

'It's true.'

'I know.' She laughed ruefully. 'And who was that man who had the grotty flat in Mile End?'

'I can't remember.'

'I just remember sitting for hours on bare mattresses, talking to weird drunken men with beards until the early morning.'

'Yes, and there was that fight once. Ended with someone falling down the stairs.'

They walked on in silence for a bit towards the bus stop, a light breeze blowing an empty crisp packet along the pavement beside them.

'God,' Rosie said with feeling. 'I'm glad we don't have to do that any more.'

'Me too,' Stephen replied. 'Shall we get a taxi?'

Justin kept a wary eye on the onions. They hissed gently in the frying pan and he stirred them with the caraway seeds anxiously, looking for signs of blackening. Although a high proportion of his cooking began with browning onions, Justin had still not quite mastered the technique of achieving the right golden, caramel glow. Inevitably, some chunks of the onion would wizen to brittle shards, giving a faint but noticeable acrid taint to the whole dish.

So far, it was going well. Justin gave the mixture another stir, releasing a pleasant scent of caraway tinged with nutty onion. There was no angry crackle as the ingredients moved in the pan, only the soft murmur of warm olive oil. Justin decided it was safe to leave for a moment.

He turned away from the pan and fetched a chunk of feta, a tub of cream cheese, a pot of double cream and some eggs from the fridge. He crumbled the feta into a bowl, then stirred in the other ingredients. The result was lumpy, streaked with egg yolk, and looked very unappetizing.

Justin began whisking. His fingers quickly became tired. At times like these he had to concede that a food processor would be useful. The mixture would have been smooth and fluffy within seconds and he could have gone back to stirring the onions. But really, how many times had he whisked anything in the past year? Almost never. And it was so wasteful to own something that you hardly ever used. Just another piece of plastic cluttering up the flat. Really, it was much more satisfying to do it this way. He carried on whisking.

Out in the hall there was a loud click as the bedroom door was pulled open. Barbara exited at an aggressive slouch. Justin expected her to go back into the living room, but instead she came silently into the tiny kitchen.

'Hi, honey,' Justin said in surprise. 'Have you come to give me a hand?'

'No,' Barbara said, opening the fridge. Justin was forced back towards the hob by the outward swing of the door.

'It would be great if you could have a go at a bit of whisking. My wrists are really aching.'

'Have you seen my rice milk?'

'It's in there, isn't it?'

'You've moved it.'

'Let me look.' Justin manoeuvred awkwardly round the fridge door and quickly located the carton.

'Here you are, see?' He handed it to Barbara, who had taken a box of cornflakes out of the cupboard. 'Barbara, what are you doing?'

'What does it look like?'

'But we're going to be eating soon. People are coming in about an hour.'

'I'm hungry.'

'Didn't you have any lunch?'

'No.'

'That was silly. I'm cooking a nice meal and you won't be able to eat it if you stuff yourself with cereal.'

'Don't lecture me.' Barbara splashed rice milk over her bowl of cornflakes and returned with it to the bedroom, shutting the door behind her.

Justin put the carton back in the fridge with a prickle of irritation. These were her friends who were coming over. The whole thing had been her idea. So why was he having to do all the cooking?

As Justin went back to the laborious whisking, the irritation began to dig harder. It wasn't as if he was asking her to do much. Just a bit of chopping and stirring. It had been a long week too. The Malawi project was entering its final stages and he was supposed to be sending it out for stakeholder review next week. If he hadn't been trying to whisk cream cheese and eggs into a light, fluffy texture, he would have been incorporating the final comments from their in-country programme head. Ideally, he would have spent most of the day on it, but even a couple of hours while Barbara did some cooking would have been helpful.

Really, it wasn't as if she was busy. She didn't seem to have done anything all week. Not even the washing up. He'd come home on Thursday night to find a huge stack of dishes waiting for him in the sink. That had annoyed him so much he had almost said something.

Justin forced the whisk through the thick peaks of creamy cheese. Surely that was ready now? A familiar sense of tiredness began to close in around him, like butter enfolding an egg white. Why didn't she just—

The smell of burning onions cut off the thought. Justin dived across to the frying pan and pushed it off the heat, stirring quickly. A harsh sizzle flared up in place of the gentle hiss, releasing more of the bitter tang.

Justin felt the frustration rising in him. He stood in the centre of the kitchen, eyes closed and hands splayed outwards at his sides, trying to force it down.

One, two, three, he counted. One ... two ... three ... It was OK, he told himself. Nothing to worry about. He was so lucky, compared to ninety per cent of the world's population.

With this effort of will, Justin stopped the anger boiling any higher. Don't think about it, that was the key thing now. Concentrate on the good things. Look at what was going well.

He sifted through the onion with a wooden spoon. Only a couple of chunks and a long stringy sliver were properly burned. He fished those out and threw them away.

Now he could make the aubergine cheesecake. This was the enjoyable bit. Everything was OK, really.

The discs of roasted aubergine were cooling on the side. They were exactly the right golden colour, Justin thought. He began arranging them in a baking tray, balancing them on their sides and filling the gaps with plum tomatoes and hand-fuls of oregano. Then he spooned the fluffy cheese mix over the top, watching it ooze invitingly into the space between the vegetables.

Justin scattered more herbs over the top and took a moment to admire the dish before putting it in the oven. That looked good, didn't it? He was already feeling hungry. This was going to be a real vegetarian feast. Thank God for Yotam Ottolenghi. His recipes were so original. Justin had heard that he wasn't really a vegetarian, which was disappointing. But never mind. Justin's dinner was going to show his guests that you didn't need any meat at all to make a delicious, healthy meal that was a really good mix of flavours and textures.

Justin still felt guilty about the argument at Matt's. Sure, Charlotte had been a bit rude about pushing the point. But, really, he blamed himself. If he hadn't let himself be provoked, the whole silly quarrel could have been avoided. Yes, she had been confrontational and aggressive about her views, but wasn't he supposed to rise above that sort of boorish behaviour? To calmly and rationally explain his position, and refuse to see a point of principle become a shouting match? But instead he had got sucked in and let it all unravel into a meaningless argument.

Well, tonight there would be no argument. Anyone eating these dishes would have to admit that vegetarian food was just as good as anything with meat in it. Better, even. Much more inventive than a great big lump of flesh. Even Charlotte and Marcus would be impressed, he felt sure. Justin wasn't particularly interested in winning the competition; he didn't think of himself as competitive like that. But he would be happy if he did his bit for vegetarianism.

Justin smiled to himself as he poured boiling water into a pan to blanch some chard. He wasn't necessarily hoping that anyone would be persuaded to give up meat – though maybe Sarah could be tempted? – just to end the mocking. Maybe, after they had praised the taste and freshness of the food, he would begin a little discussion about the moral benefits.

There wasn't much left to do for the stew now. Justin added the remaining ingredients – tomatoes, chickpeas, coriander and the chard – to the onions, and stirred them as they cooked slowly. When all the guests arrived, he would put everything in with the tamarind water to simmer together, and that would be that. He could do some rice while it was cooking. Only the salad to make now. Justin opened the cupboard to look for the quinoa.

As he poured it out, he could see Barbara emerging from the bedroom. Justin was heartened to see that she wasn't slouching any more. She was looking straight at him as she walked into the kitchen and put her empty bowl down with deliberate precision.

'Great! You must be feeling better. I've done most of it, but you could give me a hand with clearing up.'

'How long before they get here?'

Justin looked at his watch. 'Oh! Only about fifteen minutes now. I didn't realize it was so late. I'd better get moving with the salad.'

Justin reached for the boiling kettle and poured the right amount of water over the quinoa grains. Barbara stood watching him, without moving.

'Do you want to help with this?' he suggested. 'You could shell some beans if you like.'

'What are you cooking?'

'This is just the salad,' Justin replied, pleased that Barbara was now showing an interest. 'Quinoa, Beans and Radish Salad. The main dish is Swiss Chard, Chickpea and Tamarind Stew, with Aubergine Cheesecake to start.'

Barbara nodded slowly, as if she were thinking about this very deeply.

'You're cooking that for everyone?' she asked.

'Yes, but I think I've got it under control now. Although the whisking was a bit boring.'

'No, I meant . . .'

'Actually, you could put out some knives and forks on the coffee table. No point laying them out, there's no room.'

'So you're not taking her advice, huh?'

'What?' Justin was puzzled. 'Whose advice?'

'Charlotte's.'

'Oh.' He laughed. 'You mean the stuff about the sausages? That was funny, wasn't it? Could you pass the radishes? They're by the fridge.'

'You're not making them, then?'

'Of course not.' Justin squinted in concern at Barbara. 'Why on earth would I?'

'I don't know . . . I . . . I just think . . . you know, she said she wanted something and you're not even considering it.'

'Of course I'm not. She wanted meat.'

'What I'm saying is that someone coming here as a guest made a request of you.'

'Oh, so that means I have to do it, do I?'

'I don't know. I'm not saying you have to do it. But maybe you should consider it for a minute.'

'OK, let's consider it.' Justin reached past her to get the radishes himself. 'She asked for meat. We're vegetarians. I said no. What else is there to say?'

'We don't have to eat it. Why can't she have what she likes?'

'She can have what she likes anywhere else. But I don't see why I should have to be complicit in the torture of an animal in my own home.'

'You're always talking about respecting other people's belief systems. Why can't you respect hers?'

'I didn't say ...' Justin abandoned the radishes on the chopping board. 'What, do you want to cook meat for her? Is that what you're saying?'

Barbara drummed her fingers irritably on the worktop and stared into the distance. Justin was startled by the look on her face.

'All I'm saying is, why do you have to impose your moral beliefs on other people?' she asked.

'I do not! I have a great respect for diversity of—'

'Yes, you do, all the time. People just can't be doing something different from you. They're always doing something wrong.'

'That's not fair!'

'It's not your job to perfect the world, Justin.'

'What are you talking about, Barbara?' Justin stared at her, hoping her face would give him some clue. 'I'm just not cooking sausages. I'm making a nice, healthy, tasty and nutritious meal. In fact, I was just thinking before you came in that, when Charlotte eats it, she'll probably realize that not everything good has to have meat in it.'

'You see? You see?' Barbara was almost shouting now. 'Everything's about showing other people the right thing to do! Trying to make us do what you think is ethical!'

'That's not true, Barbara ... Where did this come from?

Anyway, it's not just what I think is ethical, it's what we think is ethical. Isn't it?'

'But they're the same thing!'

'Exactly.' Justin was very confused now. 'We both believe that killing other creatures for our own pleasure is wrong.'

'You're missing the point.' She was clearly disgusted with him.

'I'm not sure what you mean,' he said. 'I was just making dinner. I don't even know why we're arguing.'

'No,' Barbara said, with unmistakable sadness. 'You don't.'

'Look, honey, are you all right?' Justin came across to put his arm round her. 'I'm worried about you.'

Barbara didn't react.

'I don't know,' Justin went on. 'Sometimes I think ... Barbara, you haven't changed your mind, have you? You still think killing animals is wrong, don't you?'

'For fuck's sake, Justin!' Barbara threw off his arm with a violent shrug.

'What? What did I—'

'That's all you can fucking think about!'

'What do you mean? Of course it isn't!'

'Isn't it?'

'You know how much I care for the developing world. But animal welfare is a very important issue. If people knew the conditions—'

'Jesus, you don't get it at all!'

'And I know the health aspect is important to you as well.'

'Screw the health aspect! There are more important things than a balanced diet, Justin.'

'Barbara, this is a big thing.' Justin felt his voice getting louder and more urgent. 'Are you telling me that you don't want to be a vegetarian any more?'

'Fucking hell, Justin! No!'

'Well, what are you trying to say, then?'

Barbara paused, breathing heavily, for a second or two before she replied with unexpected vigour: 'That I don't want to be in this relationship any more!'

Justin stepped back as if she had slapped him. Barbara seemed almost as surprised as he did. They stared at each other in a silence broken only by the whirring of the oven fan.

They stayed like that for several seconds, until the doorbell rang.

Twenty

While they waited, Rosie considered what should be done with the tangled patch of grass in Justin's front garden. It clearly hadn't been mowed for ages, but even cut down it would be too patchy and full of weeds to make much of a lawn. Maybe a flower bed round the edge. But that would require someone to do some proper gardening.

That was the problem with these shared houses: no one took responsibility. Still, it was negligent of the landlord – or would it be the council? – to let things get into that state. Just look at the garden gate! Hanging uselessly off one hinge, barely covered in peeling paint.

Of course, she wasn't judging in any way. Clearly, Justin and Barbara didn't have much money and that wasn't their fault. But all the same, a bit of effort would have made a big difference. Rosie was glad she didn't live here. Gazing at the plastic bank of doorbells, she remembered how happy she was the day they moved out of the tatty, sub-divided Victorian terraced house in Finsbury Park into their own single-occupancy Edwardian villa not far from the centre of Crouch End.

'Do you think you should press it again?' Stephen asked.

'Don't be impatient.'

'Maybe they didn't hear it. They would be down by now if they had.'

'I told you we were too early!'

'What did you want us to do, wander round the housing estate for twenty minutes?'

'Well, perhaps we should give them a bit longer. They did say seven thirty.'

'It's too late now. You've pressed the bell.'

'Yes, but they haven't answered.'

Rosie spotted a patch of mould on the wall of the porch as she considered the dilemma. They had been apprehensive about the two-bus journey out to the Tottenham–Stamford Hill borders. Stephen wanted to take a taxi, but they were going to get one home and it seemed indulgent to Rosie to get two in an evening, so she had felt vindicated when they arrived at the end of the road early. They had thought about going for a drink, but the pub on the corner had a tattered Sky Sports banner hanging outside so they decided not to.

'Are you going to press the bell again, then?' Stephen asked.

'Let's give it a bit longer.'

'They can't have heard it.'

'Then maybe they're busy.'

It was still light outside, but the warmth of spring had yet to arrive and there was a sharp chill in the pale air. Rosie pressed the bell.

It took another thirty seconds for Justin to answer.

Stephen remarked immediately on how flushed he was looking. 'Slaving over a hot stove, are you?'

Justin smiled briefly, and led them upstairs. As they climbed, Rosie couldn't help noticing the scuffs and scratches on the staircase.

The flat was permeated by a warm, vegetal fug.

'That smells lovely,' Rosie said.

'Thank you.'

'Oh we love vegetarian food, don't we, Stephen? It makes such a nice change sometimes to have something that's just light and fresh and healthy.'

Justin went to get some drinks as Rosie and Stephen sat down on the sofa. Rosie inspected the cluttered living room with its multicoloured silk drapes on the wall, the large Buddha's head where the TV should go, the string of fairy lights over the door. It was a bit more hippyish than she was expecting. Barbara was always quite simply dressed, so maybe it was Justin's taste.

'Sorry, I opened yours. I didn't have anything colder in the fridge,' Justin said, handing them two tepid glasses of white wine.

'No, that's fine,' Rosie said, feeling slightly put out. It was quite a nice bottle of Marlborough Sauvignon Blanc and it really would have benefited from going back in the fridge for a bit.

'Where's Barbara?' she asked.

'Oh she's in ... She's getting changed,' Justin said. 'I'm sure she'll be out in a minute.'

'Sorry if we're a bit early.'

'No, no, it's fine. Everything's nearly ready.'

'I was worried we might be interrupting something.'

'No.'

They sat in silence for a while.

'How's your week been, Justin?' Rosie asked.

'Fine, fine. You know, busy.'

'It always is, isn't it?'

'Yes.' They lapsed into silence again. After a while Justin said: 'I'd better go and check on the main course.'

Rosie thought he seemed a bit stressed. Well, it was probably the cooking, wasn't it? This was a crucial moment, just before everyone arrived, and you had to make sure you could finish all the recipes while entertaining as well. Maybe she and Stephen should have stopped off in the pub.

They could hear every movement of the pans in the kitchen next door, so Rosie didn't feel she could say any of this to Stephen. Then there were footsteps in the hall, a door opening and whispered angry voices. The door slammed and the footsteps went back to the kitchen.

Rosie and Stephen exchanged knowing glances. The cookery row. So that's what it was. Well, it happened to everyone, and in Rosie's experience, the sooner the guests arrived, the sooner it was all forgotten.

The flat fell quiet. Rosie and Stephen sipped their wine in silence for a while, aware that any conversation would carry straight through the thin walls to the kitchen. The wine was warm, and they were left on their own, stuck in the middle of a domestic row. Rosie was pretty confident already that the evening wasn't going to be any sort of threat. The thought relaxed her.

It occurred to her then that there wouldn't be a dining room, and they would all have to eat in the living room off their knees. Almost certainly with non-matching cutlery. Well, Justin and Barbara couldn't be blamed, of course, they didn't have much money, but the rules were the rules.

'What do you make of that African mask thing?' Stephen whispered. 'Do you think we should get one like that?'

'Stephen, don't be rude.'

'It's bloody terrifying, isn't it?'

'Shh!'

'But it might be quite useful. If Jonathan isn't going to bed we could just say, "Do what you're told or the mask's coming to get you."'

'Don't be mean. It's a perfectly nice piece of African art.'

'Yes, but in the living room? It would be like having *The Scream* on your bedroom wall.'

Rosie couldn't help giggling at this, and the two of them laughed conspiratorially, leaning into each other on the sofa.

Rosie straightened up quickly as footsteps came towards them.

'Hello, Barbara! Great to see you! You look beautiful!' Rosie stood up to greet Barbara with a kiss. She did look beautiful, of course, but her shoulders were hunched forward, and if she had just changed into those jeans and vest top, Rosie dreaded to think what she had been wearing before.

Barbara smiled faintly at both of them.

'I must say, it's smelling lovely in here,' Rosie said. 'I bet we're in for a real feast.'

'Mmm,' Barbara replied.

'So how are you?' Rosie asked, as Barbara curled herself on to a cushion on the floor. 'Busy week?'

'No,' Barbara replied.

'Oh well, lucky you. It was frantic at work this week, and then I had to come home early on Wednesday because the day-care centre said Jonathan had a cold.'

'Mmm.'

'He turned out to be fine, of course, but I was in such a panic I ran out without finishing and got a bit of a ticking-off on Thursday . . .' Rosie checked herself.

What was wrong? This seemed like more than some silly bickering about how thick you chopped the carrots. There was something about Barbara's sullen silence that made Rosie want to keep babbling, to soften her up with the comforting inanities about everyday life. But she could already tell it wasn't working.

Barbara showed no inclination to restart the conversation, her eyes drifting away from Rosie and Stephen on the sofa to gaze out of the narrow window at the council block opposite. She was obviously distracted by something.

The visa! Maybe that was it. Barbara had mentioned to Rosie a while back that there had been some difficulty in renewing. With government bureaucracy it could be dragging on. That was enough to make anyone worried, wasn't it, the idea of being kicked out of the country? Poor Barbara. It must be so hard without a proper job, and not even the status of a student to fall back on. Not that being an artist wasn't a proper job, but, well . . .

A thought popped into Rosie's head. It made perfect sense. She couldn't see why she hadn't thought of it before. Maybe Justin and Barbara could get married! It would certainly sort out the visa problem. And it would be fun, wouldn't it? They were such a sweet couple. Surely Justin wouldn't wait long to propose, not in this situation. Would the wedding be in America? That would be annoying. Perhaps Rosie could have a word. If it was in London, that would be great. Barbara was so creative – the table settings would be fantastic.

Stephen was always teasing Rosie for wanting everyone to get married, but it just made everything more convenient, that was the thing. Especially with dinner parties and so on. There was none of that awkward 'Are they still together?' or 'Do we know the partner well enough?' No irritating odd numbers, either. Plus she liked the weddings. After a flurry of a dozen in eighteen months, a couple of years back, there had been almost nothing, and Rosie was looking forward to some more. Didn't they say mid-thirties was a good time, as people realized it was more or less now or never? So there should be some to look forward to soon.

Rosie often wondered why Marcus didn't get on with it. Sarah had once told Rosie that he said he didn't really believe in marriage, that it was just a piece of paper, a legal formality, so why all the fuss? Well, that was just the sort of thing men said when they were too lazy to propose. Usually, they changed their minds if their friends nagged them enough. Then it

became less effort just to get it out of the way. Rosie resolved
to start work on Marcus soon.

'Can I use your toilet?' Stephen asked, getting up from the sofa.
'Thanks,' he added, rushing gratefully towards the door. Rosie
realized no one had said anything for some time. Barbara was still
sitting cross-legged on the floor, radiating taciturn hostility.

'So, Barbara,' Rosie said with a bright smile, 'I'm really
keen to see some more of your pots.'

Barbara grimaced.

'The ones in the café were so interesting, and you said you
had some more at home. I'd really love to see them.'

'I'm not ready for that right now,' Barbara mumbled.

'Oh come on, it'll be fun. You can explain them all to me.'

'No, I . . .'

'Come on! Don't be shy!'

Eventually Barbara uncrossed her legs and went silently
out of the room. She returned with a small cardboard box of
ceramics.

'So what's this one?' Rosie asked, taking the top piece out
of the box. 'It's very pretty.'

'Nothing,' Barbara said. 'It's just a piece of trash.'

'Don't be silly. It's fascinating. Why don't you explain it to
me? Like this crack all the way down the side – I assume that's
meant to be there?'

'That was kind of the point.' Barbara said the words in one
deep sigh. 'How can you have a pot with a crack in it, right?
You can't use it. So what's the pot for? Is it just decorative?
Can it mean something? Is an object still the same thing if its
essential purpose is gone? That's what I was trying to ask.'

'How interesting!' Rosie turned the fractured pot over in her hands. 'And what's the answer?'

'I don't know.'

'Oh I see. Thought-provoking.'

'You're right. The whole thing's just garbage.'

'Stop it.' Rosie hit Barbara playfully on the upper arm. 'What about that one?' She picked out a waxy yellow vase with an irregular, dappled surface.

'This . . . ?' Barbara rubbed her left shoulder with her right hand. 'It's kind of hard to . . .' She stared at the pot. 'I guess the foundation for this was my grandmother. The texture of her skin, you see? I wanted to recreate that . . . I mean, she was ill and it didn't seem human and at the same time it obviously was . . . I don't know, I . . . I guess I tried to take that and put it in another medium, you know, to see what happened to those textures and associations when they weren't attached to a breathing body. Or even a non-breathing body. Does it still mean the same thing, you know?'

Rosie nodded very seriously.

'And then, because it's a decorative art form that's meant to be about beauty . . . what happens to that? Does it become beautiful for that reason? Was it always beautiful? I don't know . . . can it be beautiful and unsettling because it's beautiful? Does that make sense?'

'Yes, sort of,' Rosie said. 'It must be very meaningful anyway.'

Barbara snatched it back. 'Let's just—'

'And what about this one here?'

Barbara stared at it. 'That one is called "The Persistence of the Past in the Minds of the Elderly".'

'I see.' Rosie looked doubtfully at the lumpy vase gaudily painted with overlapping red and yellow stripes. 'It's very bright, isn't it?'

'It's meant to show how certain primary-coloured early memories are embedded in our minds so strongly that they can never fade. Even if everything else is gone and they start to blur into each other in old age.'

'Oh.' Rosie peered closer. 'Very clever. And this?'

'Jesus, don't make me go through them all . . .'

'Darling,' Rosie said as Stephen came back into the room. 'Barbara is just showing me her pots. Come and have a look.'

'No, please, I can't . . .'

'Great!' Stephen said with forced jollity. 'I've heard so much about them. It's nice to finally see for myself. What's that one? With the purple knobbly bits.'

Barbara's voice was flat and empty as she replied: 'That one's about my sister's wedding.'

Twenty-one

Marcus entered the living room pretty confident of what he was going to find, so he couldn't help smiling to himself when he saw the big African mask propped in the corner. Perfect. He ticked off the vibrant fabrics on the wall, the array of appropriately ethnic knick-knacks on the bookshelf.

And was that . . . Yes, it was! A beanbag! It sat bunched on the floor underneath a poster advertising the Dalai Lama's autobiography. Marcus hadn't seen a beanbag in years. It was even better than he had hoped. On his way over, he was surprised to find he was actually looking forward to the evening, so certain was he of the opportunities for condescension.

'What a very striking mask,' he said to Justin in a warm and patronizing tone.

Justin said, 'Thanks. I'd better get on with the salad,' and hurried back to the kitchen.

Rosie and Stephen were crouched on the floor with Barbara and an array of her pots. Marcus lost some of his amused certainty as he looked at them. The pots unsettled him. Yes, they were crude and childlike, but that was the point, surely?

Could they actually be good? Marcus didn't want to risk mocking them if there was any chance they might be proper art. That could bring real humiliation.

'Barbara, these are lovely!' Sarah said. 'Can I have a look?'

'I'm just putting them away.'

'Oh go on!'

Barbara finished stacking the box and stood up.

Rosie handed back the one she had been looking at. 'Barbara was just telling us that this one was inspired by a bout of chickenpox she had as a child.'

Oh come on! That had to be ridiculous, didn't it? Marcus was all ready to say something when Barbara turned and looked him in the eye. The comment withered on his tongue. He found Barbara unsettling. It didn't help that she was so attractive. Marcus always found beautiful women difficult, unless he could establish early on that they were willing to defer to his intelligence. But it wasn't just that. Barbara was unreadable, and Marcus couldn't tell if she didn't understand his jibes, or had somehow found a higher level from which to look down on him.

Sarah protested some more as Barbara carried the box away, but then the doorbell went and Justin said they were ready to eat.

Charlotte and Matt arrived within minutes of each other, but obviously not together. Marcus watched as they conspicuously avoided looking at each other. That matchmaking attempt certainly hadn't worked. Served Rosie right. Charlotte sat down on a folding chair on the other side of the room to Matt, well out of his eyeline and with everyone else in between them. Clearly, nothing happening there.

'Dinner's ready,' Justin said, putting a bottle of wine and a stack of tumblers down on the coffee table. 'I know it's not elegant, but we haven't got much space, so I hope no one minds eating off their knees. Please, sit down where you can.'

Marcus scrambled for one of the remaining chairs. It was rigid and uncomfortable, but he didn't want to end up on the beanbag. Neither did anyone else, it seemed. In the end, Barbara curled herself up on it, leaning back against the bookcase.

'Well, this is cosy, isn't it?' Marcus said as Rosie started handing round wine from the bottle Justin had brought out. 'It's just like being a student again.'

He took a sip of wine. 'Oooh! It really is like being a student again.'

'Marcus!' Sarah exclaimed.

'No, it's disgusting, isn't it?' Barbara said with sudden force. 'Justin buys it because it's Fairtrade. He hasn't noticed that it tastes like shit.'

There was a shocked silence.

'I don't know,' Rosie said carefully. 'It's not that bad. Just . . . unusual.'

'It'll do the job,' Charlotte said. 'Can I have a top-up?'

Justin came back with a plate in each hand. He signalled to Barbara to help bring in the rest, but she ignored him. Rosie jumped up and went to fetch them from the kitchen.

They settled down in uneasy silence.

'Justin,' Sarah said as they began eating, 'what was the name of that Peruvian writer you were telling me about last time?'

'Peruvian?' He looked blank. 'Oh, you mean Bernardo Hidalgo? He's Bolivian.'

'Oh! How embarrassing!'

'Don't worry about it.'

'But you were really raving about that book. What was it called?'

'*Ten Thousand Times Six*. It is brilliant.'

'What's it about?'

'It's hard to say, exactly. Some of it's set in pre-revolutionary Chile, but then part of it is about a research professor at a Canadian university, and then there's a bit in a favela in Rio de Janeiro.'

'Right.' Sarah sounded a little bit doubtful.

'I'm not explaining it very well, but it's fantastic. Has anyone else read it?' Justin looked expectantly round the room.

'Is that the one that's six hundred pages?' Rosie asked.

'Yes, I suppose it is quite long, but it's really worthwhile. Have you read it?'

'Well, my book club was thinking about it. But there's a rule against books with more than three hundred pages. So we didn't, in the end.'

'Well, it sounds great,' Sarah said. 'I'll have to note down the name so I don't forget again.'

'You can borrow it if you like.'

'Thanks, that would be great.'

Marcus was finding this difficult to take. He hadn't read the book either, but he had instantly taken a dislike to it. So he asked: 'Has anyone read the new one by Bilaj Tunek?'

There was a gratifying silence.

'It's very good,' Marcus said. He'd read only the back cover, but felt sure that a Turko-Bulgarian Nobel Prize winner beat a boring South American. 'I'd definitely recommend it. Lyrical, without ever losing sight of reality.' That was what that quote from the *Guardian* had said, wasn't it?

'What about the new Anthony Hargrave?' Rosie asked. 'Has anyone read that?'

'The one about child abuse?' Sarah asked.

'Yes. It was very harrowing.'

'God, there are so many books I need to get round to reading!' Sarah said. 'It won all those prizes, didn't it?'

Marcus felt he should say something. 'Hargrave's a total charlatan,' he declared.

'No, it's very good,' Rosie said. 'But it is a bit ... well, it's hard going.'

'Is that the one they're making a film of?' Matt asked.

'Yes, that's right!' Rosie agreed. 'It's going to have ... oh, what's his name? The one that was in *The Tudors*?'

'Oh he's hot!' Charlotte exclaimed. 'I'll see it if he's in it! Even if it is about child molesters.'

'No, actually, maybe it's not him.' Rosie hesitated. 'Maybe I mean the one from that film about Anne Boleyn ...'

'Not so hot.'

'Who's he?' Sarah asked.

'Was he the one in *The Green Lantern*?' Matt said.

'He doesn't sound very hot.'

'Hey, has anyone seen *Inception*?' Rosie asked. 'We got sent it on DVD this week, and it was totally incomprehensible.'

'I haven't seen it,' Justin said.

'It's all about trying to break into someone's dreams,' Sarah said. 'Except that you can get stuck in them and then they can hack into yours. No, wait . . . Is that right?'

'I thought it was that you die if someone wakes you up while you're in someone else's dream,' Rosie said.

Marcus felt compelled to put them right. 'It's all about the uncertainty of identity,' he said. 'All of Christopher Nolan's films are. If you can't control your subconscious, are you really you any more? What is "you" anyway?'

'What a load of bollocks,' Charlotte said.

'Well, in the end we decided to give up and watch *The Apprentice* instead,' Rosie said.

Marcus retired sullenly from the conversation. He couldn't contribute to this. How had the conversation slipped so quickly from translated fiction to reality TV? But the pause allowed him to appraise the food for the first time. He had eaten almost half of his aubergine cheesecake without really tasting it. Not a good sign.

The idea was a good one, he had to admit. But he was relieved to discover that the dish didn't live up to its name. The roast aubergine was fine, sure, if a bit monotonous. Yes, the dusting of herbs was all well and good, but the cheesy filling was just bland. Justin wasn't putting on much of an advert for a vegetarian diet.

When Justin asked if anyone wanted seconds, there was a long pause. Marcus savoured it.

'Rosie?' Justin asked. 'Would you like any more?'

'It was gorgeous, really lovely,' she said. 'But I don't think I could.'

Marcus could tell this was insincere; she was clearly being overeffusive because she hadn't thought of anything good to say about it before.

Justin went round the room, but everyone declined a second helping.

'I really couldn't,' Marcus said happily. 'It was so ... filling.'

'Are you all sure? There's only a little bit left?'

'It was too heavy, Justin,' Barbara said. 'No one wants any.'

'Right, well, I can have it for lunch tomorrow.' The forced lightness of Justin's tone could not disguise the look of surprise on his face. 'Now, does everyone mind giving me their plates? I need to wash them up for the main course.'

'We can keep the same plates,' Sarah said. 'It's no trouble.'

'The only thing is,' Marcus said, forcing down a smirk, 'I've still got quite a lot of the cheesecake left on mine.'

'Yeah, I couldn't finish it either,' Barbara said, putting her plate down slightly out of Justin's reach. 'It wasn't very good.'

'I wouldn't say that,' Marcus said carefully. He didn't quite know where this was going. 'It was certainly an interesting idea, so maybe it was the execution that was wrong.'

'Marcus ...' Sarah warned.

'Perhaps it was just over-reliant on seasoning for flavour.'

'You mean it didn't taste of very much,' Barbara said.

'I didn't say that.' Marcus was pleased by the very slight emphasis he put on the word 'say'.

'No, it was bland, Justin,' Barbara said. 'Would it have killed you to put some better herbs in?'

'Well, I'll know for next time, won't I?' Justin's voice was strained. He was staring straight at Barbara, but she wasn't looking at him now, gazing down instead at a worn patch on the carpet.

'Yeah. Next time,' she said faintly.

Marcus felt uneasy. He couldn't work out what was going on, and it was unnerving him. Normally, he would have written it off as classic host's self-criticism, designed to elicit more praise. But, well, it wasn't herself Barbara was criticizing, was it?

'Do you want any help clearing up?' Rosie asked.

'It's OK,' Justin said.

'No, go on, I'll stack the dirty plates.'

Justin let Rosie pile up half the dishes and follow him into the kitchen.

Sarah got to her feet as well. 'Can I help with the washing up?'

The room fell quiet without them. The sounds of running water and clattering crockery were very distinct.

Marcus was still unsure what was going on. Maybe Sarah was trying to find out. Usually, people conspired to keep his criticism veiled: they would pretend he wasn't being rude, and he would pretend they weren't taking offence. But he had a game plan, and he thought he might as well stick to it. When Justin came back in with a bowl of salad, he asked: 'So, Justin, what are we having for the main course?'

'Chickpea, Swiss Chard and Tamarind Stew,' Justin replied, as Marcus hoped he would.

'Tamarind?' he said in feigned surprise. 'You had that at Rosie's, didn't you?'

'Yes, we did,' Justin said.

'I thought so. You must be a big fan, to serve it again.'

'I like it, yes.'

'He puts it in fucking everything!' The violence of Barbara's reply knocked the room into silence again. Marcus didn't feel like breaking it.

Then Charlotte said: 'If only he'd do that with meat.'

Justin went back to the kitchen without reacting. After staring intently out of the window for a while, Barbara stood up and picked her way between the glasses on the floor. She went out into the hall and disappeared.

A few seconds later the front door slammed. It was pulled shut with such force Marcus could feel the vibrations through his hard plastic chair. Well, he thought with a certain shocked satisfaction, I don't think we've got much to fear from tonight's entertainment.

Twenty-two

What was that all about, Charlotte wondered without really being interested in the answer. Barbara had always struck her as a bit of a moody cow. Probably she thought of it as being enigmatic and soulful, but Charlotte knew the type from school: willowy, manipulative girls who used their pretty thinness as an excuse to behave as self-indulgently as they wanted. She'd probably decided she was allergic to cumin or something. Well, screw her. Charlotte wasn't going to pretend to care. She was pretty sure that if everyone ignored her, Barbara would slink back later on.

Charlotte poured herself another glass of wine. Of course, if Barbara didn't come back, it would make things more difficult for Justin, which was a bonus. Charlotte had promised herself she wasn't going to get sucked in to this stupid bourgeois competition – she didn't give a fuck whose napkins were the most tasteful – but she wanted to make damn sure that Justin and his sanctimonious nut roast bloody well lost.

Although, in fairness, that cheesy aubergine thing had

really hit the spot. As she arrived at Justin's flat, Charlotte had felt her hangover pushing its way back in through the protective curtain of bacon grease. She'd had to stop at the corner shop and wolf down a packet of cheese and onion crisps before she could face ringing the doorbell.

The first glass of wine was difficult. She hadn't really felt like it, and the liquid had tasted sour and alcoholic, but it was important to get started. It wasn't an evening to be faced sober. The second had been easier, and now, with the third, the hangover was at bay again. Charlotte felt her energy beginning to return. She studied Matt properly for the first time that evening. He was saying something to Stephen and didn't seem to notice her appraising him. There was less awkwardness than Charlotte had expected. All the same, she looked away before he turned round.

She took another long sip. That was more like it. The wine wasn't very good, but the feeling of it was. Tell you what, if they were having that conversation about Barbara's pots now, there was no way she would have kept her mouth shut. Load of pretentious crap. It needed saying, and Charlotte regretted not doing so. No wonder Barbara was so moody, if she spent her life churning out wanky rubbish in – where the hell even was this? Charlotte had never been to this part of London before, and certainly didn't intend to make a habit of it. It was a taxi-there-taxi-back kind of place. Charlotte had watched appalled from the window as they drove through canyon-like housing estates, with miserable-looking inhabitants shuffling about between them. They didn't even look like they'd have the wit to mug you. Twenty quid, though, and another twenty back. The evening obviously wasn't going to be worth that. Bloody Rosie.

'Make room, make room!' Sarah charged back in to fuss over the coffee table, clearing space around a big bowl of salad that seemed to be mostly beige. Justin followed carrying a big casserole dish with wisps of steam escaping from beneath the lid. He eased it into the middle of the table.

'That looks amazing, Justin,' Sarah said.

'Mmm, smells delicious,' Rosie added.

Calm down, he hasn't even taken the bloody lid off yet, Charlotte thought.

Justin removed the lid, waved away the heavy cloud of steam that billowed from the dish, and began handing round big bowls of stew.

'Do start,' he said.

'Is Barbara . . . ?' Rosie asked.

'Please. Start.'

Rosie picked up her fork.

Justin thought for a moment before adding: 'She's not been feeling too well, you see.'

'Oh I'm sorry . . .'

'She must have just gone to get some aspirin or something.'

'But I could have—'

'Please. Start.'

When everyone had started eating, Charlotte listened to another round of absurd enthusiasm.

'Mmm. Justin, this is gorgeous!'

'Delicious.'

'Absolutely fantastic!'

Jesus Christ, Charlotte thought, tone it down a notch! Could they sound any more fake? How much more obvious could it be that they were trying to compensate for Barbara storming off? Not even Justin was going to fall for this.

'Do you really think so? I'm so pleased that you like it,' Justin said.

Charlotte looked round the room, hoping someone would catch her eye in private amusement at Justin's gullibility. But only Matt had the half-smile that suggested he shared the joke. Charlotte let her eyes skate over him.

'It's really very simple,' Justin said. 'It's just chickpeas, chard, caraway seeds, tamarind paste and a few bits and pieces.'

'Is that all? But it's so rich!'

Christ. This couldn't go on.

'You know what I think would improve it?' she said.

Rosie glared at her, but Charlotte couldn't see any reason to hold back.

'Some nice cubes of aged steak,' she said.

Justin didn't react.

'This salad is lovely too,' Rosie said with grim determination. 'So fresh! What did you put into it?'

Justin had become subdued. He didn't respond.

'It's OK,' Charlotte insisted. 'But it's just a side dish, isn't it? You really need a chunky main course to go with it, don't you? Like steak.'

Justin smiled sadly, but without any sign of annoyance.

'Yes,' Charlotte tried again. 'With a nice bit of meat this would be really tasty.'

Justin sighed.

What the fuck? Why wasn't he rising to this? It had taken much less last time. Surely someone so self-righteous couldn't help but retaliate.

Charlotte had another spoonful of stew. The chickpeas popped satisfyingly between her teeth. It was quite tasty, actually – tangy, like a curry sauce. But you couldn't have just the curry sauce on its own, could you? It was all Tikka Masala and no chicken.

Quite good, that. Worth trying on Justin. Charlotte opened her mouth.

'Oh dear, I'm so sorry!' Sarah was scrambling to her feet. Her glass lay on its side next to her, a pool of wine spreading across the carpet. 'I'll get a cloth.'

'It's all right, I'll do it.' Justin perked up from his reverie, suddenly purposeful again. He dashed out to the kitchen and returned with an array of cloths, scouring pads and kitchen roll.

Justin knelt forward to mop up the wine, his skinny buttocks protruding into the ring of diners. His bottom shook with the effort of scrubbing. Charlotte shuddered involuntarily. Even Rosie sat back on her chair.

'I can't believe I was so clumsy!' Sarah said, crouching down next to Justin to study the carpet. 'Is there anything I can do?'

'No, I think it's going to be OK,' Justin replied, dabbing at the stain with paper towels. 'It was only white wine.'

'Aren't you supposed to put something on white-wine stains?' Stephen asked. 'Salt, isn't it?'

'That's red wine,' Rosie said.

'Are you sure? What's white, then? Is it lemon juice?'

'That's why I always have white wine at other people's parties,' Sarah said. 'Imagine if that had been red!'

Charlotte was appalled. What a stupid reason for choosing anything! She topped her glass up to the brim with red.

'I'm really embarrassed,' Sarah said, getting closer to Justin on the floor as he gathered the cleaning materials.

'Don't worry,' he said. 'You can hardly see it.'

Charlotte looked at the carpet. Quite clearly, you could. But the carpet was so worn and faded anyway, discoloured by the marks of numerous tenancies. Frankly, she thought, wine was probably one of the nicer stains in there.

Sarah insisted on helping Justin carry the cloths back to the kitchen. No one stepped in to restart the conversation. Charlotte watched with slight amusement as Rosie's smile became tighter the longer the silence dragged on.

'Speaking of embarrassment,' Rosie said in the end, 'did I ever tell you about the time I went to the industry awards dinner with my boss?' She didn't risk waiting for anyone to say yes before continuing. 'God, it was awful – you know how boring those work things can be – and I'd maybe had a few too many glasses of wine. Anyway, they started serving these canapés, only it wasn't a waiter with a tray, it was a finger buffet. So I thought, "Oh well, that's a bit of a faff, I can wait for dinner."'

'But then I had another glass of wine, and I thought, "If I don't eat something soon I'm going to be wasted before I sit down." So I went and picked up a plate. You know the usual sort of things they have: mini-quiches, smoked-salmon squares, prawns with satay sauce – there's always satay sauce, isn't there? And I wolfed down a couple of those to take the edge off. Ideally, I would have had one of those tiny burgers – those are the best, aren't they? – but there weren't any left.

'I was walking back across the room with a plate, looking for a quiet corner, when my boss called me over to talk to some very important woman from the Design Council or something, so I thought, "I've got to be lucid for this; better eat some more."

'And then what happened was that I was standing next to this woman while my boss was on the other side of her, talking loudly, obviously trying hard to impress her. And I had my wine glass in my left hand, and the plate in my right. But I couldn't eat anything like that. So I needed to try and get both the glass and the plate in my left hand so the right was free. I had the stem of the glass wedged in, and I was just about holding the plate between my thumb and forefinger, but I wasn't really looking at what I was doing because I was nodding vigorously, pretending to be interested in what my boss was saying. Then I pushed down on the plate to dip a prawn in some satay sauce, and the plate flipped out from between my fingers.

'There was nothing I could do. I tried to catch it, but I missed because I wasn't looking, although I did get a mini-quiche. So I just closed my eyes and thought, "Oh shit, this is going to be humiliating."

'And I waited and waited for the crash when it hit the floor. But there was nothing. I opened my eyes, looked down, and there was no plate. It had literally disappeared. I was a little bit freaked out by that, I can tell you. My boss was still droning on, and I don't think he'd noticed anything.

'Then I looked down to my right, and I saw this Design Council woman's handbag. It was a big handbag. An expensive leather one. Maybe a Mulberry, or something like that. It was undone at the top. And there, sticking out of the top of it, I could see a little pink prawn tail.

'I didn't know what to do. How can you explain that? "Er, excuse me, but I appear to have tipped a plate of canapés into your handbag. Sorry." It's not going to work, is it?

'But then I thought, "No one else has noticed. Just keep calm, and maybe you'll get away with it." So I carried on nodding, and I laughed very loudly when the boss told one of his rubbish jokes.

'I said something banal to this woman, she nodded at me, and then my boss started talking again. I thought, "Just make an excuse, leave, and you'll be clean away."

'But then the woman's phone began to ring. I heard it first, because I was so jumpy. And because it was in her handbag.'

A ripple of laughter ran round the room. Even Justin, back from the kitchen, was leaning forward to hear more. It was a good story. Why hadn't Charlotte heard it before? Clearly, this wasn't the first time Rosie had told it. Why hadn't she told Charlotte first? This was the sort of thing Rosie used to tell her immediately.

'Well, the end of this is really shaming. In my defence, I didn't have time to think. It was just instinctive.

'I stepped back as if to answer my own phone, and I put

out my hand to guide Siân a bit closer to this woman to fill the gap.'

'Who's Siân?' Charlotte asked.

'That girl who sits by our stationery cupboard. The one who sniffs all the time, but never blows her nose.'

'Oh her! She's so annoying.'

'Yes, exactly. Anyway, by the time the woman heard her phone ringing I was out of the circle and away, and when she screamed in disgust it was Siân who was standing next to her. I felt bad, but what could I do?'

'Poor Siân!' Sarah exclaimed.

'Well, yes, obviously, in a way. But she was so horrified as well that I'm sure they all believed it wasn't her. Certainly I would have done. But we never did get an award from the Design Council.'

Charlotte laughed along with everyone else. It was embarrassing, but like lots of Rosie's stories, it was self-deprecating in a way that made you think it probably hadn't been as bad as she made out.

'God, I hate finger buffets,' Stephen said with surprising vehemence. 'Quite clearly it's impossible to hold a plate, a glass and eat with your hands at the same time. So why do they persist in having them? Are they trying to make people look stupid?'

'When do you ever go to finger buffets?' Rosie asked.

'Never. Because I can't stand them.'

'You know what's really been annoying me lately?' Charlotte decided she liked the direction the conversation was going. 'People having breakfast at work.'

There was a chorus of agreement, although Matt and Justin remained quiet.

'I mean, what's the point? How much time can you possibly save by having a bowl of cornflakes at your desk? Twenty seconds? Thirty? Not even that, because then you've got to buy milk to take to work, and write your name on it with a green marker pen and three exclamation marks so that no one steals it from the fridge. And are you really going to do any work while you're spooning cereal into your face? Of course you're not. You're just going to browse the internet, aren't you? And then leave the office littered with empty bowls, with bits of rotting Cheerios stuck to the sides. What's the point? Just to say to everyone: "Hey, look, I'm so busy and important I don't have time to eat anything before rushing in to my super-important job." And then you spend the next hour e-mailing round links of baby pandas sneezing. It's pathetic.'

Marcus laughed. 'All right, then, my turn. The thing that's really been pissing me off lately is people who stand on escalators.'

'What!' Charlotte and Rosie protested at the same time.

'I just don't understand it. It's not a lift. They're basically stairs. You're meant to climb them. Why would you just stand there? Are you looking at the adverts? Are you that desperate to find out which one from *Home and Away* is doing panto this season?'

'No, it's because you can't be bothered to walk up a long flight of stairs,' Charlotte said. 'What's so hard to understand about that?'

'How lazy do you have to be not to bother walking up a few stairs?'

'About as lazy as me.'

'Half the people standing there probably go to the gym anyway. They stand on an escalator, kitbag over their shoulder, so they can get to the gym and spend half an hour on the StairMaster.'

'Got that out of your system now?' Sarah said.

'I feel a lot better.'

'Who's next?' Charlotte said. 'Matt?'

'Mobile phones that play music,' Matt said with great solemnity. 'You can't walk down the street any more without hearing some tinny R 'n' B blaring from a teenager's mobile. It makes you want to throw the thing under a bus.'

'You'd be justified in going through with that,' Marcus said.

'Who invented a phone that would be so deliberately annoying as to play music out loud? Don't they deserve punishment?'

'Absolutely.' Marcus nodded. 'Good one.'

'Right, what about you, Justin?' Charlotte said. 'Your turn. Give us something that really irritates you.'

Justin thought for a moment and opened his mouth.

'Don't say poverty,' Charlotte warned.

Justin closed his mouth. After a bit, he said: 'What about injustice?'

'You haven't really got this, have you? What about something petty that's still very aggravating.'

'Aggravating because it's so petty,' Marcus clarified. 'That would be best.'

Justin thought deeply.

'Like when you get a parking ticket because they've suspended the bay your car's in while you're on holiday,' Stephen suggested.

'Or when people spill instant coffee over the teabags in the office kitchen, so your tea always tastes faintly of coffee,' Charlotte said. 'Or when you've been working really hard all day, and the one time the boss comes over is when you're booking a holiday on the internet.'

Justin continued to ponder.

'There must be something,' Rosie encouraged him. 'Anything small.'

'OK. How about . . .' He hesitated.

'Go on.'

'OK, you know when you're on the tube or a train, and the announcer says, "Please take your newspapers with you and dispose of them"? Well, I've always thought that's a bit annoying because it seems so wasteful. Surely it's better to read a copy that someone else has finished with than to take a new one? That's the environmentally friendly thing to do, isn't it? Re-use them? So why do they tell us not to? Is it just to make their lives easier?'

'That's it, Justin, you tell 'em,' Marcus said.

'It's really annoying, isn't it?' Justin repeated with more certainty.

'That's it, well done!' Rosie said.

'Although,' Justin checked himself, 'they probably do have a good reason, don't they? After all, they can't be paid much, the people who clean trains, so maybe it's wrong to give them more work to do.'

'Are you kidding?' Charlotte spluttered into her wine. 'Public sector unions? Probably paid a fucking fortune.'

'It could be a fire hazard too,' Justin went on. 'So maybe they do have good reasons for it.'

'OK,' Marcus said. 'Full marks for effort anyway.'

'Who hasn't said anything yet?' Charlotte asked. 'Sarah, what about you?'

'I don't—'

'Wait,' Charlotte interrupted. 'I've thought of another one.'

Her audience stiffened as the front-door key scraped into the lock. They heard the door open and slam shut, then caught a glimpse of Barbara flashing past the open doorway to the living room.

Charlotte briefly lost her train of thought as the atmosphere in the room tautened. From the kitchen came the sound of Barbara scrabbling around in a cupboard.

'Yes,' Charlotte remembered what it was. 'People who wear Lycra to cycle in to work.'

But the air had gone out of the conversation. Although Charlotte was sure that at least one of them had to ride a bike, no one even seemed to consider replying. They were listening to the clatter of the cutlery drawer.

'So, Justin,' Rosie asked with a strained smile, 'how are things at work?'

Justin took a long time to reply. 'Ummm . . . Very good,' he said faintly. 'We're working on a really excellent project in Malawi at the moment.'

'Tell us about it,' Rosie said with determined interest.

'We don't want to be one of those agencies that just puts a sticking plaster on a problem and walks away,' Justin said, staring at the wall. 'We want to really settle into the life of a place, become a permanent part of their lives and keep our influence going in the long term.'

'That sounds great!' Rosie said.

'Thank you.'

Christ, Charlotte thought. What a wet blanket. You obviously want to go and find out what Barbara is doing. So go and do it! It's your fucking flat!

From the kitchen came the loud, insistent tick of the gas hob igniting. Then, slowly, something began to sizzle.

Justin couldn't take his eyes off the wall now.

After a while, Rosie said: 'What about you, Sarah? How are the kids?'

Sarah started guiltily in her chair. 'What? They're fine. Why?'

'No, I just mean how's it going at school generally?'

'Oh I see.' Sarah relaxed slightly. 'Well, it's a bit stressful at the moment, actually. Everything's about to get into gear for GCSE revision and a lot of the students are starting to realize how poorly prepared they are, and often they blame the school for that. Then you have all the ones who aren't trying, who just disrupt things for everyone else, and you have to make a decision: do I give up on them and throw them out, or do I struggle on? It's quite a stressful time for us all.'

'Oh,' Rosie said. 'Oh dear.'

'Yes,' Sarah agreed.

Rosie didn't ask her any more. There was a long silence, punctuated by the sound of hot oil spitting in the next room.

Rosie had another go. 'And Matt? What about you?'

But no one cared about the answer, because Barbara had appeared at the doorway. She advanced into the room, carrying a plate held out in front of her.

The hot, viscous smell spread out luxuriantly across the room. On the plate sat six plump sausages.

Charlotte made no attempt to stifle a delighted grin. She wasn't sure what was going on, but she liked the way it was heading.

Without saying anything, Barbara set the sausages down on the table. Warm grease seeped out of them. Barbara settled back into her place on the beanbag, propped against the bookshelf. She made no attempt at explanation.

The look on Justin's face was so astonishing that Charlotte almost got out her phone and took a picture. There was disgust there, shame, a bit of anger, maybe disappointment too. Most of all, though, was incomprehension. He wasn't looking at Barbara; he was looking at the sausages. Their blackened skin wrinkled slightly in the silence.

'B-Barbara,' he stammered. 'Those ... those don't smell like Linda McCartney.'

'No, they don't,' Barbara agreed.

'There's ... there's meat in them, isn't there?'

'Yes.' She said it very simply.

Horror spread across his face. 'Did you use my frying pan?'

Barbara exhaled impatiently. 'No, I cooked them in the fucking kettle.'

Justin didn't take his eyes off the plate. 'I just don't understand how you could do something like this.'

'It's just meat.'

'No, it's not.' He was shaking now. 'It's betrayal.'

Charlotte had to put her hand over her mouth. Sarah, for different reasons, did the same.

'I don't know what you're getting so upset about,' Barbara said in a flat voice. 'You don't have to eat it. They're for our guests.'

Rosie shifted uncomfortably on her folding chair.

'Charlotte said she would like to have some sausages with her meal,' Barbara continued. 'So here they are.'

Everyone else turned to look at Charlotte. Her face flooded with victorious elation. 'That's very thoughtful of you, Barbara,' she said. 'Very kind. Very welcoming.' Charlotte smiled warmly at Barbara, but she was still looking at Justin. Justin was still looking at the sausages.

'I'll dig in, then, shall I?' Charlotte said, reaching forward. No one said anything. She stuck her fork into the plumpest sausage. It was inexpertly cooked, blackened and charred on one side, but with a pink, raw sheen on the other. Charlotte hesitated for a moment, wondering whether they might be a bit risky. But sod it, they would be worth it.

She took an enormous bite.

'Mmm, delicious!'

The meat was bland and gooey. Charlotte reckoned it must be one of those cheap, long-life sausages you get in packets at the corner shop when the hangover's too bad to walk any further. But, just then, it tasted perfect.

Blobs of fat dribbled down the length of the sausage, and Charlotte had to catch them with the back of her hand to stop them dripping on to her lap. It was awkward, especially with everyone still staring at her, so she leaned forward and chopped the sausage into chunks, then dropped them, one by one, into her bowl of stew. Justin winced as each chunk went in.

Charlotte stirred the mixture and took a forkful. It worked really well: the sticky sweetness of the sauce enveloping the meat and steeping it in flavour.

'Mmm, really good,' she said through a mouthful. 'I recommend this.'

'Anyone else want one?' Barbara asked.

There was a very tense silence.

'Sarah?'

'No! No, thank you.'

'Rosie?'

'Thank you, but I couldn't possibly manage . . .'

'Matt?'

'Er . . . All right, then.' Matt speared a sausage and bit into it. Charlotte felt a spasm of grateful lust. His powerful jaw chewed rhythmically. It hadn't been so bad last time, had it, really? Quite fun, in fact, definitely to begin with. So what if they'd ignored each other all week? They knew where they stood.

If they went back to her flat this time, he might be up and gone before she'd even woken up. And if he wasn't gone . . . well, maybe that wouldn't be so bad.

After inspecting it closely, Marcus declined a sausage. Stephen took one and was given a sharp, disapproving look by Rosie.

'This is really good, Justin,' Charlotte said cheerfully. 'The flavours go really well together. You'll definitely have to give me the recipe.'

Justin muttered something inaudible.

'You know where I had a properly excellent sausage recently?' Charlotte went on. 'Barcelona. I wish I could remember what it was called; it was like a chorizo but with different spices. Very good. It was part of a sharing platter that was basically seven different types of pork. Fantastic.'

Charlotte ate the last lump of meat from her stew. The three remaining sausages sat cooling on the plate, their hardening skins gleaming under the lights.

'If you guys don't want them, I might have another one,' she said.

No one objected.

Charlotte leaned forward and chopped up another sausage. Both Justin and Barbara watched her intently.

'Are you all sure?' she asked, dropping the chunks into the remains of her stew. 'It's very good. Rosie? Stephen?'

They shook their heads.

'What about you, Barbara? You went to all the trouble of cooking them. Don't you want to try one?'

Barbara looked up from the plate and met Charlotte's eye. She looked at Justin, then back to the sausages. They glistened. She shifted on her beanbag.

'Barbara . . .' Justin's tone was one of urgent anguish.

She leaned forward and reached towards the plate.

'Barbara! No!'

Her fingers closed round the sausage, dimpling its fatty flesh.

Twenty-three

A rivulet of hot pork juice hung for a moment on Barbara's lower lip. Matt watched it slide down the curve of her chin until she reached up a hand to brush it away. The fairy lights caught the remains of the sticky path it traced across her skin.

Matt felt a sharp jolt of desire. Barbara was wearing a loose, faded vest top, scooping open at the front to cast appealing shadows over the swell of her chest. She lay back against the bookshelf, almost reclining, one leg cocked over the other, with an air of defiance. Matt stared.

Justin emitted another squeaky moaning sound, like a small animal caught in a trap.

'Barbara, what's the matter?' he asked. 'I just can't understand why you did that.'

'I know,' she said.

'Why, then?' Justin moaned again. 'Why would you just give up on something like that? Something you care about? A principle that was so important to you.'

She seemed to consider this herself. 'I don't know ... I guess I just wanted to try something different.'

Justin shook his head.

'To be fair,' Charlotte interrupted. 'It was a pretty tasty sausage.'

Matt smiled at this. No one else gave anything away. Charlotte caught his eye and grinned. She was in good spirits now, offering round another bottle of wine and filling up her own glass when everyone except Stephen refused.

'Does anyone want the last one?' she asked. 'Barbara? Are you sure you won't have another?'

Almost imperceptibly, Barbara shook her head.

Charlotte shrugged. Then she ate the sausage.

The silence thickened.

Rosie said: 'It's getting quite late, isn't it? I think we'd better be going.'

She looked expectantly at Justin. He didn't reply.

'Well, it's been really good to see you all ...' She gestured at Stephen, who reluctantly put down his wine glass. They stood up.

The movement stirred Justin from whatever he was thinking.

'What? Where are you going?'

'Thank you so much for a lovely evening.'

'You can't go yet. We haven't had dessert.'

'Oh ... that's OK. You've fed us so well already ...'

'But I've made Lemon Tart!' Justin stood up. 'I'll go and get it.'

They faced each other for a few seconds before Rosie conceded. She gestured at Stephen. They sat down again.

No one made any attempt at conversation. They sat quietly until the tart was served, accepting slices like prisoners receiving their rations, then offered Justin subdued praise and chewed in glum silence.

It was pretty good, actually, Matt thought. Intense lemon curd flecked with bitter rind. Matt wasn't really hungry, but like the others he carried on eating; it was either that or feel obliged to say something.

Matt accepted another glass of wine and appraised the situation. As soon as they had got through a polite amount of tart, Rosie and Stephen would leave. That was obvious. Sarah and Marcus would probably go with them. Charlotte did not seem desperate to depart. It was pretty clear what she was thinking. Matt couldn't help feeling pleased by that. She caught his eye again. At the beginning of the evening, she wouldn't even look at him. But now the option was there. Last time had been OK. Good, even, in some respects. Enjoyable and uncomplicated.

Charlotte had almost finished her dessert. Barbara, though, hadn't eaten anything. Matt had been watching. She just reclined there, using her spoon to rearrange the tart in the bowl. At first she picked out all the bits of lemon zest, and arranged them in a ring round the edge. Then she flattened out the soft filling and scraped patterns on its smooth surface with her spoon. She concentrated fully on this, not looking up. As her neck craned forward, Matt could see tiny gold hairs sticking up along the exposed length of her spine.

He watched her for some time.

Barbara's dessert was now a dirty yellowish mush. She

looked at it, disgusted, as if seeing it for the first time. In one agile movement, she sprang to her feet, left the bowl on the floor, and made for the door. Everyone looked up to watch her leave.

Matt studied Justin's face. He could see the conflict there as Justin's eyes followed Barbara out of the room. He obviously wanted to go after her, but to do so would mean abandoning his guests and acknowledging that the pleasant convention of the dinner party had been irretrievably shattered.

Matt watched Justin reluctantly turn back. Social obligation had won out. He offered them seconds.

Matt made his decision quickly. There wasn't much time to think about it. He pulled his phone out of his jacket pocket as if feeling it vibrate, and squinted in exaggerated puzzlement at the screen. When Justin asked if he wanted more tart, he waited several seconds to reply, his attention seemingly focused on the message.

'No, thanks,' he said. 'I'd better just deal with this.'

Matt kept his eye on the screen as he left the room, and pulled the door shut behind him.

At first he thought he was too late. The hall was empty. Then the bedroom door opened and Barbara came out, a big canvas bag slung over her shoulder. She was startled to notice Matt waiting for her.

He gave a concerned smile. 'Are you OK?' he asked.

'I'm fine.' Her tone was curt.

'Good. I just wanted to check that everything was all right.'

'Yes.'

He looked at her for a moment, noticing how the canvas

strap cut across the edge of her left breast, forcing it inwards slightly.

But he could tell the silent interaction was making her increasingly uncomfortable. He gestured at the bag. 'Going somewhere?' he asked. 'Because if you're popping out to get us kebabs, don't let me stop you.'

There was a long silence. She didn't react in any way. He knew it was a gamble, but he thought he had judged the odds correctly. Matt let his eyes drift up from the bag to meet hers. Finally, despite a clear effort not to, she gave the ghost of a smile back at him.

'Sorry. Cheap crack, I know.' He raised his hands in apology. 'But I've got to say, it was a pretty impressive scene you made in there.'

'Yeah?'

'Absolutely.' Matt couldn't read her tone, so he pushed on. 'Unforgettable, I'd say.'

'I feel kind of stupid.'

'There's no need. Really. Crazy, maybe, but not stupid.'

She smiled a little more this time. 'You don't think I was being a bit of a brat?'

'No. It was riveting. It certainly beat listening to Rosie and Marcus talk about office politics.'

'I did pretty much wreck the evening, though.'

'I wouldn't say so. I've never seen Charlotte look so happy.'

Barbara looked troubled. Matt moved on.

'Tell me, though, why did you do it?'

Barbara was looking at the floor. 'I don't know.'

'Really?'

Barbara thought about it. 'I guess I just felt that I needed to. Sounds dumb, doesn't it?'

'No, no, I understand.'

'You do?'

'Sure. Sometimes you have to be direct about what you want. A bit of bluntness and, well, other people might get bruised, but at least they know where they stand.'

'You reckon?'

'Yes. The alternative is that you hang around getting caught up in what other people want, what they expect of you, and after a while it starts to choke you.'

'Yes,' Barbara said quietly.

'Definitely,' Matt said with great firmness. 'As long as you know what you want.' A pause stretched out between them. 'But you do, right?' Matt said.

Barbara adjusted the strap of her bag with both hands. Matt knew it couldn't be long before Justin cracked and came out. He might as well go for it.

He gestured at the bag again. 'So where are you going?'

'I don't know,' Barbara said.

Matt nodded and counted to three.

'Look,' he said. 'Don't take this the wrong way, but it seems like you need to get out of here, clear your head for a bit. So, if you want to, to give yourself a bit of space, you could come and stay at mine.'

She didn't react, and that was good. She was thinking about it. Matt counted another slow three seconds before he went on.

'As a friend, of course,' he clarified. 'I hope you don't think

I'm being inappropriate. It just seems like you need a bit of time to think things through. I've got a very good sofa bed, I'm at work all day, and you can have some time on your own.'

Slowly, Barbara picked her gaze off the floor and looked him in the eye. He couldn't read what was there. Her face seemed completely blank. Confusion, maybe, or just exhaustion.

She shrugged. 'OK.'

The door to the living room creaked open. Justin looked at them with a faint sense of worry.

'Everything OK?' he asked.

'Yes,' Matt said.

Justin remained there, in the doorway, his eyes flicking anxiously from one to the other, and settling on Barbara's bag.

'Barbara was just showing me where the bedroom lights are,' Matt said. 'She said I could go in there to make a phone call.'

'Oh right.' Justin began to move. 'Nothing serious, I hope?'

'No, I don't think so.'

'Right, then. I'm just going to put the kettle on for some tea. Would you like some? Or some coffee?'

'No, thank you.' Matt smiled.

Justin nodded and disappeared into the kitchen.

Matt pulled the front door quietly shut behind them.

Twenty-four

Barbara had to pause on the landing to feel in the dark for the light switch. In the quiet stillness she felt violently conscious of the jostling of thoughts in her head and the strange taste in her mouth. Her fingers found the switch and clicked it on. The sausage had been much stickier than she'd expected; a lingering meaty sweetness still coated her tongue with warm, slimy fat. It was unsettling. She couldn't tell if it was nauseating or delicious. She could make no sense either of the weird sluice of emotions passing through her body.

But at least she was feeling something, then doing something because of it. Getting out of the pitiful lethargy she'd sunk into. What a shitty week. She'd been angry with herself for being so pathetic, but she couldn't find a way to shake it off.

She started with Matt down the grubby stairwell. It wasn't planned. None of it was planned. The idea of eating the sausage had just presented itself in front of her, like ideas for making things used to do. It seemed so solid.

She didn't know if Charlotte was right about the ethics. That didn't matter. The act was provocative. That was what was important. That was where art began, right?

So she'd eaten it. Just to see what it felt like. And it had worked. She couldn't describe it, but it was definitely something. There were bad things in there – guilt, self-disgust. She still didn't really want to eat meat. But it was different. That was enough for the moment.

And now here she was, beneath the unforgiving fluorescent light in the hall, squeezed up against the wall by Matt's bulk as he opened the front door. He stepped back to let her go through first and she stepped awkwardly round him into the cool night air.

That was a surprise too. But she hadn't been shocked when he said it. It made sense. She couldn't stay there, go back into that room and pretend to make conversation. Maybe this wasn't the right thing to do. But it was different. Was it sharks that had to keep moving or die? That was how she felt.

Matt walked alongside her. She still wasn't really looking him in the eye, but under the softer light of the street lamps she felt more at ease. The night was clear, and Barbara could see a couple of stars piercing the orange glow. She shivered. Matt offered her his jacket and she took it.

'If we walk towards the main road, we can probably get a taxi,' he said. 'I'd call one but it might take a while out here.'

She nodded. As they walked on, she looked at Matt sideways, as if noticing who she was with for the first time. He was a big guy, clearly direct, and most people would say he was pretty hot. Barbara wasn't sure. There was something about the line of his jaw that she couldn't find attractive. But he was responsive, even if he was too obviously trying to say the right thing.

And he wasn't Justin. That was probably key here, she thought. Justin always tried to say the right thing too, but in a completely different way.

The turbulent whirl of half-formed emotions got faster. Barbara tried to back away from it. Not now. One thing at a time. She did love Justin, in many ways. He was well meaning, kind, committed, never demanding.

She had needed that, when she had arrived. He didn't ask anything of her, always deferred to whatever she wanted. The thing was, he didn't realize how annoying that could be. He could be passionate sometimes, sure, but when that happened Barbara always felt she was an extension of his work. The rest of the time, he was always trying to placate her.

It was almost like he was scared of her. Like she was some sort of exotic creature he could never hope to understand, but only try not to provoke. It was like when she'd first asked him out. He'd been stunned, and embarrassed, hardly able to stammer out a 'yes'. Some Englishmen liked to affect that sort of Hugh Grant awkwardness as a disguise for lust. Justin wasn't like that.

Matt wasn't like that either. He didn't disguise it at all. Barbara was clear-eyed enough to know what he was aiming at. All that 'as a friend' stuff was just meant to make it harder for her to say no. But what was her aim? She didn't know. Yes, she did. To get out of there. She'd done that now. She could deal with the rest of it later.

They crossed the street. Leaving behind the long terrace of

Victorian cottages on one side, they passed into the shadow of the cliff-like housing estate that lined the other side of the road, then turned into the High Road. A low gully of grimy neon stretched away towards Stoke Newington, selling fried chicken to men in tracksuits and the occasional straggling reveller.

Barbara suddenly realized she would miss the surly squalor of London if she left, the way aggression was kept in check by indifference. She still had the option of appeal. Justin's solicitor friend had said she could have a good case. But even when she had talked about it with Justin, Barbara knew she had no stomach for fighting to stay in the country. Leaving would be easier now anyway. She wouldn't need to explain herself to anyone. She stared down the road as the 76 bus went past, seeing the details as she did when she had first arrived. The small, uneven paving squares of the sidewalk, edged with those beautiful dimpled kerbstones, weathered and faded to a smooth, pinkish grey, like granite by the seashore. Even the wobbly trajectory of the double yellow lines, spindly streaks of yellow guarding the dark asphalt.

Matt craned up and down the road looking for a taxi, while Barbara watched the ebb and flow of the street. A man in a white puffa jacket threw a half-eaten kebab into the gutter. It burst out of its orange plastic box, spraying heavy chunks of sauce-coated lettuce under the wheels of a bus.

It wasn't too late to go back. Matt had ducked into a minicab office and was negotiating with a fat man behind the stripped-pine counter. She could just turn round, walk back into the flat, go to bed. Maybe she would feel different tomorrow. They could listen to the radio, go for a walk in Abney

Park and perhaps in the evening she could work on her appeal. There was still time.

Matt came out of the office and a tatty Ford Mondeo estate cruised round from a side street. He opened the door. Barbara hesitated a moment, then stepped into the dark, cocooning warmth. It smelled strongly of peppermint.

From: Rosie and Stephen <rosieandstephen@home.co.uk>
To: Dinner at Mine <dinneratminescores@gmail.com>
Sent: 23.34
Subject: Dinner

Dear Justin (and Barbara),
Thank you so much for dinner. I'm sorry we had to leave so soon. As we explained, we got an urgent call from the babysitter about Jonathan. Fortunately, when we got home everything was fine.

We both really enjoyed the stew. It made such a nice change to have something without meat in it. I'm glad that you like tamarind so much – I hope you gave us extra points when we served it to you! The aubergine starter was quite nice. Stephen enjoyed it. I found it a little heavy and bland, I'm afraid. I have to confess that I had rather lost my appetite by the time you served pudding, although I'm sure it was delicious.

I don't know if we're meant to mark you on the sausage. Stephen said it wasn't of a very high quality, so let's not.

You were certainly a very welcoming host, although I don't see how I can avoid taking off marks for a dinner party without a table. Also there were a couple of moments of tension which made it awkward for us, as I'm sure you noticed. I'm sorry to say that you lose points there as well. So it's six out of ten. Make it six and a half. I hope Barbara will be back soon.

Yours,

Rosie and Stephen

From: Charlotte Wells <charliewells2@gmail.com>
To: Dinner at Mine <dinneratminescores@gmail.com>
Sent: 23.54
<No Subject>

What happened there, then? Buggered if I know. I was almost tempted to stick around and see if she came back. But see, Rosie, I took the hint like a good girl! (Did you lot believe that line about the babysitter? No, me neither.) Anyway: fucking great. No, seriously, Barbara, wherever you are: genius. Most satisfying sausage I ever had. Woah, not like that! I don't know if I'll ever see you again, but always remember: the sausage was great. Don't let anyone tell you otherwise. Particularly not Justin. Sorry, veg-man. Anyway, you should be grateful. Frankly, the meal was going to get a pretty crap score otherwise. But that was just brilliant. The look on Justin's face! It made it even more delicious. Screw the rest of it, for me it was all about the sausage. Full marks. Score: 10

Sent from my iPhone

From: Marcus Thompson <marcusthompson@
            taylorwilsonpartners.com>
To: Dinner at Mine <dinneratminescores@gmail.com>
Sent: 00.36
Subject: Dinner scores

The aubergine cheesecake idea was a good one, even if the mixture had not been whipped enough to give it the fluffiness the concept demanded. However, the overall meal plan was unbalanced. It began with a dish that was too heavy, and that brought out the watery, bloating aspect of the stew. The tart was certainly a mistake after that.

The chickpea stew worked well enough within its limitations, but it would have benefited from an extra, thicker flavour to firm it up a bit. The chard was over-boiled (if it had been me, I would simply have stirred it in at the end), and I found that very disappointing. A vegetarian should at least be able to cook vegetables properly.

On the plus side, the salad was simple, fresh and effective. The contrast in textures between the chewiness of the grain and the crunchy radish was pleasing. What a pity about the soggy rice, though.

The problem with the tart was that it was too sweet. A lemon tart should never be too sweet. There was no sourness at all. It just wasn't – and I'm sorry but this is the word I want – very tart.

I didn't try the sausages, but I doubt they would have improved your score.

Score: 6

Marcus

Any information in this message is strictly confidential and intended solely for the person or organization to whom it is addressed. If you have received this message in error, please notify us as soon as possible and delete it and any attached files from your system.

From: Matthew Phillips <matthewphillips@
           newgreenchambers.co.uk>
To: Dinner at Mine <dinneratminescores@gmail.com>
Sent: 00.37
Subject: Dinner with Justin and Barbara: Assessment

Comments:
Food:
Starter: Good idea (aubergine cheesecake). Effectively done.
Main Course: Interesting range of ingredients. Chard not to my taste. Somewhat watery.
Salad: Satisfactory.
Sausage: Very welcome.
Dessert: Pleasurable. Good sweetness. Lacking any marks of excellence.
Wine: Substandard, even for Fairtrade. Variety unknown.

Hosting:
– Effort: Strong.
– Conversation: Lively, animated at times.
– Ambience: Tense but pleasing.
– Outcome: Excellent.

Scores:

Starter: 8

Main: 7

Salad: 7

Sausage: 9

Dessert: 8

Wine: 6

Hosting: 10

Overall average: 7

Matthew Phillips

Barrister

New Green Chambers

Sent from my BlackBerry®

Dinner at Marcus and Sarah's

Twenty-five

Rosie composed her face into an expression of sympathetic attentiveness as she waited for Justin to answer. It put her in the right frame of mind, even though he wouldn't be able to see her. The phone rang for a good twenty seconds, and Rosie thought she might get away with just leaving a message. But then a slightly breathless voice answered.

'Hello, Justin? It's Rosie here.'

'Oh.'

Rosie waited for him to go on, but he didn't. 'I hope I haven't caught you at a bad time?' she said.

'No, it's fine. I was just getting some work done.'

'On Saturday morning? That's very dedicated.'

'Well.'

Again Rosie expected more, but didn't get it. 'I'm sorry to interrupt,' she said.

'It's fine.'

Rosie couldn't read his tone, even over the landline, which she liked to use for socially or emotionally fraught conversations, because it was easier to hear the inflections in people's voices. His replies seemed terse, though. It was almost as if he was blaming her for what had happened.

No, that was ridiculous, of course. She was reading far too much into a few syllables. How on earth could it be her fault?

It had been a rather odd end to the evening. Everyone had just done their best to get on with it and drink their coffees, determinedly ignoring the conspicuous fact that both Barbara and Matt had disappeared. Rosie and Justin had sustained a discussion about which drinks kept them awake at night.

Rosie had decided to leave before it became absolutely clear that they were not coming back. Justin had made some mild protests, and she hardly needed to deploy the babysitter excuse to overcome them. The others had taken the hint. They all praised the meal as they left.

Rosie spent all of Sunday itching to find out what had happened. But was a bit too soon to phone, and she'd managed to get through Monday as well. On Tuesday she cracked. But Barbara hadn't picked up the phone.

Later, she tried calling Matt, but he didn't answer, even when she phoned from one of the phones at work that hid your number. She begged Stephen to try, but he, very unhelpfully, refused to get involved.

Rosie was disappointed with Matt. It was so rude, just to go off like that. Not even saying goodbye to your host? That was unforgivable.

Of course it made it worse that he had gone off with Barbara. It threatened to ruin the whole competition. And obviously Justin must be devastated.

Barbara, well, she was an artist, wasn't she? She was allowed to be unpredictable. That was why Rosie had decided to cultivate her. It was always nice to have an unconventional friend. But, as she should have realized, it came with risks.

It would have been much better if Barbara had run off with a sculptor or something. Then, Rosie thought, she could even invite them round for dinner without the others. It would be very interesting to talk to a sculptor. Not that she didn't like Justin, but he could be a little, well, single-minded, couldn't he? No, a sculptor would have been nice, or even some kind of poet, at a push.

Rosie had a nagging sense that the right thing to do would be to call the whole thing off now. It would be sensitive, tactful, and it would avoid any unpleasant confrontation.

But Rosie didn't want to. She wanted to win. In some ways, it would even be helpful if everyone was in a bad mood tonight, she thought. It would depress the scores. But there was no getting round it. She had to offer Justin the opportunity to cancel. Politeness demanded it. She must at least to be able to say she had asked.

Rosie gripped the phone tighter to her ear and prepared a way through the conversation.

'How are you anyway?' she asked.

'Fine.' Justin's voice was still toneless.

'Great. We both had a lovely time last week.'

'Oh. Really?'

'I know it must have been difficult for you, with Barbara and everything.' Rosie waited, hoping for a steer on how she should go on. But Justin's reaction was impossible to detect.

'Did she . . .' Rosie decided to go for it. 'Did she ever come back?'

'No.'

'Oh.' Rosie didn't know what to say next. She wished she hadn't been so blunt. 'Well, I am sorry. Did she say why?'

'No.'

'Gosh, so have you heard from her at all?'

'Yes.'

'What did she say?' Rosie knew this was nosy, but she couldn't help herself.

'She . . . well . . . it's hard to explain.'

'Of course. I understand,' Rosie said with disappointment. She left a sympathetic pause.

'Look, I've got some e-mails I need to send . . .' Justin began.

'Yes, sorry, I won't keep you. But I just wanted to ask you about tonight.'

'Oh?'

'I know it might be difficult with Barbara there. And Matt. Not together, I mean . . . I mean, I don't know anything about it, just that they'll both be there . . .' Rosie stopped herself, aware that she had begun to panic. 'So I suppose I just wanted to check if you were still OK to come tonight.'

Justin thought about it.

'We'd all understand perfectly if you wanted to cancel.'

'Well, I'm not sure that I'm up to it, even without, you know . . .'

'Of course. I understand. That's completely fair enough.' Rosie nodded in vigorous sympathy, more for her own benefit than Justin's.

'So I think, if that's all right, I'd prefer—'

'It's entirely up to you, as I said,' Rosie cut in quickly. 'I don't want to pressure you at all.'

'OK. So . . .'

'Of course, if you didn't come, we would have to abandon the whole competition.'

'Really? Couldn't you just not include me?'

'No, it wouldn't work, because you have to have the same people voting each time, otherwise it's meaningless.'

'Oh.'

'But it's only a silly competition. It doesn't matter at all. You have to do what you feel comfortable with.'

'Yes . . . I . . .'

'I know Marcus and Sarah will be disappointed, though, because they were planning something really special. It would be a shame to have to cancel.'

'Couldn't you . . .'

'I'm sure they'll understand, though. It's only a dinner party.'

'Yes.' Justin didn't say anything else.

Rosie pressed home her advantage. 'Although it would be such a pity to see everyone's effort go to waste,' she said. 'But I would never dream of twisting your arm if you don't want to come. You should put yourself first.'

Justin took a long time to respond.

'Actually,' he said. 'Now that I think about it, maybe I ought to come.' The phone stripped his words of all tone and emotion. Rosie thought this was probably just as well.

'Brilliant!' she said. 'I mean, are you sure?'

'I don't want to be selfish about it.'

'You don't have to come if you don't want to.'

'I'm sure it will do me good to get out.'

'Really?' Rosie said, sounding concerned.

'I suppose it will take my mind off things.'

'Well, as long as you're sure.'

'It will probably be good for me.' Justin breathed heavily into the receiver, sending a blast of static crackling down the line.

Rosie now felt confident enough to push it all the way. 'No, look – don't come,' she said. 'We'll be OK. I'm sure we'll work something out.'

'No, no, I'll come.'

'Great!' Rosie closed her eyes and made a silent fist of triumph. 'And you're sure you don't feel you're being pushed into it?'

'No, not at all. I want to come.'

'That's wonderful. I must say, it's very big of you. I'm not sure I'd be able to do it if I were you.'

Justin might have sighed, but it could have been another crackle on the line.

Twenty-six

Justin sighed as he put the phone down. But he quickly told himself not to be so self-pitying. It was true that he didn't want to go out for dinner, particularly not at Marcus's house, and absolutely not if Barbara was going to be there with Matt.

But he had made a commitment, and he could see that it was unfair to try to get out of it at the last minute. Justin hoped he hadn't seemed rude on the phone to Rosie. It was nice of her to call. Perhaps he should send her a text apologizing for being so unenthusiastic.

Justin looked at his laptop, a constellation of blue and white LEDs twinkling on the coffee table. But instead of reaching for it he slumped back on the sofa and stared listlessly out of the window. On the balcony of the flat opposite, drying laundry flapped slowly in an intermittent breeze. Justin did not in fact have any more work he needed to do. When Rosie rang, he had been composing an e-mail to the office IT Services department, making some suggestions about how they could improve the archiving of old messages in Outlook.

The previous Sunday, he had gone straight into the office, feeling immediately reassured by its calm emptiness. He spent the week working even harder than usual and finished his report sooner than he had anticipated. By Wednesday evening he had nothing left to do except clear his backlog of messages. He went in early on Thursday anyway, offering to help out on other projects. For a long time, he had been meaning to clarify his thoughts about the strategic direction of the organization, and spell out some ideas for future projects, so he set these down in a series of long e-mails to the chief executive.

No one wanted to go for a drink after work so, reluctantly, he went home in the evening.

Back at the flat, he immediately noticed that things were not as he left them. Someone had come in and moved them. For a brief, delighted moment, he thought Barbara was back and called out her name. The flat was silent. When he went into the bedroom, he found that her side of the wardrobe had been emptied. There was no note. In the living room, the iPod speakers were gone. Justin thought she had given him those as a birthday present.

The sofa was still pushed against the wall of the living room. Justin crumpled on to it. He didn't want to examine what he was feeling, staring at the ransacked room, but he had to admit to himself that worrying about his moral commitment had conveniently stopped him worrying about anything else.

He briefly tried to feel guilty in turn about using his conscience to distract himself, but it didn't work. He sat very still on the sofa. The beanbag still lay against the bookshelf, where Barbara had abandoned it on Saturday.

As soon as she had left, Justin had wanted to run out after her, stop her from disappearing and make her tell him what was wrong. But the coffee was brewing, and he had to go and push the plunger down. Otherwise it would have been stewed when he served it to the guests.

He was desperate for them to leave immediately, of course, but it was obvious they could see that, so he had to insist that they stay. No one spoke while they waited for taxis. Charlotte had taken the first one. It was while they were discussing who should take the next one that Justin realized Matt had not come back. The possible reason for this dawned slowly over the silent room, bleaching the awkward pause into something far starker. Goodbyes were said very quickly. Justin was left alone with his thoughts.

But he couldn't think about Matt. Even as he tried to, his mind was repelled as if by a magnetic field from the obvious conclusion, veering off instead to go over things he might have said to upset Barbara.

As soon as the front door shut he tried to call her, but the phone went to voicemail several times. After that he washed up very thoroughly.

Yes, he'd been annoyed with her at the start of the evening, but he hadn't let it show, had he? What had he said? If only he could go back, find out what it was, and apologize.

Justin tortured himself with this thought as the dishes built up in the drying rack. Usually when she stormed off she was back within a few hours. But this time . . . and Matt . . .

Justin had always suspected that Barbara might be out of his league. So there was no point thinking about this as anything other than his fault. Even so, what she had done with the sausages . . . it was unforgivable. But she wasn't there. She wasn't giving him a chance to forgive her.

With the casserole dish soaking in the sink, Justin went back to the living room and tried Barbara again. This time her phone was off.

On Sunday morning, she had sent him a text, saying she was OK. He had replied with six messages, all of them asking questions. He hadn't heard back.

And so, on Thursday evening, finding her clothes gone, he had turned round and gone back to the office.

All Friday, he had dreaded the weekend. As he sat on the sofa after ending the call with Rosie, the days stretched out ahead of him, trackless and terrifying.

Trying not to think about it, Justin roused himself from the sofa and went into the kitchen to make coffee. He hadn't used the pot since last Saturday, and behind it in the cupboard were his and Barbara's weekend bowls. They had been made by a friend of hers, and Barbara had decreed them too delicate for everyday use. This time on a Saturday morning, he and Barbara would usually be having a late breakfast, maybe reading the *Guardian* – him the foreign pages, her the magazine – or if the weather was good, going for a walk in Abney Park.

He took both bowls out of the cupboard, but filled only one of them with cereal. Very suddenly, Justin felt his eyes welling with tears.

Twenty-seven

'What a shame!' Rosie exclaimed as she opened the door to Sarah. 'You've just missed Jonathan. He's having a nap.'

'Oh dear.' Sarah stepped into the hallway. 'I'm sorry I'm a bit later than I said. I haven't seen him for ages. I don't want to wake him, though.'

Rosie smiled tightly at her. 'No,' she said.

Sarah wondered if she had been rude. Surely not, not with such a good friend. But she found it so hard to tell what you were and weren't supposed to say about other people's children. She pulled off her jacket, feeling an itchy patch of sweat under her clothes. It was one of those early spring days when it was too cold not to wear a coat when you left the house, but by late morning a jacket felt cumbersome and a little foolish.

Rosie took the jacket, got a hanger from the hall cupboard, hung it up, and closed the door. Sarah was always amazed at her discipline in keeping this up every time. Sarah would long ago have started piling them over the banister that protruded invitingly into the hall. As she waited, Sarah felt the slight awkwardness she always felt in Rosie's new house, as if at any point she might accidentally be ruining an expensive soft furnishing.

'I'm afraid we can't really sit in the living room,' Rosie said. 'Stephen's watching TV.'

'That's fine . . .'

'I'll just get him out to say hello.'

'Oh no, don't bother.'

Sarah wondered if this was impolite as well. She didn't mean it like that; she had always liked Stephen, actually, and felt he was a calming influence on Rosie. Maybe she should say something . . .

But Rosie was already leading her into the kitchen. Sarah leaned heavily against a worktop, taking some of the weight off her feet.

'Are you all right?' Rosie asked. 'You seem a bit tense.'

'No, I'm fine. Honestly.'

'So how was the school?' Rosie asked over her shoulder as she filled the kettle with water.

'Oh God!' Sarah exhaled.

'What?' Rosie turned away from the tap. 'Was it awful?'

'No. It was amazing.'

'Right. Oh.' Rosie put the kettle on to boil.

'The facilities! Unbelievable. They have their own theatre, tennis courts, a swimming pool. A second orchestra. Can you believe that? A second one.'

'That's great, isn't it?' Rosie replied. 'Normal, green or peppermint tea? We've got something with ginger in as well, I think . . .'

'Normal, please,' Sarah said firmly.

'You always said how much you enjoyed doing your drama club with the sixth formers. Until that thing with the police . . .'

'I did! And the students really got something out of it. But that's the thing, isn't it? Those kids don't get to do it any more. Of course Tyrone shouldn't have used the knife, but he was just trying to be realistic. And so now they've had drama taken away from them, what am I going to do? Am I just going to abandon them for richer kids who can put on a full production of *Hamlet*?'

Rosie nodded understandingly. 'Chinese, Ceylon or Darjeeling?' she asked. 'I've got some English Breakfast if you fancy something stronger.'

'Yes, English Breakfast, please.' Sarah watched Rosie carefully warm the teapot with hot water. China cups and saucers were laid out on a tray, and Rosie added a plate containing four biscuits. Sarah still made tea in the same chipped mug she had taken to university.

'So are you going to take the job?' Rosie asked.

'They haven't formally offered it to me yet. But I think they will.'

'And?'

'I don't know!' Sarah's voice rose to a wail. 'I mean, the pay's great, the boys are well behaved.'

'Then what's the problem?' Rosie poured the boiling water into the pot and took an Orla Kiely tea cosy out of the drawer.

'I feel I'd be abandoning my current students. And my

future ones. Just to go and teach rich kids. They really need me in Dalston. I feel like I'm making a difference. Am I going to walk out on that for an easier life?'

Rosie nodded and picked up the tray. 'Shall we have this in the dining room?'

Sarah followed her out of the kitchen. From the living room she heard a burst of gunfire, followed by rapid dialogue from Stephen's cop show. Rosie walked quickly past the closed door.

'I see your dilemma,' Rosie said as she poured the tea. 'But you do keep saying how much the school has been getting to you recently. How tired you are . . .'

'I know, but—'

'How your energy and enthusiasm have gone, the kids are getting harder to control . . .'

'But that's—'

'How you've started dreading going in in the mornings . . .'

'Yes, but—'

'It's OK to need a change from that.'

Sarah put both hands round her cup and drank, breathing in dense fronds of steam. It took her a while to reply.

'Do you know what I asked myself as I was walking round the school?' she said. '"What would Justin do?"'

Rosie's brow creased. 'Justin?'

'Yes. It seemed like a good way to measure these things. He's committed and engaged in the world. What would he do?'

Rosie looked puzzled. 'I can't say I've thought about it.'

'I mean, I was wondering if he'd ever been tempted to leave his charity and go to work for a consultancy or a lobbyist or something like that.'

'I don't ...'

'But he wouldn't, would he? He knows what's important in a career – not money, status or a cushy time, but the knowledge that you're making people's lives better.'

'Does he?'

'It's not a matter of selling out, you see? It's about knowing that what you have is more valuable than money.'

'Have you talked to him about it?'

Sarah was taken aback. 'No. I mean, I ... I haven't spoken to him since last week. Since ...'

Rosie tutted. 'Yes, that was a shame, wasn't it? So rude of Matt. I do hope it's all right this evening.'

'I felt so bad for Justin.' Sarah put the cup down with a clatter. 'He's such a lovely guy. He didn't deserve that.'

'No, he didn't.'

'But he reacted so well to it, didn't he?'

'He's certainly been very understanding.'

'Other men would have treated that as a total humiliation. But he was so calm and dignified. Do you think he's OK?'

'Well, he said he was fine this morning.'

Sarah's hand missed her cup as she reached for it. 'Really? You've spoken to him?'

'Yes. I had to check if he was coming tonight.'

'And is he?' Sarah picked up the cup carefully.

'Yes, he's coming.'

'That's just like him, isn't it?'

'Is it?'

'The nobility of it . . . the ability to rise above his own concerns and focus on what other people want.'

Rosie broke a biscuit in half.

'Maybe he's too understanding for his own good sometimes,' Sarah went on. 'I mean, he should be angry with Barbara, shouldn't he? She behaved appallingly! To casually insult your partner like that, in front of everybody, then walk off! And that's even without whatever might have happened between her and Matt.'

'Well, I think they did, don't you?' Rosie leaned forward excitedly. 'Have you tried to phone her? I did, but she wouldn't answer. If you—'

'I can't help feeling guilty about the whole situation. If I hadn't brought Barbara into this thing, she would never have met Matt, and it would never have happened.'

'Yes, but have you spoken to her? Did she . . .'

'Oh no, I didn't think it would be right.' Sarah couldn't understand the eagerness in Rosie's voice. 'We need to show our disapproval. I mean, I always forgave her being a bit moody sometimes because of her "artistic temperament" and so on. But that doesn't excuse this, does it? That might work if you're Gauguin or someone and you're providing something of value to civilization. But Barbara's pots. Well . . .'

'I've always quite liked them.'

'Yes, they're fine – maybe enough to excuse persistent lateness when we meet for coffee, or long silences at dinner parties. But not this.'

Rosie seemed impatient with this aspect of the discussion.

'Yes, but do you think anything actually happened?' she asked with renewed enthusiasm. 'Did she and Matt . . . ?'

'I don't want to think about it! It makes me feel so bad for Justin.'

'No, but—'

'And I really do want to know what he would think about this job. I mean, I was wondering what he would say when they showed me photos of the school trip to Mount Kilimanjaro. Is it good that privileged kids are seeing Africa and raising money for the less fortunate? Or are they just using Africa as a backdrop? I mean, think of the carbon emissions. Rosie, what do you think Justin would say?'

Rosie leaned back in her chair. 'I really don't know.'

'I just feel like he'd have something humane to say about the whole thing. Wise, even. I wish could talk to him about it.'

Rosie fiddled uncomfortably with the tea-strainer. 'How's Marcus?' she asked.

Sarah was surprised by the question. 'Marcus? Oh he's fine.'

'Good.' Rosie poured them both more tea. 'And what does he think of your dilemma?'

'He can't take it seriously at all! He just laughs and says it's obvious I'd enjoy myself more if I took it, so I should just get over myself.'

'Mmm,' Rosie said carefully, taking a small bite of her biscuit.

'God, he's been disgusting about the whole competition thing.'

'Really?'

'Yes, he laughed all the way home last week. Taking the piss out of Justin and his taste in wall hangings.'

'They were quite ...'

'We had a bit of a row about it. The taxi driver even had to turn up the radio. But Marcus isn't sorry at all. That's his problem, though; he only seems to enjoy himself when he's looking down on someone.'

'Surely not,' Rosie muttered.

Sarah had always suspected that Rosie secretly thought this too. 'Don't get me wrong,' she said. 'He wasn't always like this. I mean, yes, he was always competitive – remember when we played that game of Trivial Pursuit at Stephen's birthday?'

Rosie shivered slightly.

'But at least then he could see he was being ridiculous, and laugh about it afterwards. You can't imagine how he's been about this dinner! I dread to think what he's doing at the moment. And if I try to say anything, he just snaps at me.'

Rosie shifted in her chair. 'What are you cooking tonight?'

'I don't even know. It's like he doesn't want me to get involved.' Sarah looked at her watch. 'But I'd better go back and offer to help.' She sighed. 'Otherwise I'll be blamed for that as well.'

Rosie smiled uneasily. Sarah could tell the conversation was putting her on edge. She had always felt that Rosie didn't like Marcus, and now that Sarah was moaning about him a bit, she probably wasn't sure if she could join in. Yes, that must be it.

'See you tonight,' Rosie said as she retrieved Sarah's jacket from the cupboard.

'I'm sorry I missed Jonathan,' Sarah replied.

'Next time.'

'See you later, then. It'll be great to see how Justin's getting on tonight, won't it?'

Rosie gave her that brittle smile again on the way out.

Twenty-eight

Matt sprinted through the outer gate and ran flat-out across the courtyard, holding his breath as he pushed himself as fast as he could towards the main door.

It began to open as he approached, and he had to jink sideways to avoid colliding with a young mother in a flowing headscarf, who shrank away in shock as she came out of the block, hurrying away with her two children.

Matt caught the door before it shut, hurled himself through it and let his momentum crash into the front of the lift. He reached out his hand to steady himself against the wall, panting heavily as his breathing tried to catch up with his pulse. He sank down so that the other hand rested on his knee, supporting the weight of his body, trying to bring his breathing under control. Matt could feel his heart rate still rising from the shock of the sudden acceleration, and forced himself to take deep, slow breaths until he felt the frenzied pumping level off and begin to subside.

Sometimes Matt would jog all the way up the stairs to his

flat, but his ankle was aching and he could feel the beginning of a stitch. In the lift he crouched over, both hands on his knees, waiting for his ragged breaths to even out. It seemed to take longer each time. Today it wasn't until the thirteenth floor that he could stand upright. Last year, it had been the tenth.

Matt resented having to go out running at all. He disliked the process: the undignified sweatiness, the time wasted warming up and cooling down, wearing shorts. But much more than that, he resented having become someone who had to make an effort to keep fit. That had happened only recently, and Matt knew it was a sign of age. He would notice it the day after a big dinner or a heavy night – sometimes even without them – when he would be climbing up an escalator on the tube and find himself out of breath by the time he got to the top. It wasn't anything dramatic. No one watching would have spotted it, but there it was, a sudden tightening in the chest, like a cold hand clamping round his windpipe. That had never happened when he was younger, however much he had been eating or drinking. But now he was forced to think about how fatty Marcus's cooking might be tonight.

Matt hoped he would enjoy the clean, measurable progress of running, disciplining himself to go further and faster. But the principle of personal improvement could not disguise the clammy reality of puffing uncomfortably along the pavement, dodging round groups of shoppers. And anyway, he didn't go out often enough to build up any sense of progress, instead bingeing on miles between weeks of inactivity.

The lift reached the top floor and Matt let himself into his flat, immediately flushed by the warmth in the hall. Had she turned the heating on? He pulled off his sweatshirt and put away his trainers in the hall cupboard before going to look. But the flat was empty and the boiler was idling. Perhaps it was colder outside than he thought.

Matt did a few perfunctory stretches and got into the shower. When he came out, he spent a bit longer squatting and flexing, but he knew it was useless. Whatever he did, he would be aching in the morning.

Dressed, he went into the living to look through his reference books. A precedent had occurred to him while out running and he wanted to look up the details before he forgot.

To get to the bookshelf he had to step over a scarf trailing between the sofa and the coffee table, and he exhaled testily as his foot was briefly caught in it. The book wasn't there. He snatched up the scarf with a flash of irritation.

The floor round the sofa was strewn with sweaters, a shirt and several bits of underwear. It pissed him off. Last night, and the night before, he had ignored it. Now he cracked. Matt went round the room picking them all up, feeling an ache in his lower back every time he bent over.

It was annoying verging on humiliating to be picking up after her, like some kind of domestic help. Matt folded the clothes into a rough pile and dumped them on top of the suitcase in the corner that he had designated her area, noticing a stray sock as he did so and gathering that up as well.

This wasn't really what he'd had in mind last Saturday. Where was Barbara now anyway? Perhaps it was time to talk about what was going to happen next.

Last Saturday had been good, though. Maybe not great, but definitely good. They had got back and Matt had persuaded her first to have a drink, then to tell him what was wrong. She didn't want to at first, but they had just been sitting there staring at each other, clearly past the point of polite conversation, but with nothing else to say. So after a while she had told him about the difficulties with her work, with her visa, with Justin. She'd got quite emotional in the end, particularly after her second glass of whisky.

Matt had found it moderately interesting to begin with – he had never heard anyone get animated about their frustrations with the medium of clay before. He had watched the way her body tensed as she got worked up about a point.

After a while the anger had dissipated, and when Matt could see tears on their way he moved over to the sofa and sat next to her, putting a sympathetic arm round her shoulder.

And it was good too, when it came. It had that tear-stained urgency that rarely disappointed.

Why had he done it? Well, apart from the obvious. He hadn't planned it, not exactly. He had thought about it, yes. But he hadn't planned it. There was a significant distinction to be drawn. It wasn't premeditated. He hadn't gone to Justin's flat with the intention of seducing Barbara. But the opportunity had presented itself. Matt didn't think of himself as impulsive. It was important to weigh up the pros and cons of any course of action. But if you'd done that in advance, it was much easier to act on instinct.

He'd got over the Sunday morning embarrassment with breakfast in bed. He'd brought the tray in just as she was waking up and looking round the room, and he saw the brief flash of panic in her eyes as she tried to work out where she was. As she realized, they dulled to an awkward sheepishness that stopped just short of regret.

'I've made you coffee,' he said. 'I thought you'd prefer it, but there's tea if you want.'

'Thanks. Coffee's good.'

'It's not very elaborate, I'm afraid. I hadn't stocked up. But if there's anything you particularly want I can go down to the Brazilian shop and get it.'

'No, this is great.' Barbara sat up against the pillows, pulling the duvet round herself. Matt put the tray down next to her and sat down on the edge of the bed.

'I'm going to have this toast before it gets cold, but I've brought cereal in as well if you'd like some.'

'Thanks,' Barbara said. She made no move to eat anything as Matt bit into his toast. 'Look, Matt, about last night—'

'I've cut up some fruit for you. I don't know if apple, banana and bits of a satsuma go together, but it's there if you want it.'

'OK. Thanks.' She looked at the tray, but didn't take anything.

'Here, I'll do it for you. Want a bit of everything?' He added yoghurt and chopped fruit to the bowl of bran flakes and handed it to her with a spoon.

Hesitantly, she began to eat. To hold the bowl, she had to let go of the duvet, and it began to slip slowly down, uncovering the top of her left breast. Matt forced himself not to stare.

They chewed in easy enough silence for a while. When

they caught each other's eye, he held out the coffee cup. She smiled and nodded.

'It's looking nice outside,' Matt said. 'Maybe later we could go down to Exmouth Market, or walk along the canal or something?'

'Yes, sure.'

'Great. Do you want butter and jam on your toast?'

Barbara nodded and handed him back her empty bowl. She swallowed the last mouthful and thought deeply for a while.

'Listen, Matt, I just want to—'

'It's raspberry, is that OK? I think I've got some apricot or something somewhere, although it's probably out of date by now. But I think that's OK with jam. I don't seem to have any marmalade. Remind me to buy some if we go out.'

He handed her a plate. When she was just over halfway through her toast, Matt stood up to move the tray. As he did so, he deliberately let his crooked elbow jog Barbara's. The plate flipped out of her hand and landed raspberry side down on the duvet.

'Shit, sorry!' she said.

'No, that was my fault.' Matt put the tray down and picked up the toast, leaving a sticky smear across the sheet. 'It'll come off. Would you like another piece?'

'No. I'm good.'

Matt pulled the duvet down further to inspect the stain. Barbara reluctantly let it slide. He looked up at her, grinning. 'I should probably get it off and into the wash, though. Just to be on the safe side.'

'Really?' She looked sceptically at him.

'Just to be on the safe side.' He stared at her body emerging from the folds.

In one quick movement, Matt whipped off the duvet, letting it settle on the floor behind him. He made no move to take it away. Barbara stayed where she was too, naked and poised against the pillows.

Later, when Barbara complained she was cold, Matt retrieved the duvet from the floor. No more was said about the jam stains.

Barbara went back to sleep for an hour or two, so Matt got up to do some work in his cramped study. The problems quickly absorbed him. Until he heard the shower running, he forgot all about her.

She came into the study fully dressed and serious.

'Listen, Matt, I need to make something clear.'

'Do you want some lunch?'

'No. I—'

'Are you sure? I can make some avocado salad or something.'

'No. I should go.'

'Where to?'

She stood staring at him, legs placed firmly apart as if braced for a fight.

'I don't know,' she said.

'Why don't you stay here tonight, then?' he said. 'You know, as a friend?'

She laughed sharply. 'Yeah, "as a friend".' She studied his face. 'I feel like I don't know anything about you.'

'What do you want to know?'

'I don't . . .' She seemed taken aback by the question, and fell silent for a moment as she thought about it. 'OK, your accent. Where's it from?'

'I grew up in a small village outside Preston.'

'Oh,' she said. 'Where's that?'

'It's in Lancashire,' he said. 'The north. Have you been up there?'

'I went to the Yorkshire Dales once.' She pronounced it York-shyer.

'Right. Where are you from?'

'A bunch of places. We moved around a lot.'

There was a short pause.

'You're a lawyer, right?' she said.

'Yes.'

'Do you defend criminals and that kind of stuff?'

'No.'

She stood staring at him for a few seconds and he sat staring back.

'Are you sure you don't want any lunch?'

'OK then.'

She'd insisted on going shopping and had come back an hour later and made some kind of complicated salad. Matt decided it was probably best not to bring up the question of meat. He didn't want to ask about her pots either, which left the conversation pretty stilted. In the end they talked about Pilates for the first half of the meal and the persistence of courtroom wigs for the other.

Matt didn't normally bother with the Sunday papers, but

after lunch he went out and bought both a *Sunday Times* and an *Observer*, barricading himself behind the news sections in the living room. Barbara tried one of the magazines for a while, before going to her bag and getting out a book called *How to Believe in You*. Matt raised the paper a little bit higher.

In the evening, Matt had found an unopened box set of *The World at War*, given to him by an aunt last Christmas. When they went to bed after that, Matt discovered that Barbara had found some of his old pyjamas.

Waking on Wednesday, he discovered that Barbara was asleep on the sofa. He left before she woke up and she stayed on the sofa after that, filling the living room with clothes and accoutrements that had appeared from somewhere.

Which was why Matt found himself on Saturday morning folding up a Merino cardigan and putting it next to a hair-dryer whose cord he had just wound round the handle. He had barely spoken to Barbara since last Sunday. Neither of them had made much of an effort to change that. It already seemed fairly clear to Matt that, whatever there was between them, it was fizzling out.

Yet she was still there. Matt did not know what to do about this. He considered it as he tried to fit Barbara's belongings into the suitcase that had appeared on Thursday. There was no way he could tell her to leave. Even subtly. He had already received a very disapproving e-mail from Rosie on Tuesday, which he had ignored. If Barbara was forced out of his flat in fury or, even worse, in tears, Rosie would probably feel she shouldn't forgive him.

Feeling a rumble of hunger, Matt remembered he had not

had any breakfast, and went into the kitchen to make some lunch. In the fridge he found some packaged salami, which he laid out on a plate, garnishing it with a few slices of Cheddar. Barbara had packed out the salad drawer, so Matt chopped up some tomato, cucumber and lettuce, adding a handful of bean sprouts and plenty of dressing.

A thought came to him as he turned the problem over, looking at it from all angles. He had been looking for ways out of the final dinner, from the obviously fake illness to some more exotic, and therefore more plausible, excuse. Or even just pressure of work. That was one that everyone found annoying and tried to persuade you out of, but couldn't, ultimately, argue against.

But if they went, if he made Barbara come with him, there was a chance Justin would try to get her back. Not a certainty, knowing Justin, but at least a possibility.

And he might succeed. Barbara clearly wasn't having the time of her life here. If she went, Matt thought, he would also be a wronged party. That would nullify criticism for what had happened so far. It seemed like the perfect solution, really. Matt felt pleased with himself. He added another slice of salami to his plate.

In the hall, a key scraped in the lock, and Matt heard light footsteps in the hall. They went straight past into the living room. He had never given her a key, and wasn't sure where she had found it. It seemed rude to ask.

'Hello,' he called out.

The footsteps approached the kitchen.

'Hi,' Matt said.

'Have you seen my blue sweater?' Barbara asked.

'Did you leave it on the sofa? It's probably in the suitcase. I tidied up.'

Barbara tutted, turned, went over to the living room, and came back wearing the sweater. Matt pictured the clothes that had been stacked above it scattered across the carpet again.

'I'm making some lunch,' Matt said. 'Do you want any?'

Barbara looked at his plate. 'What are you eating?'

'It's just cold meat, cheese and salad.'

'I'll take some salad.'

Matt chopped up some more tomatoes. He still hadn't raised the question of meat. Barbara had not asked for or eaten any. He couldn't help but be disappointed.

He set the plate on the table and they sat down facing each other.

'Where did you go this morning?' Matt asked.

'I was out.'

'I know. I was interested what you've been doing.'

'I went to hot yoga.'

'What's that?'

'It's like regular yoga, but you do it in a sauna.'

'Oh.' Matt ate a slice of salami. 'Why?'

'It flushes the toxins out of your body.'

'I see,' Matt said.

Barbara prodded the lettuce with her fork. 'What's the dressing on here?'

'Just a bit of oil and vinegar.'

Barbara ate a lettuce leaf. In the high stillness of the flat, Matt could hear the snap and crunch of the stalk between her teeth. He watched her cut another leaf in half, shake off the oil, and eat it without any apparent pleasure.

Matt felt obliged to look away so that they didn't catch each other's eye. They chewed silently for a while. There was no tension in the room, just a faint ambience of irritability.

In the end, Barbara spoke. 'So I guess you just worked this morning?'

'I went for a run.'

'How far did you go?'

'To Highbury and back.'

'How far is that?'

'A couple of miles.'

'What was your time?'

'I wasn't really counting.'

Did she snort slightly at that? Barbara looked down at her plate, perhaps feeling her duty was done. Matt got up and cut himself a slice of bread. He silently offered one to Barbara, but she shook her head.

Matt sat down again, hearing the chair legs scrape across the lino. 'About tonight,' he said. 'I told them we'd be there about seven thirty.'

'Tonight?' Barbara looked up sharply. 'What's tonight?'

'Dinner at Marcus's house. You hadn't forgotten?'

'I assumed we wouldn't go to that.'

'Well, I see what you mean, but I said we'd go, and it would spoil the competition if we didn't.'

'I think they would understand.' Barbara ate another piece of lettuce.

'You'd be surprised,' Matt said, mopping up the dressing

on his plate with a hunk of bread. 'Anyway, I've been working all week and I want to go out.'

'You go, then. I'll stay here.' Barbara pushed away her plate, as if suddenly disgusted by the three remaining lettuce leaves.

'I know you don't want to see Justin' – Barbara recoiled slightly at the name – 'but you have to do it sometime.'

'No, I don't.'

'And it would probably be best to do that on neutral ground,' Matt pressed on.

'You go if you want. Say I'm ill or something.'

Matt ate a bit of bread and tried another tack. 'He probably won't be there anyway, you know. Would you go, if you were him? He's probably practising his sick voice now.'

Barbara didn't smile. 'He'll go,' she said firmly.

'I can't think why he'd want to.'

'He won't want to. That's why he'll go. He'll see it as a duty.'

Matt hadn't thought of it like that. But it would explain why, when he'd texted Stephen to ask, he'd been so certain that Justin was coming.

'All right, then. But look, if you don't want to go, and Justin doesn't want to go, and you're both free tonight, why don't I ask him to come over here?'

Barbara jerked her head up. 'Jesus, no!'

'OK, it was just a suggestion. We don't have to. I just think it might be good for you.' He leaned forward across the table and reached out a hand towards her. 'I know you're feeling vulnerable at the moment . . .'

She flinched as his hand touched hers. 'No, I'm not.'

Matt grinned at her. Barbara stared down at the table, but after a while he could see she was trying not to smile.

'It's entirely understandable,' he said, keeping his hand where it was. 'I know you needed some time on your own to think things through. But I get the sense that you still aren't sure what to do.'

Barbara's smile faded.

'But look, if you don't want to have a heart to heart with Justin about everything, isn't it better to see him with other people around, so that things don't get too deep? You don't even need to speak to him. There'll be enough of us there. Just come along and use it as a chance to assess things. Observe.'

'I don't need . . .'

'I think it might be very helpful. Seeing him on safe territory, interacting with other people, will give you a better idea of what you want.'

Barbara looked up. 'Yeah?'

Matt squeezed her hand then pulled back. 'I honestly think it will help.'

Barbara studied his face. She didn't say anything. After a few moments, she got up and walked out of the kitchen. Matt was left to put her dirty plate into the sink.

Twenty-nine

Marcus swung his shopping bag on to the kitchen table, listening to it squelch satisfyingly against the wood. The fabric of the bag settled around the domed head of its contents, and a thin, salty dribble of seawater oozed out of the bottom of the bag. Marcus watched with pride as it collected into a briny pool by the pepper pot.

Leaving the bag where it was, Marcus chose four King Edward potatoes from the cupboard, washed and peeled them. Even the slight bluntness of the potato peeler did not dull his good mood. It was barely eleven o'clock and the shopping was done, the finest ingredients gathered from around the city. He had cleared the rest of the day to cook, and the process was planned out step by step. Any one of the dishes he was about to make would be the best the competition had seen; together, they were going to be spectacular. Marcus had always been confident he was going to win, but he had now moved beyond that. He now knew that if he did not, his defeat would simply devalue the whole contest.

From the fridge, Marcus took out some salt cod that had been soaking for three days. He had always been irked by those recipes that began with instructions like 'Take out the beans that have soaked overnight'. Yet now he was making one, he could appreciate the satisfying pleasure of being able to retrieve something he had prepared and put in the fridge on Wednesday. Every day since, he had changed the water it had been soaking in, getting a warm glow as he did so.

Marcus dried the cod tenderly and fried it over a low heat with the potatoes he had now mashed. It formed a thick, fishy paste, which he sampled and approved before setting it aside. Reaching round the bulbous head in the shopping bag, he took out the quails' eggs.

The local butcher had been selling these for years, and it had always annoyed Marcus that he never had a use for them. Now he lowered them reverently into boiling water. He gave them three minutes, then fished them out and put them aside to cool, as instructed, in a bowl of white wine vinegar. Several cracked immediately. He tried to peel them, but accidentally ripped the first two in half as he pulled at the shell. He slowed down, wishing he did not bite his fingernails. Chipping painstakingly at each shell, he became irritated at the fiddliness of the task, but the feeling was outweighed by satisfaction at leaving himself so much time for it.

Even so, half of the eggs were ruined. This was a shame, obviously, but there was something about the old-fashioned wantonness of destroying quails' eggs that somehow pleased him. It made him feel like a particularly sybaritic French president.

The final stage owed more to *Play School*. He scooped up a wad of the cod mixture in his left hand and balled it liberally round each good egg. There we are, first dish completed. Salt Cod Scotch Eggs. He put them in the fridge to fry later.

Marcus decided to make himself a cup of coffee before moving on to the oxtail. He tamped down the Illy in the percolator to exactly the same level as usual and put it over a medium heat on the back burner. He didn't feel especially tired, even though he had been up for five hours already. Perhaps it was knowing that everything was going perfectly so far.

Marcus didn't have a local fishmonger. Normally this bothered him only in an abstract sense. He'd considered phoning the one in Islington that was always in the papers, but then thought how much better it would sound if he was able to say casually, 'This? Yes, it should be fresh – I picked it up at Billingsgate Market this morning.'

Which was why his alarm had gone off at six o'clock and he had pulled himself out of bed with Sarah groaning semi-consciously beside him. Marcus was usually an early riser at weekends anyway; once he was awake, however briefly, things started turning over in his mind and he could not go back to sleep. His usual Saturday ritual was to leave Sarah snoring and go downstairs to make himself a cup of coffee and read *The New Yorker*, to which he had a subscription.

Instead, he downed a quick shot of espresso before heading out to one of the car club bays round the corner. Once he was outside, Marcus always enjoyed being up early. The peaceful, empty streets gave him a sense of being ahead of everyone else. He let himself into a hatchback with his touch card, set up the satnav and, with almost no traffic, was pulling into the stolid shadow of Canary Wharf in less than forty minutes.

Billingsgate Market squatted almost resentfully beneath the high, gleaming blandness of the Barclays and HSBC towers. Marcus delighted in the juxtaposition as the boxy glass buildings cast long shadows over the market in the early morning light.

The morning's peace was shattered as soon as Marcus entered the market, the icy air filled with shouting and the squeal of rubber on wet concrete. Marcus stopped to get his bearings. A porter pushing a trolley of prawns barged past him, swearing under his breath. Marcus was too taken aback to respond, and even more aghast when he realized that the porter had called him a 'fucking tourist'.

He decided to keep moving. The stalls were all the same: thick banks of white polystyrene crates laid out in long rows beneath the cavernous corrugated roof. Marcus hurried quickly between them, not wanting to dawdle and stare at the amazing variety of fish in case he was taken for a gawper on a coach party. He was there, like everyone else, to buy some rare fresh seafood at a reasonable price.

After a while the fish all began to look the same. Row upon row of glazed eyes set in shimmering rainbow flesh. Marcus walked up and down each row several times. Eventually he thought he saw what he needed tucked away at the back of a stall. He craned round to look as he went past.

'Watch where you're fucking going!'

Marcus jerked back round to see that he was about to

collide with a fat man carrying a tray of eels. He threw himself backwards as the man kept moving, staggering until he heard a loud splash below him.

Marcus felt freezing water begin to seep over the top of his Campers. He yanked his foot out of the puddle, but too late to stop the dampness spreading through his right sock.

Somewhere off to his left he heard someone laughing.

Marcus shook the loose water off his shoe. This was good. It was real. It showed this was still a proper, working market, not just a tourist attraction.

Marcus looked at the stall again. There it was. He was right. It was definitely an octopus. The stallholder held it up for him to inspect. Close to, it was slightly wizened, and the row of suckers down one tentacle was missing.

But that was OK, because it gave Marcus the opportunity to ask the question he had been looking forward to all morning.

'Have you,' he asked as matter-of-factly as he could, 'got any of the Mediterranean double-suckered variety?'

The stallholder did not blink.

'No, mate,' he said, as if it was a perfectly ordinary question. 'We had some earlier, but they all went. Got to get here early. Last of the day's catch, this. Give it to you half price.'

'No, thanks.'

Marcus walked away, his success hollow. He knew he should have got up earlier. To wake up at six and still come home empty-handed because you'd left it too late would be infuriating.

He tramped up and down the stalls. Maybe he should try

something else. Maybe one of the eels. He stopped in front of the stall. He could do it in aspic with paprika or something. A Spanish-inflected version of jellied eels. That would be good. They'd have to be impressed by that. Marcus peered closer into the beast's gaping jaw, ringed with tiny sharp teeth.

He couldn't help being slightly intimidated by it. It looked complicated. He didn't have a recipe for eel, and how easy would it be to find one?

But no, it was too high risk. If you were going to serve people eel, you really couldn't afford to fuck it up. You'd look ridiculous. Marcus walked on.

What about some of these other ones? He studied a fat, aggressive-looking fish with a pilot light above its eyes. It lay on its side on top of a crate of smaller, silvery fish as if it had personally landed them all itself.

But who knew what it would taste like? And what was the point of buying something like that if by the time it was cooked it was basically indistinguishable from cod?

Some of the stalls were beginning to pack up now, and the waft of rotting stock began to cut through the salty freshness. Marcus twice had to jump back sharply as traders sluiced down the concrete with buckets of water, sending heads, fins and bones skittering towards the drain.

Marcus did a last tour of the perimeter. If all else failed, he could just get some swordfish. As long as they gave him the sword, it would still look impressive enough.

Then, in the far corner of the market, Marcus found a man putting six small octopuses into a box. With a small but definite thrill, Marcus saw that they had two rows of suckers running up each tentacle.

'Are these Mediterranean ones?' he asked.

'Yeah, mate. Can't you see their beach towels?'

Marcus grinned politely. Banter. Right.

'Just as well I didn't ask anything about double suckers, then!'

The man stared at him blankly. 'Do you want them or not?'

'How much is it for one?'

'Six for fifty pounds.'

'But I only want one.'

'It's bulk here. Six is minimum. Give them to your friends.'

Marcus looked at the tentacles laid out in the box. Could he freeze them? How often, realistically, would he feel like defrosting an octopus?

'Come on . . . mate,' Marcus said, tripping over the unfamiliar word. 'You're clearing up for the day. You're not going to sell any otherwise. I'll take that fat one there.'

The man sighed. 'Twenty-five quid for one, then. But hurry up about it.'

Marcus hesitated. Was that a lot? Should he try to bargain? Was that insulting? Or would the man think he was an idiot if he didn't haggle? He wished he'd Googled all this etiquette earlier. It was too late to get out his iPhone now.

'That's a bit steep,' he said. 'How about fifteen pounds?'

'Twenty-five, mate. Take it or leave it.'

Marcus girded himself. The principle was established now. 'Twenty, then. Split the difference.'

The man paused, nodded, picked up the octopus and held out his hand. Marcus put a twenty-pound note in it, and the man thrust the octopus at him. It dripped seawater on to the concrete.

'Have you got anything to put it in?'

The man sighed again, but found a plastic bag, which Marcus wrapped carefully round the octopus before putting it in his canvas tote.

Walking away from the stall, Marcus swung the bag almost jauntily. The morning was a success. The squelch in his shoe didn't matter any more, because there was an octopus in his bag. How many other people could say that before eight o'clock on a Saturday morning?

As planned, Marcus headed for one of the cafés round the edge of the market to reward himself with breakfast. It had plastic tables with plastic chairs bolted to the floor, which normally would have made Marcus leave immediately, but here, he decided, it counted as authenticity. He ordered some strong tea, because he felt he should, and kippers with scrambled eggs. He had been looking forward to this bit too, hoping to be able to say to people in the future: 'You should try it. It's London's version of eating sushi at Tokyo central fish market.' So even though he actually found the kippers disappointingly greasy, he persuaded himself that this must be because they were so fresh.

Leaving just under half on his plate and his tea more or less untouched, Marcus went back to the car and drove west. There was a bit more traffic about now, but it was still before nine thirty when he arrived in Finsbury Park.

He parked the car in a side street and consulted the scrap of paper on which he had written the address. It guided him past a row of off-licences, takeaways and bagel shops on the main road, then along a one-way street opposite the mosque. Marcus stopped outside a battered black door. It was set in a red-brick wall with narrow windows too high to see through. There was no number on the door. Could this be it?

Marcus consulted the crumpled piece of paper again. L&M Wholesale. 79A. It was in the right place anyway. A Spanish colleague, Angel, had told him about it. They had been talking about the difficulty of finding good tapas in London, and Marcus had said that at least at Asturia you could pick up proper Spanish ingredients to take home. Angel had sniffed. Asturia? Yes, it's OK, but . . .

Marcus was mortified to be on the receiving end of a patronizing shrug. But Angel had made up for it by giving him the name of L&M in Finsbury Park. They were wholesalers, didn't do retail, but if you phoned up and asked nicely, they might let you come round and pick up some ingredients of superb quality at almost Spanish prices. Ever since, Marcus had been itching to try it. He had phoned up on Tuesday to place his order, and a bored and surly man had conceded that he could come by on Saturday morning.

He stepped up to the door and inspected the bell. L&M, it said, behind a layer of grime. Marcus was delighted. You didn't get much more authentic than this.

No one answered for some time. Finally a voice said, 'Yeah?'

'Marcus Thompson. Here to collect—'

'Hold on,' the man interrupted.

Marcus waited on the doorstep. From across the street, a youth in a hoodie eyed him incuriously.

The door jerked open and an unshaven man in a faded tracksuit gestured at Marcus to come in. He didn't look very Spanish. The man led him into a tatty office with three battered desks. This wasn't quite what he was expecting.

Then the man disappeared. Marcus could hear one of the three elderly computers grinding away under the desk. He sat down on a swivel chair and a strip of foam bulged through a tear in the fabric. Where were the shelves groaning with tempting produce, the legs of jamón dangling from the ceiling?

The man came back with a single plastic bag.

'That all?' he asked, with obvious contempt.

'Yes,' Marcus said.

The man exhaled loudly. 'Forty quid,' he said.

Marcus peeled off the notes.

Outside, he inspected the jar of smoked paprika and squeezed the greaseproof packages of ham. They bulged enticingly. Already he was feeling happier. Mentally he began reconfiguring the experience so that the dirty office only underlined that this was not somewhere ordinary customers went. Once he had done this, the man's rudeness was simply a sign of the efficient way he was used to dealing with busy buyers.

'Farmers' markets?' Marcus practised saying in an offhand tone as he returned to the car. 'Yes, they're all fine and everything, but if you really want proper high-quality ingredients at reasonable prices these days, you have to go wholesale.'

The rest of the shopping was pretty routine after that: to the butcher's to pick up the oxtail and kidneys, then a sweep of the greengrocer's. He was back home at about the time he normally left the house on a Saturday.

Marcus drained his coffee and returned to the kitchen work-top full of vigour and purpose. Oxtail next, he thought. Let it simmer for the rest of the day. He tossed the meat in flour and let it stand while he chopped up root vegetables and celery. That done, he browned the meat quickly in the bottom of a big Le Creuset pan, took it out again, and began building up a rich base of braised vegetables, stock and wine. When they had formed a satisfying broth, he put the meat back in, along with a muslin parcel of star anise, orange zest and an array of other spices.

Soon it was bubbling away nicely on a low heat. For this dish, more than any other, Marcus was hoping someone would ask him where he got the recipe. He wanted the chance to say, 'This? I adapted it from a Heston Blumenthal one, with some suggestions by Mark Hix. Do you think it works?'

With the oxtail done, Marcus felt he was making excellent progress. It was time to tenderize the octopus.

He pulled the creature out of its bag. With the seepage of water it had deflated, and it sprawled, shrunken and grey, on the worktop. Pushing aside the tentacles, Marcus groped tentatively into the hollow of its body. The hard, slimy flesh gave way to something gooier.

'First, turn the octopus inside out,' the recipe said. Of course. Simple, really. Marcus pushed down on the soft domed head from the outside and tried to force it through the hole in the bottom. The head buckled and then the forces balanced for a moment, until Marcus shoved harder and the creature popped, its head bursting out through the bottom of the body, sending a fine mist of entrails and fat flying across the kitchen.

Never mind; clear it up later. Marcus carried the octopus carefully to the sink, and began hacking out the internal organs now dangling precariously on the outside.

It was unpleasant work, particularly scraping off the encrusted deposits of gelatinous yellow fat. But even as he felt his gorge rising, Marcus was grimly satisfied. Cooking did not get much more real than this.

When he had cut out the eyes, Marcus put his largest pan on to boil and washed the octopus thoroughly. Its top half was looking very battered by now, but that was probably OK. He scooped up the tentacles trailing over the side of the sink and cleaned each one thoroughly, letting them drop into the bowl with eight pleasing thuds.

When the water in the pan had risen to an angry boil, Marcus hooked the creature with a wooden spoon, raising it up so that the tentacles hung to their full length – almost two feet. Pausing for a second to admire it, Marcus plunged the octopus into the boiling pot.

The water became suddenly still, and Marcus watched the end of a tentacle moving slowly in the hot eddies below the surface. Gradually, the bubbles returned. When the pot was boiling fiercely again, Marcus reached in with the wooden spoon and some salad tongs, and hauled out the octopus.

It came out wreathed in clouds of steam, re-inflated and

magnificent, the supple skin white under the spotlights. Marcus laid it aside to cool, and when it was lukewarm to the touch he plunged it back in.

He repeated this several times until the kitchen was full of salty steam. On the fourth go he left it in there, and turned the heat down to a simmer. Happy with his morning's work, he decided it was time for some lunch.

'. . . And then Dave actually started taking his shirt off on the dance floor,' Louise said. 'Everyone was cheering, of course, but he didn't realize they were taking the piss, so he whipped it off and started whirling it round his head like some sort of arthritic Chippendale.'

Charlotte started laughing as she raised the cappuccino to her lips.

'So there he was, flab flying, everyone whistling, and someone shouts, "Get 'em off!" And he starts undoing his belt. You could see the faded elastic of his boxers and everything. I swear he would have got completely naked right there if he hadn't tripped over his own trousers and landed flat on his face. The bouncers had to carry him out.'

Charlotte snorted into the coffee and felt frothy milk surge up her nose.

'You should have come,' Louise said as she pushed back her chair. 'It turned into a pretty good night. Although I do feel terrible today. Do you want to share a muffin when I'm back from the loo?'

Charlotte wiped the froth away with a napkin and nodded. Louise picked up her handbag and headed towards the Ladies'.

Charlotte did feel a little disappointed to have missed out. It sounded much better than usual.

Still, even if she'd missed a good laugh, and spent a dull evening in front of the TV watching an old episode of *Inspector Morse*, the main aim had been achieved. Charlotte felt great. She had slept for ten hours, and had not the slightest hint of a hangover.

Shopping with Louise, Charlotte had felt bright and alert, despite the crush on Oxford Street. But Louise, it was obvious, was suffering. Her eyes had that creased and sunken look that Charlotte recognized so well from the mirror. They had bought a couple of tops and Charlotte a pair of burgundy ankle boots before Louise said she had to stop for coffee.

Charlotte took another sip of cappuccino, keeping it all in her mouth this time. With an empty chair opposite her, she instinctively took out her phone. No calls, no messages, no e-mails. Charlotte kept it out anyway, preferring to fiddle with something rather than stare awkwardly into space while passers-by looked in at her through the window.

She was even looking forward to dinner at Marcus's house. No, that was putting it too strongly. But she wasn't resenting it. After last time, it was going to be entertaining. For her, at least. It would be excruciating for Justin and Barbara. And all the better for that, obviously.

She almost regretted leaving early last time. She hadn't really wanted to, but Rosie had insisted she take the first taxi. She had wanted to wait until Matt got back, but there was no way she was going to admit that to Rosie. On the way home, she had sent him a text, but he hadn't replied.

What had happened afterwards, though? She had wanted to have a proper gossip with Rosie about it in the office, like they used to, but Rosie didn't work on Mondays, Charlotte was in meetings all day Tuesday and Wednesday, on Thursday Rosie was 'working from home', and Friday was her other day off.

The thought immediately gave Charlotte something to do with her phone. She snatched it up, found 'Rosie Mob' and tapped out a text.

Did Barbara come back last Sat?

No. She ddnt come bck at all!

What happened?

Nt sure if I shd say . . .

Gossip! Tell me!

Thnk she wnt home wth Matt!

Charlotte stared at the plain black letters in their white bubble. They sat solid and impersonal on the screen.

Bastard. Fucking lecherous bastard. Charlotte felt a surge of emotion. She fought it. The feeling, whatever it was, annoyed her. She didn't want to care about it – didn't care about him – but it was insulting. Yes, that's what it was. Insulting. Fucking insulting.

What a pathetic loser. That was the first sign of a mid-life crisis, wasn't it, going round chasing after everything in a skirt? Some arty-farty neurotic with slim legs. Poor girl, though. Charlotte certainly didn't envy her. Still, she'd probably work it out soon enough and get the hell out of there. Then he'd be left on his own, stuck following his dick around wherever it fancied, as if he was just a fucking valet to his own cock. She pitied him, really.

Wanker.

Louise was on her way back from the toilet. Charlotte decided not to reply to Rosie. She thrust her phone back into her handbag.

'OK?' Louise asked as she pulled back her chair. 'Do you fancy a chocolate-chip muffin?'

'Shall we get cocktails?' Charlotte said.

Louise looked at her, surprised. 'It's three thirty in the afternoon.'

'So?'

Louise shrugged. 'All right.'

Marcus hurled the octopus as hard as he could into the sink. The whole worktop vibrated at the impact. Marcus gathered up the tentacles, raised the octopus high above his head in both hands, and threw it into the sink again. Then again, and again. After two more throws, he paused, panting hard, and wiped the sweat off his face.

Fucking thing. Why wasn't it tender? It was supposed to boil for only an hour, but when Marcus had cut the end off a tentacle to see if it was done, he might as well have been chewing a bicycle tyre. After two hours he had lost patience and switched to what was described on the internet as 'the Greek method'.

Marcus let fly again. This time the head ricocheted off the hot tap on to the draining board. He didn't know if this was working, but it was certainly better for his frustration than punching the walls.

On the next throw, a loose tentacle snapped out and whipped Marcus's favourite coffee cup off the window sill, sending it spinning over the edge of the counter to shatter on the floor.

Fucking thing! Marcus pummelled it with his bare fists in the sink. He didn't have time for this. The octopus salad was meant to be ready by now. He hacked another chunk off a tentacle and chewed it violently. That was a bit tenderer now, wasn't it?

But it was still fucking disgusting. What was he doing wrong? Nothing! This couldn't be his fault. He must have been sold a dud octopus. Marcus cursed the market trader, then cursed himself for not noticing he was being ripped off.

Why hadn't he just done the grilled squid he had wanted to do in the first place? Because it was served with pomegranate seeds, that's why. Marcus's face flushed with bitterness. Rosie had already used pomegranate, and now he couldn't serve it again without being accused of copying. Bloody Rosie. Marcus smacked the octopus resentfully. He had as good as discovered pomegranate. He'd been using it for years before it was popular. He loved that it could be light and fresh in one dish, sticky and rich in another.

And now it was everywhere. Even the corner shops in Kentish Town had started stocking it, as if people couldn't bear to be more than two hundred yards from a pomegranate any more. It had become trendy. He shivered in disgust at the thought. Could he ever use it again without people thinking he was just following the fad?

It had been exactly the same with chorizo. Marcus had been banging on for years about this fantastic Spanish sausage to people who had never heard of it. Then, without warning, it was in everything. For a while, you couldn't get a more fashionable food. And look at it now! He'd been into a petrol station the other day, and seen it in a sandwich there. A petrol station! What next? Ginsters chorizo pasties? Chorizo and onion crisps? Order something with chorizo in it now and you risked being mistaken for an estate agent. You could hardly start telling people that you liked it before it was famous, could you?

Marcus sighed deeply. Screw it, he thought, let's get the vegetarian rubbish out of the way. He stuffed the octopus back into the pot of water and dug a marrow out of the cupboard. Aggressively, Marcus chopped it in half, scored it, salted it, and put the two halves in the oven. Fucking vegetarians. He wasn't even sure they were coming until Sarah forwarded him a text from Rosie to say Justin was going to be there after all. Was whatshername, Barbara, even a vegetarian any more? Sarah had told him to assume so. But if she was going to try meat, why would she turn up her nose at his oxtail and kidneys? It was just rude. He prodded some spinach leaves into a pan, willing them to wilt quicker.

Hunched over the hob, Marcus did not hear Sarah come in.

'Wow, it's very humid in here, isn't it?' she said. 'Did you forget to take something off the boil?'

'No, I fucking didn't,' he replied.

'Don't snap at me, please. What is it, then? Is it still on? There can't be any water left in that pan.'

'It's the octopus. It's tenderizing.

'Oh, you went ahead with that, did you?'

'Why the fuck wouldn't I?'

Sarah took the lid off the pan and peered in. 'Please stop swearing at me, Marcus.'

'Well, where the hell did you think I was going at six o'clock this morning? Sainsbury's?'

'I don't know. You remember that I went out this morning as well?' Sarah had turned her back on the hob and was leaning against the worktop, arms folded across her chest.

'What?' Marcus drained the spinach water into a bowl and put the pan back on the hob.

'Have you forgotten?' Sarah asked through tight lips.

'What? Oh your school. How was it?'

'Nice of you to ask. It was amazingly luxurious. They had everything you could think of.'

'Sounds good.' Marcus put in more oil and chopped up some chilli.

Sarah waited.

Marcus added the chilli to the oil and stirred it carefully.

'Is that it?' she asked.

'What?'

'Is that your only comment? "Sounds good"? You're not going to ask anything else?'

'I don't know. Do you want to tell me anything else?'

'Not any more. I can tell you're not interested.'

'I'm cooking, for God's sake. If you want me to hold your hand, we'll have to talk about it later.'

Sarah turned to stare at Marcus's profile. He added bulgar wheat to the chilli oil and stirred it round the pan to coat the grains. From the corner of his eye, he could see her looking at him, her mouth clenched into a thin line. She obviously wanted him to say something, probably to apologize for something. He made sure every grain was covered.

Eventually, Sarah said: 'So, we can talk about cooking, can we?'

'If you want,' Marcus replied, still not looking at her.

'What are you making there?'

'It's the stuffed marrow. For the vegetarians. Assuming we still have any.'

'It smells nice.'

Was this an attempt at rapprochement? Maybe he should say thank you. And perhaps ask her about this bloody school she had been wringing her hands about for weeks. It was obvious that all she needed was a bit of reassurance. He could do that while stuffing the marrow.

Before he could say anything, Sarah added: 'Will there be enough for me?'

'What? No.' Marcus hadn't expected this. 'Not unless whatshername decides to get stuck in to the stew.'

'I think I'd prefer to eat vegetarian tonight.'

'Well, that's a vote of confidence in my main course.'

'It's nothing to do with you. I just think I need to be a bit healthier, that's all.'

'Great. Have some more carrots.'

'I think in general we eat too much meat.'

'So take a smaller portion. Eat less.'

'No, I mean in general we cook more of it than is good for us.'

'Then have salad tomorrow. But don't come in here when I'm cooking something for you and say we eat too much of it.'

Marcus added the spinach water to the pan to simmer the bulgar. He turned to Sarah and gestured at the drawer she was leaning against, forcing her to step backwards while he opened it and took out a knife.

'I don't eat that much anyway, Marcus. I won't take much of the vegetarian. I'm sure there will still be enough for the others if . . .'

'Christ! No!'

Sarah looked as if he had slapped her. 'Why the hell are you being so protective of a dish you don't even want to eat yourself?'

'Look, Sarah, shall I show you?' Marcus's voice was taut. He yanked open the oven door and took out the baking tray. 'Here are two halves of a marrow. They are what I am going to serve to two vegetarians. Do you see? Do you want me to chop them up into bits and say, "Sorry your dinner's mangled, but Sarah wanted to share"?'

'Marcus, please don't be so hostile.'

'Then don't come to me while I'm cooking you a six-course fucking banquet and say, "Actually, no, I'd prefer something else."'

She stared at him. 'Don't be rude to me, Marcus.'

'Well, don't be stupid to me, then.'

'Jesus, Marcus, what the hell is wrong with you?'

'What's wrong? I'm trying to cook four things at the same time. I've been boiling the octopus for four hours and it's still as tender as a fucking traffic warden, and now you've come in asking me to rip it all up and start again.'

He picked up the knife and began hacking up the spinach.

'OK, Marcus.' Her voice was that slow, deliberately placating tone that he found so enraging. 'I'm hardly telling you to start again, am I? Now, I can tell you're in a bad mood—'

'Well spotted!'

'OK. I'm going to leave you alone, then.'

'Yes, that's right. Off you go and leave everything to me.' He waved the knife in the direction of the door.

'I asked you yesterday if you wanted me to cook a starter or a dessert, and you said no.' The calming tone was gone now.

'I said I didn't want you fiddling with my menu plan. I didn't say, "Yes, please swan about all afternoon while I'm slaving in the kitchen."'

'Well, I certainly wouldn't want to ruin your precious menu. Not by, you know, cooking any of it. What the hell do you expect me to do?'

Marcus jabbed his knife at the spinach. 'You could cut this up. Shred some herbs. There're still some more vegetables to chop.'

'So I'm your bloody sous-chef, am I?'

'No, you're running the kitchen at the Savoy. Now either chop some vegetables or piss off.'

'Don't tell me to piss off, Marcus. And stop waving that knife around.'

Marcus slammed the knife down on the chopping board.

'OK, I'll stop. I'll drop everything I'm doing and devote the rest of the afternoon to arguing with you. Is that what you want?'

'For God's sake, Marcus. Do you want me to help or not?'

'Fine. I tell you what, you can make the romesco sauce.'

'What's romesco sauce?'

'There's a recipe in the book. It's not very complicated. It's mostly chopping.'

Sarah sighed wearily. 'All right. Fine. I'll make romesco sauce.' She opened the drawer to look for a vegetable knife. 'What's it for?'

'The asparagus.'

'The asparagus?' Sarah looked at the instructions for seeding peppers, roasting almonds and crushing garlic with a pestle and mortar. 'Don't you think you're overcomplicating things a bit?'

Marcus wheeled round with the knife in his hand.

'Right. That's it,' he said. 'Off you go.' He pointed the knife at the door.

Sarah put her knife back in the drawer. 'I can't stay in here any longer anyway. I'll come back when you've calmed down.'

'Good! Go and lay the fucking table or something.'

Sarah slammed the drawer and stalked out. Marcus heard

her muttering, not quite under her breath: 'Just because you've alphabetized your cookbooks by country doesn't mean you're Gordon Fucking Ramsay.'

He kicked the kitchen door shut quite hard.

Thirty

At first, Rosie had tried to resist the urge to be judgemental. Now, as she stood on the porch outside Marcus and Sarah's house, mentally tut-tutting at the state of the recycling bins, she decided to embrace it.

'Hello,' she said, with a too-wide smile, as Sarah opened the door.

Stephen handed over the bottle of wine they'd brought and Sarah led them into the living room.

'Marcus is still cooking,' she said. 'He'll be out to say hello in a moment, I'm sure.'

'Oh dear,' Rosie said. 'I hope he's not running late. That can happen when you try to get too ambitious.'

Sarah grimaced.

Rosie immediately felt bad about being rude to her friend. She would have expected Sarah to take it in good spirits, though, knowing it wasn't really aimed at her. Perhaps something was wrong. They sat down in silence and Sarah offered them drinks. She certainly seemed a little on edge. There was a noticeable tension in the room.

Excellent, Rosie couldn't help thinking. It could only mean that Marcus was finding things hard going in the kitchen.

There was a clatter and an oily sizzle from the next room and soon afterwards Marcus came into the room to join them. Rosie noticed the large beads of sweat below his receding hairline.

'Hello,' he said with too much jollity. 'Great to see you both.'

Rosie felt compelled to stand up and kiss him on both cheeks. Stephen and Marcus shook hands.

'Has Sarah offered you a drink?' he asked.

'I'm getting them now,' Sarah snapped, before Rosie could reply.

'What would you like?' Marcus asked.

'Glass of red wine, please,' Stephen said.

Rosie asked: 'Have you got any sherry?'

'Of course,' Marcus replied smugly. 'Fino, Oloroso or – though it's probably a bit early for this – Pedro Ximénez?'

'You don't have Manzanilla?'

'No.'

'Oh,' Rosie said, forcing her glee to sound like disappointment. 'I'll have a glass of white wine, then.'

'Sarah, will you—'

'I'm getting them!'

Sarah left the room. The three of them grinned uneasily at each other. Rosie decided to follow up with her next gambit.

'Are those shelves new?' she asked.

'Those? We got them a couple of months ago, actually. From this little workshop on Brick Lane.'

'The Turning Lathe?'

'Do you know it?'

'Yes, we thought about getting a table from there a few years ago but thought that it probably wouldn't take long to go out of style.'

Marcus got halfway through a strangled laugh.

'Excuse me,' he said. 'I'd better go and check on the amuse-gueules.'

Rosie enjoyed the flush of triumph even more than she thought she would.

In a way, it was sinking to Marcus's level. In another way, it was great. Usually, Rosie prided herself on being a considerate guest, alert to the feelings of her hosts, and helping the evening flow wherever she could. Being a good guest was an important part of life. But ever since her own dinner, with Marcus's gleeful, petty niggling over everything, the temptation had been there. Normally, she would never give in to it. But, sometimes, it was a form of social service, wasn't it? That's what she had decided. Showing Marcus what it was like to have your hard work judged and sniped at by others. In that sense, what she was doing wasn't small-minded revenge, it was education.

Leaving your guests on their own in the living room? She was going to have to deduct points for that. Leaving them without drinks? Several points.

Soon, Marcus came back, carrying a broad dish, on which

was stacked up a fat pyramid of golden, crumbling spheres. Rosie tried hard not to be impressed.

'Salt Cod Scotch Eggs,' Marcus said, putting them down on the coffee table with a flourish.

'Wow, they look delicious,' Stephen said.

'Do you know what's happened to our drinks?' Rosie added.

'Sarah!' Marcus yelled.

'I'm coming!' she shouted back from the next room.

Rosie felt her resolve weaken a little. Poor Sarah.

'I was hoping to wait until everyone was here,' Marcus said. 'But if I'd left them in any longer they would have been overcooked.'

'What a shame,' Rosie said.

'Please – try them.'

Rosie picked up one of the delicate balls. Fresh oil seeped out from between the breadcrumbs as her fingertips closed around it. She bit through it, feeling the hot snap of the crust give way to the fresh sharpness of the salted cod, then the soothing softness of the egg, the flavours recombining in unexpected ways as she chewed. It was delicious.

'Salty,' she said.

Marcus grimaced. He left to chase Sarah on the drinks.

Stephen swallowed his egg. 'These are great,' he said, reaching for a second.

'They are, aren't they?' Rosie had to agree. She ate another.

'Do you think it would be rude to have a third?'

'No, no – eat as many as you can before the others get here. I don't want them to be too impressed.'

Stephen looked at her in surprise. He was about to say something, but then just shrugged and ate another egg.

The doorbell rang as Sarah returned with the drinks. She dumped them quickly on the table to go out and answer it.

'Hi, Justin!' Rosie jumped to her feet as he came into the living room. 'Great to see you!' She kissed him on both cheeks, hoping the overenthusiasm wasn't too obvious. 'You're looking really well.'

'Hello,' Justin said.

He looked terrible, actually. Subdued and very tired. Rosie hoped it hadn't been a mistake getting him to come.

Marcus brought in a drink for him.

'Justin,' he said. 'Please try a Salt Cod Scotch Egg.'

'Scotch egg? Have they got meat in?'

'No. Not these. They've got salt cod instead of pork, and I've actually used quails' eggs to make the flavours a bit more delicate.' Marcus picked up the dish and offered the truncated pyramid to Justin.

'No, thanks,' he said.

'Go on.' Marcus thrust the plate towards him.

'I don't eat cod.'

'No?'

'I mean, apart from anything else,' Justin said, 'I couldn't eat anything that meant I was contributing to overfishing. They're emptying the seas with these industrial trawlers, and species like cod will become extinct if we carry on letting them get away with it.'

Marcus put the tray back down on the coffee table.

'But, you know, it's just a personal choice. Don't let me put you off.'

'Right,' Marcus said. 'You could have mentioned this when we asked about dietary requirements.'

'You know I am a vegetarian. And I think I did say that I don't eat unsustainably.'

There was a silence. Stephen ate a fourth Scotch egg.

Even though this awkward pause was technically Marcus's fault, and would have given Rosie another excuse to deduct points, she hated strained silences enough to feel she had to step in.

'So how are you doing, Justin?' she asked, putting a sympathetic hand on his arm to guide him towards the sofa.

'Fine,' he said flatly. 'It's been quite a busy week at work, you know, but I think I've got it all under control.'

'Great!' Rosie said a little too loudly. 'And what are you working on at the moment?'

'It's the same project in Malawi. We're sending our recommendations out to stakeholder review.'

'That sounds fascinating,' Rosie said.

'The problem is dependency, you see . . .' Justin faltered as he heard the doorbell ring. 'Er, what we're trying to do . . .'

There were footsteps and whispered voices out in the hall.

Justin froze, poised above the sofa. 'What we . . .' His train of thought ground to a halt.

'What you're trying to do . . .' Rosie prompted.

He stared at the door, waiting.

Matt stopped a couple of strides into the room and Barbara stepped out from behind him. They stood close to each other, facing Justin, their faces solemn but expressionless, like police-men come to deliver bad news.

Justin stopped blinking. He stared at them with an intensity that unnerved Rosie. No one spoke.

Rosie watched them, helpless. There were few situations, in her view, that couldn't be smoothed over with polite conver-sation. This was one of them.

Several seconds passed. Stephen took another Scotch egg and tried to chew it as quietly as he could.

Where was Marcus? This was his responsibility. He'd have to lose marks for this, Rosie thought. How long had they been standing there? It seemed like hours. It was probably about five seconds.

Eventually Matt spoke. 'Hello, Rosie,' he nodded. 'Stephen. Justin.'

Rosie and Stephen said hello. Justin did not.

Rosie wanted to go and greet them properly, but felt that to walk over to their side of the room now would count as some kind of statement. The conversation did not progress.

In the hall, the doorbell went again. Rosie almost sighed out loud with relief. Charlotte. Charlotte would get things going again. Charlotte was not someone to let other people's embarrassment put her off. Thank God they'd invited her.

Matt and Barbara moved away from the door together, retreating backwards towards the far left wall.

'Charlotte! Hi!' Rosie cried.

Charlotte's eyes scanned the room, fixing with determined hostility on Matt and Barbara. She stepped to the right of the room, creating a three-cornered staring match. Rosie felt the atmosphere of the room change again.

The silence was entrenched beyond any hope of conversation now. Rosie remained frozen. She didn't understand what was going on. What were you supposed to do in a situation like this? What could you possibly say?

Marcus appeared in the doorway. 'Do you want to come through?' he said. 'The asparagus is ready.'

Thirty-one

Look at them. Charlotte stared across the table. Clinging together like that. Making sure they sat next to each other. Like it's the first day of primary school and they're terrified someone's going to steal their dinner money.

Matt and Barbara had sat down on the far side of the table. Charlotte took the place directly opposite Matt, forcing him to look away. Barbara gazed down at her David Mellor cutlery.

It was pathetic, really. They couldn't even look her in the eye. Good. Let them squirm. Charlotte kept staring across the table. Barbara probably didn't even know, did she? She probably just drifted through life, thinking that because she was beautiful she could do whatever the fuck she liked. For some reason, that mostly involved pots. And now walking out on her boyfriend just because some sleazebag asked nicely.

But it wasn't really her fault. She was obviously a little bit dim and couldn't be blamed for that. Normally, looking like she did, there was probably no reason for her to worry about it.

No, it was Matt who was the wanker. Charlotte wasn't upset. What was there to be upset about? Some boring northern git she had never really fancied anyway had found a new squeeze. Well, fine. Who the hell cared?

She'd had to come tonight. She couldn't not, in the circumstances. She couldn't chicken out and have him thinking she was sitting at home, sobbing herself to sleep. Because she wasn't. She was just irritated, that was all. That's all he was: an irritant. A pebble in her shoe. It was important that he realized that.

He still wasn't looking at her.

Justin took the place next to Charlotte. The table wasn't really big enough for them all, and he was squashed in far too close. Charlotte planted her elbow firmly on the table to mark her territory, forcing him to shift further towards Rosie.

Perhaps she should be a bit more sympathetic, considering. He had just lost his girlfriend, in the most humiliating way you could think of. But no, fuck it, he was still Justin.

Sarah came round putting plates in front of them.

'Asparagus – what a lovely treat!' Rosie said. 'I thought it was still far too early in the year.'

'No,' Marcus replied. 'It isn't.'

'Really? But it's not May yet. Still, I suppose some of the air-freighted ones aren't bad these days. What are they Spanish? Peruvian?'

'They're English.'

'Really?' She sounded amazed. 'Well, you'll have to tell me where you get them so early.'

'From the local greengrocer's.'

'They must be terribly efficient.'

'They are.'

Charlotte bit the heads off a couple of stalks. They were fine. She wasn't much of an asparagus fan, and never enjoyed more than a couple of bites of the plump, fibrous tubes. She used them to mop up some of the spicy sauce – also fine – and put down her fork, impatient for some proper food.

'What is the sauce?' Rosie asked.

'It's a romesco,' Marcus said. 'A Spanish recipe of peppers, almonds, pine nuts and garlic.'

'Oh it's very nice,' Rosie said. 'And I must say, a really inventive way of dealing with such early season asparagus.'

'Thank you,' Marcus said warily.

'Of course, when you can get properly tasty, high-season asparagus, I much prefer to serve them plain, with just a bit of melted butter. Otherwise it's very easy to overcomplicate things, isn't it?'

Marcus stood up sharply. 'Has everyone finished?' He started collecting the plates without waiting for an answer.

Charlotte watched Rosie trying to hold back a smile as she handed up her plate. Yes, OK, she'd pissed Marcus off. Charlotte could see why she would be pleased with that. But, you know – being rude about someone's asparagus? Really? Was this what things had come to? People should just make up their minds. Either you were pretending to be polite, or you should just fucking go for it. Doubting the provenance of someone's vegetables? What kind of pathetic middle ground was that?

Jesus, she'd had enough of this. These people. And where was the next course? She was starving now.

Marcus left the room with the plates. No one seemed to feel like saying anything. Charlotte worked her way through another glass of wine.

Eventually Sarah said: 'It's been so cold recently, hasn't it?'

'Very cold,' Rosie agreed.

'Whatever happened to spring?'

'It's late this year.'

There was a pause.

'Usually, by this time of year, we've had some beautiful sunny days,' Sarah said.

'Not this year.'

'No.'

Sarah tapped the tabletop a couple of times with her index finger. 'They said on the news that it should be warmer next week.'

'That would be nice.'

'Yes.' Sarah nodded. 'It feels like such a long time since it was summer.'

The room lapsed into silence. Soon, Marcus came back with plates. Rosie asked if she could help. Marcus told her to sit down.

Charlotte peered at the absurdly gussied-up bit of meat on toast in front of her.

'Devilled Kidneys on Brioche,' Marcus announced.

Jesus. She looked at Justin's plate, on which a selection of chopped vegetables had taken the place of the kidneys. At least she wasn't having that.

As they all silently began to chew, Sarah made another attempt at conversation.

'So,' she said breezily. 'What has everyone been doing today? Anyone been up to anything exciting?'

'I was out shopping today,' Charlotte began.

'Oh yes,' Sarah responded brightly.

'Looking for a new dress ...'

'Lovely!'

'For a friend's wedding.'

'Oh yes?' Sarah's enthusiasm faltered very slightly.

'It's the season, isn't it?' Rosie agreed.

'That's right,' Charlotte said. 'I've got one next week, then they start coming thick and fast.'

'A couple of years ago was the peak for us,' Rosie said. 'We had one every other week that summer.'

'I've got that this year,' Charlotte said. 'Everyone seems to be settling down, don't they?'

Rosie did not reply immediately to this.

Charlotte speared a bit of kidney. No one seemed to want to meet her eye. They were all staring at their plates, and she was pretty sure it wasn't because of the food. Charlotte was rather pleased with the effect. Sod it, why not? Why shouldn't she get a bit of her own back? Watch and learn, Rosie.

'What about you guys?' she asked. 'Any of you got any decent weddings coming up? Marcus and Sarah?'

'No, nothing,' Sarah said quickly.

'What, not even your own? When are you two going to get round to it?' Charlotte grinned playfully across the table. 'Come on, Marcus, what's the hold up? She's not going to hang around for ever, you know.'

Marcus bared his teeth and ate a piece of kidney.

'You shouldn't let him get away with it, Sarah,' Charlotte chided. 'Tell him to get a move on.'

'It's not important,' Sarah mumbled.

Charlotte let this hang.

Rosie jumped in to help her friend.

'Weddings these days are so expensive, though, aren't they?' she said. 'Not just for the people getting married, either. You've got the hen night – a whole weekend, sometimes – and then you've got to go to a country house somewhere. Often it's a relief not to have to go to too many, isn't it?'

Charlotte hadn't really meant to hit such a raw nerve. She had no particular reason to dislike Sarah, and didn't want her to think she was being picked on. So Charlotte needed to hit her real target. It was only fair.

'Does anyone find—?' Rosie was saying.

'Matt?' Charlotte interrupted. 'Barbara? What about you? Any weddings this summer?'

'Not for me,' Matt said.

Look at him. Shaking his head and smiling like that. Acting all casual, like he's having a nice chat. But he's not enjoying this. He's not enjoying this at all. You can tell by his eyes.

'Barbara? What about you?'

Barbara was gazing at her plate. Salad on toast. So she'd gone back to the veggies, had she? How disappointing.

'Barbara? Any weddings?' Charlotte watched the top of her head.

'No,' she said quietly, still staring downwards.

Justin looked up in wounded surprise.

'Oh,' he said. 'Aren't you coming to Samina's, then?'

Barbara retreated further towards her meal.

'She'll be very disappointed if you don't.' Justin sounded hurt.

'I don't know. Maybe,' Barbara whispered. 'Let's talk about it later.'

'You don't have to sit with me if you don't want to. But I don't think you should let down your friend.'

Charlotte didn't need to say anything. She took a long, satisfying draught of wine. The table was dead. Had she gone too far? Justin didn't really deserve it, however annoying he was. But look at Matt! He had the face of someone who's just realized he's run over a puppy and is wondering whether anyone has noticed. Well, Charlotte wasn't going to let him get away with hiding the body in the recycling bin. He needed to take some responsibility.

'Matt, you could go with her!' Charlotte exclaimed, as if she had just cracked a difficult detective mystery.

'Mmm,' he said.

'That would be a nice friendly thing to do. You wouldn't want Barbara to miss her friend getting married, would you?'

He thought he could get away with not answering this. He smiled quickly and picked up his fork. But Charlotte didn't want him to escape. The others were just collateral damage.

'Would you?' she pressed.

'No,' he said.

'But Samina might not have space for you,' Justin protested. 'You can't just invite yourself.'

'Quite right, Justin. It's very rude of him, isn't it?' Charlotte said. 'You'll have to ask Samina, Matt. Will you do that?'

Matt glared at her. It tasted better than anything she'd eaten all night.

'Of course, if it came to it, you could always go instead of Justin,' she said. 'Justin wouldn't mind, would you, Justin? After all, Matt's getting used to taking your place.'

Sarah jumped to her feet.

'Has everybody finished?'

'No, they haven't,' Marcus said. 'Stephen and Matt are still eating theirs, Barbara's hardly started, and—'

'I think this course is over, though, don't you?' Sarah said. 'What did everybody think of that?'

Marcus looked expectantly round the silent table.

'Oh yes,' Rosie said. 'Very daring.'

Charlotte surrendered her half-eaten kidney with the sense of a job well done. As an added bonus, Marcus, having failed to solicit any praise for the dish, went off to the kitchen in an obvious huff.

Charlotte emptied her glass, feeling the wine settle easily on top of the afternoon's vodka and rum. Next to her, Justin fiddled with his knife, turning it over and over between his fingers with a strange look on his face.

Marcus came back into the dining room, propped the door open with his chair, and left again. A few seconds later he came steaming back in, carrying a huge salad dish criss-crossed with sliced tentacles.

'Octopus Salad with Dill and Caperberries,' he announced.

He waited for appreciative murmurs. It was undeniably impressive, but Charlotte did her best not to let her face flicker.

Marcus reached behind himself like a surgeon gesturing for forceps, and Sarah handed him a set of salad tongs. Not without reluctance, he shattered the precise arrangement of octopus and began serving.

'Not for me, thanks,' Justin said as his turn came.

'What?' Marcus paused, plate in mid-air. 'Why not?'

'I'm a vegetarian.'

'It's not meat.' Marcus shoved the plate towards him. Justin recoiled.

'I don't eat fish.'

'It's not fish, it's an octopus.'

'I'm afraid—'

'Oh come on!' Marcus slapped the plate down in front of him. 'Stop whingeing and just eat the bloody thing. You'll enjoy it.'

'I'm sorry, but you're being rude. You should have asked.'

'What, "Excuse me, do you not eat fish, including but not limited to crustaceans, cephalopods, molluscs, bivalves and related sea-dwelling creatures?" Should I have asked you for a taxonomy?'

'Don't get cross with me, Marcus,' Justin said in a calm, condescending tone. 'It's an animal that happens to live in the sea. Would you have served me seared blue whale and expected me to eat it?'

That sounded awesome, Charlotte thought.

'Look, it's just a bleeding octopus, not Flipper the dolphin.'

'Research has shown that octopuses have extremely well-developed nervous systems.'

'Research has also shown that they're extremely bloody tasty.'

Justin pushed his plate away. Marcus pushed it back. They glared at each other.

'Marcus,' Justin said, 'I have been very polite about a lot of things, I think you would have to admit. But I am not going to eat this.'

Sarah said: 'Marcus, I think you should respect Justin's decision. Shall we carry on?'

'I'll go and throw it back in the sea, shall I?'

'Please,' Sarah said. 'Don't be—'

'See how well its central nervous system has coped with being boiled for six hours and marinaded in lemon juice.'

Justin flinched and looked away. Marcus stood leaning over him. Justin picked up his fork. For one thrilling moment, Charlotte thought he was about to give up and dig in to the octopus.

But instead he set the fork down next to his knife, pushing them together in fastidious alignment.

'You know,' he said in a very solemn tone, 'I'm getting worried that this whole contest is not very sustainable.'

There was an uncertain silence round the table. You can fucking say that again, Charlotte thought.

'I mean, look at this,' Justin continued, his voice getting firmer and louder. 'Quails' eggs, endangered cod, air-freighted asparagus—'

'It is not air-freighted!'

'Then more meat, overfishing, herbs from the other side of the world, and now a sea creature mutilated for fun ... And how much of this is organic?'

'As much as is practical,' Marcus said.

Justin scanned the table with hard, unforgiving eyes. 'What about Fairtrade?'

His gaze stopped at Matt. He leaned forward in his chair. Charlotte let him have the space.

'What about you, Matt? I bet not much of your meal was Fairtrade?'

Matt relaxed pointedly in his seat and smiled in a superior way.

Christ, Charlotte thought. That was irritating. Even if he was doing it to Justin.

'Come on, then,' Justin pressed. 'Was any of it?'

'No, it wasn't. You're right,' Matt said.

'Why not? Did you even think of it?'

Matt paused before replying. 'I've never really been convinced by the benefits of Fairtrade,' he said.

'Oh!' Justin exclaimed in delighted shock. 'Right. I see. So, as long as you're getting your produce cheaply, who cares if the farmer makes a living? Is that right?'

'No,' Matt replied coolly. 'It's more that guaranteeing an artificially high price for basic goods only hinders the diversification of developing world economies.'

'Ha!' Justin sneered back at him. 'The neo-liberal argument. Let multinational corporations do it all.'

'That's hardly what I said.'

'God, I've heard this sort of thing so many times! Read a copy of the *Economist* and you think you don't have to care any more.'

'It's not about who cares the most, it's about what works,'

Matt replied in his calm and rational tone, which set Charlotte's teeth on edge. He said something about oversupplied markets. God, he was irritating.

'What a convenient way to make sure you don't have to worry about where your food comes from!' Justin went for heavy sarcasm. He wasn't very good at it. Charlotte was finding it hard to decide which of them was being more annoying.

'Some people would say,' Matt replied, 'that Fairtrade isn't really about helping the poor at all, but helping liberals like you feel better about yourselves.'

Justin's body began to shake slightly.

'I've been there, you know,' he said quietly. 'I've been there. I've seen the difference it makes.' He leaned towards Matt, his voice rising towards a shout. 'You sit here, making your dinner-party arguments, yet you know nothing about it! You've never been to a Ugandan coffee cooperative! Have you?'

'Look, never mind the Ugandans,' Marcus interrupted. 'Can we focus on the octopus, please?'

Justin ignored him. 'No. You haven't. I have. And let me tell you something. I'd like to see you argue with the people there. I'd like to see you try. Because you can't. You can't argue with people whose lives have been transformed. With children going to school for the first time, elderly people retiring with dignity, mothers getting medical treatment at a brand-new clinic. Are you going to argue against that? Are you? I'd like to see you stand there looking at the smile on a farmer's face as he tells you how he can feed his family properly for the first time, and tell him, "No, economic theory says it's all a mistake." How do you think he'd like that?'

The echoes died away slowly off the hardwood surfaces of the dining room. Justin was panting a little.

In the face of such vehemence, Matt was starting to look uneasy. 'Maybe Marcus is right,' he said. 'Let's enjoy the food.'

'Thank you!' Marcus said. 'I haven't heard any of you compliment it yet.'

Justin continued to stare at Matt. Charlotte could tell Matt was rattled. It was a glorious sight. The supercilious half-smile was gone, and the teeth on the left side of his mouth were bared in an uncomfortable grin. His shoulders had risen as he hunched forward. His eyes flicked sideways towards Barbara. Was he looking for support? But Barbara didn't notice. She was gazing out of the window, and didn't look particularly interested in taking sides. Though she too had declined the octopus.

Charlotte realized she wasn't getting the best out of things. She was irked by Justin and was tempted to have a swipe at him. But that was entirely the wrong approach. Never mind what he was saying, look at the effect he was having. A few more hits like that and Matt would be on the ropes.

'Yeah!' she said slowly, making Matt look at her. 'What sort of heartless wanker do you have to be not to like Fairtrade? I bet you're the sort of person who asks for the twenty-five pence donation to be taken off the charity pizzas in Pizza Express.'

Matt looked pleasingly taken aback. 'You can't just rely on these silly emotional arguments,' he said. 'It's ridiculous to do something if it doesn't actually work.'

Oh yes. He was really needled now.

'It's not ridiculous if you're a poor African farmer, is it?' Charlotte said, trying to look serious. 'Because it does work. Didn't you hear the man? What a difference it makes to their lives?'

'I didn't realize you were that interested, Charlotte,' Matt said.

Something about his voice meant that Charlotte found herself putting real feeling into her next words: 'You see, I think you need to learn how to make sacrifices for others, Matt. You don't know how to do that, do you? You just try something different as soon as you get bored, and sod the consequences.'

'Come on, Charlotte,' he said, uneasy now. 'You can't really pretend you care.'

'You haven't had the opportunity to find out, have you?'

Matt hesitated. Charlotte could hear Justin's angry breaths getting louder as he prepared to say something. He drank some water, but it didn't seem to calm him down.

When Justin spoke, there was an unexpected strength to his voice. 'That's the real problem, Matt: you don't care about the results of your actions. It's so convenient for you to pretend these things aren't important. Then you can just carry on doing whatever you like, taking whatever you want, and never mind anyone else.'

'Yes, well, it's very convenient for you to be able to feel superior to everyone else, isn't it?'

'You know . . .' Justin closed his eyes and seemed to have difficulty speaking. 'This kind of . . . moral blindness really sickens me. I don't understand how you can not see what this is about. What you're doing is so clearly wrong. Morally wrong.'

'Justin . . .' Rosie said reprovingly.

'No, it's all right,' Matt said. 'Let him say it. I don't know what happened to being non-judgemental, though.'

'Some things are wrong. You have to be judgemental about that.'

There was a pause.

'How's the octopus?' Marcus said.

'Fuck the octopus!' Justin shouted.

Marcus almost choked on his tentacle.

Thirty-two

Justin's tense upper body tilted backwards to allow Sarah to clear away his untouched plate of octopus. Light flashed off an oily sucker and he caught a salty gust of warming flesh as it went past his nose, prompting a lurch of revulsion.

A deep-lying nausea began to rise up towards his throat. Justin's surging feelings formed into an acrid bile that needed somehow to be expelled. He struggled for breath.

How could they all sit there politely listening to the argument like it was a debate on *Newsnight*? This wasn't a game; it was a matter of justice. Wasn't it obvious? He was on the side of the powerless. He was the victim. Why wouldn't they respect that?

His anger rose as he looked round the table. They all avoided his eye. Guilt. That's what it was. His gaze stopped at Matt, with a shudder of loathing. The power of it was new and surprising. But, looking at him, Justin couldn't understand why he hadn't felt it before. Matt's fat, beefy lips twitched upwards as he tried to hide a sneer. His elbows and forearms were braced aggressively across the table. Justin had no doubt that beneath it his legs were planted wide apart, his crotch jutting forward.

It was a type Justin had always despised. A man so arrogant that he barely noticed other people unless they were useful to him. Not even a bully, but something almost worse: the sort of person who saw the struggle between the oppressor and his victim as no more than an amusing game, treating both sides with the same easy condescension. He needed to see that selfishness did not always pay.

Justin couldn't bear to look at Barbara. His eyes seemed to skate past her without being able to focus. If he tried to concentrate on her face he felt a queasy stabbing pain in his gut, like he had just eaten a pot of rancid yoghurt. She hadn't looked at him all evening, either. Justin couldn't see the pain on her face – if anything she seemed a little bored – but he knew that Barbara found it difficult to express these things.

In some ways, he didn't blame her for what she'd done. She was obviously suffering from an artistic crisis, and what right did he have to insist that she carried on like that? He loved her. He wanted what was best for her. If that turned out to be someone else, it would be wrong of him to stand in her path.

In other ways, he was beginning to hate her. It wasn't that he had never thought about something like this happening. He had, often. He had always suspected that, really, she was never quite at ease with him. So he'd always been careful, not pushed back too much against her bad moods, each time fearing that it could be the final shove.

He hadn't tried to talk to her since last time. The thought of trying filled him with weariness. He could ask for an explanation, but what could she tell him that he didn't already know? There was no point making protestations and pleas, either. If she didn't want to come back, trying to persuade her would only make both of them sicker.

But Matt! That was where the bitterness cut through and began to make the wound sting. Someone who was, what? Richer? Taller? Stronger? Someone who stood for all he and Barbara had agreed they despised. It was almost as if she was deliberately insulting everything he valued.

Rosie broke the long silence as Marcus came in with a big casserole dish.

'Wow, Marcus, that does smell powerful!'

He pulled off the lid and a cloud of heavy steam escaped, wafting thick, meaty aromas around the table.

Justin began to feel sick again.

'Braised Oxtail with Salsify,' Marcus announced with a satisfied smile. 'A reason to be pleased it's still so cold outside.' He began ladling it out on to plates.

'It does look very filling,' Rosie said. 'I'm not sure how much I can manage.'

'The idea for the recipe came from Heston,' Marcus went on, as if he had been asked. 'But I've adjusted it with a couple of good ideas from Mark Hix and a few touches of my own. Justin, you've got some marrow coming.'

The sticky, sweet stench of stewing meat intensified as they began to eat. Justin began to feel even more disgusted.

Sarah placed in front of him a plate containing half a

slightly shrivelled marrow. An unidentifiable liquid was seeping out across the china. But then he saw the same thing put
in front of Barbara. Immediately, Justin felt a surge of hope.
She hadn't changed completely. There was, perhaps, still some
solidarity there.

He picked up his fork and clenched it in his fist.

'Shall I tell you, Matt,' he said as he prodded the thick rind
of the marrow, 'what the problem with you is?'

'If you like,' Matt said, with a faint smile.

'Yes, please do,' Charlotte added.

'The problem with you,' Justin said, sawing the squeaking
marrow–cheese with his knife, 'is that you put your own
interests first, and then you rationalize your behaviour into
the only inevitable, logical response.'

Matt's expression did not change. 'Not like you, then,' he
responded quickly. 'Your self-interest always has to become a
moral crusade.'

The casual ease of the answer filled Justin with a stabbing
fury. 'I can't believe you! You sit here and lecture me—'

'I'm not lecturing anyone.'

'After all you've done, you have the nerve to sit there and
dismiss me – no, worse – dismiss everyone who—'

'I'm not dismissing anything,' Matt said with the same
despicable calm. 'I'm simply saying you shouldn't be inflexi-
ble about your moral judgements.'

'You self-centred—'

'At best,' Matt pushed on, 'these kinds of arguments are a
sideshow, a distraction from the real problems that need to be
addressed.'

'You selfish bastard! You don't care about anyone else, as long as you get what you want!'

'The oxtail's very nice, by the way, Marcus,' Matt said.

'Thank you,' Marcus said. 'How's the marrow, Justin?'

'Bland and watery.' Justin pushed his plate away. 'Look at us all, sitting here, stuffing our faces and bickering. Is this really the most we can hope for out of life?'

'God, I hope not,' Charlotte said.

'Why don't we talk about something else?' Sarah suggested.

'Yes, good idea,' Matt agreed. 'Justin may be getting a warm glow of righteousness out of this, but he's not making it much fun for everyone else.'

'Who cares about having a nice time! We're talking about the most important things in life, here!'

'Yes, but Justin,' Rosie said, 'that doesn't mean you have to be rude.'

'That's right, Justin,' Matt said. 'You can't stop being polite just because people are suffering. They're always suffering.'

Justin threw his fork down. The sound was muffled as it sank into the stuffed marrow.

'I can't believe such callousness! I can't believe it. There's no way I can eat while listening to this.'

No one else replied. They were all still eating. All concentrating on their food like it was the only thing that mattered. Justin was astonished. The last thing he could think of now was food. Look at Stephen, tucking into his casserole like that, eating it in great steaming forkfuls. What was wrong with these people?

'Come on,' Sarah said soothingly. 'Let's not let an argument spoil the evening.'

'It's a bit late for that,' Charlotte said.

'I'm sorry,' Justin said unapologetically, 'but there's no way I can keep silent while being provoked.'

Charlotte reached out and patted Sarah's arm sympathetically.

'It is a shame Matt's fucked up your evening, isn't it?' she said. 'That makes it pretty much everyone here that he's screwed now. Doesn't it, Barbara?'

Everyone's eyes swivelled towards Barbara. Justin's too. He couldn't help it. Such disgusting crudeness. But on the other hand . . .

The tense pause lasted about three seconds.

Then Barbara pushed back her chair, scraping it sharply across the oak floor, and, without saying anything, stormed out of the room.

Justin felt his throat rise again in a whirlpool of curdled emotion as he agonized over what to do. Should he go after her? No, it was too late. She wasn't going to come back. He could see that. It would be too painful. Was he going to make her spell it out?

But then, what did he have to lose? There were only a few things she could say that would make it worse. Though what if she said them?

Seconds passed. He heard Rosie and Sarah say something, heard Charlotte interrupt them.

'Well, we might as well stop setting a dessert spoon for her,' she said. 'This is becoming a bit of a habit.'

Justin scrambled away from the table, tangling his foot round the chair leg and almost tripping as he rushed to the door.

Barbara had her coat on and was standing in the hall. Was she waiting for him?

'Barbara, I ...' he began.

'I'm sorry, Justin,' she said.

'But do you ... Will you ...' He struggled to get the words out.

'I know I've been a bitch,' she said.

'That doesn't matter.'

'You're a really sweet guy, Justin.'

He took a deep breath. 'Are you going to stay?'

'I'm not staying here. I can't.'

'No, I understand. Can I come with you?'

Her hand reached for the latch of the front door. 'I'm sorry,' she said.

'But ...' he began, thinking of so many things to say.

She pulled the door open, slipped through, and was gone.

The heavy wooden door filled his vision.

As it moved in and out of focus, Justin became aware that Matt was standing next to him.

'Oh well,' Matt said. 'Looks like we both lost. No hard feelings?'

The flash of rage was so instant and powerful that Justin was already swivelling round before he realized what was happening. He felt his right fist clench and his left shoulder drop. There was still time to abort. But Matt's fat lip was already beginning to curl. Justin put all his strength behind it.

Thirty-three

The impact was surprisingly painful. An angry scraping of lip impaled on teeth. But the blow was not hard and it was more the shock that made Matt stagger back several paces.

After the pain came astonishment, wonder, and then a slow, rising exultation. As he put his hand to his mouth and felt blood seeping through his fingers, Matt knew that he had won.

Justin was open-mouthed, blinking at him, as if not quite comprehending what he had done. Matt looked questioningly back at him, then saw to his delight that Rosie was standing in the doorway to the dining room, her mouth a perfect O of surprise. Her brow folded slowly into a reproving frown.

'Matt, are you all right?' she asked.

'Yes, I'm fine,' he said, a hint of laughter in his voice.

'Are you sure?'

'Yes, absolutely fine,' he said as breezily as he could through a mouthful of blood. 'I think I might just need to clean up a little, that's all.'

'What happened?'

'Nothing, really.'

'But he hit you!'

'Yes.' Matt felt no need to elaborate.

'Justin, why did you hit him?'

Justin was breathing heavily. Matt could see his lips twitching slightly. 'I don't know,' he whispered.

'What's that, Justin?' Rosie spoke loudly and firmly, as if to her toddler.

Matt put his hand to his mouth again as Justin struggled to speak, not so much to wipe away the blood as to cover a smile. Justin was realizing that he had lost his position of moral superiority. Matt suspected that he had no idea what to do without it.

Justin shrugged. 'He deserved it,' he said.

'Where's Barbara?' Rosie asked.

'She's gone,' Matt said.

'Oh.' Rosie nodded, then adopted the same condescending tone again. 'Now, Justin, I know you're upset, but that's no reason to hit anyone. You know that violence isn't the answer.'

'No. But . . .' Justin tailed off.

'Do you think you can apologize to Matt?'

Justin started. 'I . . .'

'It's all right, Rosie,' Matt said with a magnanimous wave. 'It doesn't matter. All forgiven.'

'Are you sure?'

'Yes, it's no problem.' Matt moved over to pat Justin on the arm. Justin recoiled from his touch and Matt enjoyed looking

down at him from his unexpected perch on the moral high
ground. They both knew that every sympathetic gesture only
rubbed it in further. Matt almost hoped Justin would hit him
again.

'No hard feelings, eh, Justin?' he said.

Justin jerked upright. 'I'd better go,' he said.

Matt left it to Rosie to reply. She failed to think of any
reason to object.

'What's going on out here?' Marcus's face appeared in the
doorway over Rosie's shoulder. 'It's time for pudding.'

A fat drop of blood crested the bulge of Matt's chin, and he
made no attempt to stop it as it rolled off the edge and hit the
floor with a soft, wet plop.

'Oops, I'm sorry,' Matt said. 'I'd better clean that up.'

'What the hell's going on?' Marcus checked his wooden
floor wasn't damaged before looking expectantly from Matt
to Justin.

'Justin hit him,' Rosie said.

'Oh.' Marcus didn't seem quite sure what to do with this
information. 'Well, I hope it's made you both hungry because
the apple fritters are ready.'

'I'm going to go now,' Justin said.

'What? You can't.'

'It's OK. I'm not hungry. Thank you for your hospitality,
but ...'

'I don't care if you're hungry or not. We have to do the
scores.'

'Marcus,' Rosie said. 'Maybe you should just let him ...'

'I haven't gone through all this to let him give up now,'

Marcus snapped. 'We can do it while eating pudding if you like, but we're bloody well going to do it.'

Justin crumpled further into himself, and shuffled after Rosie back to the table.

'I'll just go and wash my face,' Matt said.

In the bathroom, he checked the inside of his lip and saw it was already beginning to heal. He wiped the drying blood off his chin, and savoured his luck. Matt even felt a bit sorry for Justin. He tried so hard to present himself as the noble victim, but it was difficult for people to see you as noble when you were that desperate. And then the punch. It was a tactic that might have worked if he'd tried it from the beginning. People would have understood it. But after basing everything on the moral aura of being wronged, it was a disaster. With one right hook, he'd given it all away. Now Matt could claim victimhood.

After splashing his face with water, Matt went back to the dining room. It was obvious that everyone knew what had happened. They stopped talking and stared at him as he walked over to his chair. Charlotte was laughing quite openly.

'Are you OK, Matt?' Rosie asked again.

'Absolutely fine,' he said.

She was looking at him with concern across her face, her head tilted slightly to the left and a narrow crease of worry between her eyebrows. He smiled back at her with warm relief. Her disapproval seemed to be melting. Perhaps, after all, it would not be so hard to get back in her favour. It was clear that she still cared about him.

Echoes of his old feelings bounced around his chest, more

than memories, less than emotions. A long spell of her disapproval would have been difficult. Matt tried to decide what she was thinking as their eyes met. But it seemed only to be motherly concern.

Matt drained his glass and let wistfulness seep through him. He did still think about Rosie. Not every day, but sometimes. It had been his decision to end it all those years ago. She had been talking about moving in together, but he'd been only twenty, for God's sake. Far too young to be tied down. He'd wanted some time to enjoy himself. No, that wasn't it. He'd wanted some time when he didn't have to care about anyone else. A year later she'd moved in with Stephen.

He didn't regret it. There was no point regretting anything. He would certainly never do anything now. It would be too irrevocable. Matt couldn't be sure he wouldn't want to walk away again, and there would be no coming back after that.

A sharp cry of 'Fuck!' from the kitchen cut through his introspection. Matt guessed that Marcus had burned himself on a pan. He realized it was the first thing anyone had said since he and Justin had sat down.

A few moments later Marcus came through with a tray.

'Right,' he said with weary determination. 'Apple Fritters with Cinnamon and Mascarpone.'

They smelled good, in fact. Thick, warm and syrupy. Matt discovered that being punched in the face had made him hungry again. He attacked the pudding greedily. Next to him, Barbara's place remained conspicuously empty, while Justin prodded glumly at his fritter with a spoon. Still no one said anything.

About halfway through her fritter, Rosie did. 'Yes, it's interesting this, isn't it?' she said. 'The mix of styles. Sort of American we're on to now, with the syrup? After a bit of Spanish and British. Would you call this fusion?'

'I certainly would not,' Marcus replied, as if his family had been insulted.

'No? What is it, then, this mix?'

'It's not a mix. It's perfectly consistent. It's classic English food with a heavy Spanish inflection.'

'Inflection? Would that be the octopus?'

'I wouldn't expect you to understand. Nigella's never done it on TV. Is the apple straightforward enough for you?'

'It's a bit sweet, actually.'

'You know what?' Marcus said. 'Shall we just do the scores now?'

There was a shuffling round the table as people took out their phones. Justin said his didn't do e-mail, so Marcus went to get his laptop. The silence became looser as everyone began composing their verdicts.

Matt did not take long to structure his judgement. His thumbs moved quickly over the keypad of his BlackBerry. He pressed send and saw a tick appear next to the message, confirming that it was gone. The others were still hunched over their devices. Rosie and Stephen were whispering urgently to each other as Rosie made notes on a spiral pad. Justin typed slowly.

Charlotte's fingers were flying over her screen. She was grinning malevolently as she typed and Matt couldn't help but laugh silently as he thought about what she must be writing. Matt didn't put his BlackBerry down. She had been good fun, Charlotte, hadn't she? He hadn't really meant for it to be over so quickly. If Barbara hadn't come along, it probably wouldn't have been.

She would be impossible to live with, of course, and had a clear double chin as she looked down at her iPhone. But that was OK; he wasn't thinking about it as a permanent thing, just a bit of fun. She was entertaining and lively. It was worth a try, wasn't it?

His thumbs began moving over the keypad again. How to phrase it? Nothing too specific. There was no need to over-commit. Should he apologize? Yes, it would definitely be helpful. It would allow some ambiguity about his intentions. He tapped out a couple of sentences. Yes, that would do.

'Sorry about last week. Do you want to go out for a drink after this to make up for it?'

He sent it as a text. There was no indication of whether it had arrived. Charlotte was still fiddling with her phone. She didn't look up. He couldn't read her face.

She lay the phone on the table and pushed it away slightly: far enough to signal she had finished the message, but near enough to see any reply.

For several seconds Matt held his phone cupped in his palm, ostentatiously not looking at it. Then it vibrated power-fully in his hand, sending a shiver all the way up his arm. He clicked on the message.

'Fuck off,' it read. There was a little emoticon of a clenched fist.

From: Matthew Phillips <matthewphillips@
      newgreenchambers.co.uk>
To: Dinner At Mine <dinneratminescores@gmail.com>
Sent: 22.31
Subject: Assessment of dinner cooked by Marcus and
Sarah, by M Phillips

Food:

Asparagus: Somewhat bland. Sauce enjoyable. 7

Kidneys: Intense flavour. Well spiced. Juice combined
pleasingly with brioche. 9

Octopus Salad: While visually impressive, the dish was a
disappointment. Tough and over-chewy, with flavour quickly
lost. Other ingredients somewhat meagre. 6

Oxtail Stew: Satisfying thickness. Sharpness of the
vegetable complementing meat well. 9

Apple Fritters: Enjoyable. Perhaps too heavy considering
other courses. 7

Ambience /Hosting:

Wine: Pleasant Tempranillo. Not plentiful, however. 7

Conversation: Aggressive, hostile. Often intellectually inco-
                  herent. 5

Company: Generally adequate, apart from one episode of
violence. 7

Overall average: 7

Matthew Phillips

Barrister

New Green Chambers

Sent from my BlackBerry®
 From: Rosie and Stephen <rosieandstephen@home.co.uk>
To: Dinner At Mine <dinneratminescores@gmail.com>
Sent: 22.34
Subject: Dinner

Hi Marcus and Sarah,

It feels a bit odd doing this while you're watching us. You're staring, actually. It's a little bit off-putting. If I were you, I would choose this moment to go and make some coffee or something. That would be tactful.

Of course, you must be very upset that the evening wasn't a success. Please don't worry, though; a lot of it wasn't your fault. We're not going to hold you entirely responsible. You can't be blamed for Justin and Matt.

Although, a good host should probably know how to separate guests who aren't getting on. I don't mean to judge, but there were at least a couple of moments when you could have headed the whole argument off.

The problem is, I think, that Marcus is not very warm as a host. It's all very well aiming for technically impressive food – we'll come to that later – but so much of the enjoyment is about atmosphere. It's your task to create that. I'm sorry to say you didn't do a very good job. It obviously doesn't come naturally, but it doesn't even feel like you were trying. I mean, if no one's saying anything, you have to jump in there and get the conversation going again.

And not to harp on, but people were running out of wine. You just can't let that happen. I know you were distracted by all the dishes you were trying to do, but no one ever said this was easy. Perhaps you'll blame Sarah for that, I don't know.

Anyway, I can see Matt's finished already so I'd better get on to the food. Stephen certainly liked the salty cod balls, or whatever they were. Such a pity there weren't enough for everyone else. Myself, I found them too salty.

I know you said the asparagus was local, and I'll take your word for it. Perhaps that's why it wasn't at its best, so I can see why you felt you needed to jazz it up with that sauce. But really, that was gilding the lily a bit. (Although it isn't lily season either!)

The kidneys certainly did what it said on the tin. Strong, powerful flavours. Personally, I found them a bit too aggressively meaty. But that's just my taste. Stephen loved them.

And then the octopus! There's no denying it looked impressive. But by this point you should have been aware of the danger of trying too hard. I think I once had the same dish in Moro, so I could see what you were trying to do. And I suppose many people would say that it's better to be ambitious and fail than to achieve mediocrity, wouldn't they? Personally, I prefer something tasty.

I'm afraid that by the stew it was all getting a bit much for me. I certainly wasn't hungry any more, and I found it far too rich. The spices didn't really cut through the stickiness in the way I think you were going for. Although Stephen liked it.

I don't have much to say about the pudding. You can't really go wrong with apple fritters, can you? Although they were a little too sweet.

Well, I suppose it's the moment of truth now. Exciting to think we'll find out who's won any moment now, isn't it? Not that that would affect our scoring at all. So: seven out of ten.

Yours,

Rosie and Stephen

From: Justin Davidson <justindavidson@AfricAid.org.uk>
To: Dinner At Mine <dinneratminescores@gmail.com>
Sent: 22.35
Subject: Sustainability Concerns

Dear All,

I'm sorry, but I'm not sure what I'm meant to write now. It's becoming increasingly hard to pretend that food is the most important thing here.

I know you're all judging me for hitting Matt. It's true that violence doesn't solve anything. But he deserved it. I just don't think that we, as a society, should be tolerating that kind of selfishness and greed. This is someone who just reaches out and takes what he wants, not caring about what that does to everyone else. People have the right to resist aggression, don't they?

I know I'm meant to be talking about the food. Not that I could really eat very much of it. But in fact I've been getting concerned that, from the planet's point of view, we're all a little bit like Matt. We all just reach out and take what we want: we kill animals, plunder fish from the sea, spew pollution into the atmosphere flying asparagus halfway round the world. We all know it can't go on. At least, I hope we do. And for what? So that we can say somebody has won. Why does anyone have to win? That's the lesson I think we all need to learn from this.

I'd like to leave now. I know some of you will still want a score. I don't see what good it will do anyone. So: 6½.

From: Charlotte Wells <charliewells2@gmail.com>
To: Dinner At Mine <dinneratminescores@gmail.com>
Sent: 22.36
<No Subject>

Christ. Well, I'm glad that's over. One more of those things and I'd be in serious danger of stabbing someone. I won't say who.

Was this the worst of the lot? The sad truth is that it probably wasn't. At least it was entertaining. Justin, you may be one of the most annoying men on the planet, but I was right behind you there. Shame it didn't turn into a fight, though. God, I would have loved that.

The food was OK, actually. A proper amount of meat this time. If Justin had eaten a couple of those kidneys and built himself up a bit, we'd all have been picking Matt's teeth out of the Danish furniture. And I did like the stew. I realize it was probably meant to be ironic in some awful way, but you know what? It was a nice, tasty stew.

You had to let us all down with the octopus, though, didn't you? Just in case we were in any doubt that you were a massive cock, you had to bring out a fucking octopus on a plate. I mean, why not just shout, 'Look at me!', get your knob out and garnish that with parsley? Apart from anything else, I'm sure it would have been less effort for you. It tastes of rubber, for Christ's sake. (Yes, yes, I mean the octopus.) You can poncify it however you like, but it's still basically like chewing the end of a pencil.

And look! My glass is empty. Are you offering to top it up? No, you fucking well aren't. You're glaring at us all like we're taking some kind of exam. Well, we're not. We're marking you. Then I'm getting the hell out of here.

Score: 7 (And count yourself lucky. It was the punch that got you that extra point.)

Sent from my iPhone

Thirty-four

'Come on, have you finished yet?' Marcus blurted.

His whole body was tense, right leg jiggling with nervous excitement, and Sarah felt an acute spasm of repugnance. It surprised her with its intensity. She hadn't realized things had got that far. There was no doubt that this bloody competition had brought out the worst in Marcus, and she hadn't liked him for a lot of it. But it was still a shock for her to look at him leaning forward over the table, an impatient snarl on his face as he demanded that Rosie hand over the laptop, and feel so completely revolted.

'Nearly there,' Rosie said.

'Hurry up, you're not reviewing us for *Time Out*,' Marcus said. 'All I need is a score. Preferably a high one.' There was no laughter in his voice as he said it.

'All right, calm down . . . There,' Rosie said. 'I've sent it.'

'Give it to me, then.' Marcus almost snatched the MacBook from her hands.

'Right,' he said. 'The password.'

Sarah had forgotten about this bit. She felt a surge of frustration as Marcus typed his two characters and pushed the computer across the table to Rosie.

'Charlotte, you're next,' he said.

Slowly, the laptop made its way round the table, two digits at a time. The solemnity of the absurd ritual almost made Sarah laugh out loud. This is what the Freemasons would be like if it was run by computer nerds. Sarah tried to catch Rosie's eye to see if her mocking amusement was shared, but Rosie was already craning forward as the computer moved back to Marcus, stretching across to see at the same time as he did what came up on the screen.

There were fifteen new messages. Rosie sprang from her seat and crouched in next to Marcus where she could read them. Charlotte, then Matt, got up and came round to stand behind her. Stephen shifted his chair a little bit closer. Only Sarah and Justin stayed where they were. Sarah tried to catch his eye in shared scepticism, but he was gazing away across the room.

In profile he was perfectly defined against the uplighters, and seemed deeply contemplative. Wise, perhaps. And he was right, wasn't he? There were far more important things to worry about. There was a lot Sarah could learn from him, she was sure.

But at the same time, despite her silent rage at Marcus, the glowing messages drew her in. She watched as Marcus and Rosie worked their way through them, picking out the scores. Each wrote them down on their own piece of paper. Sarah leaned in closer. Hmm, Rosie was doing well, wasn't she? A very generous mark from Justin.

'The duck was not overcooked,' Rosie said briskly as she read Marcus's e-mail.

'Yes, it was,' he replied.

'It was pink in the middle.'

'Mine wasn't.'

Oh God, Sarah sighed, Marcus could be such a dick sometimes. Look at that message. 'For which points must be deducted.' Who the hell did he think he was?

Although, actually, Charlotte had been a lot ruder in her first e-mail. Yes, she was drunk, but did she really think everyone was that boring? Sarah sneaked a look upwards. Charlotte didn't seem at all ashamed; she was even grinning. Sarah was surprised to find herself hurt. She had quite liked Charlotte, despite her unfortunate views. She was good company and fun, at least; but now it turned out . . . Well, there we are. Justin was right about her as well.

The silence hardened like boiling sugar. Marcus and Rosie had totted up Rosie's score, and Rosie looked a little disappointed before quickly hiding the emotion with a bright smile.

'Well done, Rosie, good score,' Marcus said, with a smirk that he didn't try to hide. He clearly thought he was going to win.

They moved on to the second evening. Everyone, except Justin, leaned in a little closer. Marcus and Rosie again wrote down the marks independently. Marcus gave a quiet but triumphant snort as the numbers came up short.

'Bad luck, guys,' he said.

Neither Charlotte nor Matt looked particularly distressed.

'No one spotted the tart, though,' Charlotte said.

'What do you mean?' Marcus asked.

'I knew it!" said Rosie.

'Ah, but you didn't, did you? Otherwise you would have said.'

This puzzled Sarah, but no one stopped to ask what it meant because Rosie had moved on to Justin's scores. Marcus impatiently clicked forward to his own marks.

Rosie seemed to have written quite a lot. Marcus scanned through it quickly, looking for the number.

'What do you mean, I'm not warm enough as a host?' he protested.

'I'm sorry, but that's what I think,' Rosie said.

'What the hell do you want, dancing? If the atmosphere was wrong, blame these guys!' Marcus gestured dismissively towards Matt and Justin. 'Seven! That's absurd. What does that even mean, "trying too hard"?'

'Shall we look at the next e-mail?' Rosie replied.

'Seven! Jesus, did no one appreciate what I was trying to do?'

'And a six and a half,' Rosie said, not without enjoyment.

'I might as well have just defrosted a lasagne!'

But he went quiet as they opened the last e-mail. Sarah gasped quietly as she read Charlotte's penultimate paragraph, but Marcus scrolled quickly over it, pretending he hadn't noticed. Really, quite disgustingly crude, Sarah thought, as she tried to stifle a laugh.

Another seven. Rosie and Marcus both wrote it down. Marcus added the scores quickly in his head, making sure everyone noticed. He stared at them. Rosie was using the calculator on the laptop. Marcus grabbed the computer from her and added the scores again. It came out the same.

'You got twenty and a half,' he told her.

'Yes,' she agreed. 'So did you.'

They both looked at the scores again, as if they might suddenly change.

'Well, what do we do now?' Rosie asked.

'It can't be right,' Marcus said.

'Should we have some kind of tie-breaker?'

Rosie was clearly much happier with the draw. Sarah realized that Rosie's main fear had probably been losing to Marcus, whereas Marcus was outraged not to have won. It was pathetic really, Sarah thought, as he began aggressively clicking back through the e-mails, hoping for some kind of error.

'Matt!' Marcus shouted in triumph. 'Your sub-marks don't add up! If you look you'll see they average to just over seven, but you've given me only a seven. So I'll just round that up, and—'

'No,' Matt said with easy firmness. 'The mark's a seven. The breakdown is just for your reference.'

'Come on, at least make it seven and a half. That's only fair.'

'It's a seven.'

'But . . .' Marcus struggled to get the words out. 'I mean, I did more courses, so . . .'

'Trying too hard!' Rosie sang out cheerfully.

Sarah looked at Marcus's score sheet. She noticed he hadn't even bothered to add up Justin's marks. He certainly didn't look like he was about to do it himself, so Sarah picked up the biro and did it for him. Six, plus six, then remember to average Matt and Charlotte's marks, making eight and a half . . . There it was. Twenty-one.

'OK, let's settle this *MasterChef*-style,' Marcus was saying. 'Twenty minutes in the kitchen to make anything you want.'

'That's not really fair if it's your kitchen,' Rosie replied.

'Excuse me!' Sarah interrupted.

'What?' Marcus snapped. 'We need to work out who won here.'

This heightened her enjoyment in the announcement.

'Justin's got twenty-one,' she said. 'He's won.'

There was an incredulous pause. 'Well,' Sarah added. 'Him and Barbara.'

Justin was still staring up at the curtain rail. He didn't seem to have heard.

'Justin!' Sarah repeated louder. He turned round slowly. 'You've won!'

He blinked at her.

'Oh,' he said, in a tone that she would not have described as victorious.

'This can't be right,' Marcus said. 'We all ate the same meal, didn't we? Someone must have pressed the wrong button. Come on, what marks did you all mean to give?'

Justin added: 'Can I go now?'

Sarah experienced an acute pang of an emotion she struggled to identify. It was fiercer than sympathy, but not quite desire. Whatever it was, Sarah knew instinctively that she should feel guilty about it. It wasn't the sort of feeling you were supposed to have about someone who wasn't your boyfriend.

'Wait a minute,' Marcus said. 'Come on, Justin, even you can't really think your cooking was better than mine. And honestly, if the rest of you do it shows you know absolutely nothing about food.'

'Shut up, Marcus,' Charlotte said.

Sarah silently thanked her.

'Face it, Marcus,' Charlotte continued, 'Justin won. You lost. You're a loser.' She went across and patted Justin on the shoulder. 'Congratulations, Justin. What does it feel like to be a winner?'

'I don't feel much like a winner,' Justin said.

There it was. That feeling again.

'I think we're all finding it hard to believe,' Charlotte said. 'But I'm sure Barbara would be very proud. Now I think I'm going to dash.' Her hand whipped away from Justin as she made for the door. 'Thank you for dinner, Marcus and Sarah,' she said. 'Perhaps I'll see you at one of Rosie and Stephen's parties sometime. Although perhaps not.'

She vanished into the hall. After a moment's hesitation, Rosie followed her. Sarah could hear their brief exchange drifting in from the hall.

'So nice to see you, Charlotte,' Rosie said. 'I'm sorry you didn't enjoy it as much as I'd hoped. Maybe you'd like to come round for dinner at ours sometime, just the three of us. Maybe we could ask—'

'No, Rosie,' Charlotte interrupted. 'Next time we see each other outside of work, it's going to be in a pub.'

Sarah heard the door slam. She noticed that Matt was looking pensively out into the hall. He seemed to be deciding whether or not to go after her.

Rosie came back into the dining room.

'I can't believe I wasted all that effort!' Marcus exclaimed, still fruitlessly studying the computer. 'And those ingredients!'

This time Justin did get up to leave. He said goodbye, but Marcus had started adding up all Matt's sub-scores again and didn't bother to respond.

Stephen and Matt called taxis, but Justin insisted he would take the bus. He went out into the hall on his own.

Watching him slowly looking for his coat, Sarah suddenly felt choked with nerves. This was how she had felt the first time she had stood in front of a class.

Was she really going to do it? It didn't seem possible. But it hadn't seemed possible then, and she'd marched into the classroom and done it. She sneaked a look at Marcus. He was muttering quietly to himself. She caught something about 'double-suckered Mediterranean variety' and knew he wasn't going to stand in her way.

Sarah jerked back her chair, pushed past Rosie and rushed into the hall without looking back. She closed the door behind her.

Justin was zipping up his fleece.

'Thank you for dinner, Sarah,' he said without looking up at her. 'I—'

'Justin, before you go,' she interrupted.

'Yes?' He looked at her now.

'I . . .' She hadn't planned how to say it. 'I . . . Look, maybe this isn't the right time. Too soon or something, I don't know. But . . .' she tailed off.

'What?'

'I want to see you again, Justin.'

'Oh.' He looked surprised, or maybe slightly nervous. 'Well, um, maybe, you know, once things have settled down a bit, you and Marcus could come round to ours . . . mine. We could . . .'

'No, Justin,' she said. 'Without Marcus.'

'What do you mean?'

'I mean just us. The two of us.'

'The two of us?'

'Yes.'

She held his gaze. His mouth opened. For a moment nothing came out. She braced herself. Then his brow wrinkled and he said, 'What do you want to do?'

Sarah felt herself sinking. It wasn't going to plan. The memory popped into her mind of the moment when the fat kid at the back of the class made a joke about her breasts, and she'd blushed and stammered, and the whole of 5B had scented blood. She tried to blank it out.

'I thought maybe we could go out somewhere,' she said. 'A meal maybe . . .'

Uncertainty flashed across his eyes.

'No, not a meal. A film. We could go and see a film. How about the new Kiarostami?'

'Oh. I mean . . . I don't know . . .'

'Don't you like Iranian cinema?'

'Yes! It's not that ...'

She couldn't let a silence develop. She had to press on.

'Or, I remember you telling me about your Amnesty letter-writing group. It sounded fascinating. Marcus isn't into that sort of thing, so, if you don't mind, I'd very much like to come.'

Relief flooded his face.

'Oh,' he said, louder and firmer this time. 'For a minute I thought you meant ... Tuesdays. We meet on Tuesdays. It's a really friendly group. I know you'll like them, and it's great that you want to come along and help. It's Burma next week.'

'Great,' Sarah said. She sounded flat and tired.

'I'll forward you the e-mail,' Justin said, and closed the door behind him.

Sarah stood alone in the hall for a while. When the others came out, fussing for coats, Sarah barely noticed them as she said goodbye.

She trudged back into the dining room. Marcus was scowling at the leftovers.

'What a travesty,' he spat bitterly at the remains of his apple fritter. 'An absolute fucking travesty! Justin! What was the point of any of this if Justin is going to win?' He sucked down the last of his wine without any sign of enjoyment. 'He clearly knows nothing about food. He can't even stop his own girl-friend walking out on him.'

Sarah studied the emerging bald spot on the back of his head. 'Come on,' she said, reaching for a bowl of half-eaten fritter. 'Let's throw all this away.'

Thirty-five

Stephen let his eyelids droop and his head rest against the window of the taxi. His cheek was pressed against the glass, and he smiled sleepily at the kebab shops flashing by outside as they accelerated up Junction Road. They slowed only briefly at Archway roundabout. The traffic was light and Stephen knew that within fifteen minutes they would be home. Rosie was always in a hurry to leave, so within twenty minutes, half an hour at the most, he would be in bed. Ten hours of uninterrupted sleep ahead of him.

Feeling warm and affectionate, he reached across the vinyl seat and took Rosie's hand. She was looking out of the other window with a pinched expression.

'Well, that didn't go very well,' she said.

Stephen squeezed her hand.

'I knew it was a bad idea to have Justin and Matt both there.'

'Mmm.'

'I should have asked Marcus to postpone, I suppose.'

'Mmm.'

'Matt behaved terribly, of course.'

'Mmm.'

'Barbara too. Although, to be honest, I'm not so surprised about her.'

Stephen closed his eyes. He knew he didn't really need to reply.

'Justin, though!'

Stephen chuckled drowsily.

'I know! Exactly! Who'd have thought he had it in him!'

He stroked the back of her hand.

'Such a pity Matt and Charlotte didn't take to each other. I had a really good feeling about that.'

'Mmm.'

'There must be somebody we can set her up with, though. Are you sure there aren't any of your friends at work who ...'

Stephen grunted.

'Yes, OK. Sorry.' Rosie fell silent.

Stephen opened his eyes to see they were approaching the clock tower. Not far to go.

Ten hours. Jonathan rarely woke during the night now, and although he was always out of bed early, on Sundays it was Rosie's job to look after him. By the time Stephen woke at nine or ten, Jonathan would be watching his permitted allowance of cartoons and Rosie would come and bring Stephen a cup of tea.

When he got up, they would take Jonathan for a walk in Priory Park, or maybe up to Ally Pally if the weather was good. Perhaps for lunch they would try that new pub on the corner of the park, the one that now had all those *Harden's* and *Time Out* stickers on the door. It had been an old man's boozer before, but the new owners had sanded down the floorboards and started doing daily specials, written up on a big blackboard behind the bar. Stephen had heard it was good.

There was no DIY to do this week, so in the afternoon he could lie on the sofa and read, or maybe watch some of the box set of the American version of *The Office* that Rosie had got him for Christmas. Then in the evening a detective show, *Foyle's War*, maybe, or if they were feeling really adventurous, the Swedish version of *Wallander*.

He looked fondly at Rosie and lazily stroked her upper arm. Perhaps, when they got home . . . But no, she obviously wasn't in the mood. Stephen didn't mind. He was too tired anyway. Maybe in the morning, though, during that really loud cartoon about lasers. Yes, that would be nice.

His hand moved slowly down the fabric of her dress. Next weekend, they would stay in. No more of these stupid dinner parties. On Saturday, he would cook for her. She would like that. They'd have some wine, watch a film. He wouldn't have to see any of these people for ages.

And Matt. Well, Stephen could no longer see what he had worried about. What did it matter what had happened a decade ago? Rosie was disapproving of Matt now, yes, but it was more than that. There was nothing to envy. Matt's life somehow seemed so unappealing. Tawdry, but tiring too. Stephen couldn't see how he had the energy or why he would want it. Without the rivalry, maybe they could go back to being friends. His hand moved further down Rosie's dress.

'Of course, I can't help thinking it's partly my fault,' she said abruptly.

'Mmm?' Stephen's hand stopped moving.

'I mean, obviously I chose the wrong group of people.' She was still looking out of her window. 'That's the first task of any hostess, you see, to get the mix right. But it's so hard when you don't really know the partners.'

Stephen laughed silently.

'Yes, all right. I know I can't really make excuses when the guests have started hitting each other.'

She smiled in spite of herself and Stephen watched the dimple appear on her right cheek, as pleasing as always. Stephen closed his eyes again and felt the taxi slow and begin to turn. It lurched over a speed bump. They were almost home.

'I knew I should have invited Mike and Tony.'

Stephen opened his eyes.

Rosie patted his hand, still gazing out of the other window.

'I know you did. And then there're the Wilkinsons, who we haven't seen for ages, and that nice couple from the nursery.'

She looked round at him now and picked his hand off her lap.

'Yes,' she said brightly. 'Perhaps we should invite them all round for dinner?'

COUNTY LIBRARY
LOUTH
SERVICE